"Read between the lines, and the story acquires timely dimensions, though you need not do so to have good fun with the book...[Baggott] successfully imagines and populates a whole world, which is the most rigorous test of a fantasy's success. It's a bonus that the hero of the piece is a young girl, which ought to serve as inspiration for more than a few readers."

—*Kirkus Reviews*

"Julianna Baggott has created a mesmerizing, nightmarish apocalyptic world, populated by denizens who suffer out bleak existence bearing the literal marks of what was closest to them in their previous life...Sure to haunt the imagination of readers for a long, long time."

—Matt Bondurant, author of *The Wettest County in the World*

"[A] compelling tale of love and revolution...Baggott's imagery is matchless...A sure hit for fans of *The Hunger Games* and *The Host*."

—*Library Journal* (starred review)

"Laden with haunting imagery, powerful prose, and well-written characters, PURE is sure to win the hearts of teenagers and adults alike."

—Examiner.com

"From the first page on, there are no brakes on this book. It's nearly impossible to stop reading as Baggott delves fearlessly into a grotesque and fascinating future populated by strangely endearing victims (and perpetrators) of a wholly unique apocalypse. And trust me, PURE packs one hell of an apocalypse."

—Daniel H. Wilson, *New York Times* bestselling author of *Robopocalypse*

"It's a concept which jars at first, but then becomes a constant and poignant reminder of a world irretrievably lost...Baggott tells what might have been an overly grim tale with crystalline precision."

—*Guardian* (UK)

"I loved this book!...[It] runs the full emotional gamut of any work of literary fiction, but against a savage and wildly inventive post-apocalyptic backdrop that makes it Much. More. Fun...a thriller of a plot, a Dickensian cast of characters, suspense, a twist, and more."
—Laini Taylor, author of *Daughter of Smoke and Bone*

"This is a fabulous, disturbing, gripping, dark adventure."
—*Herald Sun* (Australia)

"PURE is like a combination of all those awesome YA dystopian novels we've been reading—but for adults." —*BookPage*

"This is a great post-apocalyptic horror thriller in which Julianna Baggott paints a vivid dark world...Brutally gruesome with dark humor, readers will appreciate walking in and out of the Dome with Pressia and Partridge as their guides in a trek on the wild side." —Alternative-Worlds.com

"PURE is an inventive and fun riff on both post-apocalyptic adventures and the coming-of-age story...Baggott's characters are interesting...She does a fine job of pacing the action while allowing time for the emotional aspects of the story to unfold...plenty of surprises...The world Baggott has created is fantastical: futuristic and devastated, dystopian and still hopeful...a strong and energetic novel." —BookReporter.com

PURE

JULIANNA BAGGOTT

GRAND CENTRAL
PUBLISHING

NEW YORK   BOSTON

Grand Central Publishing
Hachette Book Group
237 Park Avenue
New York, NY 10017

www.HachetteBookGroup.com

Printed in the United States of America

RRD-C

Originally published in hardcover by Grand Central Publishing.

First trade edition: September 2012
10 9 8 7 6 5 4 3 2

Grand Central Publishing is a division of Hachette Book Group, Inc.
The Grand Central Publishing name and logo is a trademark
of Hachette Book Group, Inc.

The Hachette Speakers Bureau provides a wide range of authors for speaking events. To find out more, go to www.hachettespeakersbureau.com
or call (866) 376-6591.

The publisher is not responsible for websites (or their content)
that are not owned by the publisher.

The Library of Congress has cataloged the hardcover edition as follows:
Baggott, Julianna.
   Pure / Julianna Baggott. — 1st ed.
     p. cm.
   Summary: In a post-apocalyptic world, Pressia, a sixteen-year-old survivor with a doll's head fused onto her left hand meets Partridge, a "Pure" dome-dweller who is searching for his mother, sure that she has survived the cataclysm.
   ISBN 978-1-4555-0303-2
   [1. Science fiction.]   I. Title.
   PZ7.B14026Pu 2012
   [Fic]—dc23

2011010209

ISBN 978-1-4555-0305-6 (pbk.)

For Phoebe, who made a bird of wire

PURE

PROLOGUE

*T*here was low droning overhead a week or so after the Detonations; time was hard to track. The skies were buckling with dark banks of blackened cloud, the air thick with ash and dust. If it was a plane or an airship of some sort, we never knew because the sky was so clotted. But I might have seen a metal underbelly, some dull shine of a hull dipping down for a moment, then gone. We couldn't yet see the Dome either. Now bright on the hill, it was only a dusky glow in the distance. It seemed to hover over the earth, orb-like, a lit bobble, unattached.

The droning was some kind of air mission, and we wondered if there would be more bombs. But what would be the point? Everything was gone, obliterated or swept up by the fires; there were dark puddles from black rain. Some drank the water and died from it. Our scars were fresh, our wounds and warpings raw. The survivors hobbled and limped, a procession of death, hoping to find a place that had been spared. We gave up. We were slack. We didn't take cover. Maybe some were hoping it was a relief effort. Maybe I was too.

Those who could still stagger up from the rubble did. I couldn't—my right leg gone at the knee, my hand blistered from using a pipe as a cane. You, Pressia, were only six years old, small for your age, and still pained by your wound raw at the wrist, the burns shining on your face. But you were quick. You climbed up on top of some rubble to get closer to the sound, drawn to it because it was commanding and coming from the sky.

That was when the air took shape, a billowing of shifting, fluttering motion—a sky of singular, bodiless wings.

Slips of paper.

They touched down, settling around you like giant snowflakes, the kind kids used to cut from folded paper and tape to classroom windows, but already grayed by the ashen air and wind.

You picked one up, as did the others who could, until they were all gone. You handed the paper to me and I read it aloud.

We know you are here, our brothers and sisters.
We will, one day, emerge from the Dome
to join you in peace.
For now, we watch from afar, benevolently.

Like God, *I whispered,* they're watching over us like the benevolent eye of God. *I wasn't alone in this thought. Some were awed. Others raged. We were all still stunned, dazed. Would they ask some of us to enter the gates of the Dome? Would they deny us?*

Years would come to pass. They would forget us.

But at first, the slips of paper became precious—a form of currency. That didn't last. The suffering was too great.

After I read the paper, I folded it up and said, "I'll hold on to it for you, okay?"

I don't know if you understood me. You were still distant and mute, your face as blank and wide-eyed as the face of your doll. Instead of nodding your own head, you nodded the doll's head, part of you forever now. When its eyes blinked, you blinked your own.

It was like this for a long time.

PRESSIA

CABINETS

Pressia is lying in the cabinet. This is where she'll sleep once she turns sixteen in two weeks—the tight press of blackened plywood pinching her shoulders, the muffled air, the stalled motes of ash. She'll have to be good to survive this—good and quiet and, at night when OSR patrols the streets, hidden.

She nudges the door open with her elbow, and there sits her grandfather, settled into his chair next to the alley door. The fan lodged in his throat whirs quietly; the small plastic blades spin one way when he draws in a breath and the opposite way when he breathes out. She's so used to the fan that she'll go months without really noticing it, but then there will be a moment, like this one, when she feels disengaged from her life and everything surprises.

"So, do you think you can sleep in there?" he asks. "Do you like it?"

She hates the cabinet, but she doesn't want to hurt his feelings. "I feel like a comb in a box," she says. They live in the back storage room of a burned-out barbershop. It's a small room with a table, two chairs, two old pallets on the floor, one where her grandfather now sleeps and her old one, and a handmade birdcage hung from a hook in the ceiling. They come and go through the storage room's back door, which leads to an alley. During the Before, this cabinet held barbershop supplies—boxes of black combs, bottles of blue Barbasol, shaving-cream canisters, neatly folded hand towels, white smocks that snapped around the neck. She's pretty sure that she'll have dreams of being blue Barbasol trapped in a bottle.

Her grandfather starts coughing; the fan spins wildly. His face flushes to a rubied purple. Pressia climbs out of the cabinet, walks quickly to him, and claps him on the back, pounds his ribs. Because of the cough, people have stopped coming around for his services—he was a mortician during the Before and then became known as the flesh-tailor, applying his skills with the dead to the living. She used to help him keep the wounds clean with alcohol, line up the instruments, sometimes helping hold down a kid who was flailing. Now people think he's infected.

"Are you all right?" Pressia says.

Slowly, he catches his breath. He nods. "Fine." He picks up his brick from the floor and rests it on his one stumped leg, just above its seared clot of wires. The brick is his only protection against OSR. "This sleeping cabinet is the best we've got," her grandfather says. "Just give it time."

Pressia knows she should be more appreciative. He built the hiding place a few months ago. The cabinets stretch along the back wall that they share with the barbershop itself. Most of what's left of the wrecked barbershop is exposed to the sky, a large hunk of its roof blown clean off. Her grandfather stripped the cabinets of drawers and shelves. Along the back wall of the cabinets he's put in a fake panel that acts like a trapdoor, leading to the barbershop itself, a panel that she can pop off if she needs to escape into the barbershop. And then where will she go? Her grandfather has shown her an old irrigation pipe where she can hide out while OSR ransacks the storage room, finding an empty cabinet, and her grandfather tells them that she's been gone for weeks and probably for good, maybe dead by now. He tries to convince himself that they'll believe him, that she'll be able to come back, and OSR will leave them alone after this. But of course, they both know this is unlikely.

She's known a few older kids who ran away—a boy with a missing jaw, then two kids who said they were going to get married far away from here, and a boy named Gorse and his younger sister Fandra, who was a good friend of Pressia's before they left a few years ago. There's talk of an underground that gets kids out of the city, past the Meltlands and the Deadlands where there may be other survivors—whole civilizations. Who knows? But these are only whispers, well-intended lies meant to comfort. Those kids disappeared. No one ever saw them again.

"I guess I'll have time to get used to it, all the time in the world, starting two weeks from today," she says. Once she turns sixteen, she'll be confined to the back room and sleep in the cabinet. Her grandfather has made her promise, again and again, that she won't stray. *It'll be too dangerous to go out*, he tells her. *My heart won't take it.*

They both know the whispers of what happens to you if you don't turn yourself in to OSR headquarters on your sixteenth birthday. They will take you while you're asleep in bed. They will take you if you walk alone in the rubble fields. They will take you no matter whom you pay off or how much—not that her grandfather could afford to pay anyone anything.

If you don't turn yourself in, they will take you. That isn't just a whisper. That's the truth. There are whispers that they will take you up to the outlands where you're untaught to read—if you've learned in the first place, like Pressia has. Her grandfather taught her letters and showed her the Message: *We know you are here, our brothers and sisters . . .* (No one speaks of the Message anymore. Her grandfather has hidden it away somewhere.) There are whispers that they then teach you how to kill by use of live targets. And there are whispers that either you will learn to kill or, if you're too deformed by the Detonations, you'll be used as a live target, and that will be the end of you.

What happens to the kids in the Dome when they turn sixteen? Pressia figures that it's like during the Before—cake and brightly wrapped gifts and fake, candy-stuffed animals strung up and beaten with sticks.

"Can I run to the market? We're almost out of roots." Pressia is good at boiling certain kinds of roots; it's mostly what they eat. And she wants to be out in the air.

Her grandfather looks at her anxiously.

"My name isn't even on the posted list yet," she tells him. The official list of those who need to turn themselves in to OSR is posted throughout the city—names and birthdates in two tidy columns, information gathered by the OSR. The group emerged shortly after the Detonations, when it was Operation Search and Rescue—setting up medical units that failed, making lists of the survivors and the dead, and then forming a small militia to maintain order. But those leaders were overthrown. OSR became Operation Sacred Revolution; the new leaders rule by fear and are intent on taking down the Dome one day.

Now the OSR mandates that all newborns are registered or parents are punished. OSR also does random home raids. People move so frequently that they've never had the ability to track homes. There's no such thing as addresses anymore anyway— what's left is toppled, gone, street names wiped away. Without her name on that list, it still doesn't feel quite real to Pressia. She hopes that her name will never appear. Maybe they've forgotten she exists, lost a stack of files and hers was in it.

"Plus," she says. "We need to stock up." She needs to secure as much food as she can for them before her grandfather takes over the market trips. She's better at bartering, always has been. She worries what will happen once he's in charge.

"Okay, fine," he says. "Kepperness still owes us for my stitch work on his son's neck."

"Kepperness," she repeats. Kepperness paid up a while ago. Her grandfather sometimes remembers only the things he wants to. She walks to the ledge under the splintered window where there's a row of small creatures she's made from pieces of metal, old coins, buttons, hinges, gears she collects—little windup toys—chicks that hop, caterpillars that scoot, a turtle with a small snapping beak. Her favorite is the butterfly. She's made half a dozen of them alone. Their skeletal systems are built from the teeth of old black barber combs and wings made from bits of the white smocks. The butterflies flap when they get wound up, but she's never been able to get them to fly.

She picks up one of the butterflies, winds it. Its wings shudder, kicking up a few bits of ash that swirl. Swirling ash—it's not all bad. In fact, it can be beautiful, the lit swirl. She doesn't want to see beauty in it, but she does. She finds little moments of beauty everywhere—even in ugliness. The heaviness of the clouds draping across the sky, sometimes edged dark blue. There's still dew that rises from the ground and beads up on pieces of blackened glass.

Her grandfather is looking out the alley door, so she slips the butterfly in the sack. She's been using these to barter with since people have stopped coming to him for stitching.

"You know, we're lucky to have this place—and now an escape route," her grandfather says. "We were lucky from the start. Lucky that I got to the airport early to pick you and your mother up at Baggage Claim. What if I hadn't heard there was traffic? What if I hadn't headed out early? And your mother, *she was so beautiful,*" he says, *"so young."*

"I know, I know," Pressia says, trying not to sound impatient, but it's a well-worn speech. He's talking about the day of the

Detonations, just over nine years ago when she was six years old. Her father was out of town on business. An accountant with light hair, he was pigeon-toed, her grandfather liked to tell her, but a good quarterback. Football—it was a tidy sport played on a grassy field, with buckled helmets and officials who blew whistles and threw colored handkerchiefs. "But what does it mean, anyway, that my father was a pigeon-toed quarterback if I don't remember him? What is a beautiful mother worth if you can't see her face in your head?"

"Don't say that," he says. "Of course you remember them!"

She can't tell the difference between the stories her grandfather's told her and memory. Baggage Claim, for example. Her grandfather has explained it again and again—bags on wheels, a large moving belt, security circling like trained herding dogs. But is it a memory? Her mother took the full brunt of a plate-glass window and died instantaneously, her grandfather has told her. Has Pressia ever really recalled it or only imagined it? Her mother was Japanese, which explains Pressia's black shiny hair, almond-shaped eyes, and her even-toned skin, except for the skin that's the shiny pink crescent-shaped burn, curved around her left eye. She has a light dusting of freckles because of her father's side of the family. Scotch-Irish, her grandfather calls himself, but none of these things means much of anything to her. Japanese, Scotch, Irish? The city where her father had been on business—the rest of the world, as far as anyone could tell—was decimated, gone. Japanese, Scotch, Irish—these things no longer exist. "BWI," her grandfather says, emphatically, "that was the name of the airport. And we made it out of there, following the others who were still alive. We staggered on, looking for a safe place. We stopped in this city, barely standing, but still here because it's not far from the Dome. We live a little west of Baltimore, north of DC." Again, these things mean nothing. BWI, DC, they're just letters.

Her parents are unknowable, that's what kills Pressia, and if they're unknowable, how can she know herself? She sometimes feels like she's cut off from the world, like she's floating—a small lit fleck of swirling ash.

"Mickey Mouse," her grandfather says. "Don't you remember him?" This is what gets him the most, it seems, that she doesn't remember Mickey Mouse, the trip to Disney World that they were just returning from. "He had big ears and wore white gloves?"

She walks to Freedle's cage. It's made of old bike spokes and a thin metal sheet that serves as the cage's floor and a small metal door that slides up and down. Inside, on a perch, sits Freedle, a mechanical-winged cicada. She fits her finger between the thin bars and pets his filigree wings. They've had him for as long as Pressia remembers. Old and rusty, his wings still sometimes flutter. He's Pressia's only pet. She named him Freedle when she was little because when they let him flit around the room, he had a squeaking call that sounded like he was saying, "Freedle! Freedle!" She's kept his parts working all these years, using oil the barbers once used to keep the shears running smoothly. "I remember Freedle," she says. "But no oversize mouse with a thing for white gloves." She vows one day to lie to her grandfather about it, if only to put the whole thing to rest.

What does she remember of the Detonations? The bright light—like sun on sun on sun. And she remembers that she was holding the doll. Wasn't she too old for a doll? The doll's head was attached to its tan cloth body and rubber arms and legs. The Detonations caused a shearing blast of light in the airport that flooded her vision before the world exploded and, in some cases, melted. There was the tangle of lives and the doll's head became her hand. And now, of course, she knows the doll head because it's part of her—its blinky eyes that click when she moves, the sharp black plastic rows of eyelashes, the hole in its plastic lips where the plastic bottle is supposed to fit, its rubber head in place of her fist.

She runs her good hand over the doll's head. She can feel the ripple of her finger bones within it, the small ridges and bumps of her knuckles, the lost hand fused with the rubber of the doll's skull. And in the lost hand itself? She can feel the thick, dulled sensation of her good hand touching her lost hand. That's the way she feels about the Before—it's there, she can feel it, the light sensation of nerves, just barely. The doll's eyes click shut; the hole within the pursed lips is dusted with ash as if the doll itself has been breathing this air. She pulls a woolen sock from her pocket and covers the doll's head. She always covers it when she goes out.

If she lingers, her grandfather will start telling stories of what happened to the survivors after the Detonations—bloody fights in the hulls of giant Super Marts, the burned and twisted survivors battling over camping stoves and fishing knives. "I've got to go before they close up their stalls," she says—before night patrols. She walks to where he's seated and kisses his rough cheek.

"Just to the market. No scavenging," he says, then lowers his head and coughs into his shirtsleeve.

She has every intention of scavenging. It's what she loves most, picking up bits of things to make her creatures. "I won't," she says.

He's still holding the brick, but it strikes her now as sad and desperate, an admission of weakness. He might be able to knock out the first OSR soldier with it, but not the second or the third. They always come in packs. She wants to say aloud what they both know: It won't work. She can hide in this room, sleep in the cabinets. She can pop off the fake panel whenever she hears an OSR truck in the back alley and run. But there's nowhere else to go.

"Don't be gone long," he says.

"I won't." And then, to make him feel better, she adds, "You're right about us. We are lucky." But she doesn't really feel it. The people in the Dome are lucky, playing their buckled-helmet sports, eating cake, all connected and never feeling like lit flecks of swirling ash.

"Remember that, my girl." His throat fan whirs. He'd been

clutching a small handheld electric fan when the Detonations hit—it happened during summer—and now the fan is with him forever. Sometimes he labors to breathe. The spinning mechanism gets gummed with ash and spittle. It will kill him one day, the ash mounting in his lungs, the fan chugging to a halt.

She walks to the alley door, opens it. She hears a screech that sounds almost bird-like; then something dark and furred scurries over nearby stones. She sees one of its moist eyes, staring at her. It snarls, unfolds heavy, blunt wings, and scuttles upward, taking to the gray sky.

Sometimes she thinks she hears the droning engine of an airship up there. She catches herself searching the sky for the slips of paper that once filled it—oh, the way her grandfather described it, all those wings! Maybe one day there will be another Message.

Nothing is going to last, Pressia thinks. Everything is about to change forever. She can feel it.

She glances back before stepping into the alley, and she catches her grandfather looking at her the way he does sometimes—as if she's already gone, as if he's practicing sorrow.

PARTRIDGE

MUMMIES

Partridge is sitting in Glassings' World History class, trying to concentrate. The classroom's ventilation is supposed to increase based on the number of bodies present at any given time, and academy boys—all of those rambunctious engines of energy—can make a room stuffy and warm if not kept in check. Luckily, Partridge's desk is situated not far from a small vent in the ceiling, and it's like he's sitting in a column of cool air.

Glassings is lecturing about ancient cultures. He's been going on about this subject for a month solid. The front wall is covered with images of Bryn Celli Ddu, Newgrange, Dowth and Knowth, the Durrington Wall, and Maeshowe—all Neolithic mounds dating back to around 3000 BC. The first Dome prototypes, as Glassings puts it. "Do you think we were the first to think up a Dome?"

I get it, Partridge thinks, ancient people, mounds, tombs, blah, blah, blah. Glassings stands in front of the class in his taut suit jacket with its academy emblem stitched in place and a navy-blue necktie, always tied too tightly. Partridge would rather hear Glassings' take on recent history, but that would never be allowed. They know only what they've all been told—the United

States didn't make the first strike but acted in self-defense. The Detonations escalated, leading to near-total destruction. Because of precautions taken by the Dome experimentally as a prototype for sustainable living in the face of detonations, viral attacks, and environmental disaster, this area is likely the only place in the world with survivors—the Dome and the wretches just outside of it now governed by a flimsy military regime. The Dome watches over the wretches and one day, when the earth has rejuvenated itself, they will return to take care of the wretches and start anew. It's kept simple, but Partridge knows that there's much more to it, and he's pretty sure that Glassings himself would have a lot to say on the subject.

Sometimes Glassings gets caught up in a lecture, unbuttons his suit jacket, walks away from his notes, and looks at the class—his eyes locking onto each boy's for just a moment as if he wants them to understand something he's saying in a deeper way, to take some ancient lesson and apply it to today. Partridge wants to. He feels like he could, almost, if only he had a little more information.

Partridge lifts his chin and lets the air cool his face, and he remembers, suddenly, his mother setting out a meal for him and his brother, glasses of milk with bubbles that clung to the edges, oily gravies, the airy, soft innards of bread rolls. Food that filled your mouth, that sent up puffs of steam. Now he takes his pills, perfectly formulated for optimal health. Partridge sometimes swirls the pills in his mouth, remembering that even the pills he and his brother took back then were tangy-sweet and gummed in your teeth and were shaped like animals. And then the memory is gone.

These quick visceral memories are sharp. They come at him these days like sudden blows, the collision of now and past, uncontrollable. It's only gotten worse since his father stepped up his coding sessions—the strange mix of drugs coursing through the bloodstream, the radiation, and, worst of all, being trapped in body casts so that only certain parts of his body and brain are exposed during a given session. *Mummy molds.* That's what some of Partridge's friends started calling the casts after one of Glassings' recent lectures on ancient cultures that wrapped their dead. For coding sessions, the academy boys are lined up and taken to the medical center, shuttled into private rooms. There, each undresses and fits himself into a mummy mold—confined in the hot suit—and then, after, they get back into their uniforms to be shuttled out again. The technicians warn the academy boys that as the body becomes accustomed to the new skill sets, they can expect some vertigo, sudden losses of balance that will subside as strength and speed take hold. The academy boys are used to it— a few months off from the sports teams because they've become temporarily ungainly. They tip and fall, sprawled on the turf. The brain will be just as uncoordinated, hence the strange sudden memories.

"Beautiful barbarism," Glassings says now about one of the ancient cultures. "Reverence for the dead." It's one of those moments when he isn't reading from his lecture notes. He stares at his hands spread open on his desk. He isn't supposed to make asides—*beautiful barbarism*, that kind of thing could be misinterpreted. He could lose his job. But he's quick to recover. He tells the class to read aloud from the prompter, in unison. "The sanctioned ways of disposing of the dead and collecting their personal items in the Personal Loss Archives…" Partridge joins in.

A few minutes later, Glassings is talking about the importance of corn to ancient cultures. Corn? Partridge thinks. Really? Corn?

That's when there's a knock at the door. Glassings looks up, startled. All the boys stiffen. The knock sounds again. Glassings says, "Excuse me, class." He straightens his notes and glances at the small black beady eye of one of the cameras perched in the corner of the room. Partridge wonders if the Dome officials got wind of his comment *beautiful barbarism*. Can it happen that fast? Will that do him in? Will they haul him away, right now, in front of the class?

Glassings steps out into the hall. Partridge hears voices, murmurs.

Arvin Weed, the genius of the class, who sits in front of Partridge, swivels around and gives him an inquiring look, as if Partridge must know what's going on. Partridge shrugs. People often think Partridge knows more than everyone else. He's Ellery Willux's son. Even someone that high up must let things slip now and then, that's what they figure. But no. Partridge's dad never lets things slip. That's one of the reasons he got to be high up in the first place. And since Partridge has been boarding here at the academy, they rarely even talk on the phone, much less see each other. Partridge is one of the boys who stays year-round, like his brother, Sedge, who went through the academy before him.

Glassings walks back into the classroom. "Partridge," he says, "collect your things."

"What?" Partridge says. "Me?"

"Now," Glassings says.

Partridge's stomach lurches. He shoves his notebook into his backpack and stands up. All around him, the other boys start whispering. Vic Wellingsly, Algrin Firth, the Elmsford twins. One of them makes a joke—Partridge hears his name but can't make out the rest—and they all laugh. These boys all tend to stick together, "the herd"; that's what they're called. They're the ones who'll go all the way through training to the new elite corps, Special Forces. They're destined. It isn't written anywhere, but it's understood.

Glassings tells the class to pipe down.

Arvin Weed gives Partridge a nod, as if to say, *Good luck*.

Partridge walks to the door. "Can I get the notes later?" he asks Glassings.

"Sure," Glassings says, and then he pats Partridge on the back.

"It'll be fine." He's talking about the notes, of course, keeping up with the class, but he looks at Partridge in that way Glassings has, a deeper meaning, and Partridge knows that he's trying to set his mind at ease. Whatever's coming—*it'll be fine.*

In the hall, Partridge is met by two guards. "Where to?" he says.

They're both tall and muscular, but one of them is a bit broader than the other. This one says, "Your father wants to see you."

Partridge feels cold suddenly. His palms are clammy, so he rubs his hands together. He doesn't want to see his father; he never does. "The old man?" Partridge says, trying to sound light-hearted. "A little father-son time?"

They walk him down the shiny halls, past the oil paintings of two headmasters—one fired, one new—who both look pasty, austere, and somewhat dead, then down to the academy basement, which is on the monorail line. They wait in the airy underground, silently. This is the monorail that takes the boys to the medical center, where Partridge's father works three times a week. There are floors in the medical center reserved for those who are sick. They're kept cordoned off. Sickness is treated very seriously in the Dome. Contagion could wipe them all out, and so the slightest fever can result in short-term quarantine. He's been to one of those floors a few times—a small, boring, sterile room.

The dying? No one visits them. They're taken to a floor of their own.

Partridge wonders what his father wants with him. He's not one of the herd, not destined for anything elite. That was Sedge's role. When Partridge entered the academy he wasn't sure if he was better known for his father or his brother. It didn't matter. He didn't live up to either reputation. He never won a physical challenge and he sat the bench during most games, regardless of the sport. And he wasn't intelligent enough to go into the other training program—brain augmentation. That was reserved for the smart ones like Arvin Weed, Heath Winston, Gar Dreslin. His grades have always been borderline. Like most of the boys going in for coding, he was clearly garden-variety, basic overall enhancement to better the species.

Does his father just want to check in on his garden-variety son? Maybe he was struck by a sudden desire to bond? Will they even have anything to talk about? Partridge tries to remember the last time they ever did anything together for fun. One time, after Sedge's death, his father took him swimming in the academy's indoor pool. He remembers only that his father was an excellent swimmer, he slid through the water like a sea otter, and when he came up for air, toweling off, Partridge saw his father's bare chest for the first time in as long as he could remember. Had he ever seen him only half dressed before? His father's chest had six small scars on it, on the left side, over his heart. It wasn't from an accident. The scars were too symmetrical and tidy.

The monorail comes to a stop, and Partridge has a fleeting desire to run. The guards would hit him with an electrical charge to his back. He knows that. He'd have a red burn spread down his back and arms. His father would be told, of course. It would only make matters worse. Why run anyway? Where would he go? In circles? It's a Dome, after all.

The monorail delivers them to the entrance of the medical center. The guards show their badges. They sign Partridge in, scan his retinas, and walk through the detectors into the center itself. They wind the halls until they come to his father's door. It opens before the guard has time to knock.

A female technician is standing there. Partridge can see beyond her to his father, who is lecturing half a dozen technicians. They're all looking at a bank of screens on the wall, pointing out chains of DNA coding, close-ups of a double helix.

The technician says "Thank you" to the guards and then ushers Partridge to a small leather chair to the side of his father's massive desk, which is on the opposite side of the room from where his father and the techs work.

His father is saying, "There it is. The blip in the behavioral coding. Resistance." The techs are all darty-eyed geese, terrified of his father, who's still ignoring Partridge. This is nothing new. Partridge is used to being ignored by his father.

He looks around the office, notes a set of original Dome blueprints now framed and hung on the wall over his father's desk.

Why is Partridge here, he wonders again. Is his father showing off, trying to prove something to Partridge? It's not like Partridge doesn't know that his father is smart, that he commands respect, even fear.

"All of his other types of coding have gone so well. Why not the behavioral coding?" his father says to the techs. "Anyone? Answers?"

Partridge taps his fingers on the arms of the chair, glancing at the wisps of his father's gray hair. His father looks angry. In fact, his head seems to shake with anger. He's noticed anger flaring up like this in his father ever since Partridge's brother's funeral. Sedge died after his coding was complete and he'd made it into Special Forces, the new elite corps made up of only six recent academy graduates. "A tragedy," his father calls it, as if giving it a proper name makes it acceptable somehow.

The technicians look at one another and say, "No, sir. Not yet, sir."

His father glares at the screen, his brow knotted, his fleshy nose reddened, and then he looks at Partridge, as if seeing him for the first time. He dismisses the technicians by waving them off. They leave hurriedly, scuttling out the door. Partridge wonders if they are flooded with relief each time they leave his father's presence, the way he is. Do they all secretly hate the old man? Partridge wouldn't blame them.

"So," Partridge says, fiddling with a strap on his backpack. "How are things?"

"I'm sure you're wondering why I've called you in."

Partridge shrugs. "Happy belated birthday?" His seventeenth birthday was almost ten months ago.

"Your birthday?" his father says. "Didn't you get the gift I sent?"

"What was it again?" Partridge says, tapping his chin. He remembers. The gift was a very expensive pen with an illuminated bulb on top. *So you can study late,* his father wrote him in a little note attached to the gift, *and get an edge over your classmates.* Does his father remember the gift? Probably not. Was the note even written by his father? Partridge doesn't know his father's handwriting. When he was a kid, his mother used to write riddles to help them find where she'd hidden presents. She told him that it was a tradition his father started when they were first dating—little rhyming riddles and gifts. Partridge remembers this because it struck him that they'd been in love at some point, but weren't anymore. Partridge doesn't remember his father even being there for his birthdays.

"I didn't call you in for anything birthday-related," his father says.

"So I guess next comes a fatherly interest in my schooling. You're going to ask, *Are you learning anything important?*"

His father sighs. Does anyone else speak to him this way? Probably not. "Are you learning anything important?" he asks.

"We weren't the first to invent Domes, I guess. They're prehistoric—Newgrange, Knowth, Maeshowe, et cetera."

His father sits back. The leather of his seat creaks. "I remember the first time I saw a picture of Maeshowe. I was a kid, fourteen or so. I saw it in a book on prehistoric sites." He stops speaking and raises his hand to his temple, which he rubs in a small circle. "It was a way to live forever, to build something that lasts. A legacy. It stuck in my mind."

"I thought having kids was a man's legacy."

He looks at Partridge sharply. "Yes, you're right. And that's one reason I've called you in. There's some resistance to certain aspects of your coding."

The mummy molds. Something is wrong. "What aspects of my coding?"

"Sedge's mind and body took to the coding so effortlessly," his father says. "And you're close to him genetically, but—"

"What aspects?" Partridge asks.

"Oddly enough, the behavioral coding. Strength, speed, agility, all the physical aspects are going well. Are you feeling effects? Mental and/or physical? Lack of balance? Unusual thoughts or memories?"

The memories, yes, he's thinking of his mother more, but he doesn't want to tell his father this. "I felt really cold," he says, "right around the time I heard that you'd called me in. My whole body, really cold."

"Interesting," his father says, and maybe for a split second he's injured by the comment.

Partridge points to a framed wall hanging. "Original blueprints? They're new."

"Twenty years of service," his father says. "A gift."

"Very nice," Partridge says. "I like your architectural handiwork."

"It saved us."

"Us?" Partridge says under his breath. They are the only ones left now, a family shrunken down to an embattled pair.

And then as if this marks a natural segue, his father asks questions about Partridge's mother before the Detonations, the weeks leading up to her death, a specific trip to the beach that she and Partridge had taken alone, just the two of them. "Your mother made you swallow pills?" his father asks.

There are people on the other side of the wall-mounted computer screen, most likely. It has an observation mirror's blank stare. Or maybe there aren't. Maybe his father's waved them off too. They are being recorded, though. They have to be. A beady-eyed camera is mounted in each corner.

"I don't remember. I was a kid." But Partridge remembers blue pills. They were supposed to make the flu go away, but they seemed to make it worse. The fever made him shiver under the blankets.

"She took you to the beach. You remember that, right? Just before. Your brother didn't want to go. He had a ball game. They were in the championships."

"Sedge used to love baseball. He loved a lot of things."

"This isn't about your brother." His father can barely say his brother's name. Since Sedge's death, Partridge has kept count of how many times he's heard his father say it—only a handful. His mother died while trying to help survivors get to the Dome on the day of the Detonations, and his father used to call her a saint, a martyr, then slowly he stopped speaking of her almost completely. Partridge remembers his father saying, "They didn't deserve her. They took her down with them." There was a time when his father used to talk about the survivors as "our lesser brothers and sisters." His father used to call the leaders in the Dome, including himself, "benevolent overseers." Language like this still comes up from time to time in public addresses, but in everyday chatter the survivors outside the Dome are called "wretches." He's heard his father use the term many times. And Partridge has to admit, he's spent a lot of his life hating the wretches for taking his mother down with them. But lately, in Glassings' World History, he can't help but wonder what really happened. Glassings hints that history is malleable. It can be altered. Why? To tell a nicer story.

His father says, "This is about your mother giving you pills, making you swallow something, during the dates of your absence."

"I don't remember. I was eight years old. Jesus. What do you want from me?" Even as he says it, he remembers the sunburns they both got though it was overcast and how, when they were sick, his mother told him a bedtime story, a swan wife with black feet. His mother, he sees her in his mind often—her curly hair, her soft hands with their bones as fine as a bird's bones. The swan wife was a little song, too. It had a tune. It had words that rhymed and hand motions. His mother said, "When I tell you the singing version of the story, hold this necklace in your hand." He gripped it tight in his fist. The edges of the swan's flared wings were sharp, but he didn't let up.

One time he told the story to Sedge. This was in the Dome, a day when Partridge missed his mother sharply. Sedge said it was a girl's story. It was for kids who believed in fairies. "Grow up, Partridge. She's dead and gone. Don't you see that? Are you blind?"

His father now presses him. "We're going to have to do more tests on you. Batteries of tests. You'll be poked with so many needles, you'll feel like a pincushion." *Pincushion*—it's one of those words that no longer mean anything. A cushion for pins? Is this some kind of a threat? It sounds like one. "It would help us out if you could tell us what happened."

"I can't. I'd like to, but I don't remember."

"Listen to me, son." Partridge doesn't like the way his father says the word *son*, as if it's a rebuke. "You need to get your head screwed on right. Your mother..." His father's eyes are weary. His lips are dry. He seems to be talking to someone else. He's speaking in a voice that he uses on the phone. *Hello, Willux here.* He crosses his arms on his chest. His face goes slack for a moment as if he remembers something. There's the shaking of his head again. Even his hand seems to quiver with anger. He says, "Your mother has always been problematic."

A look passes between them. Partridge doesn't say a word, but his mind keeps repeating. *Has always been. Problematic. Has always been.* This isn't the past tense. This isn't the way you talk about the dead.

His father recovers. "She wasn't right in the head." He rubs his hands on his thighs and then leans in. "I've upset you," his father says. This is strange too. He never talks about emotions.

"I'm fine."

His father stands up. "Let's get someone in here to take a picture of us. When was the last time?" It was probably at Sedge's funeral, Partridge thinks. "Something you can have in your dormitory so you're not homesick."

"I'm not homesick," Partridge says. He hasn't ever felt like home was home, not here in the Dome, so how can he miss it so badly that he's sick?

His father calls a tech in anyway, a knobby-nosed woman with bangs, and tells her to get a camera.

Partridge and his father stand in front of the newly hung blueprints, shoulder-to-shoulder, stiff as soldiers. There's a flash.

PRESSIA

SCAVENGING

Even a block away, Pressia can smell the market—spoiled meat and fish, rotted fruit, char, and smoke. She can make out the hawkers' shifting shadows, and she knows them by their coughs. This is how death is sometimes measured. There are different kinds of coughs. They rattle crisply. They begin and end with a wheeze. They begin and can't end. They churn up phlegm. They end in a grunt—this is the worst kind, her grandfather tells her. It means the lungs have taken on fluid—death by infection, drowning from within. Her grandfather rattles by day, but at night he makes the grunting cough in his sleep.

She sticks to the middle of the alley. Passing the lean-tos, she hears a family fighting, a man's loud bellow, something metal banging against a wall. A woman screeches, and a child starts to cry.

As she reaches the market, she sees that the hawkers are closing up. They've dragged metal signs in from the highway for rusted roofs and lean-tos. They shutter stalls with waterlogged press-board, load their wares in gimp pushcarts, drape their stalls in ragged tarps.

Pressia passes a whisper clutch—a circle of huddled backs, hissing, an occasional hoot, then more whispers. She glimpses their faces mottled with metal, shiny glass, rippled scars. One woman's arm looks sealed in leather, cuffed at the wrist where it meets her skin.

She sees a group of kids, not too much younger than she is. Two of them—twins, both with mangled, rusty legs exposed a bit below their skirts—are swinging a rope for a third with one whittled arm who hops between them. They chant:

Burn a Pure and breathe the ash.
Take his guts and make a sash.
Twist his hair and make a rope.
And use his bones to make Pure soap.
Washy, washy, washy. One two three.
Washy, washy, washy. Pure is me.

Pure is the name for those in the Dome. Children are fixated on Pures. They're mentioned in all of their childish rhymes, usually dead. Pressia knows this rhyme by heart. She skipped to it when she was little. She's wished for that soap, stupidly. She wonders if these kids do, too. To be Pure—what would it look and feel like? To erase the scars, to have a hand again, not a doll?

There's a little boy with eyes too far apart, eyes lodged almost on the sides of his head, horse-like, who's tending a fire in a metal barrel with two spits of charred meat balanced on it. The beasts on the spit are small, rodent-size. These children were babies during the Detonations, hardy ones. Kids born before the Detonations are called Pre and those born after are Posts. Posts should be Pure, but that's not how it works. The mutations caused by the Detonations settled deep into the survivors' genes. Babies aren't born Pure. They are mutated, born with traces of their parents' deformities. Animals too. Instead of starting anew, the breeds only seem to get more convoluted, a mix of human, animal, earth, objects.

But there's an important distinction that the people her age make—those who remember life before the Detonations and those who don't. Sometimes after an introduction, kids her age will play I Remember, exchanging memories like currency. How intimate the memory is proves how willing you are to be open to this person—a currency of trust. Those who were too young to remember are both pitied and envied, a hateful mix. Pressia catches herself pretending to remember more than she does, borrowing other people's memories and mixing them with her own. She worries about it, though, afraid that she might build on other people's memories so much that her own are untrustworthy. She has to hold tightly to the few she has.

She looks from one face to the next, the fire casting strange shadows, glinting off shards of metal and glass in their faces, lighting up bright scars, burns, and knots of keloids. A girl looks up at her, one she recognizes but can't fix a name to, and says, "You want pieces of a Pure? All toasted to a crisp?"

"No," Pressia says, louder than she meant to.

The kids laugh, except for the boy minding the fire. He twists his spit, his fingers small and delicate like he's working something that winds up, a kind of instrument or an engine. His name is Mikel. He's not like the other children. There's something steely about him. She can tell he's seen a lot of death, his parents long gone. "You sure, Pressia?" he says, very seriously. "Just a little before you get took for good?" Mikel has a mean streak, though it's not usually directed at her because she's older. So the comment surprises her.

"Nice of you to offer," she says, "but I'll pass."

Mikel looks at her with a sad expression. Maybe he'd wanted her to yell that she wasn't ever going to be taken. In any case, she feels sorry for him. His cruelty has always made him seem vulnerable, which is the opposite of the impression he'd like to give.

Up ahead, she sees Kepperness, the man her grandfather mentioned. She hasn't run into him for a while. He's the age she imagines her father would be. He's slinging empty crates into the back of a handcart with his sleeves rolled up, exposing glass-encrusted arms, thin and sinewy with muscle. He looks at her and then away. He has a few dark tubers left in a basket. She dips her head forward to cover the scars on the side of her face. "How's your son doing? Is his neck all healed?" she asks, hoping he'll feel that he still owes her something.

He stands and stretches his back with a grimace. One of his eyes glows with a golden-orange film, a cataract from the burn of radiation, which isn't unusual. "You're the flesh-tailor's kid, right? Granddaughter? You're not supposed to be around anymore. Too old, right?"

"No," she says defensively. "I'm just fifteen." She pretends to huddle against the wind, though she's actually trying to look smaller and younger.

"That so?" He stops and stares. She focuses on his good eye, the only one he can see from. "I risked my life for these tubers. Dug 'em up right near OSR's woodland. Got a few left."

"Well, what I've got is a one-of-a-kind item. Something only someone with built-up wealth could afford. You know, not for just anyone."

"What is it?"

"A butterfly," she says.

"Butterfly?" he snorts. "There ain't many butterflies left." It's true. They're very rare. In the last year or so, Pressia has seen a few more, small signs of renewal.

"It's a toy."

"A toy?" Kids don't really have toys anymore. They play with pig bladders and knotted rag dolls. "Let me have a look."

She shakes her head. "No use looking at it if you can't pay for it."

"Let me just see it."

She sighs and pretends to be reluctant. She pulls out the butterfly and holds it up.

"Closer," the man says. She can tell now that both of his eyes were seared by the Detonations, one far worse than the other.

Pressia says, "You used to have real toys as a kid, I bet."

He nods and says, "What's it do?"

She winds it up and sets it in his pushcart. The butterfly flaps its wings. "I wonder what it was like to grow up when you did. Christmas and birthdays," she says.

"I believed in magic as a kid. Can you imagine a thing like that?" he says, tilting his head and staring at the toy. "How much?"

"Normally, I charge a lot. It's a remembrance of things past. But for you? Well, just the rest of your roots, those left over," she says. "It's all we need."

He hands her the basket and she rolls the roots into her sack, then picks up the butterfly and hands it to him.

Kepperness says, "I'll give it to my son. He won't last long." Pressia has already turned to go. She hears the ticking of the windup mechanism, and then the wings fluttering. "This will brighten him up some."

No, she thinks. Keep walking. Don't ask. But she remembers his son. He was a sweet kid. Tough too. He didn't cry when her grandfather stitched his neck, even though there was nothing for the pain. "Has something else happened to him?"

"Attacked by a Dust. He was out past the fields, near the desert, hunting. He saw its eye blink up from the earth, and then it pulled him down into the sand. His mother was with him, saved him. But he got a bite somehow. It infected his blood." Dusts are those who fused with the earth; in the city, they fused with the blasted buildings. Most of them died shortly after the Detonations—no means of sustenance, or no mouths, or mouths with no digestion. But some survived because they became more rock than human, and others proved they could be of use, working in conjunction with Beasts, those who fused with animals. When Pressia scavenges in rubble, she watches for Dusts that can reach up, clasp a leg, and pull her down. She's never been out of the city where the boy was grabbed. She has heard that land is filled with Dusts. She's heard that lots of the survivalists who thought they saw the End coming, before the Detonations, and moved out into the woods were swallowed into the trees.

She's heard that a bite is an awful way to die. The child sometimes foams at the mouth and seizes. Pressia reaches into the sack for the tubers. "I didn't know," she says. "Look, keep the tubers and the butterfly."

"No," Kepperness says, putting the butterfly in an inner pocket of his coat. "I seen your grandfather not long ago. He's not doing well either, is he? We all got someone. Deal's a deal."

She's not sure what to say. He's right. Everyone has someone who's died or dying. Pressia nods. "Okay," she says. "I'm so sorry."

He's back to loading his cart again and shakes his head. "We're all sorry." He unfolds a heavy piece of cloth and pulls it down over his wares. While he isn't looking, she upends her sack and a couple of tubers roll back into the basket.

She turns quickly and starts walking. She knows she couldn't have eaten all of them, not with Kepperness's son dying, and having charged him more than she usually gets for her work.

But still, now she has to scavenge. Kepperness was right. Her grandfather isn't well. He won't last. What if she gets taken or has to run soon? She has to make as many creatures as she can so that he can use them to barter with and survive. She presses on.

When she comes to the end of the market, she stops. There, posted on a low brick wall, is a new OSR listing. It flutters in the cold wind. Some hawkers are rolling carts down the street, a loud clattering echo. She waits for them to go, then walks toward the listing. She presses the paper flat. The print is small. She has to get close. Her eyes flit down the page.

And then she sees it.

The name PRESSIA BELZE and her date of birth.

She runs the tip of her finger over the letters.

There's no denying it now. There will be no lost file with her information in it. Here it is. Real.

She backs away, stumbling over some upturned bricks. She turns down the first street she comes to.

She's freezing now. The air is damp. She pulls her inner-layer sweater up to cover her neck, then her stretched-out sweater sleeve down over her doll-head fist, still covered by the sock, tucks it under her other arm, and then crosses both arms on her chest. This is a habit really, something she does when she's outside in public, when she's nervous. A comfort, almost.

Amid the ruins on either side, there are buildings that still have their skeletal structure, and people have made makeshift homes inside them. Then she passes a building that's fully collapsed. These are the best for digging. She's found beautiful things in the rubble before—wire, coins, metal clasps, keys—but the rubble is dangerous. The more human-like Dusts and some of the human-like Beasts who have dug out homes in the rubble keep them warm with fires, cook what they've hunted down, creating trails of smoke. She imagines Kepperness's son out in the Deadlands, an eye in the sand at his feet—then a hand shooting up from nowhere, pulling him down. She's alone. If she's grabbed and pulled down, they'll feed on her until there's nothing left.

She doesn't see any smoke and so she steps up on a pile of wobbling stones, carefully picking her way along, looking for glints of metal, small bits of wiring. She knows it's pretty much picked clean, but she manages to find what might have once been a guitar string, some pieces of melted plastic like parts to an old board game, and a thin metal tube.

Maybe she can make something special for her grandfather too—a gift worth holding on to. She doesn't want to think of the word *memento* because it reminds her that she might soon be gone, but there it is in her mind. *Memento.*

When she heads home by way of the market, all the stalls are closed. She's late. She should hurry now. Her grandfather will start to worry. At the other end of the market, she sees the boy with the wide-set eyes again, Mikel. He's cooking another beast now over the kettledrum. This one is very small, nearly mouse-size, barely worth the meat.

There's a little boy beside him. He reaches up to touch the meat. Mikel says, "Don't! It'll burn you!" He shoves the boy to the ground. The little boy is barefoot. His toes are only nubs. He scrapes his knee, screams at the sight of the blood, and starts to run to a darkened doorway. Three women step out—all fused—a tangle of cloth hiding their engorged middle. Parts of each face seem to be shiny and stiff as if fused with plastic. Groupies, that's what they're called. One of the women has sloped shoulders, a curved spine. There are many arms, some pale and freckled, others dark. The one in the middle grabs the boy's arm and says, "Shut up. Hush now. Shut up."

The woman with the curved spine who seems the least fused to the others, barely hanging on, shouts at Pressia, "You do this to the boy? You do this?"

"I didn't touch him," Pressia says, and she pulls on her sleeve.

"Time to come in," the woman says to the boy. She looks around as if sensing something in the air. "Right now."

The boy twists from her grip and runs down the street toward the empty market, crying harder now.

The one with the curved spine glances back over her shoulder, raises a bony, knuckled fist, and shakes it at Pressia. "See what you done?"

Then, behind her, she hears Mikel yell, "Beast! Beast!"

Pressia turns around and there's a wolfish Beast, this one more animal than human. It's furred, but with glass embedded along its ribs. It runs on all fours with a limp, and then it pauses and rises up on its haunches, nearly the height of a full-grown man. It has clawed feet but no muzzle—instead a pink, nearly hairless human face with a long, narrow jaw and long teeth. Its ribs rise and fall quickly. Across its chest, there is embedded chain link.

Mikel climbs on top of his oil drum and scurries up a metal roof. The Groupies in the doorway dip inside, covering the door with a slab of wood. They don't even call to the lost child, who's still running down the street alone.

Pressia knows the Beast will take the child first. He's smaller than Pressia, a perfect target. But of course, it could attack both of them. It's surely big enough.

Pressia holds tight to her sack and starts sprinting, her arms pumping and legs moving swiftly. She's a fast runner, always has been light on her feet. Maybe her father, the quarterback, was fast. Her shoes are worn through on the balls of her feet, so she can feel the ground through her thin socks.

With the market closed up, this street looks foreign. The Beast is bounding down toward her. She and the little boy are the only ones out now. The little boy must sense that something's changed, danger in the air. He turns and his eyes grow wide with fear. He stumbles and, terrified, he can't get up. Closer now, she can see that his face is scalded near one of his eyes, which shines whitish blue, like a marble.

Pressia runs to him. "Come on!" she says, grabbing under his arms and lifting him up. With only one hand that's good for gripping, she needs the boy's help. "Hold tight!" she says.

She's looking wildly in every direction for something to climb.

Behind them, the Beast is closing in. There's only rubble on either side of her, but up ahead she sees a building that's only partially collapsed. It has a barred gate on its metal door—a door to a shop that once had a plate-glass front, like the barbershop. She remembers her grandfather telling her it had been a pawnshop and explaining how people looted them first because they had guns and gold, though gold eventually became worthless.

Its door is slightly open.

The kid is screaming now, loud and shrill, and he's heavier than she expected. His arms are clamped tightly around her neck, choking off her breath. The Beast is so close that she can hear its panting.

She runs to the door of metal bars, throws it open, swings around and slams it shut, the child still holding on. The door locks automatically.

They're in a small bare room, just a few pallets on the floor. She covers the kid's screaming mouth with her hand. "Quiet," she says, "just be quiet!" and she backs up to the far wall. She sits down with the boy in her lap in the darkened corner of the room.

The Beast is at the door in an instant, barking and clawing through the bars. This Beast has no speech, no hands, despite its human face and eyes. The door rattles loudly. Frustrated, it crouches and growls. And then it turns its head, sniffs the air. And, distracted now, it runs off.

The boy bites her hand as hard as he can.

"Ouch!" Pressia says, rubbing her palm on her pants. "What was that for?"

The boy looks at her wide-eyed as if it surprised him too.

"I was kind of expecting a thank-you," she says.

There's a loud bang from the other side of the room.

Pressia gasps and turns. The boy looks too.

A trapdoor has been slapped open and a guy's head and shoulders have popped up from a room below. He has mussed hair and dark, serious eyes. He's a little older than Pressia. He says, "Are you here for the meeting or what?"

The boy screams again, as if this is the only thing he knows how to do. No wonder the woman told him to shut up, Pressia thinks. He's a screamer. And then he runs to the barred door.

"Don't go out there!" Pressia says.

But the boy is too quick. He unlocks the door, shoots through it, and takes off.

"Who was that?" the guy asks.

"I don't even know," Pressia says, standing up. She can see now that the guy is standing on a rickety, folding ladder leading to a basement. There's a roomful of people down below.

"I know you," he says. "You're the flesh-tailor's granddaughter."

She notices two scars running up one side of his face, maybe her grandfather's stitching. She can tell that the stitching isn't very old, only a year or two. "I don't remember meeting you."

"We didn't meet," he says. "Plus I was pretty banged up." He points to his face. "You might not recognize me. But I remember seeing you there." He looks at her in a way that makes her blush. There's something familiar maybe, just in the dark shine of his eyes. She likes his face, a survivor's face, a sharp jaw, his scars long and jagged. His eyes—there's something about them that makes him seem both angry and sweet at the same time.

"Are you here for the meeting? Seriously, we're starting. There's food."

It's her last time out before she turns sixteen. Her name is on the list. Her heart is still pounding in her chest. She saved the boy. She feels courageous. And she's starving. She likes the idea of food. Maybe there will be enough so she can steal some for her grandfather, unnoticed.

There's a howl not too far off. The Beast is still near.

"Yes," Pressia says. "I'm here for the meeting."

He almost smiles, but stops short. He's not the kind to smile too easily. He turns and shouts to those below, "One more! Make room!" And Pressia notices a fluttering motion beneath the back of his blue shirt, rippling like water.

She remembers him now, the boy with birds in his back.

Partridge

METAL BOX

A̲ll the boys from Glassings' World History class are quiet, which is strange because field trips usually bring out the worst in them. Only their footsteps clatter and echo up and down the alphabetized rows of metal boxes. Even Glassings, who always has something to say, has gone mute. His face is taut and flushed as if he were choking on something, grief or hope? Partridge isn't sure. Glassings shuffles off, disappearing down one of the aisles.

The air in the Dome is always dry and sterile, a static presence. But in the Personal Loss Archives, the air feels faintly charged, almost electrically. Partridge can't put his finger on it. Of course, he tells himself, it's not possible that the items of the dead stored here are different from any other molecular arrangement of items, but still it seems almost as if they are.

Or maybe it isn't the personal items of the dead or the air. Maybe it's the academy boys who are charged, each looking for a specific name. All of them lost someone in the Detonations, like Partridge did. If, out of that person's entire life, some artifact of their existence survived, it was put in a metal box, labeled, alphabetized, trapped here forever—to be honored? And then there are those boys who know someone who's died since the Detonations in the Dome itself. Partridge has someone like that too. When you lose someone in the Dome, though, not much is made of the loss. These losses are to be taken in stride. In the face of such great global losses, how can anyone take a personal loss too personally? And serious illnesses are rare, or maybe more accurately well hidden.

Glassings has put in the request for this field trip many times over the years. Finally he got the okay, and here they are. A recorded voice-over narration kicks in overhead on unseen speakers, a woman saying, "Each person who dies is afforded one small metal box of personal items. Bodies are cremated because space is at a premium. We must reduce each footprint. This is what's allowed until the land is habitable again and we regain our rightful place as full participants and re-creators of the natural landscape."

"Can we open the boxes?" Arvin Weed calls out. "I've found an aunt."

"Auntie Weed!" one of the other boys shouts, mockingly.

"Yes," Glassings says, distracted by his own search, no doubt. "It's not every day you get access like this. Be respectful. Don't touch anything." This means that if Glassings finds the metal box he's looking for, he's opening it. Partridge assumed they wouldn't be allowed to open anything, that he'd only see rows of metal boxes. His heart beats harder in his chest. He walks faster, before Glassings changes his mind, before one of the docents comes in and tells them not to. He's almost running. He feels dizzy. It seems like all the boys are almost running now, skidding around corners, teetering due to the coding's effect on their equilibriums.

He makes it down the long rows to the end of the alphabet—Willux. He finds his older brother's name—SEDGE WATSON WILLUX—and his dates, so final and finite, in tidy print. He runs his fingers over the raised type. The ink isn't faded like some of the others. Sedge has only been gone for a year. In some ways it seems like forever and then, in almost the same moment, it's as if he's still here, and there's been some kind of clerical error. He remembers the last time he saw him. They were at his induction dinner. Sedge and the five other newly graduated academy boys were the first of the new elite corps. Sedge was wearing his uniform. The coding was in full effect. He was taller, broader, his jaw thicker. He told Partridge that he was too skinny. "Double up on the protein bars," he said, and there was a moment when he looked at Partridge and said, "You remember the stories you used to tell? Fairy tales?" Partridge nodded. "I think about them sometimes still." Sedge laughed. And then, just before he left, Sedge hugged Partridge and whispered in his ear, "Maybe this won't happen to you." At the time, Partridge thought it was a mean thing to say, like he wasn't man enough to make it through the training. But after Sedge was found dead, Partridge wondered if it was a sincere wish, a hope.

Partridge doesn't know what happened to the other five boys inducted that day. He's heard rumors that they are in intensive training and their families only get letters from them. Partridge assumes that their families don't complain; they have to be relieved that their kids are still alive.

Partridge fits his fingers in the handle, but for some reason he can't bear to open the box. Sedge is gone. In the small print below his name, a line reads CAUSE: GUNSHOT WOUND, SELF-INFLICTED. Unlike life before they lived in the Dome, suicide doesn't have as dark a stigma. Resources should go to the healthy and those with a strong will to live. The dying aren't given many resources; that would be impractical. One day, hopefully not too far off, they will all return to the world outside, the New Eden, as some call it, and they'll need to be hardy. Sedge's suicide was tragic because he was young and strong, but the act alone of taking his own life was a sign of defectiveness, and there was something admirable in the act—or so that was the rhetoric thrown at Partridge—that Sedge saw this defect in himself and spared himself for the good of the whole. Partridge hates this kind of talk. *My brother is dead*, he wants to tell them. *He was the murderer and the victim. We'll never get him back.*

Partridge doesn't want to see what his brother has been reduced to. The contents of a metal box. He can't bear it.

His mother's box is next—ARIBELLE CORDING WILLUX—and he's surprised that she's allowed to exist here at all. Unlike Sedge, Partridge will take any memory of her he can find, fitted into a box or not. He pulls the small metal handle, unhooks the box, and carries it to the narrow table in the middle of the row. He lifts the lid. He hasn't asked his father many questions about his mother. He can tell that it makes his father uncomfortable. Inside the box, Partridge finds a birthday card with balloons on the cover without an envelope written by his mother to Partridge on his ninth birthday—but his ninth birthday hadn't happened yet—a small metal box, and an old photograph of him and his mother at the beach. What shocks him is how real these things are. She must have moved them into the Dome before the Detonations. Each of them was allowed to bring in a few small items that were special to them. Of course, their father said it was just in case of emergency—an emergency that he said would likely never happen. These were things from the box his mother must have brought in with her.

She existed. He thinks of his father's line of questioning. Had his mother interfered with his coding? Had she fed him pills? Did his mother know more than his father had given her credit for?

He opens the card and reads her handwritten message. *Always walk in the light. Follow your soul. May it have wings. You are my guiding star, like the one that rose in the east and guided the Wise Men. Happy 9th Birthday, Partridge! Love, Mom.*

Did she know she wasn't going to be with him on his ninth

birthday? Was she planning ahead? He tries to hear the words in his mother's voice. Is this the way she talked about birthdays? Was he her guiding star? He touches her scrawl, written so hard that he can feel the grooves her pen made.

He picks up the small metal box and sees a small windup tab on the back, next to the lid's hinges. He opens the lid. A few plinking notes rise up—a music box. He shuts the lid quickly, hoping everyone was too engrossed in their own finds to notice.

Hidden under the music box, Partridge finds the thin chain of a necklace and pendant—a swan made of gold with a bright blue stone for an eye. He picks up the chain, and the swan pendant spins. He hears his father's voice again, "Your mother has always been problematic." *Has always been.*

Partridge knows he has to get out to the other side. If she exists—if there's the smallest hope—he has to try to find her.

He looks up and down his row—empty. He picks up each small item and slips them, quickly, one by one, into his blazer pockets, then fits the box back into its slot, the sound of metal against metal and then a clunk.

PRESSIA

MEETING

THE MEETING ROOM IS SMALL and cramped. It holds only a dozen people, all standing, and when Pressia descends the ladder, they shift and sigh, annoyed that she's here taking up room. She figures they're mad that there's another person they'll have to share food with. The room smells like vinegar. She's never had sauerkraut but her grandfather has described it, and she wonders if that's what they'll be eating. Her grandfather has taught her that it's a German food.

The guy who appeared from the trapdoor moves to the back wall. Pressia has to inch around the group to be able to have a clear view of him. He's broad and muscular. His blue shirt has a few tears. The elbows are worn through. Where the buttons are missing, he's punched holes in the fabric and tied them with string.

She remembers the first time she saw him. She was heading home down the alley from a day of scavenging and heard voices through the window. She stopped and looked in. She saw this boy—two years younger than he is now but still strong, wiry— lying on his side on the table while her grandfather worked on his face. The scene was blurred by the splintered window, but still she was sure that she saw the small quick wings of birds—rumpled gray feathers, a quick glimpse of a pair of small orange claws tucked up under a downy belly—lodged there in his back. The boy sat up, put on his shirt. Pressia walked to the door and stood just out of sight. The boy said that he could bring her grandfather a weapon as payment. Her grandfather told him to keep the weapon. "You need to protect yourself. Plus," he said, "one day you'll be stronger, and I'll only be older, weaker. I'd rather you owe me a favor."

"I don't like owing favors," the boy told him.

"Too bad," her grandfather said. "That's what I need."

The boy then left in a hurry, and when he turned the corner he ran into Pressia standing there. She pitched backward and he grabbed her arm to steady her. He was gripping her arm with the doll-head fist. He noticed it and said, "Sorry." For bumping into her or because of her deformity? She pulled her arm away from him. "I'm fine," she told him. But she was embarrassed because he probably knew she'd been spying on him.

Here he is now, the boy who doesn't like to be indebted but owes her grandfather. The boy with birds in his back.

He starts the meeting. "There's a new person with us." He points to Pressia. Everyone turns and looks at her. Like everyone else, they have scars, burns, large red knotted tissue, almost rope-like. One of the faces is connected to a jawline that holds a drape of twisted skin, so textured it almost seems like bark on a tree. She only recognizes one face—Gorse, who disappeared a few years ago with his little sister Fandra. Pressia looks around for Fandra, who had fine golden hair and a shriveled left arm. They used to joke that they were perfect for each other—Fandra had a good right hand and Pressia had the left. But she doesn't see her. Gorse catches her eye and looks away. The sight of him makes Pressia giddy. The network of the underground—maybe it not only exists but actually works. She knows now that at least one has survived, and all the people in the room look older than she is. Is this the underground? Is the boy with the birds in his back the head of it?

And what do they see when they look at her? She tucks her head to her chest, turning the crescent-shaped scar away from view, and she pulls her sweater sleeve down over the doll head. She nods at the group, hoping they'll look away soon.

"What's your name?" the boy with the birds in his back asks.

"Pressia," she says and then immediately regrets it. She wishes she'd used a fake name. She doesn't know who these people are. This is a mistake. She knows it now, clearly. She wants to go, but feels trapped.

"Pressia," he says under his breath, as if he's practicing it. "Okay," he says to the group, "let's get started."

Another boy in the crowd raises his hand. His face is partially disintegrated from infections where the metal on his cheek, something that once was chrome but is now rust-mottled, meets the puckered skin. There's a ridge of angry festered skin. If he doesn't get antibiotic ointment, he could die of it. She's seen people die of simple infections like this. The medicine is sometimes sold at certain stalls in the market but not always, and it's expensive. "When are you going to let us look in the footlocker?" he asks.

"After I'm done, like always, Halpern. You know that."

Halpern looks around, embarrassed, and picks at a scab on his cheek.

Pressia sees the footlocker now for the first time. It's pushed up against a wall. She wonders if that's where the food is kept.

Pressia notices the girls in the audience. One has exposed wires in her neck. Another has a hand twisted solid with the handle of a bike, the metal sawed off and poking up from her wrist like a protruding bone. She's surprised that they don't hide these things. One could wear a scarf, the other a sock like Pressia does. But their expressions are tough, self-possessed, proud almost.

"For those of you new to the meeting," the guy with the birds in his back says, glancing at Pressia, "I'm one of the dead." This means he's listed among those dead from the Detonations. OSR isn't looking for him. It's a good thing, all in all. "My parents were both professors who died before the Detonations. They had dangerous ideas. I have the remains of a book they were working on together, which is where I get a lot of my information. After they died, I was sent to live with an aunt and uncle. That's where I was living when the Detonations hit. They didn't survive. I've made it myself since I was just about nine years old. My name is Bradwell and this is Shadow History."

Bradwell. She remembers hearing whispers about him now, some conspiracy theorist, evangelizing out by the Rubble Fields. She heard that he challenged a lot of the ideas about the Detonations and the Dome, especially those who worship the Dome, having confused it with a deity, a benevolent but distant god. Even though she wasn't a Dome worshipper, she immediately hated the idea of him. Why have conspiracy theories? It's over. Done. Here we are. Why spin your wheels?

As he launches into his talk, pacing with his hands in his pockets, she starts to hate the reality of him, too. He's cocky and paranoid. He spouts off his theories about the Dome officials, stating that he has proof that they caused total destruction so that they could wipe out all but a fraction of the world's population while they were Dome-protected, that the Dome was designed for this purpose—not as a prototype for a viral outbreak, environmental disaster, or attack from other nations. They wanted only the elite to survive in the Dome while they waited for the earth to renew itself, at which point they'd return. A clean slate. "Did you ever wonder why we're not experiencing a full nuclear winter? Well, because it was orchestrated to avoid one. They used a cocktail of bombs—the Low Orbiting Focused Enhanced Radiation Neutron System satellites known as LoFERNS, and the High Orbiting Focused Enhanced Radiation Neutron System satellites, or HiFERNS, with electromagnetic pulse—EMP—magnification." He discusses the difference between atomic and nuclear bombs that were also used in the cocktails, and pulses designed to knock out all communications. "And how did Dusts come about? The bombs disrupted molecular structures. The cocktails included the distribution of nanotechnology to help to speed up the recovery of the earth—nanotechnology that promotes the self-assembly of molecules. The nanotechnology, speeded up by DNA, which is an informational material but also excellent at the self-assembly of cells, made our fusing stronger. And the nanotechnology that hit the humans trapped in rubble or scorched land helped them to regenerate. Even though they couldn't completely free themselves, the human cells of the Dusts grew powerful and learned to survive."

He explains one conspiracy after the next, linking them so quickly Pressia can barely understand him. But she isn't sure that she's even supposed to understand the theories. The talk isn't designed for newcomers. This is a group of those already converted. They nod along, like this was a bedtime story, and they have it memorized so they can pass it on to others. Pressia recites the Message in her head: *We know you are here, our brothers and sisters. We will, one day, emerge from the Dome to join you in peace. For now, we watch from afar, benevolently.* And then the old cross, the one her father called an Irish cross. It may not be word from the benevolent eye of God, as so many have thought of the Dome, but it's certainly not the Message of an evil force. Their sin is that of surviving. She can't blame them for that. She's guilty of the same.

It dawns on her that if she's heard of Bradwell, OSR has to know that he exists. Panic pricks across her skin. It's dangerous for her to be here at all. Bradwell is almost eighteen and even though he's listed among the dead, he has to be a prime target for OSR. As he talks, a few things are clear. He hates OSR, which he sees as feeble, weakened by their own greed and evil, incapable of taking down the Dome or effecting any real change. "Just another corrupt tyrant," he says. He especially despises that there's no transparency. The names of the highest-ranking officials in OSR are unknown. They let the grunts do their dirty work in the streets.

If anyone heard him talking this way, he'd be shot—probably publicly. They all would be considered enemies of OSR, punishable by death. She wants to go, but how? The ladder to the trapdoor in the ceiling is folded up. She'd have to make a scene. She'd have to explain herself. But what's worse? What if there's a raid and she's stuck down here with these people?

At the same time, she desperately wants to know what's in the footlocker. The guy named Halpern obviously wants to get into it. It must hold valuables. Where's the food? Mainly she wants Bradwell to stop speaking. He's talking about the things no one ever speaks of, the Detonations and their effects—the updrafts and downdrafts uprooting houses, the cyclones of fire, the reptilian skin of the dying, bodies turned to char, the oily black rain, the pyres to burn the dead, those who died days later, starting with a nosebleed and later decaying from within. She tries to will him to shut up in her mind. *Please stop! Stop! Now!*

He starts to glance at her as he speaks, and moves closer to her side of the room. He squints like he's tough, but as he gets angrier—talking about how the political movement called the Return of Civility, overseen by the national military arm called the Righteous Red Wave, was all part of the lead-up to the Detonations, the rule of everything in the name of fear, the massive prisons, sanatoriums for the sick, asylums for dissidents, their remains sprawling in every direction once you left the gated suburbs—his eyes are teary. He'd never cry, she can tell that about him, but he's complicated. At one point he says, "It was sick, all of it." And then he pokes a sarcastic dimple in his cheek and says, "You know God loves you because you're rich!"

Is this what it was like back then, really? Her father was an accountant. Her mother had taken her to Disney. They lived in the suburbs. They had a little yard. Her grandfather has drawn her pictures of it all. Her parents weren't professors who had dangerous ideas. So what side were they on? She steps back again toward the ladder.

"We have to remember what we don't want to," he tells them. "We have to pass down our stories. My parents were already gone, shot to death in their beds. I was told it was intruders, but I knew better, even then."

And now Bradwell speaks as if he's talking to her alone, like she's the only person in the room. His eyes hook on to hers and hold her there. It's a strange feeling, like being tethered to the earth—not a fleck of ash at all. He tells his story—his I Remember.

After his parents were shot, he was shipped to live with his aunt and uncle in the suburbs. His uncle had been promised three spots in the Dome, had been told a route to take into the Dome when the alarm sounded, a private route that wound around the barricades. He had tickets even. He'd paid good money for them. They stocked the car with bottled water and cash.

It happened on a Saturday afternoon. Bradwell had walked far from home. He wandered a lot those days. He doesn't remember much—only the bright flash, the heat coursing through his body, like his blood was on fire. The shadow of the birds rising up behind him . . . And so that is, in fact, what she saw two years ago when he was being stitched up on the table. Ruffling beneath his shirt, they are wings.

Bradwell's body was burned and blistered, raw. The birds' beaks felt like daggers.

He made it back to his aunt and uncle's house, amid smoldering fires and air thick with ash, people crying from rubble. Others wandered, blood-covered, their skin melted away. His uncle had been working on the car, making sure it was in tiptop shape for the special route around the barricades. He was under the car when the Detonations went off, fused with the engine. It lodged in his chest. His aunt was burned, suffering, and afraid of Bradwell's body, his birds. But she said, "Don't leave us." The smell of death, burned hair and skin—it was everywhere. The sky was gray, clotted with ash. "There was sun but the sky was so clouded with dust, day looked like dusk"—that's what Bradwell said. Does Pressia remember this simple thing? She wants to. After sun on sun on sun, it was dusk, day after day.

Bradwell stayed with his aunt in the garage, which was scalded, rickety, but strangely intact—lined with charred boxes, the fake Christmas tree, the shovels, and tools. His uncle was nearly dead, but he tried to explain to his wife how to get him free. He said things about bolt cutters and a hanging pulley that they could rig to the ceiling. But who could his wife go to for help? Everyone was either gone or dead or dying or trapped. She tried to feed her husband, but he refused to eat.

Bradwell found a dead cat on the charred lawn, put it in a box, and tried to bring it back to life, uselessly. His aunt was hoarse and winded—a little insane by then, most likely. She was dazed, weak, tending to her own burns and wounds, watching her husband slowly die.

Bradwell stops talking for a moment, looks down at the floor and then back at Pressia. He says, "And then one day, he begged her. He whispered, 'Turn on the engine. Turn it on.'"

The room is silent and still.

Bradwell says, "She held the keys in her hand and shouted at me to get out of the garage. And I did."

Pressia feels light-headed. She puts her hand on the cement wall to steady herself. She looks up at Bradwell. Why is he telling them this story? It's sick. I Remember is supposed to be a way of giving people gifts, small sweet memories, the kind Pressia likes to collect, needs to believe in. Why this? What good does this do anyone? She glances around the room at the others. They don't seem angry, like she does. Their faces are, if anything, calm. Some have their eyes closed as if they want to picture it all in their minds. This is the last thing that Pressia wants, but she does see it all—the flock of birds, the dead cat, the man trapped under the car.

Bradwell goes on, "She turned the key. For a few moments, the motor chugged. When she didn't come out to get me, I went in. I saw the blood and my uncle's waxy blue face. My aunt curled in the corner of the garage. I packed up the bottled water and put cash in a bag and taped it to my stomach. And I went back home, to my parents' house, burned to char, and found the footlocker they'd hidden in a protected room. I dragged the footlocker with me back into the dark world and learned how to survive."

His dark eyes flit across the crowd. He says, "We each have a story. They did this to us. There was no outside aggressor. They wanted an apocalypse. They wanted the end. And they made it happen. It was orchestrated—who got in, who didn't. There was a master list. We weren't on it. We were left here to die. They want to erase us, the past, *but we can't let them.*"

That's the end. No one claps. Bradwell simply turns around and pops the lock on the footlocker.

Silently, they form a line and, one by one, with reverence, they go up to take a look inside. Some reach into the footlocker and pull out papers—some colored, some black and white. Pressia can't tell what they are. She wants to see what's in the locker, but her heart's pounding in her chest. She has to get out. She sees Gorse talking to people in the corner. It's great that he's alive, but she doesn't want to find out what happened to Fandra. Pressia has to get out of here. She walks to the back of the room and pulls on the rickety ladder. It unfolds from the ceiling. She starts to climb up. But there's Bradwell at the bottom. "You didn't come for the meeting, did you?"

"Of course I did."

"You had no idea what it was about."

"I have to go," Pressia says. "It's later than I thought. I made this promise and—"

"If you knew about the meeting, then what's in the footlocker?"

She says, "Papers. You know."

He pinches the frayed cuff of her pants and gives a little tug. "Come and look."

She gazes up at the trapdoor.

"The latch locks automatically, both ways, once it's shut," he says. "You have to wait for Halpern to unlock it anyway. He's got the only key." He holds out his hand, offering help, but she ignores it and steps down on her own.

"I don't have much time," she says.

"That's fine."

There's no longer a line. Everyone is holding the papers and talking about them in small groups, Gorse among them. He looks at her. She nods, and he nods back. She has to talk to him. He's standing by the footlocker. She wants to see inside it. She walks up to him.

"Pressia," he says.

Bradwell is behind her. "You two know each other?"

"We did," Gorse says.

"You disappeared and you're still alive," Pressia says. She can't hide her amazement.

"Pressia," he says. "Don't tell anyone about me. Don't."

"I won't," she says. "What about—"

He cuts her off. "No," he says, and she understands Fandra is, in fact, dead. She's thought that Fandra was dead ever since they disappeared, but she didn't realize how hopeful she'd become since seeing Gorse that maybe she was alive, that maybe Pressia would see her again.

"I'm sorry," she says.

He shakes his head and changes the subject. "The footlocker," he says. "Go have a look."

She steps toward the locker, people on either side of her, shoulder-to-shoulder. She feels shaken. She peers inside. It's filled with ash-smeared folders. One labeled MAPS. Another labeled MAN-USCRIPT. The top folder is opened and inside there are pieces of magazines and newspapers and packages. Pressia doesn't reach in. She can't touch them at first. She kneels down and grips the edge of the footlocker. There are images of people so happy they've lost weight that they've wrapped their stomachs with measuring tapes; dogs in sunglasses and party hats; and cars with huge red bows on their roofs. There are smiling bumblebees, "money-back guarantees," little furry boxes with jewelry in them. The pictures have some wear and tear. Some have burn holes, blackened edges. Some are fogged gray with ash. But still they're beautiful. This is what it was like, Pressia thinks. Not all that stuff Bradwell has just told them. This was it. These are pictures. Proof. Real.

She reaches down and touches one. A picture of people wearing glasses with colored lenses in movie theaters. They watch the screens, laughing, and eat from small colorful cardboard bins.

Bradwell says, "It was called 3-D. They watched the flat movie screens but with the glasses on, the world jumped out at them from the screen, like real life." He picks up the picture and hands it to her.

When she holds it, her hands start to shake. "I just don't remember it in detail like this. It's amazing. I mean." She looks at him. "Why do you say all that other stuff when you've got these pictures right here? I mean, look at these."

"Because what I said was the truth. Shadow History. This isn't."

She shakes her head. "You can say what you want. I know what it was like. I have it in my head. It was more like this. I'm sure of it."

Bradwell laughs.

"Don't laugh at me!"

"I know your type."

"What?" Pressia says. "You don't know anything about me."

"You're the type who wants it all back the way it once was, the Before. You can't look back like that. You probably even love the idea of the Dome. All cushy and sweet."

It feels like he's scolding her. "I'm not looking back. You're the history teacher!"

"I only look back so we don't make the same mistakes again."

"As if we'll ever have the luxury," she says. "Or is that what you're planning with your little lessons? A way to infiltrate OSR, bring down the Dome?" She shoves the picture at his chest and walks to Halpern. "Unlock the trapdoor," she says.

Halpern looks at her. "What? Does it lock?"

She looks over at Bradwell. "You think that's funny?"

"I didn't want you to go," Bradwell says. "Is that so wrong?"

She walks quickly to the ladder, and Bradwell does too.

He says, "Here, take this." He holds out a little piece of folded paper.

"What is it?"

"Have you already turned sixteen?"

"Not yet."

"This is where you can find me," he says. "Take it. You might need it."

"What? In case I need a few more lectures?" she says. "And where's the food anyway?"

"Halpern!" Bradwell calls out. "Where's the food?"

"Forget it," Pressia says. She pulls the ladder down.

But as she puts her foot on the first rung, he reaches up and slips the piece of folded paper into her pocket. "It can't hurt."

"You know, you're just a type too," she says.

"What kind?"

She doesn't know what to say. She's never met anyone like him. The birds on his back seem restless. Their wings shiver under his shirt. His eyes are brooding, intense. She says, "You're a smart boy. You can figure that out."

As she climbs the ladder, he says, "You just said something nice about me. Are you aware of that? That was a compliment. You're sweet-talking me, aren't you?"

This only makes her angrier. "I hope I never see you again," she says. "Is that sweet enough for you?" She climbs high enough to give the trapdoor a shove. It flies open and cracks against the wood. Everyone in the room below stops and stares up at her.

And for some strange reason, she expects to look into the room overhead and see a house with flowers stitched into the sofa, bright windows with wind-swelled curtains, a family with measuring-tape belts eating a shiny turkey, a dog smiling at her in sunglasses, and outside, a car wearing a bow—maybe even Fandra, alive and combing her fine golden hair.

She knows that she'll never forget the pictures she saw. They're in her mind forever. Bradwell too, with his mussed hair, his double scar, and all the things that poured from his mouth. Sweet-talking him? Is that what he accused her of? Can that even matter now that she's heard the Detonations were orchestrated, that they were left to die?

There is no sofa, curtains, family, dog, or bow.

There's only the room with the dusty pallets and the barred door.

PARTRIDGE

TICKER

Partridge's roommate, silas hastings, walks to the mirror attached to the back of the closet door and slaps his cheeks with aftershave. "Don't make this one of those things where you have to study right up to the last minute. It's a dance, for shit's sake." Hastings is a clean-cut kid. He's bony and way too tall, and so he's all arms and legs and always looks oddly angular. Partridge likes him all right. He's a good roommate—fairly tidy, studious— but his one flaw is that he takes things personally. That, and sometimes he's a nag.

What's made things tense is that Partridge has been avoiding Hastings, saying he has to study more, complaining about pressure his dad's put on him. But in reality, he's been trying to find time alone— when Hastings is shooting hoops or goofing off in the lounge, things Partridge used to do with him—so that he can study the blueprints from the photograph taken in his father's office, the one his father sent to Partridge's academy postal box. Sometimes he winds up the music box and lets it play itself out. The music is the tune to a little song his mother used to sing about the swan wife, the one she taught him on that trip to the beach. Could that be just a coincidence? He feels like it means something more. This is what he's hoping to do for a few minutes once Hastings is gone, listen to the song and study the blueprints while all the other boys are arriving at the dance.

Right now Partridge is stalling. He's still wrapped in a towel, his hair wet from the shower. He's got his clothes laid out. Partridge blew up the picture of him and his father so that he could see the details of the blueprint. He found the air-filtration system, fans built into tunnels at twenty-foot intervals. After lights-out, he illuminates the blueprints with the small dim bulb that sits on the top of the special pen his father gave him as a gift for his birthday. It came in handy after all.

He's been blowing Hastings off too because his father made good on his threat. There have been lots of tests, batteries of tests, just like Partridge's father said there would be. Partridge has become a pincushion. He has a new understanding of what that means—he feels perforated. His blood, his cells, his DNA. His father has scheduled a test so invasive that Partridge will have to be put under—another needle in his arm that will be taped down and made into a shunt, connected to a clear bag of something that would render him unconscious.

"I'll be there eventually," Partridge says. "You go on."

"Have you looked out on the commons?" Hastings asks, leaning up to the window that overlooks the grassy lawn dividing the girls' dorms from the boys'. "Weed is sending messages with his laser pen to some girl. Can you imagine that dork asking out a girl dork via laser-pen messages?"

Partridge glances out at the lawn. He sees the small sharp zig-zags of a red pinpoint moving through the grass. He looks up at the lit windows of the girls' dorms. Someone over there knows how to read this stuff. It's amazing how inventive they have to be to get a chance to talk to girls. "Everybody's got to have an angle, I guess," Partridge says. Hastings has no angle with girls so he's really in no position to judge Weed on this one, and he knows it.

"You know," Hastings says, "it breaks my heart that you can't even walk down to the dance with me, your compadre. Little by little, you're killing me."

"What?" Partridge says, trying to play dumb.

"Why don't you tell me the truth, huh?"

"What truth?"

"You've been blowing me off because you hate me. Just say so. I won't take it personally." Hastings is famous for saying that he won't take personal insults personally, and he always does.

Partridge decides to tell him a little truth, just one, to appease him. "Look, I've got a lot weighing on me. My dad is bringing me in for a special mummy mold session. All the way under."

Hastings touches the back of his desk chair. His face goes a little pale.

"Hastings," Partridge says. "It's me. Not you. Don't take it so hard."

"No, no." He flips his hair out of his eyes, a nervous habit. "It's just, you know. I've heard rumors about these kinds of sessions. Some of the boys say that this is how you get bugged."

"I know," Partridge says. "They can put lenses in your eyes and recording devices in your ears and you're a walking, talking spy whether you know it or not."

"These aren't just your typical chipping devices so some high-strung parents know where their kid is at all times. These are high-tech. The sights you see and things you hear are monitored on full-color high-definition screens."

"Well, it's not going to be like that, Hastings. No one's going to make Willux's kid a spy."

"What if it's worse?" Hastings says. "What if they put in a ticker." A ticker is supposedly a bomb that they can plant in anyone's head. It's controlled via remote. If you suddenly become more of a risk than your value, they flip a switch. Partridge doesn't believe in the ticker.

"It's just a myth, Hastings. There's no such thing."

"Then what do they want to do to you?"

"They just want biological info."

"They don't need to put you under for info. DNA, blood, piss. What more could they want?"

Partridge knows what they want from him. They want to alter his behavioral coding, and for some reason they can't. And it has to do with his mother. He's told Hastings more than he wanted to. Mainly, he can't tell anyone that he's planning to get out. He knows how to get out of the Dome. He's done the research, the calculations. He's going to go out through the air-filtration system. There's only one more thing he needs, a knife, and he's going to get it tonight. "No need to panic, Hastings. I'll be fine. I always am, right?"

"You don't want a ticker, man. You do *not* want that."

"Look, you're all dressed up, Hastings. Don't worry about it. Go have fun. Like you said, *It's a dance, for shit's sake!*"

"Okay, okay," Hastings says and lopes to the door on his long legs. "Don't leave me alone down there forever, okay?"

"If you'd stop bugging me, I could go faster."

Hastings gives a salute and shuts the door.

Partridge sits down heavily on his mattress. Hastings, that idiot, Partridge says to himself, but it doesn't help. Hastings has freaked him out, talking about the ticker; why would officials want to off their own soldiers? He could have told Hastings that he should watch out for himself. Hastings' behavioral coding has probably already been altered a little. It might even be one of the reasons why he doesn't want to be late for the dance. Punctuality is a Dome virtue.

Partridge can't imagine how it would feel to start acting differently, just in the littlest of ways. "It's just like growing up. A maturation." That's what parents think of the behavioral coding—for boys at least. Girls don't get coding, something about their delicate reproductive organs, unless they're not okayed for reproduction. If they aren't going to reproduce, then brain enhancements can start up. Partridge doesn't want to change at all. He wants to know that what he does comes from himself—even if it's wrong. In any case, he has to get out before they find a way to mess with his behavioral coding or else he'll never do it. He'll stop himself. He might not even have the impulse to get out anymore. But what's outside the Dome? All he knows is that it's a land filled with wretches, most of whom were too stupid or stubborn to join the Dome. Or they were sick in the head, criminally insane, virally compromised—already institutionalized. It was bad back then; society was diseased. The world has been forever changed. Now most of the wretches who survived are atrocities, deformed beyond human recognition, perversions of their previous life-forms. In class, they've been shown pictures, stills frozen from ash-fogged video footage. Will he be able to survive out there in the deadly environment among the violent wretches? And it's possible that once he's out, no one will come looking for him. No one is allowed out of the Dome for any reason—not even for reconnaissance. Is this a suicide mission?

Too late. He's made up his mind. He can't afford any distractions right now—from Hastings or himself. He hears the ventilation system click on and checks his watch. He stands and climbs the short ladder to his bunk. He pulls out a small notebook wedged between the mattress and the railing. He opens the book, notes the time, shuts it, and pushes it back into its spot.

Wherever he is now, whether he's lying there in his mummy mold undergoing radiation or waiting for another vial to be taken from him or during his classes or in his dorm room at night, he studies the patterned hum of the filtration fans—the dull whirring that vibrates throughout the Dome at timed intervals. He makes notations in a book he's supposed to use to keep track of his assignments and his coding sessions. He barely noticed the

sounds before. But now that he's begun, he can sometimes antici-
pate the quiet tick just before the motors kick in. He knows now
that the air-filtration system leads out of the Dome and that the
fan blades turn off at certain times for a period of three minutes
and forty-two seconds.

He's going out because his mother might exist. "Your mother
has always been problematic." That's what his father said, and
ever since Partridge stole his mother's things from the Personal
Loss Archives, she's felt even more real. If there's a chance she's
out there, he has to try to find her.

He gets dressed quickly, pulling on his pants and shirt, looping
and tightening his tie. His hair is so short it doesn't need a comb.
Right now he has to concentrate on one thing: Lyda Mertz.

LYDA

CUPCAKE

WHEN LYDA HELPED DECORATE the dining hall with stream-
ers and gold-foil stars glued to the ceiling, she hadn't yet had a
date. There were a few people she would have been willing to go
with, but Partridge was the only one she wanted to ask her. When
he did, standing by the small set of metal bleachers out by the athletic fields during a rare moment when she wasn't being corralled
by one of the teachers, Lyda had thought, Wouldn't it be nice if it
was a little chilly and we were both windblown and the sky was
blustered, like a real fall day? But of course, she didn't say this. She
only said, "Yes, I'd love to go with you! That sounds great!" And
she fit her hands in her pockets because she was afraid he might
try to hold one and her palms were now sweating.

He looked around after she agreed, as if he was hoping no one
had heard them, as if he might take it back if someone had. But he
said, "Okay then. We can just meet there."

And now here they are, sitting next to each other at the skirted
tables. Partridge looks perfect. His eyes are such a beautiful gray that
whenever he glances at her, she feels like her heart might burst. Still,
he's barely glanced at her even though they're sitting side by side.

They've piped music in overhead, all the oldest songs on the sanctioned list. This one, swirling now, is a melancholy but kind of creepy song about someone who is watching every step and every breath someone else takes. It makes her feel a little paranoid, overly scrutinized, and she's self-conscious enough about the dip of her dress's neckline.

Partridge's roommate is leaning up against the far wall, talking to a girl. He looks over and sees Partridge, who gives him a nod. Hastings smiles goofily and then turns back to the girl.

"Hastings, that's his name, right?" Lyda says. She's trying to make conversation, but also doesn't mind lingering on Hastings, maybe to hint that she and Partridge could be sitting closer, whispering.

"That's a small miracle," Partridge says. "He doesn't have a natural way with the ladies." Lyda wonders if Partridge has a natural way with the ladies but, for some reason, isn't turning on the charms for her.

Because it's a special occasion, their food pills—bullets, as the academy boys call them—have been replaced by cupcakes sitting on all the tables on small blue plates. She watches Partridge fit large forkfuls into his mouth. She imagines that it must feel like near suffocation by eating—a rarity. Lyda nibbles her cake, savoring it, making it last.

She tries to start up the conversation again. This time she talks about her art class, which is her favorite. "My wire bird has been chosen to be in the next display in the exhibit in Founders Hall—a student art show. Do you take art classes? I've heard they don't let the boys take art, only things that have real-life applications, like science. Is that right?"

"I've taken art history. We're allowed to have some culture. But really, what good would it do us to know how to make a wire bird?" he says, gruffly. He leans back in his chair, arms crossed.

She says, "What's wrong? Is it something I said?" He seems to be disgusted with her, so why did he ask her to be his date anyway?

"It doesn't matter now," he says, as if she did say the wrong thing, and he's punishing her for it.

She pokes the cupcake with her fork. "Look," she says, "I don't know what your problem is. If something is wrong, tell me."

"Is that what you do? Look for people's problems? Try to drum up new patients for your mother?" Lyda's mother works in the rehabilitation center where some students are taken if they're having mental adaptability issues. Every once in a while one returns, but usually they're gone forever.

Lyda's stung by the accusation. "I don't know why you're acting like this. I thought you were decent." She doesn't want to storm off, but she knows that she has to now. She's told him that he's not decent. Where is there to go from here? She throws down her napkin and walks off to the punch bowl. She refuses to look back at him.

PARTRIDGE

KNIFE

PARTRIDGE FEELS GUILTY BEFORE LYDA WALKS OFF, but he's relieved once she has. It's part of his plan. He wants the key that's in her pocketbook. He's acted like a jerk in the hope that she would walk away from him, leaving the pocketbook behind. But he almost apologized to her a few times. It was harder than he'd thought. She's prettier than he remembered—her small sharp nose, freckles, her blue eyes—and it surprised him. Her looks aren't the reason he asked her to be his date.

He moves so his hands are more behind his back, slips the ring of keys off the strap of her pocketbook and into the pocket of his suit jacket. He pushes his chair back angrily like this is part of the fight and walks off as if to the bathroom, then quickly down the hall.

"Partridge!" It's Glassings. He's wearing a bow tie.

"You're scrubbed up," Partridge says, acting as normal as possible. He likes Glassings.

"I brought a date," he says.

"Really?"

"So hard to believe?" Glassings says with a joking pout.

"With that bow tie, anything's possible," Partridge says. Glassings is the only professor he can joke with like this—maybe the only adult at all. He surely can't joke with his father. What if Glassings were Partridge's father? The thought flickers through Partridge's mind. He'd tell him the truth. In fact, he wants to tell him everything. By this time tomorrow, he'll be gone. "Are you going to dance tonight?" Partridge asks, unable to look Glassings in the eye.

"Of course," he says. "You okay?"

"Fine!" Partridge says, not sure what he's done to tip Glassings off. "Just nervous. I don't really know how to dance."

"I can't help you there. I'm blessed with two left feet," Glassings says, and here the conversation stalls awkwardly for a moment. And then Glassings pretends to straighten Partridge's necktie and collar. He whispers, "I know what's going on, and it's okay."

"You know what's going on?" Partridge says, trying to sound innocent.

Glassings stares at him. "C'mon, Partridge. I know what's what."

Partridge feels sick. Has he been that obvious? Who else knows his plans?

"You stole the stuff from your mother's metal box in the Personal Loss Archives." Glassings' face goes soft. He smiles gently. "It's natural. You want to have some of her back. I took something from one of the boxes too."

Partridge looks at his shoes. His mother's things. That's what this is about. He shifts his weight and says, "I'm sorry. I didn't mean to. It was an impulse."

"Look, I'm not telling anyone," Glassings says quietly. "If you ever want to talk, come to me."

Partridge nods.

"You're not alone," Glassings whispers.

"Thanks," Partridge says.

Then Glassings leans in close and says, "It wouldn't hurt you to chum up to Arvin Weed. He's on to something in that lab, making great strides, you know. Smart kid, going places. Not to choose your friends for you, but he's a good egg."

"I'll keep that in mind."

Glassings gives him a gentle punch in the shoulder and walks off. Partridge stands there for a minute. He feels derailed, but he shouldn't. It was a false alarm. He tells himself to focus. He pretends he's lost something. He taps his suit pockets—where the keys are hidden—and his pants pockets, and then shakes his head. Is anyone even looking? He then turns down the first dim hallway, the route back to the dorms. But once he's around the corner, he turns again to the doors of Founders Hall. He pulls out Lyda's keys, picks the largest one, and fits it in the lock.

Founders Hall is the main exhibit space, now home to a Domesticity Display. Partridge pulls out his light-up pen and lets it glide over the nested metal spoons for measuring, a small white timer, and plates with elaborately designed edging. Lyda is in charge of the Domesticity Display. That's why he chose her, a calculated move on his part to get the keys, which sounds worse than it is. Partridge reminds himself that no one's perfect. Not even Lyda. Why did she say yes? Probably because he's Willux's son. And that fact has clouded all of his relationships. Growing up in the Dome, he can never be sure if people like him for himself or for his last name.

His light reflects a row of sharp glints—the case of knives. He walks over quickly. He runs his fingers over the lock, lifts Lyda's key ring, the keys clinking in the dark. Because of the coding, he hears the keys too crisply in his mind like high-pitched bells. He tries one key after the next until one glides in. He twists it. There's a small pop. He lifts the glass lid.

Then he hears Lyda's voice. "What are you doing in here?"

He looks back and sees the soft outline of her dress, a silhouette. "Nothing," he says.

She touches the light switch and turns on the electrical wall sconces, set to dim. Her eyes catch the light. "Do I want to know?"

"I don't think so."

She looks over her shoulder at the door. "I'll look away and count to twenty," she says. Her eyes lock onto his, as if she's confessing something. He wants to confess too, suddenly. She looks beautiful at this moment—the tight fit of her dress around her narrow waist, the shine of her eyes, the petite red bow of her lips. He trusts her with a rush that he can't explain.

He nods and then she turns her back and starts counting.

The display case is lined with soft velvety material. The knife has a wooden handle. He runs his finger along the blade—duller than he'd have liked. But it will do.

He tucks the knife into his belt, hidden by his blazer. He locks the case and walks to the door. "Let's go," he says to Lyda.

She looks at him for a second in the dim light, and he wonders if she's going to ask him questions. She doesn't. She reaches up and hits the light switch. The room goes dark. He gives her the keys, his hand brushing hers. They walk out together, and she locks the door behind them.

"Let's do what normal people do," Partridge says as they walk down the hall together, "so no one suspects."

She nods. "Okay."

He slips his hand in hers. This is what normal people do, hold hands.

When Partridge steps back into the decorated dining hall, he feels like a different person. He's only passing through. He's leaving. This won't last. His life is going to change.

He and Lyda walk to the middle of the dance floor, under the fake gold stars attached to the ceiling, where the other couples sway. She reaches up and knits her fingers behind his neck. He wraps his hands around her waist. The silk of her dress is soft. He's taller than she is and lowers his head to be closer. Her hair smells like honey, and her skin is warm, maybe flushed. When one song ends, he starts to back away, but stops when they're face-to-face. She rises up on her tiptoes and kisses him. Her lips are soft. He can smell her flowery perfume. He kisses her back, runs his hands up her ribs a little.

And then, as if she's just realized that they're in a crowded room, she pulls away and glances around.

Glassings is eating off a cake plate, loading up. Miss Pearl is idling by the entrance.

"It's late," Lyda says.

"One more song?" Partridge asks.

She nods.

This time he holds her hand, pulls it to his shoulder, and tilts his head so it's touching hers. He closes his eyes because he doesn't want to remember what he sees, only what he feels.

Pressia

GIFTS

ON THE MORNING OF HER SIXTEENTH BIRTHDAY, Pressia wakes up having slept fitfully in the cabinet. She can hear Bradwell's voice asking her if she'd turned sixteen yet. And now she has. She can still remember the feel of the raised print of her name on the official list as she touched it with her fingertip.

She could stay in the darkened cabinet all day. She could close her eyes and pretend that she's a speck of ash that's floated far up into the sky and she's only looking down on this girl in a cabinet. She tries to imagine it, but then she's distracted by her grandfather's ragged cough, and she returns to her body, her backbone against the wood, her clamped shoulders, the doll-head fist tucked under her chin.

It's her birthday. There's no way around it.

She climbs out of the cabinet.

Her grandfather's sitting at the table. "Good morning!"

Before him are two packages. One is simply a square of paper laid on top of a small mound, topped with a flower. The flower is an ash-choked yellow bell. The other package is something rolled up and wrapped with a cloth, tied with string, knotted in a bow.

Pressia walks past the gifts to Freedle's cage and fits her fingers through the bars. The cicada flutters its metal wings, which tick against the bars. "You shouldn't have gotten me gifts."

"Of course I should have," her grandfather says.

She doesn't want a birthday or presents. "I don't need anything," she says.

"Pressia," he whispers, "we should celebrate what we can."

"Not this one," she says. "Not this birthday."

"This gift is from me," her grandfather says, pointing to the flower-topped gift. "And I found this other one beside the door this morning."

"Beside the door?" Anyone who wanted to know her birthday could. It's written on the lists posted around the city. But Pressia doesn't have many friends. When survivors approach sixteen, alliances break down. Everyone knows they have to fend for themselves. In the weeks leading up to Gorse and Fandra's disappearance, Fandra was cold to Pressia, breaking ties before she had to say goodbye. Pressia hadn't understood it at the time, but now she does.

Her grandfather rolls the gift toward Pressia to reveal scribbling on the cloth.

She walks to the table and sits in the opposite chair. She reads the scribbling: *For you, Pressia.* And it's signed *Bradwell.*

"Bradwell?" her grandfather asks. "I know him. I stitched him once. How does he know who you are?"

"He doesn't," she says. Why would he get me a gift? she wonders. He thinks I'm only a type—the type who wants it all back the way it once was, the Before, who even loves the idea of the Dome. And what's so wrong with that? Isn't that what any normal person would want? She feels a strange angry heat spread under her ribs. She pictures Bradwell's face, the two scars, the burn, the way his eyes tear up and then he squints so he looks tough again.

She ignores his gift and instead pulls her grandfather's toward her so it's right in front of her.

"I want to tell you," he says, "that I wish it were something beautiful. You deserve something beautiful."

"It's okay," she tells him.

"Go ahead and open it."

She leans over the table, pinches the paper, and lifts it with a small flourish. She loves gifts even though she's embarrassed to admit it.

There sits a pair of shoes, thick leather stretched over smoothed wood.

"Clogs," her grandfather says. "They were invented by the Dutch, like windmills."

"I thought there were mills for grain," she says. "And paper. Mills for wind?"

"They were shaped like lighthouses," he says. He's explained lighthouses. He grew up near ships. "But instead of lights at the top, they had fans, to turn wind into power. Once upon a time we were going to use a lot of them for energy."

Who would mill wind? she wonders. And who would name a shoe a clog? As if someone were going to shove the shoe down a pipe.

"Try them on," her grandfather says.

She sets the clogs on the floor and slips her feet into the wooden grooves. The leather is still stiff, and when she stands, she notices that the wood soles make her taller. She doesn't want to be taller. She wants to be small and young. Her grandfather is replacing her old shoes with new ones that seem like they'd never wear out. Does he think they're coming for her soon? Does he think she'll run away in these shoes? Where to? The Rubble Fields? The Meltlands? The Deadlands? What lies beyond that? There are rumors of fallen train cars, tracks, caved tunnels, large airy factories, amusement parks—there wasn't only Disney—zoos, museums, and stadiums. There were bridges, once; one of them used to span a river that's supposed to exist west of here. Is all of it gone?

"When you were two years old, you had a pony at your birthday party," her grandfather says.

"A pony?" she says, clomping around in the heavy shoes, feeling hooved herself. She's wearing woolly slacks and socks and a sweater. The wool to make her clothes comes from sheep herded outside the city where there are small swatches of prickly grass cropping up from the earth, and stands of trees that edge up to OSR land where some survivors hunt new breeds, winged things and furred beasts that claw bulbs and roots, and feed on one another. Some of the sheep are barely sheep. But even deformed, horns twisted and spiked, unfit to eat, their wool is good. Some survivors have made a living off of it. "Why a pony? Where would they put a pony?"

"It walked circles in the backyard, giving rides." This is the first she's heard of a pony. Her grandfather has told her stories of birthdays. Ice cream cake, piñatas, water balloons. Where did this come from?

"My parents hired a pony to walk in circles?" They're strangers to her. The smallest glimpse awakens some kind of insatiable hunger.

He nods. He looks tired suddenly, very old. "Sometimes I'm glad they never had to see this."

Pressia doesn't say anything, but his words burn deeply. She wants her parents here. She tries to keep certain moments of her life in her head so that she can tell them all of this one day, just in case. Even though she knows they're dead, she can't stop herself. Even now she thinks that she'll tell them about this day, clogs and talk of windmills. And if she ever sees them again, even though she knows she won't, she'll ask them questions. They'll tell her stories. She'll ask them about the pony. She wants them to be watching over her somehow, seeing all of this, the way certain religions believe in heaven and the soul living on. Every once in a while, she can almost feel them watching—her mother or her father? She's not sure. And she can't confess it to anyone, but it is a comfort.

"And this other gift? From Bradwell?" Her grandfather is part teasing and part suspicious, a tone she's never heard before.

"It's probably something stupid or mean. He can be mean."

"Well, are you going to open it?"

Part of her doesn't want to, but that would just make the gift loom larger. To get it over with, she quickly pulls the string on the bow and it comes loose and falls to the table. She brings the string to Freedle's cage and slips it between the bars. Freedle likes small things to play with sometimes, or he did at least when he was younger. "Have at it," Pressia says.

Freedle's eyes snap to the string. He flaps his wings.

Pressia walks back to the table, sits down, and unrolls the cloth.

It's a clipping—the one that she found in Bradwell's footlocker and loved, the one of people wearing glasses with colored lenses in movie theaters, eating from small colorful cardboard bins, the one that made her hands shake for reasons she couldn't explain, the one that she was looking at when he told her that he knew her type. Pressia's heart kicks up in her chest. She's a little breathless. Is this just some kind of cruel gift? Is he making fun of her?

Pressia needs to calm down. It's only paper, she tells herself.

But it isn't only paper. It existed way back when she had a mother and a father and she rode a pony in her backyard in circles. She touches the cheek of someone laughing in the theater. Bradwell was right after all. She is a type. Was this his point in giving her the gift? Well, fine then. This is what she wants and will never have. The Before back again. Why not envy the people in the Dome? Why not wish she were anywhere but here? She wouldn't mind wearing 3-D glasses in a movie theater and eating from boxes with her beautiful mother and accountant father. She wouldn't mind having a dog in a party hat and a car with a bow and a measuring-tape belt. Is that so wrong?

"The movies," her grandfather says. "Look at that, 3-D glasses. I remember seeing movies like that when I was young."

"It's so real," Pressia says. "Wouldn't it be nice if—"

Her grandfather cuts her off. "This is the world we live in."

"I know," she says and looks at Freedle in his cage, rusty Freedle. She gets up and walks away from the picture. She stares at her row of little creatures on the window ledge. For the first time, they strike her as childish. She's sixteen now. What does she want with toys? She looks at them sitting there. She then looks at the magazine picture—3-D glasses, velvet seats. Compared with that shiny world, her little butterflies look dull. Sad excuses for toys. She picks up one of the newest butterflies and holds it in her hand. She winds it and lets its wings sputter, noisy clicking. She puts the butterfly back on the ledge and raises her one good hand, lightly pressing it against the window's splintered glass.

PARTRIDGE

3 MINUTES AND 42 SECONDS

FOR A WHILE AFTER GLASSINGS' FIELD TRIP to the Personal Loss Archives, Partridge hadn't known how he was going to gain access to the air-filtration system. But then he realized that one of the access points to the system was connected to the coding center where all the academy boys from his level went for weekly coding sessions in their mummy molds.

And so that's how he's decided to work it.

He lines up at morning bells, carrying his backpack with him; it holds his mother's things, plus a container of soytex pills, a few bottles of water, and the knife he stole from the Domesticity Display. He's wearing a hooded jacket and a scarf even though it's a little warm.

As usual, the boys are shuttled on the monorail. He steers clear of the herd. He's never really had many friends in the academy. Hastings is an exception, not the rule. Partridge was too famous when he arrived—because of his father and his older brother. But then Sedge killed himself, and Partridge was famous in a very different way.

Now he shuffles past the herd and takes a seat between Hastings, who usually sleeps the entire trip, and Arvin Weed because he's always reading large science files on his handheld—things that the science teacher hasn't covered and probably won't, nanotechnology, biomedicine, neuroscience. If you get him talking, he'll mumble about self-generating cells and synaptic firings and brain plaque. Because Arvin spends most of his time in the school science lab—*on to something, making great strides*, as Glassings put it, *a good egg, going places*—he's almost invisible even when he's in plain sight. While Arvin is clicking through documents, Hastings has already balled up his jacket for a makeshift pillow.

Partridge hasn't gone unnoticed, though. Vic Wellingsly, one of the herd, shouts down the train car, "So Partridge, rumor has it you're going under today. You going to get a ticker or what?"

Partridge looks at Hastings, who looks back wide-eyed. He then gives Wellingsly a dirty look.

"What?" Wellingsly says. "Was I not supposed to say anything? Is this not common knowledge?"

"Sorry," Hastings mutters to Partridge, flipping his hair out of his eyes. Hastings wants to fit in with the herd. It's not surprising that he traded in this information for a little recognition. Still, it pisses Partridge off.

"So?" Wellingsly says. "Tick, tick, tick?"

Partridge shakes his head. "Just the regular," he says. "No big deal."

"Imagine Partridge with a ticker," one of the Elmsford twins says. "They'd flip the switch just to put him out of his misery. A mercy killing!"

The herd laughs.

Arvin glances up from his book as if, for a moment, he's thinking of standing up for Partridge, but then he slouches and keeps reading. Hastings closes his eyes and pretends to sleep.

The other Elmsford twin says, "Partridge's head like an exploding melon!"

"All over Lyda Mertz's dress," Vic says. "So sorry, Lyda. Partridge here must've gotten excited."

"Leave Lyda out of it!" Partridge says, sounding angrier than he wanted to.

"Or what?" Vic says. "You know I'd be happy to beat your ass."

"Really?" Partridge says, and everyone knows what he means— *You're going to beat up Willux's son? Would that be a wise thing to do?* Partridge hates himself for saying it. It just came out so fast. He hates being Willux's son. It makes him a target as much as it protects him.

Vic doesn't say anything. The train car goes quiet. Partridge wonders if they'll look back at this moment after he's gone or dead—depending how things go. He's got to make it past huge sets of fan blades. He could get chopped to death, a chopped melon. What will they think of him then? That he was a coward who died trying to run away? That he was defective, like Sedge?

He looks out the window. The scenery shifts past—the playing fields, the academy's stone walls, the tall stacked homes, shopping complexes, the office buildings, and, farther out, the automatic threshers at work in the fields—and then they enter the dark tunnel. He imagines the sick wretches clawing at him, the poisoned land and water, the ruins. He won't die out there, will he? It's a risk he has to be willing to take. He can't stay here, knowing his mother might be alive out there, knowing that if he stays, he'll be altered, deep down, in ways he'll never even really remember.

As if someone has hit a light switch, their car goes dark before the automatic lights flicker on, as they head straight to the heart of the coding center. The brakes hiss, and the boys are slightly bucked, then settle, then stand.

They are quiet in the halls. Some say halfhearted see-yas.

Partridge grabs Hastings before he heads off. "Hey," he says. "You can't do that."

"I'm sorry," Hastings says. "I shouldn't have told him. He's all mouth."

"No," Partridge says. "It's not about me. It's about you. You're going to have to stand up to them one day."

"Maybe," Hastings says.

"You will and you can do it. I know it." Partridge feels bad about leaving Hastings behind. He'll be a little lost without him. He doesn't want him to fall into the herd by accident, where he'll be the one they kick around for laughs. "I might miss dinner tonight, to study," Partridge says. "Go with Arvin Weed. Sit at his table, okay?"

"You're arranging my social circles now?"

"Just do it. Okay? Remember I said this."

"You're being weird," Hastings says.

"No I'm not."

Two escorts walk up and lead them in opposite directions.

"See you later, weirdo," Hastings says.

"Bye," Partridge says.

He's led to a small white room—no windows. The mummy mold sits on the examination table. It's a perfectly smooth cast, hinged at the back so that Partridge can climb inside. Above and beside it, there is equipment—robotic arms, pincers, vacuum tubing—all shiny chrome, newly polished. A desk with a computer and a chair-on-wheels sit in one corner. On the desk, there's a vase with a fake flower bowing from the lip. A reminder of home or nature? Partridge wonders. The Dome doesn't usually go for those kinds of soft touches.

And suddenly Partridge has second thoughts. He doesn't have to go through with this. No one has to know. He could have dinner with Hastings and ask Lyda to help him return the knife. He remembers the feel of her narrow waist and her ribs as his hands moved up her silky dress while they kissed. He'd love to smell her honeyed hair again.

Someone has probably noticed that the knife is missing—a teacher or janitor. Lyda could be in one of the headmaster's offices right now, being interrogated. If he's caught, his father will be furious. He might be pulled out of the academy. He might be sent to the rehabilitation center to talk to someone like Lyda's mother, Mrs. Mertz. And Lyda? She'll be in trouble too, if he's caught. He'd have to tell them how he gained access to the display.

He could confide in Glassings. But what would Glassings do? He'd lead him to the library stacks where they'd have a quiet conversation, perhaps using the small squares of scrap paper and tiny pencils. Glassings would sweat the way he does sometimes, small beads on his forehead that he pushes back into his receding hairline. He'd advise him to keep quiet, no doubt. He'd be nice about it.

The cast is there, waiting for Partridge, a perfect mold of his body. It surprises him how big he is. Just a few years ago he'd been the shortest in his class, and pudgy too. But the cast is so long and lean that it seems like it would belong to someone else, someone older, more like Sedge. If Sedge were still alive, would Partridge be taller than him now? He'll never know.

He wants to go back, but it's already too late.

He only has a few minutes before the tech arrives. Cool air is streaming through the vents. He pulls the rolling chair away from the computer desk and situates it under the duct. He stands on the chair, hoping for steadiness. He unscrews the duct cover lodged overhead, and pushes it into the ceiling. He quickly reaches up, curling his hands over the metal frame, and then, kicking the chair back to the desk on his way, he pulls himself into the dark duct. On his hands and knees, he replaces the cover over the hole. It won't fool anyone long, but it may buy him a few minutes.

It's darker in the ducts than he expected, and louder. The system is on, vibrating manically. He crawls as fast as he can. He has to make it to the first set of filters by the time the system stops. At that point, he'll have only three minutes and forty-two seconds of downtime to make it through the first filter, the tunnels and the rows of fans, and at the end of that, the second barrier of filters. He'll have to cut his way out into the world. That is, if he's made it in time and the blades haven't chopped him to death by then.

Just as the blueprints indicated, he can crawl out of the duct-work and step into the massive air-purification tunnel itself. He stands upright, his head barely skimming the ceiling. Its sheet metal is perfectly rounded—and he thinks of the word *kettledrum*. But he's not sure what the word means. What does a kettle have to do with a drum?

Just ahead, there's the first set of pink filters, tautly drawn, like a dense fixed curtain, blocking his way. Partridge is surprised that the filters are so pink, pink as a tongue, and that everything here is now so brightly lit. He wonders why. For maintenance purposes?

He pulls out the kitchen knife and thinks of Lyda, her voice counting to twenty slowly in the dimly lit room, his finger running over the blade. He starts sawing through the filters. The fibers are tough with thick strands running through them, like muscle in meat. The fibers begin to break loose. The particles spin and rise, reminding him again of something else from his childhood, but he can't think of what—something like snow?

Partridge has heard the fibers are barbed and can settle into your lungs, starting up an infection. He doesn't know if this is true or not. He's come to mistrust everything presented as fact. Still, he doesn't want to take unnecessary risks. He pulls out his scarf, ties it around his mouth.

He gets enough of the filters perforated and shoulders his way through. His hooded jacket now dusted pink, he sees the series of monstrous fans in front of him, the fan blades sharp and still.

He runs to the first set of blades and without touching them finds a low triangle between the blades, and he dips through. His boots slip on the slick surface, and he falls on one hip with a thud that echoes, the clumsiness of coding. He scrambles to his feet quickly and takes the next fan and the next, finding a rhythm. Has the tech already figured out that his body cast is empty? Has someone sent out a shrill alarm? Has Special Forces been alerted? Partridge knows that once word gets out that Willux's son—his only *living* son—is missing, there will be no end to the search.

He moves faster through the series of tunnels and fans as if it were an obstacle course. He remembers a backyard, maybe his own backyard from his childhood or maybe someone else's. There was a green lawn with blades of grass that you could rip right out of the ground, and trees with bark that wasn't smooth or polished. There was a dog even. His older brother and someone else, a tall girl, had set up a course with ropes they were supposed to swing on and hoops to dive through and a ball that they had to shoot into a bucket at the end. There were drinks in boxes with tiny straws. The necks of the straws were like little accordions, and they bent to fit in your mouth.

His head feels suddenly heavy, and his body shifts. He grabs one of the blades to steady himself. It's so sharp that the edge draws blood. His blood dots the floor. He's only seen himself bleed a few times, at the dentist's office, for example, when the machines were too forceful and his foamy spit turned pink. His vision narrows to a white seed of light and then comes flooding back.

He glances at his watch. Thirty-two seconds left. It hits him that he might not make it. He could die here, chopped to bits, and now because he's broken through the filters, his body will be sent out, his blood carried by the strong current of air with the other smaller fibers. They'll turn red with his blood. The operators will have to shut things down. Some people will have to be moved to temporary housing. Rumors will spread. The real story will be buried. They won't mention a word about a problem with the air filtration because everyone would assume that the wretches had risen up, organized biological warfare. They might even think that OSR, that flimsy militaristic regime, had made a hit. There would be mass panic. They'd come up with some other rationale, and, as for Partridge, they'd make up some story, hopefully something noble. Poor Willux, his father would be given condolence cards. There wouldn't be a real burial. Just like last time, with his brother. No one wants to see a dead body, no beautiful barbarism here. Poor old Willux, his wife and two sons now all dead, three boxes in the Personal Loss Archives.

Partridge staggers forward, sliding along the surface, throwing himself through the blades. There's another knick on his cheek. He hears distant ticking. The motor. He jumps through the second-to-last fan and sprints. He can see the final set of pink filters at the end of the tunnel. He wants to get out. He wants to feel it all again, wind and sun. He wants to find his old street, his old house—gone, he knows, blown up, but still. There is resistance in his behavioral coding. Why? What does it have to do with his mother? He found her things in the box, and everything changed. He has the envelope filled with her possessions—the swan necklace on a gold chain, the birthday card, the metal music box, and the photo—locked in a plastic pouch. He feels it all there on his back.

The final fan clicks backward, just one single inch, and Partridge dives through the last set of blades just as the fans begin to roar at his back, and the wind is drawn in like a deep unending breath from the other side of the last set of filters. The current is drawing him backward now. This is how his memory has felt, a long inhale that pulls him back. He falls to the ground but sets his boot heels and, hand over hand, pulls himself away from the blades. His strength coding is kicking in. He feels a surge of power. When he's close enough, he reaches out and stabs the filters with his kitchen knife and drags his body forward against the wind. The pink fibers break loose and stream past him into the fans and he thinks of the word *confetti*.

PRESSIA

KNOCK

Pressia is working late at night on her small creatures. Her grandfather is asleep by the alley door, sitting upright in his chair, the brick on his thigh. He's taken over the bartering and, ever since, she's needed more creatures to sell for smaller returns. Sometimes he's too sickly to make it to the market at all and they both feel useless, something they both hate. She marks time by hunger now. During these late nights, she's begun to realize that she could die here slowly, wasting away in an ash-laced cabinet in a cramped room. She looks at her grandfather, his wired stump, his closed eyes, the sheen of his burns, the labored rise and fall of his chest, the soft wheeze of ash in his lungs, the spinning fan in his throat. His face is clenched even while dreaming.

She keeps Bradwell's gift, the magazine picture, on the table. She sometimes hates the people in their 3-D glasses—an ugly reminder of what she'll never have—but can't seem to put the picture away.

Ever since she opened the gift, there have been more memories, quick flashes: a small tank with fish swishing back and forth, the feel of the woolen tassel on her mother's pocketbook, that soft yarn in her fist, a heating duct under a table that seemed to purr. She remembers sitting on what must have been her father's shoulders as he walked under flowering trees, being wrapped in his coat as she was asleep and being shuttled from the car to her bed. She remembers brushing her mother's hair with a wire brush while a song played on a handheld computer—the image of a woman singing a lullaby about a girl on a front porch, and someone is begging her to take his hand to ride with him into the Promised Land. Just her voice, no instruments at all. It must have been her mother's favorite lullaby. She played the recording every night before Pressia fell asleep. At the time, Pressia got tired of the song, but now she'd sacrifice almost anything to hear it again. Her mother smelled like soap made out of grass—clean and sweet. Her father smelled like something richer, more like coffee. The picture of the people in the theater, for some reason, jolts her memories, and she'll miss her parents so deeply that sometimes she can't breathe. Even though she doesn't remember them in any whole way, she remembers the feel of being enveloped by her mother—the softness of her body, the silkiness of her hair, the sweetness of her scent, the warmth. When her father wrapped her in his coat, she felt cocooned.

This is what she's thinking about, her fingers quickly attaching wings to the skeletal frame of a butterfly, when there's a knock at the door. The knock is sharp, the singular rap of a knuckle. There's no engine noise of an OSR truck. Who can it be?

Her grandfather is sleeping soundly, deep rattling snores. She gets up and tiptoes to her grandfather, which is hard to do in Dutch-invented clogs; did these Dutch never have a reason to tiptoe? She grabs his shoulder and shakes it. "Someone's here," she whispers.

He startles awake just as another knock sounds out in the small room.

"Into the cabinet," he says. They've worked it that she hides

there if someone comes to the door, and if he taps his cane—
shave and a haircut, two bits—she should escape through the fake
panel. Pressia assumes that the little rhythm has something to do
with barbershops, which may be why her grandfather's chosen it.
That's their sign.

Pressia walks quickly to the cabinet and climbs in. She leaves
the smallest crack in the door so she can see.

Her grandfather hobbles to the door with his cane and peers
through a small hole that he's cut out of the wood. "Who is it?" he
asks.

There's a voice on the other side, a woman's voice. Pressia can't
make out what she's saying, but it must appease her grandfather
in some way. He opens the door, and the woman walks in quickly,
breathlessly. He shuts the door behind her.

Pressia sees the woman in small glimpses—the rust on the
gears embedded in her cheek, a sheen of metal cast over one of
her eyes. She's thin and short with blunt shoulders. She's holding a
bloody rag to her elbow. "Death Spree!" she tells Pressia's grandfather. "Unannounced! We just had one not but a month ago! I
barely got away."

A Death Spree? It makes no sense. The OSR announces Death
Sprees—they let the soldiers form tribes for twenty-four-hour peri-
ods so they can kill people, carry their bodies to a circle staked out
in an enemy's field, tallying the dead for points. Those with the
most win. OSR sees it as a way of winnowing the weak from the
general population. They announce Death Sprees about twice a
year, but they'd just had one. It was the time Pressia's grandfather
chose to strip the cabinets and make the fake panel so his handiwork
wouldn't be heard over the stomping, hooting wildness. There
have never been two Death Sprees so close together and never unannounced. She assumes the woman's crazy or perhaps in shock.

"You sure about a Death Spree?" Pressia's grandfather says. "I
haven't heard any chants."

"How else did I get this wound? It was out past the Rubble Fields heading west, still going strong. I ran here instead of home." The woman has come to be stitched up, but it's been so long since her grandfather has done any stitching, he has to look for his kit, which sits at the end of the cabinet, and dust it off.

The woman says, "By God, what a day. First all them whispers, now a Death Spree!" She sits down at the table and looks at Pressia's creatures. She sees the picture and touches it lightly with one finger. Pressia wonders if she'll ask about it. She wishes she'd thought to swipe it from the table before climbing into the cabinet. "You heard them new whispers. Didn't you?"

"Can't say that I've been out today." He sits down across from the woman and looks at the gaping flesh.

"You didn't hear?"

Her grandfather shakes his head and starts swabbing his instruments with alcohol. The room fills with its antiseptic tang.

"A Pure," she says, lowering her voice. "A boy with no scars, no marks, no fusings. They say he was full-grown, this boy—tall and thin and with hair shorn close to his head."

"Not possible," her grandfather says. This is what Pressia's thinking too. People like to make things up about Pures. It's not the first time she's heard this one. And nothing's ever come of the other whispers.

"He was spotted in the Drylands," the woman says. "And then he was gone."

Pressia's grandfather laughs, which turns into a cough. He turns his head and coughs until he's gasping.

"You okay to be doing this?" she asks him. "You've got the weeping lungs?"

"I'm fine. It's the throat fan. I collect too much dust and have to get it out."

"It ain't polite to laugh anyways," she says.

Her grandfather starts stitching now. The woman winces.

"But how many times have we heard this one before?" he says.

"It's different this time," the woman says. "It's not drunk Groupies. It was three different spotters. Each saw him and then reported. They say he didn't see them, and they didn't approach because they sensed he was holy."

"It's the whisper clutches. That's all."

They go quiet for a moment as her grandfather stitches the wound. The woman's face becomes rigid, the gears locking up. Pressia's grandfather blots the bleeding. He works quickly, daubing the wound with alcohol, then wraps it.

When he says, "All done," the woman rolls her shirtsleeve down over the bandage. She hands him a small tin of meat and then pulls up a piece of fruit from her sack. It's bright red but wears a thick skin almost like an orange. "It's a beauty. Isn't it?" She hands it to him, as payment.

"Nice doing business with you," Pressia's grandfather says.

The woman then pauses. "Believe what I told you or not. But listen, if there's a Pure who got out, then you know what."

"No," he says. "What? You tell me."

"If there's a way out, it means there's also a way in." Pressia gets a sudden chill. Then the woman lifts her finger to her ear. "Hear that?" she says.

And now Pressia does hear something, the far-off chanting of a Death Spree. What if the woman isn't crazy? Pressia wants this whisper about the Pure to be true. She knows that whispers can be useful. Sometimes they contain real information. But usually they're fairy tales and lies. This is the worst kind of whisper, the kind that draws you in, gives you hope.

"If there's a way out," the woman says again, very slowly and calmly this time, "it means there's also a way in."

"We'll never get in," Pressia's grandfather says impatiently.

"A Pure," the woman says, "a Pure here among us!"

And this is when they all hear a truck rumbling in the alley. They're still and quiet.

A dog outside barks viciously, a gunshot, and then no more barking. Pressia knows which dog it was. She recognized its bark—a dog that's been beaten so much, it only knows how to cower or attack. She always felt sorry for it, and would sometimes feed it small bits of food—not from her hand, though, because it couldn't be completely trusted.

She holds her breath. Everything grows quiet except for the low rumbling idle of the truck in the alley. In the morning, someone will be gone.

Her grandfather taps the floor—*shave and a haircut, two bits*—with his cane. Pressia isn't ready to go. She doesn't want to leave her grandfather. He moves quickly to his chair. He picks up the brick and holds it in one hand.

The woman holds her wound and moves to the window where she peeks out. "OSR," she whispers, terrified.

Pressia's grandfather gazes at Pressia, their eyes meeting through the small crack of the cabinet door. His breath is quick, his eyes wide. Lost. He looks lost.

Shot through with fear, Pressia wonders what will happen to him without her. Maybe OSR are coming for someone else, she thinks. Maybe the boy named Arturo or the twin girls who live in the lean-to. Not that she wants it to be the twin girls in the lean-to or Arturo. How can she wish the OSR on someone else?

She can't move.

In the alleyway, she hears a muffled cry, boots scraping the pavement. *Not here*, she whispers to herself. *Please, not here!* She's waiting for the rev of the truck's engine, the pop of its clutch, but it's still there, a constant rumbling in the alley.

Her grandfather taps the rubber stopper on his cane again—harder—*shave and a haircut, two bits!*

She has to go. But before she does, she draws a circle, then two eyes and a smiling mouth with her finger in the ash collected on the cabinet door. She wants it to mean, *I'll be back soon.* Will he see it and understand? What if she doesn't come home soon? What if she is not fine and never will be again?

Pressia takes a deep breath and then she pushes the doll-head fist against the fake panel. It gives a little, then pops loose and clatters to the dusty barbershop floor. Light washes into the cabinet.

Pressia's heart hammers in her chest. She looks around the shadowed hull of the barbershop. Most of the roof was blown off and now gives way to the dusky night sky. She feels unprotected coming from the tight embrace of the cabinets to this openness.

There's only one chair left in the barbershop, a swivel chair with a foot pump that can make the seat higher or lower. The counter in front of this one chair is still perfectly intact, too. Three combs float in a dust-covered glass tube filled with old cloudy blue water like they're suspended in time.

She moves quickly into the shadow of this wall and slides along it, passing the bank of shattered mirrors. She hears another rumbling truck. It's strange that there is more than one. She squats down and holds her breath. She doesn't move. She hears a radio playing in the truck, a tinny version of an old-fashioned song with a screaming electric guitar and pumping bass, one she doesn't know. She has heard that when they take people, they tie their hands behind their backs and tape their mouths. But do they turn on the radio while they're driving away? For some reason, this seems like the worst of it.

She crouches as low as she can. She tries not to breathe. Are they coming for her alone, one truck blocking the alley and another on the street running parallel? All the mirrors are broken except a handheld one that sits on that counter. She asked her grandfather about the handheld mirrors once, and he said they used them to show the customers the backs of their heads. She doesn't know who would ever want to see the back of their head. Who would ever need to?

From this spot, she can see the Dome again, up on the hill due north. It's an orb—shiny and bright, dotted with large black weapons, a glittering fortress, topped with a cross that shines even through the ash-choked air. She thinks about the Pure, the one who was supposedly spotted in the Drylands, tall and lean, with short hair. It has to be only a whisper. It can't be true. Who would leave the Dome to come here and be hunted?

The truck is inching along. A searchlight floods the room. She doesn't move.

The light hits a triangular shard and for a second there, staring up at her, are her own eyes, almond-shaped like her Japanese mother—*so beautiful, so young.* And her father's freckles over the bridge of her nose. And then there is the burned crescent that half circles her left eye.

If she goes, what will happen to Freedle? Freedle is going to give out one day.

The searchlight slides on and then the truck rumbles past with OSR and a black claw painted on its side. Pressia stays completely still as the growling motor and the radio song fade into the night. The first truck is still in the alley. She hears shouting, but not her grandfather's voice.

She peeks out through the large holes where the plate-glass windows used to be. It's dark and cold. No one is on the street. She slides along the shadow of the wall again to the front door's blasted hull. There sits a big strange rusted tube painted with pale red and blue spiral stripes. It's shattered and warped. Her grandfather says it's something that was attached to all barbershops, a symbol that once meant something. She walks out the door, staying close to the crumbled wall.

What was the plan? Hide. The huge old irrigation pipe that her grandfather once showed her is three blocks away. He thought she'd be safe there. But is anyplace safe now?

Bradwell, she thinks. The underground. She has the map to his place that he slipped in her pocket still folded there. He might be home, preparing for his next lesson in Shadow History. What if she shows up and says thank you for the gift, pretending it was meant as a kindness not a cruelty? Would he take her in? He owes her grandfather for stitching him up, but she'd never go there asking for a favor. Never. Still, she decides to try to make it all the way there. Fandra didn't survive, but her brother did.

On the floor, next to the door, is a small charred bell. It surprises her. She picks it up but its clapper is missing and so it doesn't make a sound. She could make something out of it, one day.

She holds the bell so tightly that its edge digs into the meat of her hand.

PARTRIDGE

HOOF

PARTRIDGE HEARS THE SHEEP before he sees them, rustling from dark brambles in the woods in front of him, errant bleating. One stutters in a way that reminds him of Vic Wellingsly laughing at him on the monorail car. But that was in another world. The sun's gone down, and all warmth has been leached from the air. Partridge is on the outskirts of the city now, the hunkered char of its remains. He smells smoke from fires, hears distant voices, an occasional shout. A scuttle of wings rattles overhead.

He's made it through the stretch of sandy dust fields where he drank all his water and twice thought he saw an eye in the earth, a singular blinking eye that was quickly lost in dust. A hallucination? He can't be sure.

He's skirting the edge of the woods. If the earth can be that alive, the woods are too dangerous. He assumes that's where some of the wretches must live. He thinks of his mother, the saint, as his father used to call her, and the wretches she supposedly saved. If she's still alive, are they?

A large oily black bird dips close to his head. He sees its sharp beak on a crooked hinge, its claws ratcheting open and closed, midair. Astonished, he watches it until it flies out of sight into the woods. He thinks of Lyda's caged wire bird, and he's filled with guilt and fear. Where is Lyda now? He can't help but feel that she's in danger, that her life has changed. Would they just ask her questions and then let her return to her normal life? She has nothing to tell, really. She knows he took the knife, but after that it will seem like she's holding something back, that she knows more than she's saying. Did anyone see them kiss? If so, that will make her look guilty. He remembers the kiss. It comes back to him again and again—sweet and soft. She smelled like flowers and honey.

Then the sheep emerge from the trees, hobbling along on dainty, mangled hooves. He squats in the brambles to watch them. He assumes they're feral. They wander to a gutted seam in the earth pooled with rainwater. Their tongues are quick, almost sharp looking, some shining like razors. Their fur is beaded with water, matted in hunks. Their eyes rove out of sync, and their horns—sometimes too many horns to count, sometimes a row of horns, a spiked ridge down the beast's back—are grotesque. Some horns grow like vines, spiraling one another, then veering off to one side. In one case, the horns have grown backward, like a mane, and have fused into the backbone so the head is locked in place.

As terrifying as the beasts seem, Partridge is thankful to know that the water is drinkable. He has a ragged cough—from breathing the barbed fibers? From the sandy ash? He'll wait for the sheep to walk off and refill his bottles.

But the sheep aren't feral. A shepherd with a stubbed arm and bowed legs tromps out of the woods, calling gruffly and wielding a sharp stick. His face is marred with burns, and one eye seems to have slid and settled into the bone of his cheek. His boots are heavy, coated in mud. He herds the sheep, brutally whacking and poking them, making guttural noises. The man accidentally drops the stick, bends to pick it up. His face—rippled with burns and welts—turns, and his eyes lock on Partridge. He grimaces. "You," he says. "You thieving? Meat or wool?"

Partridge wraps his face with the scarf, pulls up the hood, and shakes his head. "I just need water." He motions to the puddle.

"Drink that and your stomach will rot," the man says. His teeth shine, dark pearls. "Come here. I got water."

The sheep—their gray haunches—recede into the woods with the shepherd driving them. Partridge follows. The woods are blackened still, but there's greenery bursting up in small clutches. Soon enough, they come to a lean-to and a pen of mesh and stakes. The man herds the sheep in. Some buck and he whips them on the snouts. They bleat. The pen is so small that the sheep are wedged in, clotting the space with wool.

"What's that smell?" Partridge asks.

"Dung, piss, rot, sour wool. A little death. I got liquor," he says, "homemade. It'll cost you."

"Just water," Partridge says, his breath making the scarf damp. He pulls a bottle from his backpack and hands it to the man.

The man stares at the bottle for a moment and Partridge worries that there's something about it that tips the shepherd off, but he then hobbles into the lean-to. Partridge sees inside of it for a moment, the warped door propped by mud. The pink sheen of skinned animals hanging from the walls. With their heads chopped off, he can't identify them. Not that their heads would have necessarily helped him.

Partridge feels a sting on his arm. He swats it, and there is an armored beetle of some sort with thick pincers. He flicks it, but the beetle seems rooted. So he digs his fingers in and pinches it off his skin.

The man returns with his bottle, now filled with water.

"Where are you coming from?"

"The city," Partridge says. "I should be getting back."

"What part of the city?" the man asks. His sunken eye blinks slower than the other. Partridge shifts his vision between the two.

"The outskirts," Partridge says, and he starts to walk back the way he came. "Thank you for the water."

"I've suffered a recent loss," the man says. "My wife, diseased. She's dead, fresh dead. I need a warm body here. It's the work of more than one."

Partridge looks at the penned sheep. One of the sheep has a spade-like hoof, rusty and dented. He digs in the corner. "I can't."

"You're not natural. Are you?"

Partridge doesn't move. "I've got to head back."

"Where's your marks? What's you fused to? I see nothin' on you."

The man picks up his stick and points it at Partridge. Partridge sees the scars on his face clearly now, a frenzy of nicks.

"Hold steady," the man says slowly, crouching.

Partridge turns and runs back the way he came. His speed kicks in, the motion of his arms and legs fast and steady as pistons. He heads out of the woods the way they came, and then his foot catches on a soft log. He falls to the ground. Here, again, is the puddled rainwater where the sheep had been drinking. He looks back at the log and sees that it isn't a log at all. It's a bundle of reeds—some green, some a rusty brown. He thinks of the threshers out beyond the academy. He listens for the shepherd, hears nothing. He walks to the reeds, sees the shine of wire that binds them. He stares until he sees a pale glimmer, something wet and still. He reaches down, his hand shaking. He smells something sickly sweet. He parts the reeds—they're damp, almost rubbery—and exposes a human face, whitish gray on one cheek while the other is dark red, the flesh seemingly broiled, the mouth purplish from a lack of air and blood. It's the shepherd's wife—*diseased, fresh dead*. This is how he's buried her.

What part of her is wet and still? Her eye—a dark, luminous green.

LYDA

REHABILITATION

THE WHITE PADDED ROOM IS CHILLED. It reminds Lyda that there once was a container within the large box of the refrigerator before the Detonations. There are only small fridges now that people mostly eat soytex pills. But the little box in the big fridge was where her mother kept the round heads of lettuce. Were they too dainty to withstand the common area of the refrigerator? She thinks of the flared, rippled edges of the outer leaves like a skirt hem twirling.

Her mother has been to visit her twice, unofficially. During those visits, her mother was relatively quiet, but Lyda could read her anger. Her mother chatted about the neighbors and her kitchen garden, and once, very quietly, she said, "Do you have any idea how much your actions will cost us? No one can look me in the eye." But she hugged her too, at the end of each visit, rough and quick.

Today her mother will arrive as an administrator for an evaluation. She'll walk in like all the others wearing a lab coat and carrying her small handheld computer—a shield in front of her chest, hiding her tightly wrapped bosom. Beneath the press of her brassiere and the fatty meat of her breasts, there's a heart. Lyda knows it's there, beating furiously.

The room is small, square, outfitted with a bed, a toilet, and a miniature sink. A fake window shimmers on one wall. She remembers her mother fighting for this improvement in quality care a few years ago. She led the discussion in front of the board. Someone had done research that sunlight helps those with mental illness. But of course, real lit windows were out of the question. This was a compromise. The window shows shifts of light timed with a caged wall clock. Lyda doesn't trust the clock or the window image. She thinks that time is manipulated when she sleeps. It goes too quickly. Perhaps it's the sleeping medication. The longer she stays in confinement, the more serious they are categorizing her mental illness, and her chance of release shrinks. She takes pills in the morning to wake her too, and others to calm her nerves, even though she tells them that her nerves are fine. Are they? Under the circumstances, she figures they're not too bad. Not yet at least.

Regardless of whether she gets out or not, there is the stain. Who would allow her to marry into their family now? No one. Even if they did, she wouldn't be permitted to have children. Ill fit for genetic repopulation—the end.

The fake sunlight image of the window flickers as if birds have fluttered by. Is it part of the program? Why would she even think of birds passing by a window? There are so few birds in the Dome. Occasionally one will escape the aviary. But this is rare. Were the birds from her imagination? Some deep recess of memory?

The hardest thing so far, aside from the gnawing panic, is her hair. It was shorn when she arrived. She has calculated that it will take three years, at least, to return to the length it once was. The few girls she's known to come back from rehabilitation have worn wigs at first. Their faces stiff with fear of relapse and the fake shine of their hair make them seem alien, more reason to fear them.

She now wears a white scarf on her head—white to match the thin cotton jumpsuit that balloons around her, snapping up the front—one size fits all. The scarf is knotted at the nape of her neck where she has an itch. She slips her fingers below the knot and scratches.

She thinks of Partridge, his hand fitted in hers as they walked back down the corridor to the dance. He appears so quickly in her mind sometimes that her stomach flips. She's here because of him. Each question she's been asked leads back to that night. The truth is that she barely knows him. She can say this again and again, and no one ever believes her. She says it now in the quiet space of her holding cell, *I barely know him.* She doesn't even believe herself. Is he alive? She feels like her body would know, somehow, deep down, if he was dead.

At three o'clock, there's a knock and, before she can answer, the door opens. The team walks in—two doctors, both female, and her mother. She looks at her mother, awaiting some acknowledgment. But her mother's face is as still as the academy's holding pond. She looks at Lyda, but not really. Her stare rests on the wall beside her, shifts to the floor, the sink, and back to the wall.

"How are you feeling?" asks the taller, more willowy doctor.

"Fine," Lyda says. "The window's nice."

Her mother flinches, almost imperceptibly.

"You like it?" the willowy doctor says. "That was a really important improvement for us."

"We are going to ask you some brief questions once more," the other doctor begins. She's squat and chops her words. "We've been told to look into the nature of your relationship with Rip-kard Willux."

"Your boyfriend, Partridge," the willowy doctor adds as if Lyda wouldn't recognize his name.

"Just a few questions," her mother says. "We'll keep it short." Is her mother telling her to keep her answers short, too?

"I don't know where Partridge is," Lyda says. "I've told every-one that, again and again." There have been several interroga-tions, each a little more hostile than the one before it.

"Ellery Willux himself is, of course, very invested, as you can imagine," the willowy doctor says. Just saying his name thrills her, Lyda can tell. "It's his son we're talking about."

"You might aid in finding the boy," her mother adds, cheerfully, as if to say that this might redeem them as a family.

The fake image of the window flickers again as if with wings—or is it that the program has a glitch? Is it stuttering? *You might aid in finding the boy.* Is he lost? Is he gone? Like an aviary bird? Like the bird she made of wire that might now be on display in Found-ers Hall in lieu of antique egg timers, aprons, and knives. Or has her wire bird been disqualified because she's no longer a student attending the academy?

"You've stated that you showed him the Domesticity Display after hours in the exact manner that you would have when lead-ing a tour midday," the squat doctor says.

"But is this completely accurate? A boy and a girl in a dark room, having skipped out on a dance, music playing," the wil-lowy doctor adds. "We were all young once." She winks.

Lyda doesn't answer. She's learned to answer questions with questions. "What do you mean?"

"Did he kiss you?" the willowy doctor asks.

Lyda feels heat rise in her cheeks. He didn't kiss her. She kissed him.

"Did you two embrace?"

She remembers his hand on the dip of her waist, lightly touch-ing her ribs, the swish of fabric across her stomach. They danced to two songs. They have plenty of witnesses. Mr. Glassings and Miss Pearl were chaperones. Partridge bowed his head as they danced, and she felt his breath on her neck. There was a knife in his belt, hidden from view by his jacket. Yes. The kiss? Did people notice? They held hands on the walk to her dormitory. Many people saw them. Was someone looking out a window? Were there other couples walking down the path?

"Whether you liked him or not," the squat doctor says, "do you think he might have had deep feelings for you?"

Lyda's eyes tear up. No, she thinks. No, he didn't have feelings for me. I was just a convenient date. He'd been surly from the start. He was only kind to her because she'd let him get away with stealing from the display cases—a knife. A knife he used for what purpose? No one will tell her. And he danced with her because he wanted them to appear normal, to fit in and not draw any attention to themselves. Do they worry that he might be dead? Do they think he's wandered off and killed himself like his brother? She looks at her mother now, pleadingly. *What should I do?*

"Did he love you?" the willowy doctor repeats.

Lyda's mother nods. It's not even a nod really. It's more of a slight jerk, as if she were trying not to cough. Lyda wipes her eyes. Her mother is telling her to say yes, to tell them that Partridge loved her. Would this make her more valuable? If she has any value at all, it would only be because he's alive. If they think that he loves her, then perhaps they will use her—as a dispatch? A go-between? A lure?

She grips her knees, the fabric bunching between her fingers, and then she smooths the fabric flat. "Yes," she says, lowering her eyes. "He loved me." And for a moment, she pretends it's true, and she says it again, louder. "He said so. He told me he loved me that night."

The window flickers again. Or is it her vision?

PRESSIA

SHOE

To get to Bradwell's house, Pressia crosses the street and heads down the alley that runs parallel to the market. Off in the distance, she hears the chants of the Death Sprees. Sometimes she pretends the chants are part of a wedding party. Why not? They rise and fall and sound like a celebration—why not of love? Her grandfather told her about her parents' wedding—white tents, tablecloths, a tiered cake.

But she can't think about that now. She tries to gauge the positions of the Death Spree teams, and decides that they must be in the Meltlands where the gated suburbs once stood. She knows people who grew up there. She's heard about them in games of I Remember—identical homes, ticking sprinklers, plastic playground equipment in everyone's backyards. That's why they're called the Meltlands—each yard dotted with a large, colorful melted knot of plastic that was once a sliding board, swing set, and lidded sandbox in the shape of a turtle.

She tries to figure out by the chant which team it is. Some are more vicious than others. But she's never really learned to tell them all apart. Her grandfather refers to the different chants as birdcalls, each one supposedly distinctive. She doesn't know if chants are starting up or coming to an end in the enemy's final field. Luckily the chants are off in the southern part of the Meltlands, which isn't the direction she's headed. Now that she listens more closely, they could be even farther. Maybe they're out by the prisons, asylums, and sanatoriums, their scalded infrastructures of steel, rubbled stone, and the trimming of barbed wire. The kids have a singsong about the prisons.

> The deathy houses all fell down.
> The deathy houses all fell down.
> The sick souls wander 'round and 'round.
> Watch out! They drag you underground.

She's never seen the fallen structures herself. She's never been that far.

No one is out on the streets. It's cold and dark and damp. She pulls her thick sweater up around her neck, tucks the sock-covered doll-fist under her arm, and walks quickly to another alley. She kept the hollow bell. It's shoved down deep in her sweater pocket.

On top of the Death Spree chants, she's listening for Groupies. There's something about the restlessness of never being able to get away from one another that makes them take to the streets at night. Some Groupies use their collective strength to hunt people down and rob them—not that she and her grandfather ever have much to take. She listens for OSR trucks too. They're the reason she's chosen to walk in the narrowest alleys instead of the streets.

She crosses to another alley and then, because she feels charged with adrenaline, she starts running. She can't help it. The streets are so quiet with only the distant chanting that she wants to drown it out with the sound of her heart in her ears. She heads down one alley but hears an OSR engine. She doubles back and heads in the opposite direction from the chanting. She crosses from one alley to another and another—twice she catches a glimpse of an OSR truck and has to change directions.

When she arrives at the Rubble Fields, she's turned around. She stands in the shadow of a hobbled brick building that's part of a wrecked row. She has to decide whether to go around the Rubble Fields, which will take an extra hour at least, or to cut through. The Rubble Fields used to be the center of the city, densely packed with tall buildings, trucks and cars, an underground metro system, and aboveground crowds crossing at traffic lights.

Now there are hills of collapsed stone. Beasts have dug burrows and small caves in them. Pressia can see tendrils of smoke rising up from gaps here and there. The Beasts have lit fires to keep warm.

She doesn't have much time to worry about what to do next, because an OSR truck roars up the street and parks abruptly in front of the building closest to her. She edges around the corner and presses her back against the brick.

The passenger door pops open. A man in a green OSR uniform jumps out. His foot is gone. One of his pant legs is cuffed. And instead of a knee, there's the neck bone of a dog, its furred cranium, its bulged eyes, jaw, teeth. Is the man's leg part of the dog's vertebrae? It's impossible to say where the man's leg once was. The dog is missing a back leg and its tail, but he skitters in place of the man's foot. They've learned how to walk with a quick, uneven limp. He goes around back and opens the door. Two more OSR soldiers jump to the street in their black boots. They're armed with rifles.

"This is the last stop," the driver shouts out. Pressia can't see his face behind the glass, but it seems as if there are two men in there, one head close to the other—or maybe behind it. Is the driver a Groupie? She hears another voice echo the driver, "Last stop." Has it come from the other head?

Her heart hammers. Her breath's gone shallow.

The three men storm into the building. "OSR!" one shouts. And then she hears their boots pounding through the house.

The soldier driving the truck cranks the radio, and she wonders if it's the same truck that was in her alley earlier that night.

Down the street, a bunch of voices rise up. There's a figure, someone wearing a hooded coat, a face hidden by a scarf. It's too dark to make out much else. The figure shouts, "Stop! Leave me alone!" It's a boy's voice, muffled by the scarf. He's over sixteen by the looks of him. OSR will take him if they see him.

Then she sees the Groupies emerge from a side street. What used to be maybe seven or eight people is now one massive body, an assortment of arms and legs and a few glints of chrome, their leering faces—burned, wired, sometimes melded, two faces in one. They're drunk—she can tell that much by the way they're stumbling around, the slurriness of their curses.

The soldier behind the wheel glances in his rearview mirror, but then, disinterested, takes out a pocketknife and starts cleaning his nails.

"Give us what you got!" one of the Groupies says.

"Hand it over!" another says.

"I can't," the voice in the hood says. "It's nothing anyway. It wouldn't mean anything to you."

"Then give it!" one of the Groupies says.

And a hand shoots out and shoves the hooded figure. He falls to the ground and his bag flips from his hand, landing a few feet away. That's what they're after. If it's not important, he should give it to them. Groupies can get vicious, especially when they're polluted.

The hooded figure reaches for the bag so quickly and surely, his hand seems like an arrow that shoots from his body and then back again. The Groupies are confused by this sudden action. Some try to rear backward, but the others won't let them.

Then the hooded figure stands up so unnaturally fast that he stumbles backward as if his body is out of sync. While he's off balance, one of the Groupies kicks him in the stomach, and then they all move in—one massive body.

They could kill him, and Pressia hates the hooded figure for not just giving them his bag. She presses her eyes shut. She tells herself not to get involved. Let him die, she tells herself. What's it to you?

But she opens her eyes and looks out at the street. She sees an oil drum on the other side. The soldier behind the wheel is whistling to the song on the radio, still picking his nails with the knife. And so she takes off her heavy shoe—the clog with its wooden sole—and throws it at the drum as hard as she can. Her aim is good, and she hits it dead-on. The drum gives out a low loud gong.

The Groupies look up, their dull faces clouded with fear and confusion. Is it a Beast from the Rubble Fields? A team from an OSR Death Spree, lying in wait? They've been ambushed before; she can tell by the way they whip their heads around. And of course, they ambush people themselves.

The distraction gives the hooded figure enough time to scramble to his feet again, more slowly and deliberately this time, and run up the hill away from them. He runs fast, with extreme speed, even with a limp in his stride.

For some reason she can't understand, he runs straight for the back of the truck, crawls under it, and freezes.

The Groupies look up the street now. They see the truck, maybe for the first time, and with a few grunts they skulk back in the direction they came from.

Pressia wants to yell at the hooded figure. She created a diversion to save him from the Groupies—in front of the OSR even—and he crawls under their truck?

The soldiers in the house come pounding out again.

"Empty!" the one with the dog leg shouts to the driver.

The other two soldiers climb into the back of the truck, as does the one from the passenger seat. The driver puts away his knife, gives a nod. The other head shifts and bobs over his shoulder. He revs the engine, puts the truck in gear, and pulls off.

Pressia looks up and sees a face appear in the truck's back window—a face, half hidden with shadow, a face encrusted with bits of metal, and a taped-shut mouth. A stranger. Just a kid, like her. She takes a step toward the boy in the truck—she can't stop herself—out of the shadows.

The truck turns the corner. Silence fills the alley.

It could have been her.

Now with the truck gone, the hooded figure is exposed, lying on the street. He looks up and sees her. His hood has slipped off, and there is a shorn head. He's tall and lean without a mark or a scar or a burn on his clean, pale face. A long scarf twists in a loose swirl to the ground. He grabs his bag and scarf, quickly stands up and looks around, dazed and lost. And then he staggers, as if head-heavy, and he stumbles backward toward the gutter. He falls— the thick clunk of his skull on cement.

A Pure. Pressia hears the old woman's voice in her mind. *A Pure here among us.*

PARTRIDGE

SKULL

NOW, HERE, BREATHLESS. The stars look like small bright punctures—almost lost in the dark-dust air—but they aren't punctures. It isn't the ceiling of the cafeteria decorated for a dance. The sky overhead is endless. It isn't contained.

Home? Childhood?

No.

Home was a big airy space. Tall ceilings. White on white. A vacuum cleaner always purring in distant rooms. A woman in sweatpants working it back and forth against the furred floors. Not his mother. But his mother was always nearby. She paced. She waved her hands when she spoke. She stared out windows. Cursed. She said, "Don't tell your father." She said, "Remember, keep this just between the two of us." There were secrets within secrets. She said, "Let me tell you the story again."

The story was always the same. The swan wife. Before she was a wife, she was a swan girl who saved a young man from drowning. He was the young prince. A bad prince. He stole her wings and forced her to marry him. He became a bad king.

Why was he bad?

The king thought he was good, but he was wrong.

There was a good prince too. He lived in another land. The swan wife didn't yet know he existed.

The bad king gave her two sons.

Was one good and one bad?

No. They were different. One was like the father, ambitious and strong. One was like her.

Like what? How?

I don't know how. Listen. This is important.

Did the boy—the one like her—have wings?

No. But the bad king put the wings in a bucket down a dark, old dry well, and the boy who was like the swan wife heard ruffling down that well, and one night he climbed down the well and found the wings for his mother. She put them on, and she took the boy she could—the one like her, who didn't resist her—and flew away.

Partridge remembers his mother telling him the story on the beach. She had a towel around her shoulders. It ruffled at her back like wings.

The beach was where they had their second house. It's where they were in the photograph he found in her drawer in the Personal Loss Archives. They didn't go when it was cool except this once. The sun must have been warm because he remembers being sunburned, his lips cracked. They got a flu. Not a virulent one that would send them to an asylum; this was just a stomach flu. His mother took a blue blanket from the linen closet and wrapped him in it. She was sick too. They both slept on the sofas and threw up into little white plastic buckets. She put a wet cloth on his forehead. And she talked about the swan wife and the boy and the new land where they found the good king.

Is my father the bad king?

It's just a story. But listen. Promise me you'll always remember it. Don't tell the story to your father. He doesn't like stories.

Partridge can't lift his head. He feels pinned to the ground, and the memory wheels across his mind. And then it stops. His head is abuzz, a cold bright pain at the back of his skull. His heart is as loud in his ears as the automatic threshers at work in the fields beyond the academy. He used to watch the threshers from the lonesome dormer window at the end of the hall in his dorm when Hastings went home for weekends. Lyda—is she there now? Can she hear the threshers? Does she remember kissing him? He remembers. It surprised him. He kissed her back, and then she pulled away, embarrassed.

There is wind on his skin. This is the real air. The wind whips over his head, flutters the fine fuzz of his hair. The air churns darkly as if stirred by unseen fan blades. He thinks of fan blades—shiny and quick in his mind. How did he get here?

PRESSIA

GRAY EYES

THE PURE STAGGERS TO HIS FEET and stands in the road. He glances around for a moment, up and down the row of burned, hollowed-out hulls, over the Rubble Fields with their wisps of smoke threading up into the night air, then at the buildings again. He looks at the sky, as if trying to get his bearings that way. Finally, he pulls the strap on his bag over his shoulder and loops the scarf once around his neck and jaw. He glances at the Rubble Fields and heads toward them.

Pressia tightens the wool sock over the doll-head fist, pulls her sweater sleeve down, and steps out of the alley. "Don't," she says. "You'll never make it."

He whips around, scared, and then his eyes fall on her, and he's obviously relieved that she's not a Groupie or a Beast or even an OSR soldier—though she doubts he knows the names of any of these things. What's there to be afraid of where he comes from anyway? Does he even understand fear? Is he afraid of birthday cakes and dogs wearing sunglasses and new cars topped with big red bows?

His face is smooth and clear, his eyes a pale gray. And she can't quite believe that she is looking at a Pure—a living, breathing Pure.

Burn a Pure and breathe the ash.
Take his guts and make a sash.
Twist his hair and make a rope.
And use his bones to make Pure soap.

That's what comes to mind. Kids sing the song all the time, but no one ever thinks they'll see a real Pure, no matter how many stupid whispers there are. Never. She feels like there's something light and airy and winged inside her chest, locked in her ribs, like Freedle in his cage, like the homemade butterfly in her sack.

"I'm trying to get to Lombard Street," he says, a little breathlessly. Pressia wonders if the quality of his voice is different. Clearer, sweeter? Is that the voice of someone who hasn't been breathing ash for years? "Ten Fifty-four Lombard, to be exact. Large row houses with grillwork gates."

"It's not good to stand out there in plain sight," Pressia tells him. "It's dangerous."

"I've noticed." He takes a step toward her and then stops. One side of his face has been lightly dusted with ash. "I don't know if I should trust you," he says. It's a fair statement. He's almost been beaten by Groupies; he's bound to be a little nervous now.

She sticks out her foot, the one missing its shoe. "I threw my shoe to distract the Groupies who were about to kill you. I've already saved you once."

He looks down the street to where he was getting shoved around. He walks over to Pressia in the alley. "Thanks," he says. He smiles. His teeth are straight and very white, like he's lived on fresh milk his whole life. His face, this close up, is even more startling because of its perfection. She can't tell how old he is. He seems older than she is, but then he seems young in a way too. She doesn't want to be caught staring and so she looks down at the ground. He says, "They were going to tear me apart. I hope I'm worth your lost shoe."

"I hope my shoe isn't lost," she says, turning away from him a little so that he can't see the side of her face that's burned.

He tugs on the strap of his bag. "I'll help you find your shoe if you help me find Lombard Street."

"It's not easy finding streets here. We don't go by streets."

"Where did you throw your shoe? Which direction?" he asks, heading back toward the street.

"Don't," she says, although she needs the shoe, the gift from her grandfather, maybe the last gift he'll ever give her. She hears a truck engine to the east and then another in the opposite direction. And there's still another not far off, or is it an echo? He should stay out of sight. Anyone could see him. It's not safe. "Leave it."

But he's already in the middle of the street again. "Which way?" he says and opens his arms wide, pointing in opposite directions, like he wants to be a living target.

"The oil drum," she says, just trying to hurry him up.

He spins around, sees the oil drum, and runs to it. He turns a half circle around the drum and then bends over. When he pops back up, he's got her shoe. He holds it over his head like a prize.

"Stop," she whispers, wishing he'd get back in the shadows.

He runs to her and gets down on his knee. "Here," he says. "Give me your foot."

"It's okay," she says. "I can do it." Her cheeks are flushed. She's embarrassed and mad at him too. Who does he think he is, anyway? He's a Pure who's been kept safe, who's had it easy his whole life. She can put on her own shoe. She's not a child. She bends down, rips her shoe out of his hand, and puts it on herself.

"How does this sound? I helped you find your shoe so you help me find Lombard Street or *what used to be* Lombard Street."

She's scared now. It's settling in that he is a Pure and that this is too dangerous, being with him. The news of his presence will keep spreading, and there's no way to stop it. When people find out that there's a Pure here for certain, he will definitely become a target—his arms stretched wide or not. Some people will want to use him as an angry sacrifice. He represents all of the people from the Dome, the rich and the lucky who left them behind to suffer and die. Others will want to capture him and leverage ransom somehow. And the OSR will want him for his secrets or to use him as bait.

And she has her own reasons, doesn't she? *If there's a way out, that means there's a way in.* That's what the old woman said, and maybe it's true. She knows that he could be of use. Wouldn't he offer her some leverage with the OSR? Could she get out of having to report to headquarters? Could she negotiate medical help for her grandfather too, while she's at it?

She tugs on her sweater sleeve. The Dome will send out people to look for him, won't they? What if they want him back? "Do you have a chip?" she asks.

He rubs the back of his neck. "Nope," he says. "I never got one as a kid. I'm fresh as the day I was born. You can look if you want." The chip implants always leave a small raised bump as a scar.

She shakes her head.

"Do you have one?"

"It's defunct now. Just a dead chip," she says. She always keeps her hair long enough to cover the small scar. "They don't work here anyway. But it's what all good parents did back then."

"Are you saying my parents weren't good parents?" he says, half joking.

"I don't know anything about your parents."

"Well, I don't have a chip. That's what you wanted to know. Are you going to help me or what?" He's a little angry now. She's not sure why, but she's glad to see that she can rile him. It tilts a little power in her direction.

She nods. "But we'll have to use old maps. I know someone who has them. I was on my way to his place. I can take you there. Maybe he can help."

"That's fine," he says. "Which way?" He turns and starts for the street.

She grabs his jacket. "Wait," she tells him. "I'm not going out with you like that."

"Like what?" he says.

She stares at him, disbelieving. "Uncovered."

He puts his hands in his pockets. "So it's obvious."

"Of course it's obvious."

He doesn't say anything for a moment. They stand there. "What was that thing that attacked me?"

"A Groupie. A big one. Everyone out here is deformed in some way, fused so that we aren't exactly what we were before."

"And you?"

She looks away from him and answers a different question. "People's skin is often littered. Glass is sharp, depending on how it's embedded. Plastic can stiffen up, making it hard to move. Metal rusts."

"Like the Tin Man," the Pure says.

"Who?"

"He's a character in a book and this old movie," he says.

"We don't have that stuff here. Not much survived."

"Right," he says. "And what's that singing?"

She'd blocked it out, but he's right. Chanting voices from the Death Spree carry on the wind. She shrugs and says, "Maybe people singing at a wedding." She's not sure why she would say something like this. Did people sing at weddings—like her parents' church wedding and white-tent reception? Do they still sing in the Dome?

"You'll have to watch out for OSR trucks too."

He smiles.

"What's funny?"

"Just that they're real. In the Dome, we know they exist. OSR. That they started as Operation Search and Rescue, a civilian militia, and then became a kind of fascist regime. Operation . . . what is it now?"

"Sacred Revolution," Pressia says, flatly. She can't help but feel like she's being made fun of.

"Right!" he says. "That's it!"

"Do you think that's quaint?" she says. "They'll kill you. They'll torture you and shove a gun down your throat and murder you. Do you understand that?"

He seems to accept this, and then he says, "I guess you hate me. I wouldn't blame you. Historically speaking . . ."

Pressia shakes her head. "Please don't give a group apology. I don't need your guilty conscience. You got in. I didn't. The end." She puts her hand in her pocket and feels the hard rim of the bell. She considers adding something a little gentler, to relieve his guilt, something like *We were kids when it happened. What could we do? What could anyone do?* But she decides not to. His guilt gives her some leverage, too. And the fact is that there's some truth to his guilt. How did he get into the Dome? What kind of privilege allowed it? She understands enough of Bradwell's conspiracy theories to know that ugly decisions were made. Why shouldn't she blame the Pure a little?

"You've got to wear the hood and the scarf over your face," she tells him.

"I'll try to blend in." He quickly winds the scarf around his neck, covering his face, and lifts the hood. "Good now?" he says.

It's not really enough. There's something in his gray eyes that makes him different, something that he probably can't do anything about. Wouldn't anyone know at a glance that he's a Pure? Pressia feels certain that she would. He's hopeful in a way that no one here is hopeful, but there's also some deep sadness in him. In some ways, he doesn't seem Pure at all. "It's not just your face," she tells him.

"What is it?" he says.

She shakes her head, letting her hair fall to cover the scars on one side of her face. "Nothing," she says. And then without thinking, she simply asks, "Why are you here?"

"Home," he says. "I'm trying to find my way home."

For some reason, this makes Pressia furious. She pulls her sweater up under her chin. "Home," she says. "Here outside the Dome on Lombard Street?"

"Right."

But he left this place. He deserted his home. He doesn't deserve to get it back. She decides to veer away from talk of home. "We have to take the shortcut through the Rubble Fields. We have no choice," she tells the Pure. She's trying not to look at him now. She tightens the sock and tugs on her sweater sleeve. "We could run into Beasts and Dusts who might try to kill us, but at least it'll take us off the streets where we might run into those who'll try to capture you. Plus it's faster."

"Capture me?"

"People already know you're here. There are whispers all over the place. And if any of those Groupies weren't too polluted to see your face, well, they'll spread the whispers even more. We'll have to move fast and quietly so we don't give them a lot of warning and we'll have to—"

"What's your name?" the Pure asks.

"My name?"

He sticks his hand straight out in front of himself, aiming it at her like a gun, with his thumb up in the air.

"What are you doing that for?"

"What?" He shoves the hand at her again. "I'm introducing myself. People call me Partridge."

"I'm Pressia," she tells him and then she gives his hand a smack. "Stop pointing your hand at me like that."

He looks confused and shoves his hand in one of the pockets of his hooded jacket.

"If there's anything of value in that bag, you better hide it under your coat at all times." Pressia starts walking quickly toward the Rubble Fields, and he follows closely behind. She gives instructions. "Stay away from the rising smoke. Walk gently. Some people say that the Dusts can feel vibrations. If you get grabbed, don't scream. Don't say a word. I'll keep looking back."

There's an art to walking through the Rubble Fields, being light-footed, quick to shift your weight from one side of your body to the other, but not overcompensating in any one direction. She's mastered these skills from her years of scavenging and knows how to keep her knees loose, her feet flexible, so that she can maintain her balance.

She heads out across the rocks and she can hear him following behind her. She's keeping a lookout for eyes in the stones. She can't get too worked up about the eyes, because she also has to constantly route a path around smoke-fires and glance backward at Partridge. And she listens for the OSR truck engines. She doesn't want to get to the other side just to wind up caught in headlights.

She realizes that this is her value to him. This is what she's worth. She's his guide and she doesn't want to tell him too much because she wants him to rely on her, to need her, and maybe to become indebted. She wants him to feel like he owes her something.

She's doing all of this—shifting, looking for Dusts, veering away from smoke, and glancing back at the Pure, his hood flapping around his darkened face in the wind—and she's thinking about Bradwell too. What will he think of her bringing a Pure to his door? Would that impress him? She doubts it. He doesn't seem like he'd be easy to impress. But still, she knows he's devoted his life to unraveling the past. She hopes he has the right old maps, and that he knows how to apply them to what's left of this city. What good do street names do for a city that's lost everything, including most streets?

That's what she's thinking about when she hears the scream from behind her. She turns around and sees that the Pure is already down; one leg has been dragged into the rubble out of sight. "Pressia!" he shouts.

The guttural noises of Beasts rise up all around them.

"Why did you scream?" she shouts at the Pure, realizing she's screaming now too, but unable to stop herself. "I told you not to scream!" She looks out across the Rubble Fields. Heads have already popped up from the smoke holes. The Beasts know that they've gotten one. They will all want in on the feast. Out here, there are other outcasts too. Creatures so fused or burned or scarred that no one can identify them anymore. They've lost something elementally human. And cut off from others, they've become vicious.

Pressia picks up rocks and hurls them at one Beast's head and then another. They duck and reappear. "It's stronger than you," she yells. "You can't try to hold on. You have to be willing to go down and fight it. Get a rock in each hand and kick it! I'll cover you!" She hopes he can fight, but she doubts they teach that kind of thing in the Dome. What would they need to protect themselves against? If he doesn't know how to fight, she can't go down after him. There'd be no one to fend off the Beasts. They'd gather in a large hungry crowd waiting at the hole to kill them both as soon as they made it back up, if they could make it back up.

Partridge looks at her, wide-eyed with fear.

"Do it!" she says.

He shakes his head. "I'm not going down to fight it on its own terms," he says.

"You don't have a choice!"

But then Partridge claws at the stones, pulling himself forward, inch by inch. He grabs a loose stone, which gives, and the creature—likely a Dust—jerks him as if he's slipped down a rung of a ladder. But his other hand keeps its grip, and although the Dust has a hold on one of his legs, the Pure is kicking it hard with his free boot. His hands flexed, he pulls his leg to his chest with brute strength and drags the Dust up from the hole. She's never seen anything like it, didn't know it was possible.

Squat and barrel-chested, this Dust is a hunched creature with hardened armor made of stone. Its face is dug out—pitted eyes, a small dark hole for a mouth. It's the size of a small bear. Used to darkness and tight spaces, it looks slightly confused up here, a little dazed. But then it locks onto Partridge and crawls toward him. Pressia hurls rock after rock at the Beasts so they know that she and Partridge aren't just victims here to pick away at like vultures. They'll have to fight. She hits two Beasts square-on—one with a cat-like head who yowls and disappears for good. The other is furred but thickly muscular. It takes the blow, arches, and goes back under the rubble.

Partridge is fiddling with his backpack, rummaging around with his strangely fast movements. Why do his hands move so quickly? How is it possible? And yet he's so clumsy. If he'd slow down, he'd be able to find what he's looking for more easily. His hands flutter in the bag, and this only gives the Dust time to crouch back on its haunches and pounce. The stone weight of the creature lands on Partridge's chest and sends him crashing on the rocks behind him. The Dust has knocked the air out of him, and he's stunned, breathless. But Pressia can see what he pulled from the bag: a knife with a wooden handle.

Pressia keeps throwing rocks at Beasts circling closer. "Look for something human on him," she cries out. "You can only kill it if you can find the part of it that's alive and pulsing."

The Dust has him pinned to the rocks and lifts its blunt stone head, ready to slam it into the Pure's skull, but the Pure shoves him off with surprising force, and the Dust lands hard—stone against stone—on its back, revealing a slip of pale raw pink skin on his chest. Beetle-like, the Dust is stuck on its back, its small stumped stone-encrusted arms and legs flailing.

The Pure moves in fast. He fits the knife into the pink center, stabbing the Dust's belly, in between the stone plates, driving the knife in deep. The Dust gives a hollow moan as if its voice echoes in its own stony shell. Dark, ashen blood spills out of the wound. The Pure saws the knife back and forth, as if he's cutting into a loaf of bread, then pulls it out and scrapes it on the rocks.

The foul stench of the Dust's blood is carried by the wind. The Beasts, fearful, retreat quickly into their smoky holes.

Pressia is breathless. Partridge stares at the Dust. The knife is shaking in his hand, his eyes vacant. He's covered in dust and soot. There's a trickle of blood coming from his nose. He wipes it with the back of his hand and stares at the red smear left there.

"Partridge," she whispers. His name sounds strange in her mouth, too personal. But she says it again. "Partridge, are you okay?"

He pulls the hood back up over his head, sits on the rocks, trying to catch his breath. He wraps his arms around his bag. "Sorry," he says.

"Sorry for what?" she asks.

"I screamed. You told me not to." He rubs at the soot on one hand with his thumb, then stares at it. "The dirt," he says, his voice strangely peaceful.

"What about it?" she asks.

"It's dirty."

PRESSIA

WIND

ON THE OTHER SIDE OF THE RUBBLE FIELDS, Pressia takes out the folded map that Bradwell slipped into her pocket at the meeting, and studies it for a minute. They're only five blocks from Bradwell's place. They stick to side streets, alleys. Everything is quiet. She hears no trucks. Even the chanting from the Death Spree is gone. At one point, there's a baby crying, but then it quiets down.

Partridge is taking everything in, but Pressia can't imagine what's so interesting. It's all burned hulls, smashed glass, melted plastic, charred metal, and the sharp edges of things poking up from ash.

He lifts his hand in the air like he's trying to catch snow. "What is this stuff in the air?" he asks.

"What stuff?"

"The gray stuff."

"Oh," she says. She doesn't even notice it anymore. She's gotten used to it swirling in the air day in and day out, settling like thin lace over everything that sits still long enough. "Ash," she says. "There are a lot of names for it—black snow, the earth's silk lining—like a purse turned inside out. Some call it the dark death. When it billows and then settles, some call it a blessing of ash."

"A blessing?" Partridge says. "We use that word a lot in the Dome."

"I imagine you'd have lots of reasons to." It's not a nice thing to say, but she's already said it.

"Some," he says.

"Well, it's soot and dust and bits left from the blast," Pressia says. "It's not good to breathe."

"You're right about that," he says, pulling his scarf up over his nose and mouth. "You breathe it in and it stains your lungs. I've read about it."

"Are there books about us or something?" This makes Pressia angry—the idea that this world is a subject of study, a story, instead of filled with real people, trying to survive.

He nods. "Some digitized documentation."

"But how can you know what things are like here when you're all in a Dome? Are we your little scientific subjects?"

"It's not me," he says, defensively. "I'm not doing it. It's the people in charge. They have advanced cameras that shoot footage for security purposes. The ash makes the shots kind of unclear. Some of that footage is chosen to be frozen into stills. And there are reports about how bad things are here and how lucky we are," he says.

"Luck is relative," Pressia tells him. *For now, we watch from afar, benevolently.* That's what the Message said. So that's what they meant, after all.

"But they don't really capture it. Like the dusty air." He waves a hand around. "And how it gets on your skin. The air, itself, it's cold. And wind. No one can really explain wind. How it can come up really fast and it stings your face a little. And it moves the dust in the air around. They can't get all of that."

"You don't have wind?"

"It's a Dome. A controlled environment."

Pressia looks around and thinks about wind for a moment. And she realizes that there's a difference between soot and dust—something burned or having been ripped apart or demolished—and they move differently in the wind. It never really struck her before, but she finds herself saying, "Soot flutters up on almost any shift in the wind, but dust is heavier. It will weigh itself down more quickly."

"That kind of thing," Partridge says. "That's what they can't get at."

Pressia pauses a moment and then asks, "Do you want to play I Remember?"

"What's that?"

"You don't play it in the Dome?"

"Is it a game?"

"It's just what it says. When you meet someone and you're getting to know them, you ask them what they remember about the Before. Sometimes it's all you can get out of a person, especially old people. But they play the game the best. My grandfather remembers a lot of things." Pressia isn't good at the game. Although her memories are brightly colored, crisp, sometimes tactile—like she can almost feel the Before—she can never quite express those sensations. She thinks about playing the game with her mother and father one day. They'll fill in the gaps between the small tank with fish, the tassel on her mother's pocketbook, the heating duct, the wire brush, the smell of grass soap on her skin, her father's coat, her ear to his heart, and her mother brushing her hair, her mother singing the song on the computer, the lullaby about the girl on the porch and the boy who begs her to come with him—did the girl ever have the courage to go? She wants to play the game with Partridge. What would a Pure remember? Aren't their memories clearer, less muddied by this version of the world they live in?

He laughs. "We'd never be allowed to play a game like that. The past is the past. It would be impolite to bring it up. Only little kids do that kind of thing." And then he quickly adds, "No offense. It's just the way we are."

Pressia takes offense anyway. "The past is all we've got here," she says, picking up her pace a little. She thinks about Bradwell's speech. *They want to erase us, the past, but we can't let them.* This is how forgetting works. Erase the past, never speak of it.

He strides quickly to catch up and grabs her elbow, the one that leads to the doll head. She jerks it in close to her body. "Don't just grab people," she says. "What's wrong with you?"

"I want to play the game," he says. "It's why I'm here—to find out about the past." He looks at her straight-on, his eyes taking in her face, skittering to the edge where the burn begins.

She dips her head forward so her hair blocks her face from view. "Well, here, *that's* what's impolite."

"What?" he asks.

"Staring at people. None of us wants to be looked at."

"I didn't mean to . . ." He looks away. "I'm sorry."

Pressia doesn't respond. It helps that he feels like he's done her wrong and owes her something, and good too that he needs her as a social guide here—the dos and don'ts of this culture. She is trying to ratchet up his dependence on her.

They walk a little farther in silence. She's punishing him, but then decides she should be forgiving too, and so she asks a question that's been on her mind. "Okay," Pressia says, deciding to fake it, "we once bought a new car with a giant red ribbon on top of it. And I remember Mickey Mouse and his white gloves."

"Huh," he says. "Right."

"Do you remember dogs wearing sunglasses? They were funny, right?"

"I don't really remember dogs wearing sunglasses," he says. "Nope."

"Oh," she says. "Your turn."

"Well, my mother used to tell me a story about the swan wife, and there was a bad king in the story who stole her wings and, well, I guess I thought my father was the bad king."

"Was he a bad king?"

"It was a fairy tale, that's all. They didn't get along. It was kid logic. It didn't make sense. But I loved the story. I loved her, I guess. She could have told me anything, and I'd have loved her. Kids love their parents, even the parents who don't deserve it. They can't help it."

This memory of his is so honest and real that Pressia's embarrassed that she didn't play the game sincerely. She tries again. "My parents hired a pony to come to my birthday party once when I was little."

"To give the kids rides?"

"I guess."

"That's nice. A pony. You liked ponies?"

"I don't know."

She wonders if the game has helped. Does he trust her more now that she's handed a memory over and he's given one to her? She decides to test it. "Back there with the Dust you killed, when you pulled it up from the hole and flipped it—that didn't seem normal," she says. "It didn't seem possible." She waits for him to pick up his end of the conversation. He tucks his chin to his chest and doesn't answer. "Back there with the Groupies, when you ran, it seemed faster than a human running..."

He shakes his head. "The academy," he says. "I got some special training. That's all."

"Training?"

"Well, coding, really. It didn't all take, though. I'm not a ripe specimen, turns out." He doesn't seem to want to talk about it, and she doesn't want to push. She lets the conversation lag. They walk on in silence.

Finally they come to a small collapsed storefront.

"This is it," she says.

"This is what?" Partridge asks.

She leads him around a pile of rubble to a wide metal back door. "Bradwell's place," she whispers. "I should warn you that he's fused."

"In what way?"

"Birds," she says.

"Birds?"

"In his back."

He looks at her, startled, and she likes that she's disturbed him.

She knocks, following the directions on the piece of paper— one knock, then two soft taps and then she pauses and gives another sharp knuckle-punch. She hears some noise inside. And then Bradwell knocks from the other side, the same way she did, small hollow-sounding gongs.

"He lives here?" Partridge asks. "Who could live here?"

She knocks twice. "Wait over there. I don't want you to set him off." She points to a wall, darkened by shadow.

"Does he set off easily?"

"Just go."

Partridge recedes to the shadows.

There's a scraping sound, Bradwell unlocking the door. It opens, just a crack. "It's the middle of the night," he whispers, his voice so rough she wonders if she woke him. "Who are you? What the hell do you want?"

"It's Pressia."

The door opens wider. Bradwell is taller and broader than she remembers him. A survivor, it seems, should be wiry and lithe, a body easily hidden, lean from subsisting on little. But he's had to become muscular to survive. There's the double scar running jaggedly up his cheek, his burns, but his eyes are what catch Pressia's attention. She feels a hesitation in her breath. They're dark eyes and steely, but when they take in Pressia's face they seem to soften, as if Bradwell is capable of more tenderness than she thought. "Pressia?" he says. "I thought you didn't want to see me ever again."

She turns her burned cheek away from him and feels herself blush—embarrassed by what? Why? She hears a flutter behind him—the wings of the birds lodged in his back.

"Why are you here?"

"I wanted to thank you for the gift."

"Now?"

"No," she says. "That's not why I came. I just thought I'd say it now that you're here. I mean, I'm here with you." She's yammering. She wishes she'd stop. "And I brought someone," she says. "It's urgent."

"Who?"

"Someone who needs help." And then she quickly adds, "I don't need help. It's this other person who does." If she hadn't run into the Pure, she'd be at his doorstep right now asking Bradwell to save her. And she realizes how relieved she is that she isn't coming to him by herself, for herself. There's a quiet moment. Is Bradwell going to turn back? Is he trying to decide what to do?

"What kind of help?"

"It's important or I wouldn't be here."

Partridge steps out of the shadows. "She's here for my sake."

Bradwell glances at Partridge, then Pressia.

"Get in here," he says. "Hurry up."

———

"What is this place?" Partridge asks.

"Elliot Marker and Sons Fine Selection of Meats, Established 1933," Bradwell says. "Found the little bronze placard after the Detonations. This was when some people were still lining up the dead and covering them with sheets and rolling them in rugs to be identified later, as if some government agency were just about to kick in and start up a recovery effort. The first floor—the display cases and counters, cutting area, cold storage, office—that was all gone, but I pulled the rubble from the back door at night hoping it led to the basement. And it did. The meats were spoiled but a butcher shop's got a lot of weapons."

Pressia's eyes are adjusting to the dark. She's standing in a strange cage, outfitted with straps and chains, and a slide that leads to the basement. Partridge is standing behind her. He reaches up and touches a chain. "And this is?"

"The stunning pen," Bradwell says. "Animals were brought in through the back door, then stunned, with their hooves secured by straps connected to a rod that ran along rails. Their heavy bodies would be suspended upside down, and they were brought down for processing." Bradwell jogs down the slide in his heavy boots. "Just be glad you aren't a heifer in the old days."

Pressia sits on the pen's floor, scoots to the edge, and slides down into the basement. Partridge follows her, and then they walk behind Bradwell along the side of the basement that hasn't caved in, heading toward the hint of light from the cooler at the other end of the room. "They bled animals down here, used hot vats and processing stations. The animals were pulled along the rails by a system of winches and stripped of their hides, dismantled."

"Do you ever stop giving lessons?" Pressia asks under her breath.

"What?" Bradwell says.

"Nothing."

The ceiling is still fitted with its bare rails, which lead into the meat locker—a small room, ten feet by fifteen, with metal walls and ceiling. The rails run along the ceiling in here too. Bradwell says, "I've taken down most of the huge hooks that used to dangle from them." But there are a few left. Two of the hooks are strung up with strange creatures, hybrids of some sort. They've been skinned. Bradwell's also removed any metallic or glass fusings— one is missing an arm, the other has an amputated tail. Now that they're bare with pimpled flesh, it's hard to say what they once might have been. In one corner, there is a homemade wire cage holding two rat-like creatures.

"Where did you catch these?" Pressia asks.

"The defunct sewer system. Some of the smaller pipes stayed intact under the rubble. The vermin use them. And at certain points, the pipelines end. Some break completely, and if you lie in wait at the end of one of the narrow pipes, you'll eventually catch a small beast."

"There isn't much room for them to move in these cages," Pressia says.

"I don't want them to move. I want them to get fat."

Their claws scratch against the cement floor.

The walls are lined with shelves interrupted by vertical rows of more hooks. If you tried to hang a hat on one, it'd pierce the top clean through. Partridge is eyeing the hooks.

Bradwell tells him, "Don't get too excited and start gesturing wildly or you'll get hooked and good."

The meat locker doesn't have much ventilation except for a homemade exhaust fan over a cook stove. "The shop is on the weak power grid that OSR uses to light the city," he says. A single bulb hangs from the ceiling in the middle of the room.

Wool blankets are draped over two old armchairs that he must have found somewhere out in the streets. One has melted in on itself; the other's lost one arm and its back. Both have exploding foam that he's clearly tried to stuff back in, but the stuffing just keeps trying to escape. Pushed together, this must be where he sleeps. He has a small stock of canned meats from the market and some wild berries that grow among thorns in the woods.

Pressia wonders if she's caught him off guard, showing up like this. He's tidying up now, putting away a pan, shoving an extra pair of boots under an armchair. Is he embarrassed? Nervous?

She sees the footlocker pressed up against one of the walls. She wants to open it and go rifling through. Sitting on top of it is what seems to be a reference book on butchering, processing, and preserving meats of all kinds.

"So," Bradwell says, "welcome to my home sweet home." He still hasn't gotten a good look at Partridge. He doesn't know that this is a Pure—flesh and blood. Partridge has his hood on and the scarf. He's holding tight to his bag, hidden under his coat, like Pressia taught him. Pressia is nervous now. She remembers Bradwell's talk, how much he hated the people in the Dome. She worries if this was the right decision. How will Bradwell react? It strikes her now that Bradwell might see Partridge as the enemy. What then?

Bradwell pulls the two armchairs apart. "Sit down," he says to Pressia and Partridge.

And they sit on the lumpy chairs.

Bradwell pulls up the footlocker and takes a seat. She sees the ruffle of birds on his back under his shirt. She feels for him. The birds are his body now—just as the doll head is part of hers. The birds merge with his life span. They live as long as he lives. If one has an injured wing, would he feel it? Once, when she was twelve, she tried to cut her doll head off. She thought she could free herself from it. The pain was sharp, but only at first. When she slid the razor in deep at the back of the doll's neck where it met her wrist, it wasn't as painful. But the blood flowed so brightly, and with such force, that it scared her. She pressed a cloth to it, but the cloth went red fast. She had to tell her grandfather. He worked quickly. His skills as a mortician came in handy. The stitches were even, and the scar is small.

Pressia sits back, and even though the sock hides the doll-head fist, she tugs on her sweater sleeve to be doubly sure. The Pure would see it as grotesque and maybe as a sign of weakness.

She glances at Partridge and knows he's seen the ruffle beneath Bradwell's shirt too, but Partridge doesn't say a word. Pressia imagines that he's in shock. Everything must be foreign. She's had years to get used to it. He's only had a couple of days maybe.

"So are you going to tell me who this is now?" Bradwell asks.

"This is Partridge." She says to Partridge, "Take off the scarf and hood."

He hesitates.

"It's okay. Bradwell's on our side." But is he? Pressia wonders. She hopes by saying it, she'll convince Bradwell that it's true.

Partridge pushes off his hood and unwinds the scarf.

Bradwell stares at his face, which is smudged with dirt, but unmarked. "Arms," Bradwell says.

"I don't have any weapons," he says. "Except an antique knife."

"No," Bradwell says. His face is calm, except for his eyes. They look at Partridge sharply, like someone who is about to aim a gun. "I want to see your actual arms."

Partridge pulls up his sleeves, and there is more perfect skin. There's something unsettling about it. Pressia isn't sure why, but she feels a kind of revulsion. Is it jealousy and hatred? Does she despise Partridge for his skin? It's also beautiful. She can't deny it—like cream.

Bradwell nods at Partridge's legs.

Partridge bends down and pulls up one pant leg and then the other.

Bradwell stands up and crosses his arms on his chest. He rubs the burn on his neck, agitated, and walks around the meat locker, dodging the hooks weighted with hybrids. He looks at Pressia. "You brought me a Pure?"

Pressia nods.

"I mean, I knew you were different but—"

"I thought I was a type."

"At first, I thought you might be, but then you told me off."

"I didn't tell you off."

"Yes you did."

"No, I didn't. I just disagreed with the way you'd categorized me. And I said so. Is that what you think every time someone corrects you? That they're telling you off?"

"No. It's just that—"

"And then you give them a mean birthday present, just to remind them of what you think of them?"

"I thought you liked that clipping. I was being nice."

She's quiet a moment. "Oh. Well, thank you."

"You already said thank you but I guess that was sarcastic."

"Maybe a little insincere—"

Partridge says, "Um, excuse me."

"Right," Bradwell says, but then he turns to Pressia again. "You brought me a Pure? Is *that* some kind of mean gift?"

"I didn't know where else to go."

"A *Pure*?" Bradwell says again, incredulously. "Does he know anything about what happened? The Detonations?"

"He can speak for himself," she says.

Bradwell stares at him. Maybe he's afraid of Partridge. He might despise him. "Well?" Bradwell finally says.

"I know what I've been spoon-fed," Partridge says, "but also I know a little about the truth."

"What truth?" Bradwell says.

"Well, I know that you can't trust everything you hear." He unbuttons his coat and pulls out the backpack. "I was told that everything was awful here before the bomb, and that everyone was invited into the Dome before we were attacked by the enemy. But some people refused to come in. They were the violent, sickly, poor, stubborn, uneducated. My father said that my mother was trying to save some of these wretches."

"Wretches?" Bradwell says, angrily.

"Wait," Pressia tells Bradwell. "Let's stay calm."

"That's us he's talking about!" Bradwell says to Pressia.

"This is what I was *taught*. Not what I *believe*," Partridge says.

It's quiet a moment. Bradwell stares at Pressia. She braces for a challenge, but he seems to give in. He waves his hand. "Why don't you just call us brothers and sisters? That's what you called us in the Message. Brothers and sisters, one big happy family."

"What message?" Partridge says.

"You don't know about the Message?" Pressia says.

He shakes his head.

"Should I recite it for him?" Bradwell asks Pressia.

"Let's just move on."

Bradwell clears his throat and recites the Message anyway: "*We know you are here, our brothers and sisters. We will, one day, emerge from the Dome to join you in peace. For now, we watch from afar, benevolently.*"

"When was this sent?" Partridge says.

"A few weeks after the Detonations," Pressia says, and then she turns to Bradwell. "Just let him go on."

Partridge glances at Bradwell, who doesn't say anything, and then he continues. "We lived in the city on Lombard Street, and when the alarm came to get in the Dome, my mother was out helping these . . . other people . . . trying to educate them. And my brother and I were in the Dome already, just on a tour. She didn't make it in time. She died a saint."

Bradwell grunts. "There was no alarm," he says.

Partridge looks at Bradwell sharply. "Of course there was."

"There wasn't any alarm. Believe me."

Pressia remembers the announcement of heavy traffic. That's all that exists in her grandfather's story. She glances between Partridge and Bradwell.

"There wasn't much time. I know that much," Partridge says. "But there was an alarm. People rushed the Dome. It was a madhouse, and lives were lost."

"Lives were lost," Bradwell says. "You make it sound almost accidental."

"What could we do? We were trying to protect ourselves," Partridge says, defensively. *We couldn't save everyone.*"

"No, that was never the plan."

The room goes silent for a moment. There's only the sound of the rat-like beasts' scratching nails.

"There's more to all of this than you know," Bradwell says.

"This isn't the time for a lesson," Pressia says. "Just let him talk."

"A lesson?" Bradwell says.

"You don't have to be so . . ." Pressia isn't sure of the right word.

"Pedantic?" Bradwell says.

She doesn't know what *pedantic* means, but she doesn't like his snotty tone. "So *like that*," Pressia says. "Just let him talk."

"So far, I should be calm and more specifically not *like that* . . . Anything else?" Bradwell asks Pressia. "Would you like to do surgery on my personality? How about open-heart surgery? I've got some tools."

Pressia sits back and laughs. The laugh surprises her. She's not sure why she thinks this is funny, but it just is. Bradwell is so big and loud, and she's not sure how, but she feels like she's gotten at him somehow.

"What's funny?" Bradwell says, his arms outstretched.

"I don't know," Pressia says. "I guess it's that you're a survivor. You're almost mythic, but it's just . . . You seem so easily . . . unglued."

"I'm not unglued!" Bradwell says. Then he looks at Partridge.

"You're slightly unglued," Partridge says.

Bradwell sits on the footlocker again, sighs deeply, closes his eyes, and then opens them. "There, see? I'm fine. I'm perfectly glued."

Pressia says, "What else, Partridge? Go on."

Partridge rubs at the dirt on his hands. The leather bag still sits on his lap. He unlatches the clasp on the bag and pulls out a small leather-bound book. "I came across my mother's things a few weeks ago," he goes on. "I just felt like there was this completely different world than the one I'd been taught. Her things, they still existed . . . It's hard to explain. And now that I'm here, I remember how the ugliness is what makes the beautiful things beautiful."

Pressia knows what he means—one can't truly exist without the other. She likes Partridge. He's open in ways he doesn't have to be, and it makes her trust him.

"Why are you here?" Bradwell says, pushing to the point.

"After I found her things, I kept digging. My father . . ." He pauses a moment. His face clouds over. Pressia can't read all the emotions. Maybe he loves his father. Maybe he hates him. It's hard to tell. Maybe his father is the parent he loves even though he doesn't deserve it. "He was one of the leaders on the exodus to the Dome. He's still a prominent figure. A scientist and engineer." His voice is flat, calm.

Bradwell leans into Partridge. "What's your father's name?"

"Ellery Willux."

Bradwell laughs, shaking his head. "The Willuxes."

"Do you know his family?" Pressia asks.

"Maybe I've seen the name," he says, sarcastically.

"What's that mean?" Partridge asks.

"The Best and the Brightest," Bradwell says. "Well, look at you. You come from good stock."

"How do you know my family?"

"The Detonations strike and it's just a coincidence that the Dome exists and some get in and some don't? You think there isn't some design behind it all—"

"Stop," Pressia says softly. This has to go peacefully. Pressia can't risk Bradwell losing his temper. She turns to Partridge. "How did you get out?"

"Someone framed some of the blueprints from the original

design for my dad as a gift for twenty years of service. I studied them, the air-filtration system, the ventilation. You can hear the ventilation system when it's at work. A deep bass hum that runs underneath everything. I started to keep a journal." He holds up the leather-bound notebook in his hand. "I noted when it turned on and when it shut down. And then figured out how I could slip into the main system. And I figured out that on a certain day, at a certain time, I could probably make it past the blades of the system of circulation fans when they were down—for approximately three minutes and forty-two seconds. And that, at the end of it, I'd find a barrier of breathable fibers that I could cut my way out of. That's what I did." He smiles a little. "I got windblown at the end, but not chopped to death."

Bradwell stares at him. "And you're gone. Just like that. And no one in the Dome cares? No one's out looking for you?"

He shrugs. "By now they'll have their cameras looking for me. The cameras don't work very well, though. Never have. It's the ash. But who knows if they'll come after me? No one is ever supposed to leave the Dome—for any reason. Reconnaissance is forbidden."

"But your father," Pressia says. "I mean if he's a prominent figure . . . Wouldn't they send out people to find you?"

"My father and I don't have a very close relationship. Anyway, it's never been done before. No one's ever gotten out. No one's ever wanted to—not like I did."

Bradwell shakes his head. "What's in that envelope again?"

"Personal stuff," Partridge says. "Typical mother stuff. Jewelry, a music box, a letter."

"I wouldn't mind taking a look," Bradwell says. "Might be something interesting in there."

Partridge pauses. Pressia can tell he doesn't trust Bradwell. Partridge scoops up the envelope holding his mother's possessions and places it back in his leather bag. "It's nothing."

"So that's why you wanted to come here—to find your mother, the *saint*?" Bradwell says.

Partridge ignores Bradwell's tone. "Once I saw her things, I started to doubt everything I've ever been told. I was told she was dead, so I doubted that too," he says.

"And what if she is dead?" Bradwell asks.

"I'm used to that idea," Partridge says, stoically.

"We're used to the idea too," Bradwell says. "Most people here have plenty of people they've lost."

Bradwell doesn't know Pressia's story of loss, but he knows she has one. Every survivor has one. Partridge doesn't know anything about her or what she's lost either, and she doesn't feel like acknowledging it now. "Partridge needs to find Lombard Street. That's where they lived. He can at least start there," she tells Bradwell. "He needs the old map of the city."

"Why should I help him?" he says.

"Maybe he can help us in return," she says.

"We don't need his help."

Partridge doesn't say a word. Bradwell looks at the two of them. Pressia leans toward Bradwell. "Maybe you don't, but I do," she says.

"What do you need him for?"

"Leverage. OSR. Maybe I could get off the list. And my grandfather is sick. He's all I've got. Without any help, I'm sure . . ." She suddenly feels sick, like saying aloud her fears—that her grandfather will die, that she'll be shipped to the OSR and because of her lost hand, she'll be of no use—will make them undeniably true. Her mouth is dry. She almost can't say it. But then the words tumble out. "We won't make it."

Bradwell kicks the footlocker. The birds, startled but with nowhere to go, beat madly under the shirt on his back. He looks at Pressia. He's giving in, she can tell. He might even be giving in for her sake.

She doesn't want his sympathy. She hates pity. She says quickly, "We just need a map. We can make it."

Bradwell shakes his head.

"We'll be fine," Pressia says.

"You might make it, but he won't. He hasn't adapted to this environment. It'd be a waste of a perfectly good Pure to let him go out and get his head bashed by Groupies."

"Thanks for the vote of confidence," Partridge says.

"What's the street?" Bradwell says.

"Lombard," Partridge says. "Ten Fifty-four Lombard."

"If the street exists, I'll get you to it. Then maybe you should go home, back to the Dome and Daddy."

Partridge is pissed. He leans forward. "I don't need any—"

Pressia cuts in, "We'll take the map. If you can get us to Lombard, that would be great."

Bradwell looks at Partridge, giving him a chance to finish. But Partridge must know that Pressia's right. They should take whatever help they can get.

"Yeah," Partridge says. "Lombard would be great. We won't ask for any more than that."

"Okay," Bradwell says. "It's not easy, you know. If the street didn't have any big important buildings on it, then it'll be lost to us. And if it was anywhere close to the middle of the city, it'll just be part of the Rubble Fields. I can't guarantee anything." Bradwell squats down and opens the footlocker. After a few moments of careful sorting, he comes up with an old map of the city. It's tattered; the seams have worn through to a soft fray.

"Lombard Street," he says. He opens the map on the floor. Partridge and Pressia kneel beside him. He runs his finger along the grid at one side, then puts a finger on section 2E.

"Do you see it?" she asks, and suddenly, she hopes the house is still standing. She hopes, beyond all reason, that it's the way it once was: big houses in a tidy row with white stone steps and fancy gates, windows with curtains that open to beautiful rooms, bikes locked to front gates, people walking dogs, people pushing strollers. She doesn't know why she even lets herself have this kind of hope. Maybe it has something to do with the Pure, as if his hopefulness is contagious.

Bradwell's finger stops on an intersection. "Are you always this lucky?" he says to Partridge.

"What? Where is it?"

"I know exactly where Lombard is." He gets up, walks out of the meat locker into the larger room. He kneels next to the toppled wall and pulls a few bricks away, exposing a hole filled with weapons—hooks, knives, cleavers. He pulls some out and brings them back into the cooler. He gives Partridge and Pressia each a knife. Pressia likes the weight of it, although she doesn't want to think of what it's been used for here in the butcher shop—and by Bradwell too.

"Just in case," he says, and he slips a knife and a hook onto loops stitched inside his own jacket. He then holds up a gun. "I found a bunch of these stun guns too. At first I thought they were some kind of bike pump. Instead of bullets, they've got a cartridge that delivers a stunning blow if held to the head of a cow or pig. Good for hand-to-hand combat. Good if you're attacked by Groupies."

"Can I see it?" Partridge asks.

Bradwell hands it to him, and Partridge holds it lightly, like it's a small animal.

"The first time I used it was on Groupies," Bradwell says. "I pulled the gun from my waistband, and, within the dense tangle of bodies, I found the back of a skull. I pulled the trigger and the head went limp. The Groupies must have felt the sudden shock of death throughout their shared cells. They reared and spun a slow circle, like they were trying to release themselves from the dead one. Its head was lolling and flopping, and I ran off."

"I don't know if I'd be able to do that," Pressia says, looking at the knife in her hands.

"Life or death," Partridge says. "I think you would."

"Maybe I don't know how to process a cow," Bradwell says, "but I know these weapons as well as any butcher ever did—as a means of survival."

Pressia puts the knife into the rope of her belt. She'd rather use the knife to cut wires and make her small windup toys than kill anything. "Where are we going exactly?"

"The church," Bradwell says. "Part of it still exists. A crypt." He stops, stares at one of the walls of the meat locker as if he's looking through it. "That's where I go sometimes."

"To pray?" Pressia says. "You believe in God?"

"No," he says. "It's just a good safe place. Tight walls, sound structure."

Pressia doesn't know what she thinks about God. All she knows is that people around here have pretty much given up on the idea of religion and faith, although there are some who still worship in their own ways, and some who've confused the Dome with a version of heaven. "I've heard whispers of people who meet and burn candles and write things down. Do they meet there?"

"I think they do," Bradwell says, folding up the map. "There's evidence of it—wax, small offerings."

"I've never thought that there was anything I could hope to get by praying for it," Pressia says.

Bradwell grabs his coat off a metal rail overhead. "That's probably what they pray for. Hope."

EL CAPITAN

GUNS

THE FABRIC OF THE AWNING IS WORN AWAY. All that's left are the aluminum spokes, bolted to the old asylum. El Capitan looks up through the awning's charred metal spines at the gray sky. *Pressia Belze*—the name is heavy. Why is Ingership suddenly obsessed with some survivor named Pressia Belze? El Capitan doesn't like the name—the way it draws itself out, a buzz in the mouth. He gave up looking for her. It's not his job to be out on the streets, so he came home an hour ago and sent the men back out. Now he wonders if he'll pay for that decision. Could those idiots really find the girl without him? He doubts it.

He shouts into the walkie-talkie. "Did you get her? Over."

The radio goes silent.

"Do you read me? Over."

There's nothing.

"Dead again," El Capitan says.

And then El Capitan's brother, Helmud, mutters, "Dead again."

Helmud is only seventeen, two years younger than El Capitan, and he's always been the smaller of the two. El Capitan and Helmud were ten and eight, respectively, when the Detonations hit. Helmud is fused to El Capitan's back. The visual effect is that of a permanent piggyback ride. Helmud has his own upper body, but the rest feeds into his brother—the lumpy bone and muscle of his thighs forming a thick band across El Capitan's lower back. They'd been riding a motorized dirt bike when the whitest white and the hot wind blasted them down—Helmud on the back of the dirt bike holding on to his older brother. El Capitan had rebuilt the engine himself. Now Helmud's skinny arms are draped around his brother's thick neck.

The walkie-talkie crackles to life. El Capitan can hear the truck's radio and growling gears, as if it's climbing a hill. Finally the officer's voice pops through the noise. "No. But we will. Trust me. Over."

Trust me, El Capitan thinks. He shoves the walkie-talkie into his holster. He glances back at his brother. "Like I ever trusted anybody. Not even you."

"Not even you," Helmud whispers back.

The truth is he's always had to trust Helmud. For so long, they've only had each other. They never had a father, really, and when El Capitan was nine, their mother died of a virulent influenza in an asylum like the one he stands in front of now.

El Capitan shouts into the walkie-talkie, "If you don't get her, Ingership will have our asses. Don't mess this up. Over."

It's late. The moon is lost in a gray haze. El Capitan thinks about going in to see if Vedra is still working in the kitchen. He likes the way she looks through the steam of the dishwasher. He could order her to make him a sandwich. He's the highest-ranking official on the ground here at headquarters, after all. But he knows how it will go with Vedra. They'll talk as she cuts the meat, her hands raw from all that work, so much of her scarred skin showing, her brightly seared flesh. She'll talk to him with that soft voice, and eventually her eyes will slide to his brother's face, which is always there, always gazing blankly over his shoulder.

He hates the way people can't help but look at Helmud while El Capitan is speaking, a stupid puppet bobbing behind his back, and a rage will rise up inside El Capitan—so quick and sharp he could snap. Sometimes, at night, while listening to his brother's deep breaths, he imagines rolling to his back—smothering his brother once and for all. If Helmud died, he would too, though. He knows that. They are both too large to have one die and the other live, too entwined. Sometimes it seems so inevitable, he can barely stand the waiting.

Instead of seeing Vedra in the kitchen's steam, he decides to head to the woods—what's left of it, what's growing back—to check his traps. Two days in a row, his traps have been picked clean. He caught something all right, but then something else came along and ate it.

Once he's walked behind headquarters, there are forts made of planks of wood, shears of metal on a barren dirt field, a wall built out of stones. On top of it, there's barbed wire. Beyond that, there are wrecked buildings. One had a row of columns, and two of the columns remain with nothing behind them but a sooty sky. He loves the sky more than anything. He'd wanted to be in the air force, once upon a time, as a kid. He used to know everything there was about flying; he had library books and an old flight simulation video where he logged hours upon hours of practice. He knew nothing about his own father except that he'd been in the air force, a fighter pilot, kicked out of the military on a psych discharge. "Crazy as hell," his mother used to say about him. "We're lucky he's gone." Gone where? El Capitan never knew. But he knew he was like his father in some ways—he wanted to be in the sky and he was crazy. The closest he ever got to flying was riding that motorized dirt bike, catching air after hitting a jump. He doesn't like thinking about that now.

He's no pilot, but he is an officer. He's in charge of sorting out fresh recruits. He decides which ones can be trained and which ones can't. He sends some of them to the de-education outposts to get them stripped down a little, mentally, to make them a little more willing to take orders and not stir things up. And he picks off the weak ones, keeping a few in a holding pen on the grounds. He sends reports directly to Ingership via Ingership's own personal messengers.

Sometimes Ingership sends El Capitan things to feed the weakest recruits—twisted ears of corn, pale tomatoes with innards more dust than pulp, a certain kind of unlabeled meat. He then reports to Ingership which foods make them sick, which don't. Where do the foods come from? He doesn't ask questions. El Capitan tests things on the weak recruits for his own purposes too—berries he finds in the woods, morels, leaves that could be basil or mint but never are. Sometimes the weak recruits get sick. Occasionally they die. Every once in a while, they're just fine, and so El Capitan collects those foods and shares them with Helmud.

Sometimes Ingership orders El Capitan to play The Game, letting one of the weak recruits loose so El Capitan can hunt the recruit down like a sick deer. It's a mercy really, that's what El Capitan tells himself. Why have them suffer in a pen? Better to get it over with. It's the way he'd want it, really. The Game reminds El Capitan of when he hunted squirrels as a kid in the woods near his house, but, then again, not really. Nothing's like it used to be. It's been a while since Ingership has ordered him to play The Game, and El Capitan hopes that Ingership has forgotten about it and won't ever ask again. Ingership has become unpredictable recently. In fact, just yesterday he organized his own team for a Death Spree that he decided to spring on everyone without warning.

As El Capitan makes his way toward the woods, he passes the caged pen—twenty feet by twenty feet, enclosed by chain link, with a cement floor. Recruits are huddled together in one corner of the pen. They moan and shudder until they hear his footsteps;

then one of them hushes then another, and they quiet down quickly. He can see their strange twisted limbs, the glint of various metals, the shine of glass. They're barely human when you get right down to it, he reminds himself, but still he looks away when he passes by.

"There but for the grace of God, Helmud. That could be you in there," he says.

"You in there," Helmud says.

"Shut up, Helmud."

"Shut up."

He's not sure what's got Ingership all heated up about this new recruit, Pressia Belze. Ingership wants this girl to be promoted to officer upon arrival. He wants El Capitan to await emergency orders for her, a mission, but meanwhile to bring her *into the fold*. El Capitan isn't sure what this means exactly. He's not sure how much he himself is supposed to know. Is he supposed to know, for example, that he's really just a midlevel bureaucrat? Is he supposed to know that this militia—five thousand in three facilities each and another three thousand getting uneducated—no matter how big it gets, no matter how strong, will never be able to take down the Dome? The Dome is impenetrable, heavily armed. Does Ingership know that El Capitan has lost his fire? He's given up on the idea that he might get to open fire on some of his Pure *brothers and sisters* one day. He's still just trying to survive.

But surviving is what he's known. He's been a survivalist since his mother died when he was nine. He took care of his brother, living in a fort El Capitan built in the woods surrounding their old house. He got money however he could, dealing this and that, and he stockpiled guns and ammo, including things his father had left behind.

"Remember all our guns," El Capitan says to Helmud, trudging into the woods now, headquarters looming at his back. Sometimes he feels deeply nostalgic for his guns.

"Guns," Helmud says.

Before the Detonations, there were many survivalists living off the grid in those woods. One neighbor, an old man who'd been in a war or two, taught El Capitan how to hide his guns and ammo. El Capitan did everything Old Man Zander told him to. He bought 40 PVC pipe with end caps, six inches in diameter, and some PVC solvent. He and Helmud disassembled their rifles in their house one afternoon in late winter. El Capitan remembers the driving sleet, the sound of it ticking against the windows. The two brothers rubbed the gun parts down with anti-rust oil, which gave the guns and their hands a waxy sheen. Helmud had gotten hold of the aluminized Mylar bag, cut it into smaller pieces, and wrapped the barreled actions, stocks, trigger assemblies, hand guards, magazines, scopes, mounts, and several thousand rounds of .223 along with silica gel desiccant packets. Those were El Capitan's ideas. He'd seen them in boxes of his mother's old high heels in her closet. Helmud fused the ends of the bags with an iron. They vacuum-packed the bags with the neighbor's Shop-Vac.

They packed six small cans of 1,1,1-trichloroethane to degrease it later, plus cleaning rods, patches, Hoppe's No. 9 Solvent, gun oil, grease, a set of reloading dies, and a well-worn owner's manual. Then they wrapped it all in duct tape.

They filled the pipe with the bags of ammo and the rifle pieces and supplies. They sealed up the end caps and then Helmud said, "We should paint our initials on all this."

"You think?" El Capitan said.

And so they did. El Capitan knows that they thought they might actually die before they got to dig it up, and if someone did find it, they'd be known in some small way. With a thick black permanent marker, Helmud wrote H. E. C., for Helmud Elmore Croll. As for *El Capitan*, that was a nickname his mother gave him before she left for the asylum. She said, "You're in charge 'til I get back, El Capitan." But she never came back. And so El Capitan wrote his initials, E. C. C.—El Capitan Croll—and let his baptismal name die forever.

Old Man Zander loaned them a posthole digger, and they dug deeper into a hole left from a felled oak. They buried the stuff straight up and down so it'd be harder to find by metal detectors. El Capitan drew up the map, numbering paces because Old Man Zander had suggested it, "just in case the landscape is blown clean of its markings." El Capitan thought Old Man Zander was crazy, but he followed his orders. He never saw him again after the Detonations, never looked for him either.

After the Detonations, El Capitan thought Helmud would die on his back, and El Capitan wasn't doing so well either. He was burned, blistered, bloody. He made it back to the woods near their house, though, and found the metal tip of a shovel, paced the steps out from memory. The map was long gone. He dug, holding the head of the shovel in his hands with his brother dying on his back.

When he found the guns, he thought about shooting Helmud in the head and then himself, ending it there. But El Capitan could feel his brother's heartbeat through his own ribs, and there was something about it that wouldn't let him pull the trigger.

The guns, that's how they survived. Not so much from using them—though El Capitan had to kill people for survival's sake those early months. Mainly he leveraged them to get a good position in the OSR. This was after Operation Search and Rescue became Operation Sacred Revolution, and they were looking for young fiery recruits with nothing to lose. Plus, joining the OSR meant that he and Helmud wouldn't go hungry.

The woods here still look burned out, older trees toppled and blackened. Some trees withstood the blast, shorn of their limbs; others had boughs permanently bent down by the pressure of the Detonations, trees reaching for the earth instead of the sky, as if wanting to hold on. But the underbrush has regenerated, slowly fighting for the ash-covered sun. Stubble has inched up from the tree roots, strange new bushes that El Capitan can't get used to. They have small berries that are poisonous, and their leaves are sometimes scaly. Once he found a low-lying bush nudging up from under a gutted maple, and its leaves were covered in downy fur. Not just fuzz, actual fur.

He walks from trap to trap, heading deeper into the woods. Each one has been tripped. Not a speck of blood. But the skins are there, and the bones, some of which have been snapped and sucked clean of their marrow. It makes no sense. But he's more baffled than angry. He can't think of any kind of creature who'd work this neatly, and it sets him on edge.

About twenty feet from his last trap, he hears something in the air, a deep bass hum. He stops. "You hear that?" he asks his brother, but it's like talking to himself.

The hum grows softer as if it's traveling away from him at a fast rate of speed. Is it an engine? It seems too clean to be an engine. It fades too fast.

He walks to his final trap, and there's a wild hen of some sort—dead, plump, plucked clean. But it's not in the trap. It lies there beside the trap, which has been tripped, but the hen shows no signs of having been killed by anything other than a farmer's quick twist of the neck. It seems as if it's lying there like a gift, set out for El Capitan. He nudges it with a bamboo stick. It jostles. He picks it up, and there, nestled under its body like some strange joke, are three eggs. Brown eggs. One is speckled.

He lifts the speckled egg, cradles it in his palm. It's like someone out here wants to reach out to him somehow.

When was the last time he saw an egg and held it in his palm? Maybe it was before the Detonations when his mother was still in the house, buying eggs in Styrofoam cartons.

The hen and her eggs feel like a strange miracle, and he remembers what it was like pulling the PVC from the ground, like extracting a long white bone from the earth, and how the soil was still loose, soft and tender in his hands. He found a bit of his old handsaw. He wiped the mud away and sawed off the end caps. Everything slid out, just like they'd planned—except his brother was fused to his back. Helmud wouldn't die. No, he'd be a weight El Capitan would have to shoulder forever.

But sometimes he remembers the sound of guns slipping down the inside of the PVC pipe, the weight of those Mylar bags, the heavy clicks as he assembled the rifles, one after the other, and he loves Helmud as much as he hates him. He feels like he wouldn't have made it without him. The weight of his brother has made him stronger.

The hum returns, and El Capitan squats down as low as he can. He lies flat in the brush. His brother seems to be crying softly on his back. Sometimes Helmud cries for no reason.

"Shut up," El Capitan whispers softly. "Shut up, Helmud. It's okay. Shut up."

He can see them then, strange creatures—both human and not human—shifting through the trees.

PARTRIDGE

SINGING

Out on the street, Bradwell leads the way, taking long quick strides. Pressia is next, then Partridge. Bradwell never looks back at Partridge, but Pressia does, and Partridge wonders what she thinks of him. Is he just a pawn? Does she just want to get off the OSR list, whatever that is, and get help for her grandfather, like she said? If so, fair enough. She'll help him, and he'll help her if he can. Plus, he has proof that she's got a good heart. She saved his life before she could have possibly known who he was or what he could do for her. He trusts her; that's the bottom line.

And he knows that Bradwell hates him, resents the privilege of Partridge's Dome life, and who can blame him? Partridge just hopes that Bradwell doesn't hate him so much that he'll let him get his head bashed by Groupies, as Bradwell put it. It would have been funny if it weren't such a real possibility.

Bradwell stops to look up an alley to see if it's clear.

The wind has gotten colder. Partridge pulls his coat in close to his ribs. "This is what winter feels like, right?" he says to Pressia.

"No," she tells him. "Winter's cold."

"But this is cold," he says.

"It's not winter-cold."

"I'd like to see all of this covered in snow," he says.

"The snow is dark by the time it hits the ground, already stained."

Bradwell doubles back. "They're too close," he says. Partridge doesn't know who he's talking about. "We'll have to go underground. This way."

"Underground?" Partridge asks.

Partridge doesn't like going underground. Even in the basement of the academy library, it's too easy for him to lose his bearings without the landmarks, the sun, moon, stars. Here, though, one of those fixed bearings is the Dome itself, which is brighter than everything else in the sky, its shining cross pointing directly at heaven, though, like Pressia, he's not sure what he believes in.

"If he says underground is the best way to go, it is," Pressia says.

Bradwell points to a square hole by a gutter. Its metal grate is long gone, probably stolen. He slips his legs in first and then drops down. Pressia slips in next. Her shoes clap loudly against cement. Partridge goes down last. It's dark and damp. So many puddles, he can't even try to sidestep them all. They have to just go splashing through. Every once in a while, he hears animals, their shadows scampering past, their various squeaks and chirrups.

"Seriously," Partridge says, "why are we down here?"

"You heard the chanting, right?" Bradwell says.

"Yeah," Partridge says. He can still hear it. "What's so wrong with a wedding?"

Bradwell stops, turns, and squints at him. "A *wedding*?"

Partridge looks at Pressia. "You said . . ."

Pressia says to Bradwell, "I might have told him that the chants were from a wedding."

"Why would you lie about something like that?" Bradwell looks at her, baffled.

"I don't know. Maybe I wanted it to be true. Maybe I'm a type."

Then Pressia says to Partridge, "It's not a wedding. It's a kind of game, OSR's definition of a sport."

"Oh," Partridge says, "that's not so bad. We play sports in the Dome, too. I've been a halfback in a variation of what used to be called football."

"This is a blood sport called a Death Spree, used by OSR to rid society of the weak. It's really the only kind of sport around here, if you can call it a sport," Bradwell says, walking quickly again. "They get points for killing people."

"It's better to just stay out of their way," Pressia tells him, and then—she doesn't know why, maybe just for effect—she says, "You'd be worth ten points."

"Only ten?" Partridge asks.

"Actually," Bradwell says over his shoulder, "ten's a compliment."

"Well," Partridge says, "in that case, thanks. Thanks a lot."

"If they knew you were a Pure, though, who knows what they'd do with you?" Pressia says.

They walk on for a while in silence. He thinks of what Bradwell said in the meat cooler: *And you're gone. Just like that. And no one in the Dome cares? No one's out looking for you?* They are looking for him. And they'll question the academy boys who were with him last, maybe his teachers, anyone he might have confided in. Lyda. He can't help but wonder what they've done with her.

And here it's dank. The puddles are foul. The air is stale and still. Partridge doesn't complain, but he's surprised by how much it unnerves him and how relieved he is when, finally, Bradwell stops and says, "Lombard. It should be right up there. Ready?"

"Absolutely," Partridge says.

"Wait," Pressia says. "Don't expect too much."

Does he look that naive? "I'll be fine."

"Just don't get your hopes up." She looks at him in a way he can't quite read. Does she feel sorry for him? Is she a little angry? Is she being protective?

"I don't have my hopes up," he says. But he knows that's a lie. He wants to find something—if not his mother, then something that might lead to her. If he doesn't find it, he'll have nowhere to go from here. He'll have escaped for no reason, without any way back. Bradwell told him to go back home to the Dome and his daddy. But that's not possible, is it? Could he go back to Glassings' lectures on World History? Could he and Lyda date, communicating with Arvin's laser pen on the grass of the commons? Would he be put under and altered for good? Play the pincushion? Be bugged? Would he get a ticker inserted into his brain?

This opening has an old rusty ladder propped up to it, but Partridge jumps and grabs the cement lip overhead and pulls himself up like he did to get into the tunnels leading to the air-filtration system. That seems years ago.

Aboveground, there was a row of houses here once, but now they're toppled, rubble, husks. A streetlight pole lies on the ground like a tree that was struck by lightning, fried and fallen next to the skeletons of two cars, stripped down to nothing. On the corner, he sees the steeple of the church that Bradwell had talked about. The church collapsed and the steeple fell into it. It sticks out now, tilted to one side, no longer pointing to heaven like the Dome.

"Here we are," Bradwell says flatly. "Lombard." Partridge is pretty sure there's something kind of happy in his tone or at least smug.

A breeze whips up ashy dust, but Partridge doesn't cover his face. He walks down the street a few paces. He feels lost. He runs his eyes over the remains. What does he expect to find? Some remnant of the past? The vacuum cleaner? The telephone? A hint of domesticity? His mother sitting in a lawn chair, reading a book, waiting for him with fresh lemonade?

Pressia touches his arm. "I'm sorry."

He looks at her. "I need *Ten Fifty-four* Lombard Street," he says. He kicks into some kind of autopilot. "Ten Fifty-four."

"What, are you kidding?" Bradwell laughs. "There is no *Ten Fifty-four* Lombard Street because there is no *Lombard Street.* Don't you see that? It's gone!"

"I need Ten Fifty-four Lombard Street," Partridge says again. "You don't understand!"

"I do understand," Bradwell says. "You come here to this bombed-out place to mix with all these deformed *wretches,* and you think you deserve to find your mother, just like that. You think it's your right and privilege, because you've suffered for what? Fifteen minutes?"

Partridge keeps his eyes steady, but he's breathing hard. "I'm going to find Ten Fifty-four Lombard Street. That's what I came here to do." He walks down the dark street.

He hears Pressia say, "Bradwell."

"Hear that?" Bradwell says. The Death Spree chants are still going on. Partridge can't judge how close or far off they are. Their voices seem to echo through the city. "You don't have much time!" It must be close to dawn.

Pressia catches up to Partridge.

He stops. He's found a house that lost its second story. Tarp has been tied to the old windows. He hears faint singing.

"We have to hurry," Pressia tells him.

"There's someone in there," he says.

"Seriously," she says, "we don't have much time."

He whips his backpack off his shoulders, unzips it, and pulls out a plastic pouch with a photograph inside.

"What's that?" Pressia asks.

"A picture of my mother," he says. "I'm going to see if this person remembers her." He walks up to the doorway, which no longer has a door but instead has some plywood propped against it from the inside.

"Don't," Pressia tells him. "You never know what kind you're going to come up against."

"I have to," he says.

She shakes her head. "Wrap up then."

He winds the scarf around his face, pulls up the hood, hiding everything but his eyes.

The singing is louder now, an off-kilter tune from a rattled, high-pitched voice, more like warbling than singing.

He taps on the plywood.

The singing stops. There's a rattle of what sounds like pans. Then nothing.

"Hello?" Partridge calls out. "I'm sorry to bother you, but I have a question."

No response.

"I was hoping you might be able to help me," he says.

"C'mon," Pressia tells him. "Let's go."

"No," he whispers, even though the chant sounds closer now than before. "Leave if you want to. This is all I've got. My only chance."

"Okay," Pressia says. "Hurry."

"I'm looking for someone," he calls. It's quiet a moment. He glances back at Bradwell who snaps his fingers, telling them to hurry up. Partridge tries again. "I really need your help," he says. "It's important. I'm looking for my mother."

There's another rattle inside, and then an old voice says, "State your name!"

"Partridge," he says, leaning toward the tarp-covered window. "Partridge Willux."

"Willux?" she says. It seems his name always gets a reaction.

"We lived at Ten Fifty-four Lombard," he says urgently. "I have a photograph."

An arm appears now from behind the tarp, a claw-like hand, metallic and rusty.

Partridge is afraid to give up the photograph. It's the only one he has. But he does.

The fingers pinch it, and the hand disappears.

It's dawn, he realizes. The sun is edging up the horizon.

The tarp is lifted then, very slowly, revealing an old woman's face—pale and covered in bits of glass. She hands the photograph back to Partridge without a word, but her eyes are distant, strange. Her face looks haunted.

"Did you know her?" Partridge asks.

The old woman glances up and down the street. She sees Bradwell, standing in the shadows, and she steps back, lowering the tarp a bit. The old woman's eyes lock onto Partridge's. "I want to see your face," she says.

Partridge looks at Pressia. She shakes her head no.

"I'll tell you something," she says. "But I have to see your face first."

"Why?" Pressia says, stepping closer. "Just give him the information. It's important to him."

She shakes her head. "I have to see his face."

Partridge pulls the scarf down.

The woman looks at him and nods. "What I thought."

"What do you mean?" Partridge asks.

The woman shakes her head.

"You told me you'd give me information if I showed you my face. I held up my end."

"You look like her," the old woman says.

"Like my mother?" he asks.

She nods. The chanting is getting louder. Pressia pulls on Partridge's sleeve. "We've got to go."

"Is she alive?" Partridge asks.

The old woman shrugs.

Bradwell whistles through his teeth. There's no more time to waste. Partridge can hear the footfalls of the Death Spree, that chuffing sound of boots on the streets, their voices rising and falling in unison. The air is vibrating.

"Did you see her after the Detonations?" Partridge asks.

The old woman closes her eyes, and she whispers something under her breath.

Pressia pulls on Partridge's jacket. "We have to go! Now!"

"What did you say?" Partridge shouts at the old woman. "Did you see her or not? Did she live through it?"

Finally, the old woman lifts her head and says, "He broke her heart." And then she closes her eyes and starts singing loudly—shrill, anguished notes, as if she's trying to drown out everything around her.

Pressia

SARCOPHAGUS

Pressia is running as fast as she can. Bradwell is up ahead, his shirt rustling with wings, and Partridge is sprinting beside her, jacket flapping. She knows he can move more quickly than he is—special training at the academy even though he wasn't *a ripe specimen*—but she takes it as a good sign that he's staying right with her. Maybe he's realized how much he needs her. The chants are an echo, roaring down the alleys, sometimes shot through with a high-pitched cry.

"Back down underground?" Pressia shouts to Bradwell.

"No!" he says. "They're tunneling down there, too."

Pressia looks over her shoulder and sees the leader of this team. He's shirtless, his arms and chest smeared red with blood over metal. The skin on his face is puckered and shiny. One of his arms is curled up close to his chest—withered there—but his other arm is fiercely muscular. He has shards of glass wrapped in tape around his knuckles. He might be an OSR soldier she's seen patrolling, but she'd never recognize him as he is.

He's the head of the wedge. The others fan out behind him in a loose formation. In the back there's a designated whip who will decide when it's time to fan out the back of the wedge and form a tightening circle around a victim. Pressia once saw a woman and her baby attacked in a Death Spree. Pressia had hidden herself in an old overturned mailbox that had been popped open and gutted long ago. She remembers now the way they lifted the mother's body over their heads after they'd beaten her to death, how the baby was tossed around like a ball.

Pressia's foot catches on a curb and she falls hard, skidding along the cement. Her palm burns, the doll head aches. She sees Partridge's boots stop in front of her and turn, the damp cuffs of his pants. She tries to scramble up, but she makes the mistake of looking behind her once more, and the red blood and glinting bodies of the Death Spree terrify her. She loses her footing again.

"This way!" Bradwell shouts up ahead. He doesn't know she's down. He hops over a low crumbled stone wall near the collapsed steeple.

She sees them closing in. The leader has his eyes fixed on her.

And then her body is hoisted up, and there's wind in her face. The sock fitted over her doll-head fist snags on something on the ground and it's gone. She's moving through the air, the doll-head fist exposed, and she can hear Partridge saying, "It's okay. We're close. We're almost there."

She doesn't want to be rescued by the Pure. "No," she says, "I'm fine. Let go of me!"

He doesn't answer, just grips her tighter, and she knows that if he did let her down, she'd get taken up by the Death Spree, but still, she punches his ribs with her doll-head fist. "I mean it. Let me down!" In her panicked vision, she sees Bradwell lift a piece of old cast-iron gate that's been laid over an opening that leads to a set of stairs. She closes her eyes as Partridge holds her tight and jumps down the stairs.

As soon as his feet hit the ground, she shoves him, and he sets her down. With the sock that hid the doll-head fist gone, she feels naked. She pulls the sweater sleeve over it as tightly as she can, and sits down. Her knees to her chest, she hides the doll head in her lap. It's so dark she can barely see anything.

"Sorry," Partridge says. "I had to pick you up. I had to or—"

"Don't apologize," she says, rubbing her ribs where he gripped her so tightly. "You saved me. Don't make me feel like I have to forgive you for it." That's the best she can do.

They all sit on the floor, Pressia between Partridge and Bradwell, their backs pressed against the cold wall. They huddle in a corner away from the stairs, and no one moves. She can't believe that Partridge picked her up like that. When was the last time someone carried her? She remembers her father wrapping her in a coat, carrying her in his arms. She misses him now, the feeling of being safe and warm.

The room is small and damp. Slowly her eyes adjust, and that's when she finally sees that they're not really alone. Dug into the opposite wall, there's a stone figure—a statue of a girl, sitting on top of a long narrow cement box like a casket behind a wall of Plexiglas, splintered but still intact. An engraved placard is fixed to the wall, but it's too far away to read. She has long hair, pulled back loosely from her face, and is wearing a simple full-length dress. Her perfect dainty hands are folded in her lap. She seems alone, cut off from the world. There's something deeply sorrowful about her eyes, as if she's lost people she loves but, too, she's expectant, as if holding her breath, waiting.

The chants are getting louder, the feet pounding closer. Pressia pulls her sweater sleeve more tightly over her doll-head fist. Partridge sees her do it. Maybe he wants to ask her what she's hiding. This is no time to ask. The Death Spree is overhead now. The feet are pounding so loudly all around them that a bit of the ceiling crumbles.

This is where people come to pray. Bradwell was right. On the lip of the cement casing, beside the Plexiglas, Pressia sees the pooled wax of old candles, the drippings that have melted down the wall onto the tiled floor. Pressia looks at the statue of the girl again. The girl sits on her own casket, a long box that reminds Pressia of the cabinets where she sleeps, or used to sleep. Pressia wonders if she'll ever make it back to the back room of the barbershop to her grandfather. Is he waiting for her still, the brick in his lap?

The footfalls grow thunderous. The ceiling rattles. Plaster, loose stones, clods of dirt fall to the floor. Suddenly Pressia is afraid that the ceiling is going to cave in. They all cover their heads. Partridge has put the photograph back in the plastic pouch. It sits on top of his bag, which he's hunched over protectively.

"We're going to be buried alive!" Pressia shouts.

"Which would be ironic," Bradwell says. "To be buried alive, in a crypt."

"Not funny," she tells him.

"I wasn't trying to be funny," he says.

"I'd rather not die," Partridge says. "Not now that I know my mother survived..."

Pressia looks up at him through the raining dirt. Is that what he thinks? How is he so sure? All the old woman said was that someone broke his mother's heart. It meant nothing to Pressia. She holds her breath for a moment, willing the pounding feet to stop, but they don't. She grips her knees tightly and squeezes her eyes shut.

A crowd starts cheering. There are loud whoops, war cries.

"They got somebody," Pressia says.

"Good," Bradwell says. "That will appease them. They'll move on more quickly now, carry the body to the field."

"Good?" Partridge asks. "How can it be good?"

"Good doesn't mean what you think it means," Bradwell says.

The chanting heads off into the distance.

Pressia looks at the stone coffin. "Is there a dead person in there?" she asks.

"A sarcophagus," Bradwell says.

"A what?" Partridge asks.

"Sarcophagus," Bradwell repeats. "In other words, yes. A dead person or part of one."

"We're in a tomb, aren't we?" Partridge says.

Bradwell nods. "A crypt."

Partridge is still holding the photograph in its plastic pouch.

Pressia holds out her hand. "Can I see it?"

He hands it to her.

"What?" Bradwell says. "I can't look at it but she can?"

Partridge smiles and shrugs. The photo is of a little boy about eight years old, standing on the beach—Partridge. He's holding his mother's hand and a bucket. It's windy, and the ocean is foamy around their ankles. She's beautiful, his mother is—lightly freckled with a gorgeous smile—and the old woman was right. He does look like her, the same lit-up face. Mothers, she thinks, they'll always be foreign, a land I'll never visit. "What's her name?"

"Aribelle Willux...well, originally, Cording."

She hands the pouch back to Partridge, but he shakes his head. "Bradwell can look at it."

"Me?" Bradwell says. "I didn't think I was good enough."

"You might see something that I don't."

"Like what?"

"A clue or something," Partridge says.

Pressia hands Bradwell the photo, and he starts to study it.

"I remember that trip," Partridge says. "It was just the two of us. My mother's mother passed down a house close to the beach. It was kind of cold, and my mother and I both ended up getting sick, a stomach bug. She made us tea, and I threw up in a garbage can next to my bed." He digs in his backpack and pulls out the envelope of his mother's things. "Here," he says. "Maybe if you looked at these things, you'd get some kind of insight. I don't know...Maybe if you read the birthday card. And there's a music box and a necklace."

Bradwell gives the photo back to Partridge, takes the envelope, and looks inside. He picks up the music box, opens it. A little tune starts to play. "I don't know this song," Bradwell says.

"It's weird, but, honestly, I think she made the tune up," he says. "But then how did she find a music box that played a song she invented?"

"The box looks handmade," Pressia says. It's simple and plain. She holds out her hand. "Let me see." Bradwell hands it to her. She looks inside and sees the small metal fingers striking the nubs on a metal turning spool. "I could make something like this, if I had the right tools." She closes the box, opens it, closes it again, testing the stopping mechanism.

Bradwell lifts the gold chain, looped over a few fingers. The swan spins. Its body must be solid gold, Pressia thinks. It has a long neck and an oversize jeweled eye, a bright blue stone almost as big as a marble that is visible from both sides. It's perfect, not a single flaw, untarnished—pure. Pressia can't take her eyes from it. She's never really seen something that survived the Detonations, aside from Partridge. Its blue eye is hypnotic.

Finally, Bradwell sets the necklace back into the envelope. He looks at Pressia. His face is soft for a moment like he wants to tell her something, but then he stiffens up. "I got you to Lombard. That was all I promised." He stands up, but not all the way. He's too tall for the small space. "People think it's amazing that I survived on my own since I was nine years old. But the thing is I've survived *because* I've been alone all this time. Once you start to get involved with other people, they weigh you down. You two will have to make it on your own."

"Nice sentiment," Pressia says. "Really generous and charitable."

"If you were smart, you'd walk away too," Bradwell says. "Generosity and charity can get you killed."

"Look," Partridge says. "I'm fine. I don't need someone holding my hand."

Pressia knows he doesn't stand a chance alone. He's got to know it, too. But what now? The air in the small space shifts. A bit more sunlit ash sifts down. It grazes the opening overhead and filters into the crypt. It's morning, and now it's light enough for her to make out part of the name on the placard, SAINT WI, but the rest of the name is lost. The placard is dented, the letters gone. Under that, she can make out only a few other words of any importance—BORN IN...HER FATHER WAS...PATRON SAINT OF...ABBESS...SMALL CHILDREN... THREE MIRACLES...TUBERCULOSIS...Nothing more. Pressia's parents were married in a church, their reception outside under white tents. She notices that there's a small dried flower, crisp with age, sitting on the waxy edge. A small offering? "I guess we've come to a dead end," Pressia says.

"Not really. My mother survived the Detonations," Partridge says. "I got that much."

"How do you know she survived?" Pressia asks.

"The old lady said so," Partridge says. "You were there."

"I thought she said that he broke her heart," Pressia says. "That doesn't mean much."

"He *did* break her heart. He left her here. If she'd died in the Detonations, she wouldn't have had time to have had a broken heart. But she did. He broke her heart, and this woman knew about it, knew she'd been left behind, and that my father had taken me and my brother with him. That's what she meant by he broke her heart. She might have been a saint, but she didn't *die* a saint." Partridge slips the photograph back into its pouch, fits it into a larger envelope and then an interior pocket of his backpack.

"Even if she survived the blast, which is still a big if," Bradwell says, "she might not have survived what came after. Not many have."

"Look, you might think it's stupid, but I think she's alive," Partridge says.

"Your father saved you and your brother, but not her?" Bradwell asks.

Partridge nods. "He broke her heart and mine too." The confession only sits there for a second. Partridge shakes it off. "I want to go back to the old lady. She knew more than she was telling me."

"It's light out now," Pressia says. "We have to be careful. Let me just take a look first."

"I'll go," Partridge says.

"No," Bradwell says. "I will. I'll see what kind of damage the Death Spree did."

"I said I'd go," Pressia says, standing up and brushing the debris from her head and clothes. She wants to still be of use, to make sure that Partridge knows she's worth something. She hasn't given up.

"It's too dangerous!" Partridge says, and he reaches out and grabs her. His hand clasps her wrist and pulls up the sweater sleeve, exposing the back of the doll's head. It surprises him, but he doesn't let go. Instead he looks into her eyes.

She turns her arm, showing him the doll's face in place of her hand.

"From the blast," she says. "You wanted to know before. Well, here it is."

"I see," Partridge says.

"We wear our marks with pride," Bradwell says. "We're survivors."

Pressia knows that Bradwell wishes this were true, but it's not, not for her at least.

"I'm going up to look around," she says. "I'll be fine."

Partridge nods and lets her go.

She walks up the stone steps into the light, keeping herself hidden in the church's crumbled stone remains. She crouches behind part of a wall and looks out at the street. There are a few people on the road standing in front of the old woman's house in a loose circle. The tarp has been torn from her window. The plywood door is gone. The people shuffle away.

And there on the ground is a pool of blood, glistening with shards of glass.

Pressia's eyes sting, but she doesn't cry. She immediately thinks that the woman shouldn't have been singing like that. She should have stopped. Didn't she know better? And Pressia is aware of the shift within her, from sympathy to contempt. She hates that shift. She knows it's wrong, and yet she can't help it. This woman's death has to be a lesson. That's all.

She turns away.

Then there's a sharp cuff on her arm. A grunt and breath. Someone's got her by the stomach, lifted her off her feet, and is running. At first, she thinks it must be Partridge or someone from the Death Spree. No. She hears an engine. It's OSR. She reaches for the knife that Bradwell gave her. She fits her hand around the handle, pulls it from her belt, but a hand with one dark metal finger clamps her wrist so tightly that she loses her grip. The knife clatters to the ground.

The hand with the metal finger clamps her mouth. She tries to scream, but it's muffled. Like the boy with the nubbed toes in the room above the meeting, she bites the meaty center of the hand where there's soft skin. She hears a curse so vicious that it contracts her captor's ribs, but the grip on her body only tightens. Her bite has drawn blood. Her mouth tastes of rust and salt. She flexes her back, kicks her captor's back, and tries to punch with the dollhead fist. Do Bradwell and Partridge know she's gone? Are they coming for her?

She tries to spit. She feels wind in her hair. She hears the engine. She looks up and sees the back of the truck. They've come for her. She knows she's gone.

Partridge

MOUTH

AFTER A FEW MINUTES, Partridge walks to the top of the crypt's stone steps to see how Pressia is doing. What's taking her so long? It's windy. The landscape is bare except for a stain on the ground, fresh blood littered with glass.

He turns back to Bradwell, one hand on each side of the stairwell, his arms outstretched. "Where did she go?"

"What do you mean?" Bradwell shoves past him and takes the stairs three at a time. "What the hell do you mean?"

"Pressia!" Bradwell shouts.

"Pressia!" Partridge shouts now too, even though he knows they shouldn't. It could draw attention.

Bradwell runs to the spot of blood, and Partridge follows, his stomach turning with dread. He's not sure what to do. "Do you think it's her blood?" Partridge asks, his voice choked in his throat.

"There's a scrim on top where it's started to coagulate. It's been here too long." Bradwell's eyes are wild, searching.

"She's gone," Partridge says. "She's really gone. Isn't she?"

Bradwell looks in every direction. "Stop saying that!" he says.

"You go look in the old woman's house. I'll get up high and try to get a view."

The air ripples with gray shades of ash. Partridge is disoriented for a moment. Then he sees the old woman's front door where, not long ago, he found out that his mother survived. And now Pressia is gone. It's his fault. He runs to the old woman's place. The plywood is already gone from the door. He tears through the cramped space. "Pressia!" he shouts. The old woman had nothing. A pit for fires where the house was open to the sky, a few roots in a darkened corner, rags bundled on the floor, fashioned to look like a baby; its mouth is dark brown like dried blood.

He hears Bradwell calling outside. "Pressia!"

There's no response.

Partridge runs out of the room back into the street to Bradwell. "Is she gone?" He isn't asking a question as much as demanding an answer. Bradwell seems to know everything. He should know this. "Was she taken?"

Bradwell turns and punches Partridge in the stomach, knocking the wind out of him. Partridge falls to one knee, his arm around his stomach, the knuckles of his other hand on the rock. "What the hell?" he mutters. His voice is a hoarse whisper, the air dying in his lungs.

"Your mother's dead! You hear me? You come down here and want us to risk everything for a dead woman?" Bradwell shouts.

"I'm sorry," Partridge says. "I didn't mean for—"

"You think you're the only one who ever lost someone and wanted to go home?" Bradwell is furious, the veins on his temples standing out, the strange rustling motion on his back. "Why don't you go back to your tidy little Dome and stick to the plan—just watch us die *from afar, benevolently.*"

Partridge is still trying to pull air into his chest, and it feels good to be down on the ground. He deserved to be punched. What has he done? Pressia is gone. "I'm sorry," he says. "I don't know what else to say."

Bradwell tells him to shut up.

"I'm sorry," Partridge says.

"She risked her life for you," Bradwell says.

"Yes, she did." Partridge knows that Bradwell hates the sight of him.

Bradwell grabs Partridge by the arms and pulls him up, but Partridge feels a rush of anger, and instinctively he shoves Bradwell in the chest. His motions are faster and harder than he expects, almost knocking Bradwell to the ground. "I didn't lose her on purpose."

"If you weren't here," Bradwell says, "she'd be fine."

"I know."

"I got you here," Bradwell says. "And now you owe me. You owe her. This is the mission. Not your mother. Pressia. We've got to find her."

"We?" Partridge says. "What about that beautiful speech in there about how you survived because you didn't get involved, because you've always been alone."

"Look, I'll help you find your mother if and only if we find Pressia first. That's it."

Partridge hates himself for thinking about it, but he hesitates. Maybe Bradwell was right in the crypt. Maybe it's better to go alone. Maybe that's how to best survive. Could he make it on his own? Where would he go from here? He thinks of Pressia. She threw her shoe, striking the oil drum. Without her, he'd probably already be dead. Maybe this is the way it's supposed to go. Maybe this is fate. "We have to find Pressia," Partridge says. "Of course. Because it's the right thing to do."

Bradwell says, "They took her for a reason."

"What?" Partridge says.

"How did you say you figured out how to get out of the Dome?" Bradwell asks. "A blueprint? Is that what you said?"

"One of the original blueprints," Partridge says. "It was a gift to my father."

"Let me guess. A *recent* gift, right?"

"Yes, for his twenty years of service. Why?"

"A goddamn blueprint, framed and mounted on a goddamn wall!"

"What's wrong with that?" Partridge asks, but it's like he can already sense what's wrong. He adds quickly, "I figured out the ventilation system myself. I timed it all out, three minutes and forty-two seconds."

"Did it dawn on you that you were supposed to find the blueprint?" Bradwell says.

"No. It's not like that. My father would never expect me to do something like escape." Partridge shakes his head. "You don't know him."

"Really?"

"He doesn't think that highly of me."

"True. I mean, it's a little embarrassing that they had to frame the goddamn blueprints and hang them on a wall!"

"Shut up!" Partridge shouts.

"It's the truth and you know it. You can feel it. A hot little kernel inside of your brain. It all makes sense now. Things are clicking into place. Aren't they?"

Partridge's jaw is locked, but his mind is churning. It's true. He needed things, and there was the opportunity to get them. Glassings had put in a request for a field trip to the Personal Loss Archives for years, and then, out of the blue, it's finally granted?

Bradwell asks Partridge, in a low voice, trying to sound calm, "How did you come across Pressia?"

"I don't know. She said she was dodging OSR trucks. They were everywhere."

"OSR," Bradwell says. "Jesus. You two were sheep. You were being herded."

"By OSR? You think they're taking orders from the Dome? They're not revolutionary?"

"I should have seen it. Even the Death Spree, that was planned too, probably. The teams' chants used to herd her." Bradwell paces, kicking rocks. "Did you think the Dome was just going to let you waltz off? They arranged all of it. Your daddy took care of everything," Bradwell says.

"That's not true," he says quietly. "I was almost killed by those fan blades."

"But you *weren't* killed by the fan blades," Bradwell says.

"How would they know where Pressia is? Her chip is dead," Partridge says.

"She was wrong."

"But what do they want with Pressia?"

"I want to see everything you've got," Bradwell says. "I want to know what you know. I want what's in your whole head. That's all you're worth to me, you understand?"

Partridge nods. "Okay. However I can help."

LYDA

STRIPS

From LYDA'S ROOM, she can see the faces of the other girls when they peer out the small rectangular windows lodged in the upper left corners of their doors. She's been here the longest. The other faces on this wing come and linger for a day and then they disappear—to where? Lyda doesn't know. Relocation, that's what the guards call it. When they bring Lyda food on compartmentalized trays, they say things about her relocation. They wonder why it's stalled. They say almost jokingly, "Why are you still here?" It's a mystery to them, but they aren't allowed to ask many questions. Some of them know about her connection to Partridge. Some have even lowered their voices and asked questions about him. One asked, "What was he gonna use the knife for?"

"What knife?" she said.

The faces of girls floating, seemingly bodiless, in the rectangular windows of the other holding cells are one way to keep track of the days. A new girl will come. Then another will take her place. Sometimes they leave for therapy then return; sometimes they don't. Their heads are shiny from being shaved, their eyes and noses puffed and raw from crying. They look at her and see something different. Someone who's not lost but stuck. They gaze at her pleadingly. Some of the girls try to ask questions with hand gestures. But this is nearly impossible. Guards patrol and clap their small clubs on the doors. Before a language of gestures can develop, the girls disappear.

Today, though, one of the guards comes in when it's not meal-time. She unlocks the door and says, "You're going to occupational."

"Occupational?" Lyda asks.

"Therapy. You'll weave a sitting mat."

"Okay," Lyda says. "Do I need a sitting mat in here?"

"Does anyone *need* a sitting mat?" the guard asks, and then she smiles. "It's a good sign," she whispers. "Someone's going soft on you."

Lyda wonders if her mother pulled some strings. Is this the beginning of a real rehabilitation? Does this mean someone thinks she can be made well again, even though she was never unwell?

The hall is like another world. She takes in the tiled floor, the clean grout, the swish of the guard's uniform in front of her, the bobbing Taser strapped to her hip, a janitorial closet with a large unplugged floor buffer.

There's a face behind one of the small rectangular windows, a girl whose eyes are wild with fear, and then another who's placid. Lyda categorizes them—the first one hasn't yet gotten her meds, the second has. Lyda fakes taking her pills now. After the guard leaves, she spits them out and crushes them to dust.

The guard checks her clipboard and stops to open another door not far from Lyda's. Inside, there's a new girl, a face that Lyda doesn't recognize, one who hasn't yet appeared at her rectangular window. The girl has wide hips and a narrow waist. Her head is freshly shaved. The nicks are still raw. Lyda can tell by the girl's eyebrows that she's a redhead.

"Up!" the guard shouts at the redhead. "Come on."

The girl glances at Lyda and the guard. She picks up the white head scarf in her lap, covers her head with it, tying it in the back. She follows them.

They're led to a room with three long tables and benches. Lyda sees other girls now, their whole bodies, not just faces, which surprises her. It's as if she's forgotten they have bodies. She recognizes a few from the windows in the past few days. Their heads are covered with scarves too, like hers. They wear identical white jumpsuits. Why white? Lyda wonders. It so easily shows stains. And then she thinks of this as an antiquated notion; fear of stains belongs to her old life. It doesn't exist here. It can't. Not alongside the fear of lifelong confinement.

The girls are weaving mats just like the guard said. They have plastic strips in different colors, and they work them in and out, in checkered patterns, like children at camp.

The guard tells Lyda and the redhead to take a seat. Lyda files in next to a girl on the end, and the redhead sits across from her. The redhead starts collecting strips—only reds and whites—and weaves quickly, her head bowed to her work.

The girl next to Lyda looks up at her with deep brown eyes, as if she recognizes her, then lowers her head and gets back to weaving. Lyda doesn't know this girl. Down the row, all the girls seem to turn quickly and glance at Lyda. Each one who looks nudges the next. It's a chain reaction.

Lyda is famous, but these girls know more about why she's famous than she does.

The guards have moved to one corner. They lean against the walls and talk.

Lyda glances at the guards and picks up a handful of plastic strips. Her fingers fiddle nervously. Everything is quiet for a while until the girl beside Lyda whispers, "You're still here."

Does she mean in the community craft room or the asylum?

Lyda doesn't respond. Why would she? Of course she's still here, either way.

"Everyone thought they'd have taken you out by now."

"Out?"

"Force you to give information."

"I don't have any."

The girl looks at her, disbelieving.

"Do they know where he went? What happened?" Lyda asks.

"You should know."

"I don't."

The girl laughs.

Lyda decides to ignore the laughter. The redhead has started humming as she works, a little nursery song that Lyda's mother used to sing to her, "Twinkle, twinkle, little star . . ." It's the awful kind of song that, once it gets in your head, can stick with you, especially back in solitary confinement. It could make you insane. The redhead's afflicted with the song, Lyda thinks. She hopes it isn't catching. The redhead stops humming for a minute and looks at Lyda as if she wants to tell her something, but doesn't dare. She starts humming again.

Lyda hates the redhead a little now. She turns back to the one with brown eyes who laughed at her. "What's so funny?" she asks.

"You don't know, do you?"

Lyda shakes her head.

"They say he went all the way out."

"All the way where?"

"Out of the Dome."

She keeps weaving. Out? Why would he go out? Why would anyone go out? The survivors on the outside are evil, deranged. They're vicious, deformed, no longer truly human. She's heard a hundred dark and awful tales of the girls who survived, the ones who kept some part of their humanity only to be raped or eaten alive. What would they do to Partridge? Gut him, boil him, feed on him.

She can barely breathe. She looks at the faces all hovering over their sitting mats. One girl looks at her. She's pale and smiley. Lyda wonders if she's taking medications that make her smile. Why else would anyone smile in here?

The redhead taps her sitting mat on the table, humming away, and stares at Lyda, as if she wants her attention or maybe even her approval. It's a simple white sitting mat with a red stripe down the middle. She looks at Lyda searchingly, as if to say *See? See what I made?*

The girl next to Lyda with the deep brown eyes whispers, "He's probably already dead. Who could survive out there? He was still just an academy boy. My boyfriend said he wasn't even through coding."

Partridge. She feels like he's stepped off the planet. But dead? She still believes that she'd know if he were dead. She would feel dead inside. She doesn't. She thinks of the way he held her waist when they danced, that kiss, and her stomach flips again as it always does when she thinks of him. It wouldn't happen if he were dead. She'd feel dread, grief. But she still feels hopeful. "He could do it," Lyda whispers. "He could survive."

The girl laughs again.

"Shut up!" Lyda whispers harshly at her, and she turns on the redhead and says it to her too: "Shut up!"

The redhead freezes.

The other girls look up.

The guards eye the table. "Work, ladies!" one of them says. "It's good for you! Keep at it."

Lyda looks at the colored strips. They blur and jump in her vision. She starts to cry, but backhands the tears. She doesn't want anyone to see. Keep at it, she thinks to herself. Keep at it.

PRESSIA

BLEACH

IT'S NOT THE WAY PRESSIA THOUGHT it would be. It's more like an old hospital than a military base. The air smells antiseptic, too clean. Almost bleached. There are five cots in this room, and the kids lying on them don't shift. They don't move. But they aren't asleep either. They're wearing green uniforms, starched, waiting. One has a stiff hand covered in red aluminum. Another's head is mangled with stone. Yet another is hidden under a blanket. Pressia knows that she's none too pretty either—her scarred face, her fused doll-head fist. She still has the duct tape on her mouth, her hands tied behind her back, and she's in street clothes, so they know she's new. If she could, she thinks she might ask them what they're waiting for, but then would she really want to know?

She tries to be still like them. She tries to imagine what happened after Bradwell and Partridge figured out she was gone. She wants to believe that they'd join forces and come after her, try to free her. But she knows this isn't possible. Neither of them really even knows her. Partridge ran into her by accident; he has a mission of his own. She looks back and wonders if Bradwell liked her at all or if he only ever saw a type. It doesn't matter anyway. The last thing he really had to say was that he had survived because he didn't get involved with other people's lives. Would she have tried to save him if the roles were reversed? She doesn't have to think about it for long—she would. The world, as awful as it is, seems like it's better off with Bradwell in it. He's charged from within, lit up, ready to fight, and even if he's not going to fight for her, he has energy that they all need here on the outside.

She thinks of his double scars and the angry flutter of birds on his back. She misses him. It's a sudden, sharp ache in her chest. She can't deny it; she wants him to miss her too, and to fight to find her. She hates the feeling in her chest, wishes it would go away, but it doesn't subside. She'll have to haul this ache around with her, an awful realization. The truth is that he isn't coming for her, and Bradwell and Partridge hate each other too much to stick together anyway. Without her, they likely said their good-byes quickly and went their separate ways. She's on her own now.

The hard cot is tightly made, which makes Pressia think there's a nurse lurking somewhere. Pressia has imagined hospitals like the one she was born in—one where she could get an operation to free her hand and her grandfather could get the fan removed from his throat. She imagines herself and her grandfather in side-by-side hospital beds on plumped pillows.

Lying on her side, she can pick at the wool blanket with her hand behind her back, but can't do much else. Sometimes she thinks of God and tries to pray to Saint Wi, but it won't take root. The prayer just rolls away from her.

The lights flicker.

There's a round of gunfire outside.

The guard walks by the door and stares inside. She holds a rifle in her arms, cradles it really like she's pacing the halls to get a baby back to sleep, like there's a maternity ward somewhere. She wears the regulation green OSR uniform, complete with an armband with a claw.

Pressia will have to explain herself at some point. She knows

OSR doesn't like the ones who don't hand themselves over, whom they have to hunt down and capture. But her resistance has to prove something at least, that she's tough in some way. Pressia thinks she can explain that she would have turned herself in, but she has to take care of her grandfather. That's a sign of loyalty. They want loyalty. She has to say whatever she can to stay alive.

But she's seen OSR drag people from their homes, wrestle them into the backs of trucks in front of children, in front of whole families. She's seen them shoot people dead in the streets. She wonders how Fandra died but stops herself. She has to forget this.

The guard walks in through the door. The faces all turn to her, stricken, dazed. Is this what they're waiting for? The guard isn't cradling the rifle anymore. She's pointing it at Pressia.

"Pressia Belze?" she says.

Pressia would sit up and say yes but she can't. Tape over her mouth, she nods, lying there on her side, curled like a shrimp.

The guard walks over and yanks her upper arm, pulling her to her feet. She follows the guard out of the room, but glances back at the other kids. None of them will look her in the eye, except one. Pressia can see now that he's a real cripple—one of his pant legs is empty. There's nothing there, and she knows he won't make it, not as a soldier and maybe not even as a live target. Even if these are the remains of some hospital, it's not one anymore, and maybe they use the bleach to cover up the smell of death. Pressia tries to smile at the cripple, to offer some small kindness, but her mouth is taped shut so the cripple won't ever know.

The guard is broad and squat. Her skin is scorched, burned to a high pink sheen on her face, neck, and hands. Pressia wonders if it covers her whole body. She's filled a hole in her cheek with an old coin. She walks beside Pressia and, for no reason Pressia can tell or prompting she can predict, the guard pops Pressia in the ribs with the butt of the rifle. When she doubles over, the guard says, "Pressia Belze," hatefully, as if it's a curse.

There are open doors along the hall, and inside each room there are cots, and kids waiting. It's quiet, except for murmurs, cot springs, and boot scrapes.

Pressia can tell now that this place is ancient, the tiled floors, the molding, the old doors, high airy ceilings. They walk past a lobby of some sort that has a threadbare ornate rug and a bank of tall windows. The glass is long gone and the room now swirls with wind that gets caught up in the frail bits of gauzy curtains, gray with ash. It's the kind of place people would come to wait for someone to be brought to them—a relative wheeled out, some-one imbalanced, maybe insane. Asylums, sanatoriums, rehab centers—they had a lot of names. And then there were the prisons.

Out the windows, Pressia sees planks of wood nailed together like a lean-to, a stone wall topped with barbed wire, and farther still, white pillars that are attached to nothing at all. They're just stalks.

The guard stops in front of a door and knocks.

A man's voice, gruff and lazy, shouts, "Come in!"

The guard opens the door and gives Pressia one more shove with the butt of the rifle. "Pressia Belze," she says, and because this is the only thing Pressia has heard her say, Pressia wonders if it's the only thing she knows how to say.

There's a desk and a man sitting behind it, or it's actually two men. One is big and meaty. He seems much older than Pressia, but it's hard to figure age what with scars and burns. The larger man seems old and young at the same time, but he may be only slightly older than Pressia, just wearier. The smaller man seems her age, but also weirdly ageless because of a certain vacancy in his gaze. The larger man is wearing a gray uniform, an officer of some sort, and he's eating a tiny baked chicken from a tin. The head of the chicken is still on.

And the man on his back is small. He's fused there. His skinny arms hang around the big man's thick neck, broad back to skinny chest. Pressia remembers the driver of the truck and the head that had seemed to float behind his. Maybe these are the same two.

The big man says to the guard, "Take off the tape. She needs to talk." The man's fingers are greasy with chicken fat. His nails are dirty and shiny at the same time.

The guard pulls off the tape, hard. Pressia licks her lips and tastes blood.

"You can go," the big man says to the guard.

She leaves, shutting the door with more gentleness than Pressia could expect of her. It clicks softly.

"So," the big man says. "I'm El Capitan. This is headquarters. I run things."

The small man on his back whispers, "I run things."

El Capitan ignores him, picks at the dark meat, slips some into his fat mouth. Pressia realizes she's starving. "Where did they find you?" El Capitan asks as he raises a smaller piece of meat over his shoulder, feeding the man on his back, straight into his mouth almost like a baby bird.

"I was out," Pressia tells him.

He looks at her. "That it?"

She nods.

"Why didn't you turn yourself in?" El Capitan asks. "You like a chase?"

"My grandfather's sick."

"Do you know how many people have the excuse that someone in the family is sick?"

"I'd guess a lot of people have sick families, if they have a family at all."

He tilts his head, and she's not sure how to read his expression. He goes back to his chicken. "The revolution is coming, so my question is this—can you kill?" El Capitan says this without much expression. It's like he's reading it off of a recruitment brochure. His heart's not in it.

Truth is that there's something about being hungry that makes Pressia want to kill people. It flashes up in her, this ugly desire. "I could learn how to kill." She's relieved that her wrists are still tied behind her back. He can't see the doll-head fist.

"One day we'll take them down." His voice goes soft. "That's all I want, really. I'd like to kill one Pure before I die. Just one." He sighs, rubs his knuckles on the desk. "And your grandfather?" he asks.

"There's nothing I can do for him now," Pressia says. And it hits her that this is the truth and a strange relief. She feels immediately guilty. He has the meat tin and the strange red orange from the woman he stitched and one last row of handmade creatures that he can use for bartering.

"I understand family responsibilities," El Capitan says. "Helmud"—he points to the man on his back—"my brother. I'd kill him, but he's family."

"I'd kill him, but he's family," Helmud says, folding his arms under his neck like an insect. El Capitan pulls loose a drumstick, holds it up for Helmud to nibble, but not too much, just a little; then he yanks it back. "But still," he says, "you're small, like you've never eaten a real meal. You wouldn't make it. I'd say, going with my gut, that you should be of use, but only at your own expense."

Pressia's stomach knots up. She thinks of the cripple with the missing leg. Maybe there isn't much difference between the two of them.

He leans forward, both of his elbows sliding across the desk. "It's my job to make these kinds of calls. You think I like it?"

She's not sure if he likes it or not.

Then he turns and shouts at Helmud, "Knock it off back there!"

Helmud looks up wide-eyed.

"He's always fiddling. Nervous fingers. Fiddle, fiddle, fiddle. You're gonna drive me insane one day, Helmud, with all the nervous crap. You hear me?"

"You hear me?" Helmud says.

El Capitan pulls a file off the stack. "Strange thing, though. It says in your file that you've been ordered up. To be an officer. They say we should keep your education intact, and I should roll you into training."

"Really?" Pressia says. This immediately feels like a bad sign. Do they know her connection to the Pure? Why else would she be singled out? "Officer training?"

"Most people would sound a little happier," El Capitan says, and he rubs his greasy lips then opens a box of cigars on his desk. "In fact, I'd say you're shit lucky." He lights a cigar and lets the smoke cloud around his head. "Lucky you!" he says.

His brother's face is hidden now behind El Capitan's head, but Pressia can still hear his voice. "Lucky you," he whispers. "Lucky you."

Partridge

shadow history

THEY'RE BACK IN BRADWELL'S MEAT LOCKER. It smells like smoky meat. While Partridge changed into Bradwell's clothes, Bradwell refried leftovers of a plump hybrid now sitting on the cook stove. He tells Partridge to eat. "We've got to have fuel." But Partridge has no appetite. He feels like a stranger now that he's wearing Bradwell's clothes. The shirt's too loose, the pants too short. The boots are so wide, his feet slide around. Partridge feels foreign to himself.

Partridge told Bradwell that he wasn't chipped, but Bradwell's sure there's a bug on him somewhere and has told him that he'll have to burn all of his clothes and his mother's belongings, which he's not sure he'll be able to do.

On the floor, Bradwell has set down every paper he thinks will help him find the bigger picture—printed emails from his parents, some original Japanese documentation, handwritten notes, a chunk of his parents' manuscript, and now, to add to it all, Partridge's mother's things. It's strange to see everything laid out, like pieces taken from lots of different puzzles. How could they ever fit together to create a whole? It's not possible. But Bradwell seems almost electrified by the possibilities. He's huffed down his food and now paces around the evidence. Even the wings in his back are unable to be still.

Partridge fixes his attention on the clippings of his father—a few shots of him at the mike, sometimes dipping forward with one hand pressed to his tie, a false humility that Partridge despises. His father is in the background of lots of other news-story photos, hanging at the edges. Partridge says, "I don't even recognize him, really. I mean, what was he really like?"

"Your father?" Bradwell says. "A man of short sentences, positive catchphrases, and lots of promises. A master of vague, among other things."

Partridge picks up one of the dusty clippings. He stares at his father's pale face, his reedy lips, his eyes always looking away from the camera. "He's a liar. He knows more than he's willing to say."

"I bet he knew everything," Bradwell says.

"What's everything?

"All the way back to World War Two."

"World War Two?"

"My parents studied it," Bradwell says. "Otten Bradwell and Silva Bernt. They were tagged at a young age like your dad was, young recruits for the Best and the Brightest. They were plucked out of their respective high schools a couple of states away from each other on random afternoons their senior year and taken out to lunch at Red Lobsters."

"Red Lobsters?"

"A restaurant chain, probably part of the protocol. Someone had done that level of research and had found the perfect restaurant to lure young recruits from modest backgrounds. Your dad probably was taken to a Red Lobster too when he was in high school."

Partridge can't imagine his father ever having been Partridge's age now. Impossible. He was always old. He was born old.

"But unlike your father, my parents turned it down. They used to joke that the Red Lobster didn't work on either of them. They were Red-Lobster-*immune*."

Partridge doesn't like the way Bradwell's take makes his father sound weak. He doesn't like the sound of his father's name coming from Bradwell's mouth. "Where did you find all of this stuff?" Partridge asks.

"My parents knew what was coming. They had a hidden safe room with double-enforced steel-lined walls. After my aunt and uncle died, I went back to the house, all burned up. Without thinking too hard, I knew the four-digit combination—eight-one-oh-five, the number of the house they'd first lived in, where I was born, in fact, in Philly. It wasn't easy, but I hauled the footlocker with me and finally to this place."

"My mother's stuff might be nothing," Partridge says. "But the first time I held her things in my hands, they felt important—proof, like they could lead me to her. Maybe it's stupid."

Bradwell touches the small pristine metal music box, brushes one finger over the birthday card, lightly, its design of balloons on the cover, as if the things are holy. Partridge would never tell him that's what it looks like, though. He knows that Bradwell would hate the idea that anyone would treat anything from the Dome reverently.

"I haven't seen anything like this since the Detonations, not charred or singed, not partially obliterated or ashen. They had to have been inside the Dome before the Detonations." He touches the gold pendant, the swan with its blue eye, and the smooth edges of the birthday card. "Jesus!" he says, hit by a sudden flare of anger. "What's it like to walk around perfect, huh, Partridge? No scars, no burns, no birds. To be a clean slate?"

The question makes Partridge angry. "Just because I live in a Dome doesn't mean I've never suffered. I mean, it's not like *your* suffering. What could compare to this, huh? Do you want an award for it? A medal that says First Place Suffering? You win, Bradwell. Okay? You win."

"This isn't about us."

"Then stop making it about us."

"We have to clear our heads of the most obvious and blinding assumptions. We don't want to see what's being represented. We want to see what's really here—and the shadows that live behind it. The Shadow History."

"Right," Partridge says, even though he's still angry and doesn't know how he could possibly clear his head.

"How old were you when the Detonations hit?"

"Eight and a half."

"This is for your ninth birthday."

"I know. My father never gave it to me."

"She knew she wasn't going to be with you for it, either dead . . ."

"Or still out here."

"Why did she only do one birthday? Why not all of them?"

"Maybe it's proof she's alive. She thought she'd be reunited with me for my tenth."

"Or maybe that's the only one your father kept." Bradwell went on, "If your mother's things were in the Dome before the Detonations, does that mean you packed up before the Detonations and moved in?"

"We were allowed a few personal items—not because we knew the Detonations were coming, just in case of something, anything, really."

"How soon before the Detonations?"

"We were taking a tour when the Detonations hit. We walked around what would be our little apartment. I put my small box of things—stupid stuff, a video game, a stuffed animal I won from a machine and thought was lucky—under the bunk beds."

"Well, when you all brought in your small box of things, your mother must have known then that there was a chance she wasn't going to be with you."

"I guess so."

"Willux could have stolen some things before he left his wife behind. On purpose. If so, that means the objects are valuable. Did he plant this stuff because he knew it was important, just not why? Did he want you to find it, hoping it would stir something in you?" Bradwell winds the music box and opens it. "What about this tune?"

"What about it?"

"Does it stir something?"

"Like I said, it's a kid song that I think she made up. It's nothing."

Bradwell lifts the necklace by its gold-link chain and watches the swan twist, its wings spread wide.

Partridge can feel Bradwell's energy. "Do you have any ideas?" Partridge asks. "A plan?"

Aboveground it's gotten windy, and there's the rattle of debris being kicked around. Bradwell glances overhead, then at the necklace wound around his fingers. "You know what would help?" Bradwell says. "Info about your mother."

"I doubt I can answer any questions about her. I barely knew her."

"What do you know about her?"

"She was smart and pretty. She met my father kind of young." Partridge picks up the birthday card and fiddles with the raised design on the front of it, multicolored balloons.

"Were they happily married?"

"That's kind of personal, isn't it?"

"Everything's relevant," Bradwell says.

"I think they were happy at one point. But I don't remember them laughing together or kissing each other. The air in the house was always, I don't know, stiff. They were formal with each other. Weirdly well mannered. In the end, I think she hated him."

"Why do you think that?"

He hesitates. "I don't know. Parents sometimes hate each other, right?"

"What did your mother do?"

"She was a linguist," he says. "She spoke tons of languages. My father used to say that she was also fluent in Gestures. No matter what language she was speaking, she was always waving her hands around." He waves his hands in the air. "Supposedly she took me with her to Asia for a year when I was little. Some kind of work she had there, an opportunity. She wanted to get back into her career. I was just a baby, a one-year-old or so."

"That's strange. Isn't it? Leaving your husband and one of your other kids and taking the baby to Asia to work for a year?"

"My older brother was in kindergarten already."

"Still…"

"I guess it's strange." Partridge sits in one of the armchairs. He shoves himself back in his seat. Is Bradwell goading him? "I don't know what's strange and what's normal, actually."

"Where's your brother now?"

"He's dead." Partridge says it quickly, as if this will lighten the ache in his chest.

Bradwell pauses a moment. "I'm sorry about that." It feels like an apology for a lot of things, actually, like thinking Partridge's life was a cakewalk.

Partridge doesn't lord it over Bradwell, though, and he knows he could. He says, "It's okay."

"How did he die?"

Partridge looks around without moving his head. His eyes rove—the metal walls, the hooks overhead strung with animals, the footlocker. "He killed himself."

"In the Dome?" He's incredulous. "How could anyone lucky enough to live in the Dome kill themselves?"

"It's not really that unusual. There isn't a strong stigma attached to it like there used to be. With very little death by sickness and the theory of limited resources, it's still awful, but it's not seen as selfish. In some cases, it's almost generous."

"The *theory* of limited resources?" Bradwell says. "They planned the apocalypse because they wanted the earth to survive, regenerate itself, so once they've used up their *limited resources*, they'll be ready to use the world's again. It's a sweet plan."

"Is that what you really think?" Partridge asks.

"It's what I know."

"All I know is that my brother was a good guy, and people admired him. He was of true value, and he was better than I am, really. A better person. There are worse things than killing yourself. That's all I was saying."

"There are worse things like what?"

"Why all these questions? Do we have a plan?"

Bradwell pulls out a small knife from his belt. He puts the swan pendant down on the footlocker and kneels in front of it.

"What are you doing?" Partridge asks.

Bradwell raises the butt of the knife and, in one quick motion, slams it down on the pendant. The belly of the swan cracks in half.

Before he can think about it, Partridge lunges and shoves Bradwell to the ground. He pins down Bradwell's hand with the knife, grabs his other wrist too, and uses it to apply pressure to Bradwell's neck. "What did you do?" he shouts. "That was my mother's! Do you know what that's worth to me?"

Bradwell tightens his neck muscles and strains to speak. "I don't give a shit what you value."

Partridge shoves him and then lets him go. Bradwell sits up and rubs his neck. Partridge picks up the two small pieces of the swan. The neck, the jeweled eye, and the hole to thread the pendant onto a necklace are still intact. Only the belly is halved, showing a hollow center. Partridge looks at the two halves closely.

"It's not just a pendant, is it?" Bradwell says, sitting with his back against the metal wall. "It has a hollow center. Am I right?"

"Why the hell did you do that?"

"I had to. Is there something inside?"

Partridge lifts the pendant and sees foreign markings he can't read. "I don't know," Partridge says. "An inscription. I can't make it out. It's in a different language."

Bradwell holds out his hand. "Can I look?"

Grudgingly, Partridge places the two pieces in Bradwell's palm. Bradwell eyes them closely, holding them up to the bare bulb in the middle of the room.

"Do you know what it says?" Partridge asks, impatiently.

"I've spent years teaching myself Japanese. My father was fluent and his research contains a lot of translation work. I don't speak it. But I can read it a little." Partridge huddles next to him under the bulb. "This here," Bradwell says, pointing to the first two characters: 私の. "This means 'my.'" And then he moves his finger to the next group フェニックス. "And this is a word that I would know anywhere. It means 'phoenix.'"

"My phoenix?" Partridge says. "That doesn't make sense. My father didn't speak Japanese. I never heard him call my mother by any pet names. He wasn't the type."

"Maybe it's not from him," Bradwell says.

"What does *my phoenix* mean?" Partridge asks.

"I don't know who it's from, but it's loaded. It means your mother and whoever gave her the pendant knew a lot," Bradwell says to Partridge. "Maybe she knew everything too."

"Everything? What's that mean?" Partridge says.

"Operation Phoenix," Bradwell says. "It's the name of the whole mission."

"The Detonations."

"Armageddon. New Eden. Your father's baby. A new civilization would rise from the ashes like a phoenix. Clever name, right?"

Bradwell stands up. He coughs. His neck is red. Partridge feels a little guilty now for having choked him. Bradwell hands Partridge a metal bin, probably once used for holding entrails. "Put your clothes and your mom's things in here. We've got to light 'em up. Kill any chips."

Partridge feels dazed. He hands Bradwell the small bundle of his clothes and his backpack, though he's taken all of his mother's things out of it already. "What if I just pick her things clean," he says. "I'm sure they're fine." He fiddles with the raised design on the front of the birthday card, looking for chips. He feels a small hard nub. He wets his fingers with his tongue and rubs the front cover of the card. The paper rubs off, disintegrating. And there is a very fine chip—thin as a slip of paper but hard, white plastic, a tiny sensor. "Shit," Partridge says. "Is this card even real? Did my mother really write that?" He paces a quick circle. "Glassings got permission to go on this field trip," Partridge says. "My World History teacher. Maybe they wanted me to steal the stuff. Maybe they knew I would and they planted it all."

"But the card could be real. The chip added later." Bradwell holds out his hand, and Partridge drops the chip in his palm. "We'll send them on a chase." Bradwell fixes the chip to a wire, using some kind of strong-smelling, homemade epoxy in a jar. He unlatches the cage holding the two rat-like creatures. He cups the one-eyed rat and cradles it to his chest. The rat squirms while Bradwell wraps the wire around its middle, twisting the wire ends together to keep it in place. He then carries the rat to a drain in the floor, flips off the drain's cap, and shoves it in. Partridge hears the rat hit the floor and skitter off.

Bradwell pours a strong-smelling liquid on the clothes in the metal bucket. Partridge picks up the music box and winds it one last time.

Bradwell lights the bucket. A blaze flares.

When the song plays out, Partridge hands him the music box. Bradwell drops it in. They stand there watching the flames.

"Where's the photograph?" Bradwell asks.

"Really? Even that?"

Bradwell nods.

Partridge doesn't take it out of its protective pouch. He can't look at it again. He consoles himself with the fact that he has the image burned into his mind. He holds it over the bucket, lets it fall, and looks away. He doesn't want to see the flames peel away his mother's face.

Partridge then holds up a piece of the pendant that still has the loop intact where it's attached to the necklace, the part of the pendant with the blue gem. "What if Pressia comes back here?" Partridge says. "I want her to know that we're looking for her, that we haven't given up on her. We could leave half of this pendant for her. We'd take the half with the inscription. She'd have the half with the blue stone."

Bradwell walks to the spot where the weapons are hidden. He kneels down, removes the bricks, and pulls out knives, cleavers, hooks, and a stun gun. "I don't know about that."

"I can't burn this," Partridge says. "I just can't."

Bradwell is sorting weapons. "Fine. Keep half, leave half. Heat it enough to fry chips. We've got to move fast now. The more time we lose, the less chance we have of getting to her." He fits a butcher knife and a hook into straps in his jacket and in his belt loop.

"Where are we going?" Partridge asks, lowering the necklace into the flames.

"There's only one person who I know for certain isn't controlled by the Dome," Bradwell says. "She lives in the Meltlands, which are vast. She's the only person who's got power and who we can trust."

"If the Meltlands are vast," Partridge says, "how do we find her?"

"That's not the way it works," Bradwell says, handing Partridge a meat hook and a knife. "We don't find her. She finds us."

PRESSIA

GAME

NOW PRESSIA SITS ON THE EDGE of her cot and waits. For what? She doesn't know. She has her own green uniform. It fits. The pants have pleats and cuffed hems. The cuffs brush the boots just right when she walks. The boots are heavy and stiff. She wiggles her toes in them. The socks are wool and warm. She doesn't miss the clogs. She'd never tell her grandfather this, but she loves these boots, tough ones that stay on your feet.

She's embarrassed to admit that it all feels so good—clothes that are warm and fitted. Her grandfather told her that her parents took a picture of her on the first day of kindergarten, dressed in a school uniform, standing next to a tree in the front yard. This uniform makes her feel solid, protected. She's part of an army. She has backup. And she hates herself for this undeniable feeling of unity. She hates OSR. She does. But her dark secret, one she'd never admit to anyone, especially not Bradwell, is that she loves the uniform.

Worse still, the band tied around her upper arm has a magical hold over the other kids in her room. It has a black claw emblem stitched on it, OSR's symbol, the same kind that's painted on their trucks, their notices, anything official. The claw means power. The kids stare at it as much as they do her doll-head fist, as if the two cancel each other out. She hates that the uniform doesn't let her hide her doll-head fist. The sleeves stop right at her wrist. But she's so powerful because of the black claw armband that she almost doesn't care. In fact, she has the inexplicable desire to whisper to them that if they, too, had doll-head fists, they'd be lucky enough to get the claw band on their arms. It's all a twisted mix of pride and shame.

Another thing that shames her is that she's eaten so well. Her dinner last night and early breakfast this morning were brought in on trays. Both times it was a soup of some kind, dark, oily broth, and there were some pieces of meat floating in it, onions too. A greasy whirl to it all. And two heels of bread, a fat wedge of cheese, and a glass of milk. The milk was fresh. Somewhere around here there's a cow that gives milk. The eating strikes her as a kind of giving in, betraying all she's believed in. If she's going to get out, though, she'll need her strength. That's how she rationalizes it to herself at least.

The other kids got only bread, thin cheese wedges, and cups of cloudy water. They eyed her with suspicion and jealousy.

None of the recruits says anything. Pressia can tell that they've gotten punished for it. But she's wondering if there isn't a different set of rules for her. It's the first time in her life she's ever felt lucky. *Lucky you!* That's what El Capitan said. *Lucky you!* She knows not to trust it. Not to trust anything. The special treatment has to do with the Pure. There's no other explanation, right? Otherwise she'd be a live target, probably dead already. But what, exactly, they expect from her isn't clear.

After the guard looks into the room and strolls on, Pressia feels bold and breaks the silence. "What are we waiting for?"

"Our orders," the cripple whispers.

Pressia doesn't know where he got his information, but it sounds official. Pressia is waiting to roll into training. Officer training.

The guard appears at the door, says a name, Dirk Martus, and one of the kids gets up and follows her.

He doesn't come back.

The day stretches on. Pressia thinks about her grandfather sometimes. She wonders if he's eaten the strange fruit the woman used to pay him for his stitching. She thinks of Freedle. Has her grandfather oiled his gears? She thinks of her butterflies on the sill. Has he used them in the market? How many are left?

She tries to imagine Bradwell at his next meeting. Will he think of her at all? Will he at least wonder what became of her? What if one day she's the officer who stumbles on one of those meetings? He never came for her, and this would be her chance to turn him in. She'd let him go, of course. He'd owe her his freedom. Most likely, they'll never see each other again.

She listens to the gunfire in the distance and tries to establish some loose pattern that it might follow, but she doesn't find one.

She thinks about food, of course. She hopes there's more of it. It's disturbing how much she longs to be taken care of. If she can keep things going here, she might become an officer and be able to get protection for her grandfather. She could save him still, if she can save herself.

"Pressia Belze." The guard appears in the door frame again.

Pressia gets up and follows her out the door.

This time, they all watch Pressia go.

Out in the hall, the guard says, "You been invited to play The Game."

"What kind of game?" Pressia asks.

The guard looks at her like she wants to pop her with the butt of her rifle, but Pressia is going to become an officer. She wears the armband with the claw. "Not sure," the guard says. And Pressia realizes that the guard is telling the truth. She doesn't know because she's never been invited to play The Game.

The guard walks her down a hall and leads Pressia out through a back door, and she is now standing in the cold. It's midmorning. Pressia is surprised that she's lost track of time.

Down a slope, there's a forest, charred and stripped by the Detonations. She can see the ghostly image of the forest as it once was—taller trees, darting birds, rattling leaves. "It must have been beautiful here during the Before," she says.

"What?" the guard says.

Pressia's embarrassed. She wishes she hadn't said it aloud. "Nothing."

The guard says, "There, down there. See him?"

In the shadows, Pressia spots El Capitan. His brother, Helmud, from this distance, makes El Capitan look like a humpback. The tip of his lit cigar glows. He's got a rifle at his chest, strapped around him and Helmud.

Pressia turns to the guard. "You play The Game out there?" Had she been expecting a card game? Her grandfather once explained the game of pool to her—the colored balls, bank shots, corner pockets, cues.

"Yep, out there," the guard says.

Pressia doesn't like forests and underbrush.

"What's the name of this game?" Pressia asks.

"The Game," the guard says.

Pressia doesn't like the way the guard says it, but Pressia pretends she isn't nervous. "Very original, like naming a pet cat Cat."

The woman stares at her for a moment, blankly, then hands her a jacket that's been hooked over one arm.

"For me?"

"Put it on."

"Thanks."

The guard doesn't say anything. She dips back inside and shuts the door.

Pressia loves the jacket—the way it puffs around her, like walking inside warm risen bread. Nothing gets through it, not the cold, not the wind that whips up and then dies. These are the little things that people should really appreciate, simple pleasures. That's all she has right this minute. The jacket is warm, and sometimes you should just be thankful for that. When was the last time she felt warm like this in a jacket? She knows she could die out here. This whole officer thing is bullshit. The Game could be a game where she's the one who gets trapped. She knows this. But still, she thinks, at least she'd die in a warm coat.

She walks down the slope, wondering what she should say to El Capitan. Should she call him El Capitan? It's a strange name. Did he make it up himself? If Pressia calls him El Capitan, will it just sound forced or, worse, a little insincere? She wouldn't want El Capitan to think she's making fun of him. It's only a matter of time before he realizes that she has no real ties to the Pure. She met him on the street. She got him to his old address, a pile of rubble. By the time El Capitan figures that out, she hopes she's on his good side—if good sides matter here. She decides not to say his name at all.

When she gets to the bottom of the hill, she stands there for a moment, not sure how to start. El Capitan puffs on the cigar and his brother stares at Pressia with his wide-set eyes.

El Capitan looks disgusted and already weary. He sizes Pressia up out of the corner of his eye and shakes his head as if disagreeing with the wisdom of all this but resigned to it anyway. He hands Pressia an extra rifle and says, "I'm guessing you can't shoot."

Pressia holds it like it might be a musical instrument or a shovel. She's never seen a gun this close up before, much less held one. She says, "I've never had the pleasure."

"Like this," El Capitan says, taking the rifle from her hand gruffly. He shows Pressia how to hold the rifle and look through the sight, then hands it back to her.

She holds the trigger with her good hand and then balances the long part of the gun on her doll-head fist.

The doll head gives El Capitan pause; she can tell. But he's used to deformities. And he's had his fair share of comments, hasn't he? A man who carries his brother on his back? He only says, "Can you at least flex it to your wrist, create a firm grip?"

Pressia can, of course. She's had to develop a grip over the years.

But then he nudges one of her elbows, adjusting her stance. For a moment he seems almost brotherly, and Pressia can't help but think of how her grandfather once taught her to swing an imaginary golf club by wrapping his arms around her, and lacing his fingers around hers. There were sloping green lawns that went on forever, he told her, and the golf clubs themselves were fitted with little specially made knit hats. But this gentleness doesn't last. El Capitan looks at her and says, "I don't get it." He drops his stub of cigar and rubs it out under his boot heel.

"What?"

"Why you?"

She shrugs, and he looks at her suspiciously, then coughs and spits on the ground. "Don't fire it right now. We don't want to announce our location. Just practice," El Capitan says. "Take a deep breath before you pull the trigger, let it out, just halfway. Then fire."

"Fire," his brother whispers, startling Pressia. She'd almost forgotten he was there.

Pressia takes aim and thinks about her breathing. She draws it in, holds it, imagines the crack of the gun, then lets her breath out.

"Don't forget that," El Capitan says, and he pushes her barrel down. "And don't point it at me while we're walking."

Pressia thinks of Helmud. Shouldn't El Capitan refer to himself as plural? *Just don't point it at us—right?*

El Capitan slaps her on the back. "Follow me."

His brother whispers, "Follow me."

"But what's The Game?" Pressia asks.

"No real rules, just a game of tag. Hunt down your foe. Then shoot instead of tag."

"What are we hunting down?"

"*Who* are we hunting down," El Capitan corrects her.

Pressia tries to think of the jacket, like walking in warm bread. "Who then?"

"An incoming. Someone like you. But this one isn't as lucky as Pressia Belze." She doesn't like the way he keeps calling her lucky. It's like he's mocking her.

Pressia glances at Helmud.

"Is the incoming armed?" Pressia asks.

"Unarmed. Those were the orders. I'm starting you out at level A," El Capitan says. "Think of this as part of your officer training."

They're on a worn path that cuts through the woods, downhill. "Who sent the orders?" she asks, worried that this is too bold. Officers are supposed to be bold, though, she tells herself.

"Ingership," El Capitan says. "I was hoping he'd forgotten about The Game. It'd been a while. But orders are orders."

What if he didn't shoot the incoming but let the incoming go free? Do orders have to be orders? Maybe this is why she's in officer training. She's supposed to learn not to ask these kinds of questions.

Pressia hears a sound behind them. Is it the incoming she's supposed to shoot? El Capitan doesn't turn around and so Pressia doesn't either. She doesn't want to shoot an incoming, someone just like her but not lucky. Pressia knows that she's not lucky for good. This is just some kind of error. At some point someone, maybe this

Ingership, will call down from some other level and say they got the wrong girl. *Not Belze*, they'll say. *We meant someone else.* And then she'll be out here in the woods being hunted down by El Capitan and an officer-in-training who's never had the pleasure of shooting a gun before. Pressia's never liked games. She's never been good at them. Bradwell—she wishes he was out here with her. Would he kill an incoming? No. He'd figure out how to take a stand, do the right thing, make a statement. She's just trying to stay alive. There's nothing wrong with that. In fact, she kind of wishes he could see her now, but just a picture, a girl in the woods with a gun. At least she's giving the impression that she can take care of herself.

After a while, El Capitan stops. "You hear that?"

Pressia does hear something, the faintest rustling, but it's just wind through leaves. She looks to her right and sees a shape. It limps from one tree to the next then slips out of sight. A saying from Pressia's childhood echoes in her head, *Come out! Come out wherever you are!* It fills her with nervous dread. She mentally urges the shape to stay hidden. *Don't come out. Don't come out.*

El Capitan walks in the opposite direction into the brush and stops. He points his gun at something on the ground. "Look here," he says.

Pressia walks up and sees writhing reddish fur and then shining eyes, a dainty piggish snout with wiry whiskers but fox-like body. The animal is locked in a small steel trap.

"What is it?"

"Hybrid of some sort. It's genetically mutated, upscale though. Its generations turn over quicker than ours. See there." He nudges the animal's claw, and there's a metal glint to it. "Survival of the fittest."

"The fittest," Helmud says.

"Just like us, right." El Capitan looks at her. He expects her to agree and she does.

"Right."

"That's what'll happen to our DNA over time," El Capitan says.

"Some of us will produce offspring with mergers that make us stronger, and others will die out. This one's still good to eat."

"Are you going to shoot it?" Pressia asks.

"Shooting it is bad for the meat. So don't, if you can avoid it." El Capitan looks around and picks up a rock. He holds the rock over its head for a moment, taking aim, and then bashes the skull so that it caves in. The animal twitches. Its metal claw clenches, then its eyes turn dull and glassy.

The brutality makes Pressia feel sick, but she refuses to show it. El Capitan keeps an eye on her, gauging her toughness. Or so it seems.

"I caught a dog-size rat a couple weeks back with a tail made of chain. It's sick out here. Perversions of all kinds."

"Perversions," his brother says.

Pressia is shaken. Her hand is trembling. To hide it, she grips the gun tightly. "Why did you ask me out here?" Pressia says. "Just to play The Game?"

"It's all a game now," El Capitan says, unlocking the trap. "You lose, you're dead. Winning means you just keep playing. Sometimes I wish I'd lose. Tired. I get tired, that's all. Do you know what I mean?"

She does but she's surprised he's said it aloud, something so honest and vulnerable. She remembers the time she made the cut to her wrist. Was she trying to cut herself loose from the doll head or was she really just tired? She wonders for a moment if he's testing her. Should she tell him that she has no idea what he's talking about, that she's tough, officer material? There's something in the way he looks at her, though, and she can't lie. She nods. "I know what you mean."

El Capitan motions to the dead animal, picks it up, pulls a cloth sack from the interior of his jacket, and drops in the beast. The sack is immediately splotched red, a bright seeping of blood. "This is the first time I've found a whole beast to eat in a week."

"What do you mean?"

"Something's been getting to my traps and eating what's there before I pick up what I need."

"What do you think it is?"

El Capitan resets the trap with his boot. He talks over his shoulder to his brother. "We can trust her, right? We can trust this Pressia Belze?"

"Belze, Belze!" his brother says excitedly, but it sounds like *bells, bells* to Pressia, like he's expecting something to start ringing.

"Look," El Capitan says, "I'm willing to be generous with you. We can have our own meat, you and me. Not have to rely on that shit they serve here daily." He stares at Pressia. "That chicken looked pretty good to you the other day, no?"

Pressia nods. "But my meal wasn't bad. Better than the others'."

"The others don't know a damn thing," El Capitan says. "They never will. But you . . ." His eyes rove the forest.

"What about me?"

"Stick close," he says. "I hear 'em. Sometimes they move so fast, it's like hummingbirds. You hear 'em?"

Pressia strains to hear something, anything. *Don't come out. Don't come out wherever you are.* "What am I listening for?"

"The air goes electric when they're around." El Capitan hunches over and walks slowly, quietly.

Pressia follows him. She likes the weight of the gun in her hand now. She's relieved it's not just a golf club. She wishes her grandfather had taught her about guns rather than imaginary wedges, nine irons, putters.

El Capitan squats down in some brush, nods to Pressia to get next to him. "Look at that."

There's a field where a house used to sit. Now it's a broken mound. Beside it, there's a lump of plastic that probably used to be a jungle gym. There's also a huge metal fist, curled in on itself, as if a metal ladder had gotten wrapped up in it. Pressia couldn't define the thing.

"There they are." El Capitan is strangely calm, transfixed.

Moving in the shadows of trees on the other side of the field, she sees quick bodies. Nothing like the limping figure that was hiding behind trees, these are large, fleet, and shifting in a pattern. She sees two and then a third. They emerge from the woods, and she can see that they are men, young with broad faces. They wear tight-fitting dark ashen camouflage suits that leave their arms bare. Their sleek hairless skin, so pristine, seems to glow. Their arms are rippled with muscle but also guns, thick black metal, attached, if not built in. They tilt their heads as if hearing things from far off and sniff the air. Their bodies are muscular. Two have barrel chests. The other has enormous thighs. They all have short hair. When they aren't moving with great speed with their breath steaming behind them in the chilled air, they lope almost elegantly. They have oversize hands—no, claws—but are still human. Normally, Pressia would be terrified, but because of the creatures' odd elegance and El Capitan's rapt fearlessness, she isn't.

"I've seen these three before. Maybe they like to be able to triangulate a victim."

"Who are they?" Pressia whispers.

"You don't have to whisper," El Capitan says. "They know we're here. If they wanted to kill us, they would have."

Pressia watches one of the young men leap onto the plastic mound. He looks off in the distance as if seeing for miles. "Where did they come from?"

The creatures move restlessly, and El Capitan seems agitated, almost boyish. For the first time, he seems closer to her age. He says, "I was hoping that they'd show, but I didn't know for sure. Now you saw them too. I'm not alone."

Pressia thinks of the brother on El Capitan's back and thinks, You're never alone.

"They're looking for something or someone." El Capitan turns to Pressia. "But you wouldn't happen to know anything about that, right?"

Pressia shakes her head. "About what?"

"It's interesting that they show up the same time you do."

"I don't know what you're talking about. I've never seen anything like them before in my life." Pressia thinks of the Pure standing there in the middle of the street, just the way he'd been described. Is that who the creatures are looking for? "I don't even know what they are."

"Somebody's learned how to take every trait that they want from other animals or things and merge or fuse them with a human," El Capitan says. "Hyper-brain, hyper-body."

"The Dome?" Pressia says.

"Yeah, the Dome. Who else? But they know we're here," El Capitan says, "so why don't they kill us? We're the enemy, right? Or at least worth eating."

"Worth eating," his brother says.

Pressia watches the creatures, their sudden bursts of speed, the strange hum—El Capitan was right about that. There's a buzz in the air.

"See that one there?" He points to the one who seems to be looking directly at them. "That one looked at me like that last time too. He's got something more human in him than the others. You see it?"

Pressia isn't so sure. They all seem so completely foreign to her that she has trouble seeing their humanness. "I guess so," she says.

"They fused them with some nice toys, huh?" El Capitan says. "The guns are state-of-the-art, and I wouldn't be surprised if there were some computer chips lodged in them somewhere, smart guns. But there are animals involved. Whatever they merged them with, they became animals on a deep level. Maybe they merged them with wildcats and bears. Maybe hawks for vision.

Maybe they even gave them some echolocation sonar like with bats. See how they twist their heads?" El Capitan says. "No matter what, they became bloodthirsty."

"Bloodthirsty," his brother whispers.

And at the mention of this word, the three creatures turn in unison and stare at Pressia, El Capitan, and his brother in the brush.

"Don't move," El Capitan says.

Pressia doesn't even breathe. She closes her eyes and thinks of the coat—warm inside it. She thinks, If I die here, at least . . .

But then some other sound grabs the creatures' attention and they run toward it. Humming fills the air. They burst off through the trees.

The air goes still.

Pressia turns to El Capitan. "Why did you show me this?"

El Capitan stands up, stares at his boots. "Ingership sent your emergency orders."

"Who is Ingership exactly?"

El Capitan gives a grunting laugh. "He's the man with the plan." He squints at Pressia. "I never got orders like this before— to take some runt and send 'em up to officer, just like that. And a girl at that. Ingership wants to meet you—in person. And then there are these creatures, coming around. It has something to do with you," he says accusingly.

"But I don't know how it could have something to do with me. I'm nothing. A wretch, like everybody else."

"You know something. You have something. They need you somehow. It's all interrelated," he says, twirling his fingers in the air. "I just can't see how. There are no coincidences, right?"

"I don't know," Pressia says. "I think there probably are coincidences."

"Better I make nice with you now, though," El Capitan says. "For my own sake."

"For my own sake," his brother says. And El Capitan glances over his shoulder at his brother, who sits there with his head tilted.

Just then there's a loud chunk not too far off, a cry, some urgent rustling.

"Caught us something," El Capitan says.

Pressia closes her eyes for a second, then stands up and follows El Capitan back to the trap.

There on the ground is the crippled boy from Pressia's room, the only one who'd look at her when she first arrived. He must have been crawling because it's his upper body that's caught. The metal teeth have sunken into his ribs. He's bleeding through his thin jacket. He turns and stares at Pressia. He coughs up blood.

"Well, it's not really sporting," El Capitan says. "But you could shoot him just for practice."

The boy looks at Pressia. His face contorted with pain, his neck cords taut and blue.

Pressia doesn't say anything. She lifts the rifle, shakily.

"Take a few steps back, at least," El Capitan says. "So you have to aim a little."

Pressia steps back and so does El Capitan. Pressia raises the gun, looks through the sight. She takes a deep breath and then lets out just half of it. She stops breathing. But before she pulls the trigger, she realizes that she could lift the gun—up and to the right—and kill El Capitan and his brother. If she's got this one shot, that's what she should do with it. She knows it the way she's always known the most important things in her life. She could shoot and run.

Pressia pinches her left eye and takes aim. She holds the boy's head in her sight. And then, calmly, just the way El Capitan taught her, she breathes in again, lets the breath halfway out, but she doesn't fire.

She says, "I can't kill him."

"Why not? He's right there."

"I'm not a killer," she says. "Maybe we can carry him back and someone can help him. You have doctors here, don't you?"

"But that's not The Game," El Capitan says.

"If you need to kill someone for The Game, you can kill me. I can't kill him. I just can't. He's never done anything to me."

El Capitan swings his own rifle around to the front. He tucks it under his arm. And for a moment Pressia thinks he's taking her up on her offer. He's going to kill her. Her heart pounds louder, drowning out all the noise around her. She shuts her eyes.

But then the crippled boy on the ground mutters through his blood-filled mouth, "Do it!"

Pressia opens her eyes. El Capitan has taken aim at the boy. She thinks of shoving El Capitan, tackling him, as if she could. But the boy wants to die. His eyes are pleading. He's asked El Capitan to do it. And so she watches El Capitan's ribs rise then fall and half-way through the exhale, he pulls the trigger.

The boy's head skids across the ground. His face is gone. His body goes limp.

And Pressia starts breathing again.

PARTRIDGE

CAGE

To get to the meltlands, Partridge and Bradwell have to go through the fallen city, and passing by Pressia's house isn't much of a detour.

"I want to check in with her grandfather," Bradwell says. "I know where she lives."

Partridge is completely covered; none of his skin shows. In fact, Bradwell has told him to stoop his shoulders as if hunched and walk by dragging one leg. They'd normally stick to side streets and underground, but there's no time for that now.

They're pushing their way through the crowded market stalls, the more crowded and bustling the easier to fit in, Bradwell explained. On every side, there are people who seem part robotic. Partridge sees exposed gears and wires, pieces of skin melded with glass and plastic. He sees the back of a hand shining with the tin of an old can of soda, a chest made of the white metal of machinery—a washing machine? There's a bulbous growth on the side of a head, skin attaching an earpiece to an ear. He sees a hand fold open, revealing an embedded keypad. Someone else uses a cane because he has a dead leg that he rolls in front of himself. Sometimes there's simply fur on one forearm, a hand that's twisted and small like a paw.

But what surprises him the most are the children. There aren't many young kids in the Dome. Large families are discouraged, and some aren't allowed to have children at all, if there are obvious flaws in someone's genetic makeup.

"Stop gawking," Bradwell hisses at Partridge.

"I'm just not used to seeing kids," Partridge whispers. "Not so many of them."

"They siphon off resources, right?"

"It sounds bad when you put it that way."

"Just keep your eyes straight ahead."

"That's harder than you'd think."

They walk on a bit farther. "How do you know where Pressia lives? Did you stop by a lot?" he asks, trying to distract himself.

"I met her a week or so before her birthday and later I dropped off a gift."

Partridge wonders what would constitute a gift here. Too, he wants to see where Pressia lives. He feels guilty for wanting to get a feel for everyday life, like a tourist, but he does. He wants to see how things work. "What did you give her?"

"Nothing that would mean anything to you," Bradwell says. "Their place is just up ahead. It's not far." Partridge is getting used to Bradwell. By this comment, he means, *Shut up and stop asking questions.*

The alley is narrow. It smells of animals and rot. The houses are built into the fallen buildings. Some are no more than plywood propped up on rocks.

"This is it," Bradwell says. He walks to a window that looks newly broken. There are still small shards of glass sticking out from the frame. They both look through it into a small room, a table, an upended chair, a bundle of cloth on the floor that might be a kind of bed. Along the back wall there are cabinets, the doors all opened wide. He sees the EMPLOYEES ONLY sign on an interior door. "What kind of shop was it?"

"Barbershop, but that's blasted. The back office is all that's left."

Partridge spots a birdcage on the ground, its bars dented on one side. There's an empty hook overhead. "Looks abandoned," Partridge says.

"It's not good," Bradwell says. He walks to the door and knocks lightly. The door isn't shut all the way. Bradwell's knock causes it to ease open.

"Hello?" Partridge calls out. "Anyone here?"

"He's been taken," Bradwell says, walking around the room. He opens and closes the cabinet, walks to the table. He sees something hung on the wall, walks closer.

"Maybe he's just out," Partridge says, walking up beside Bradwell.

Bradwell doesn't say anything. He's staring at a picture that's been framed with uneven strips of wood and hung on the wall. "People wearing sunglasses in a movie theater?" Partridge says, lifting it from its small hook for a closer look.

"Three-D glasses," Bradwell says. "She loved this picture. I don't know why."

"Was this the gift you gave her?"

Bradwell nods. He looks shaken.

Partridge turns the picture over and, on the back, there's another piece of paper. It's creased with old fold marks and ash-gray. He can barely read the words. *"We know you are here, our brothers and sisters. We will, one day, emerge from the Dome to join you in peace. For now, we watch from afar, benevolently."* He looks at Bradwell.

"The Message," Bradwell says, glancing at the small piece of paper. "An original."

Partridge feels a chill on his arms. His father okayed the Message. This was part of the plan, from the outset. *Brothers and sisters.* He places the frame back on its hook. His stomach churns.

"They took him," Bradwell says, and he walks to the window ledge. The floor is littered with glass and small broken pieces of metal and wire, some white cloth. Bradwell picks something up and cups it in his hands.

"What is it?" Partridge asks.

"One of Pressia's creatures," Bradwell says. "She makes them. Her grandfather showed me some. He was proud of her."

Now Partridge can tell that it's a butterfly with gray wings and a small windup tab on its wire ribs.

"She bartered with them in the market. Her grandfather might have tried to save them. There was a struggle." He's right. Partridge can imagine it now with the busted window, the cage knocked from its hook, the overturned chair. "This is the only one left."

Partridge walks to the dented birdcage on the ground. He lifts it by a small ring attached to the top and puts it back on the hook.

"Whatever was in this cage is gone now," Bradwell says.

"Maybe it's better off," Partridge says. "Let loose, freed."

"You think?" Bradwell says.

Partridge isn't so sure—to be in a cage or set loose into this world? This is a question that he should be able to answer. Does some part of him wish he was back in the Dome?

LYDA

FINGERS

LYDA IS AT THE SMALL RECTANGULAR WINDOW, looking out. What else is there to do? Sit on her sitting mat? It's a mix of every color, a hideous mishmash. She's hidden it under her covers because she can't stand to stare at it.

The fake window shimmering on the wall is filled with late-afternoon light. It flickers as if leaves are creating a dappled effect. Is it the same projected window in every cell? There's something about the window that makes her feel deeply manipulated. Cut off from any real bearings, it seems as if the asylum now controls the sun itself. And even within the Dome, they rely on the sun as a true measure of day and night. Without it, she feels even more lost and alone.

Lyda's room sits at the end of the hall. She has a view of the rectangular windows in the doors on either side of the hallway. All of the windows are empty now. Some of the girls may be in therapy sessions. There is a communal meal that some of them are escorted to. Others are on their beds or pacing or thinking about their own projected windows.

But then someone appears, down the row of windows. The redhead. Her face is soft and pale. Her eyebrows are so fair that they're barely there. It gives her a blank expression. She stares at Lyda with her eyes full of worry, that same, strange expectant look she had in the craft room.

Lyda feels guilty now for having told her to shut up. The girl was only humming, only trying to pass the time. What was so wrong with that? She decides to make amends and raises her hand to the window, waves.

The redhead lifts her hand too, but then presses the fingers of that hand to the glass. Starting with her pinky, she lifts and presses each finger, one at a time, in a row, to a rhythm. She's crazy, Lyda thinks, but since there's nothing else to look at she keeps watching. Pinky, ring, pause. Middle, index. Pause. Then quickly, thumb, pinky, ring. Middle, index, pause. Thumb, pinky, pause. Then quickly again, ring, middle, index, thumb, pinky. Then in threes, ring, middle, index, pause, thumb, pinky, ring, pause, middle, index, thumb, pause, pinky. This is when Lyda realizes that it's a song. But it isn't that she's playing the notes on a piano, only the rhythm of the song.

And Lyda knows what song it is. That horrible, awful, stick-in-your-head-and-drive-you-insane "Twinkle, Twinkle." Disgusted, she rolls away from the window and, with her back to the wall, slides to the floor.

What if this is her life forever? What if relocation orders never come? She looks up at the fake window. Has it turned to dusk? Will she one day know the most minute shifts of fake sun, from morning to night?

She crawls to her mattress and pulls the sitting mat out from under her covers. She rips the plastic strips apart. She'll redo them. She'll make something pretty. She'll do and make. This will ease her restlessness. She sorts the strips by colors and tries to think of a design that would make her happy. She'd love to stitch a message into the sitting mat. *Save me*, that's what she would write. *I'm not crazy. Get me out of here!*

But who would ever see it? She'd have to hold it up to the window and hope that one of the other girls could read the message. And that's when she thinks of the redhead. What if she isn't crazy? What if the song holds a message?

She runs all of the words to the song over in her mind. *Up above the world so high. Like a diamond in the sky?* She starts weaving the plastic strips—blue, purple, red, green, creating a checkered pattern. The song is in her head now and meaningless. Just stuck there. It loops, wordlessly, and then as her fingers move back and forth, finding a rhythm, the words to the song return. But they aren't "Twinkle, Twinkle." They're the alphabet. She'd never noticed before that the two songs share a tune.

A, B, C, D, E, F, G...Letters, language.

She stands up, letting the remaining plastic strips for the sitting mat fall to the floor. She runs to the window, and there is the redhead's pale face, waiting for her.

Lyda presses her fingers to the window. She runs through the alphabet to the rhythm of the tune until her finger lands on *H*, and then she runs through it again, stopping on *I*.

The redhead smiles and this time, she waves.

It's dusk. Lyda is losing light. She makes a question mark on her window. What does the girl want to tell her so badly? What is it?

The girl starts to spell. It's a slow process, and Lyda nods each time she gets a letter. She whispers the letter under her breath, to help her remember where she is in a word. At the end of each word, the redhead draws a line on the window.

She writes, M-a-n-y / o-f / u-s. / W-e / w-i-l-l /

A guard patrols the hall. They both leave their windows. Lyda lies down in bed under her covers, pretends to be asleep. We will what? Lyda thinks. What?

She listens to the guard's shoes retreat down the hall, returns to the window. The redhead isn't there, but after a few moments, she reappears.

She writes: O-v-e-r- *Overcome?* Lyda wonders. Will she overcome this imprisonment? Is this a message of hope for all those who are stuck here, feeling lost forever?

No. The redhead's message goes on. She spells out, t-h-r-o-w. We will *overthrow?* Who will they overthrow?

Lyda taps her letters as quickly as she can, g-u-a-r-d-s. She makes another question mark with her finger on the window.

The redhead looks at her with her blank face, and shakes her head vehemently. No, no, no.

Lyda writes a question mark on the glass. Who? She needs to know.

It's nearly dark in the room. Lyda can only barely make out the redhead's finger on the window. The redhead taps out four letters. D-o-m-e.

Lyda stares at her. She doesn't understand. She puts her finger on the glass again and draws another question mark.

The redhead taps out T-e-l-l / h-i-m.

PARTRIDGE

DARTS

THE PRISONS, ASYLUMS, AND SANATORIUMS have all collapsed, one colossus after the next, like piles of wrought-iron bones scorched bare, and the houses in the gated communities are charred or obliterated completely. The plastic jungle gyms and pirate ships and mini castles turned out to be durable. Large indistinct blobs of color, they dot the blackened, nearly flattened terrain of dust and ash like warped sculptures, things Partridge has seen images of in his Art History class.

Art installations, that's what Mr. Welch called them. And, in some strange way, they please Partridge now. He imagines Welch, who resembles in some ways a shrunken version of Glassings in World History. Welch would sometimes stand in front of the projector to explain something with the blur of colors on his reedy frame, his sunken chest, his shiny bald pate. He was one of the judges who picked Lyda's bird. Partridge will probably never see Welch or Glassings or Lyda again. He'll never see the bird. And Pressia?

Bradwell is out in front of Partridge, his hand resting on the hilt of a knife in his jacket. And Partridge has a hook and a butcher's knife from Bradwell, as well as the old knife from the Domesticity Display, but still he feels vulnerable out here, slightly imbalanced. The coding is gaining its foothold in his body. Sometimes he feels it surge as it tries to take hold of his muscles, drill into his bones, fire through his synapses. It's a feeling that he can't describe—a thickening of blood coursing through his body, something foreign within him. He was immune to the behavioral coding because of the blue pills his mother fed him at the beach, but still the rest of the coding exists in the chemicals of his brain. Can he trust his own brain? Right now he feels foggy on details. "What's this trustworthy woman like again?" Partridge asks.

"Hard to say," Bradwell tells him.

"Haven't you two met before?"

"Nope," Bradwell says. "I know the rumors, though."

"Rumors?"

"Yep. She's our only shot," Bradwell says. "That is, if we're not killed by her protectors first."

"Her protectors could kill us?"

"They wouldn't be protectors if they didn't protect her."

"Shit," Partridge says. "You've got me out here based on rumors?"

Bradwell spins around. "Let's get this straight. *You've* got *me* out here, looking for Pressia, who you got out, too."

"Sorry," Partridge says.

Bradwell starts walking again. Partridge follows. "It's not really rumors anyway. Myth is more accurate. Do you have a better idea?"

He knows that Partridge doesn't have any better ideas. Partridge is a stranger here. He's got nothing.

Sometimes Partridge imagines that this isn't real, that, instead, it's just some elaborate reenactment of destruction, not the actual destruction itself. He remembers once being in a museum on a class trip. There were miniature displays with live actors in various wings, talking about what things were like before the Return of Civility. Each display was dedicated to a theme: before the impressive prison system was built, before difficult children were properly medicated, when feminism didn't encourage femininity, when the media was hostile to government instead of working toward a greater good, before people with dangerous ideas were properly identified, back when government had to ask permission to protect its good citizens from the evils of the world and from the evils among us, before the gates had gone up around neighborhoods with buzzer systems and friendly men at gatehouses who knew everyone by name.

In the heat of the day, there were battle reenactments on the museum's wide lawn that showed the uprisings waged in certain cities against the Return of Civility and its legislation. With the military behind the government, the uprisings—usually political demonstrations that became violent—were easily tamped down. The government's domestic militia, the Righteous Red Wave, came to save the day. The recorded sounds were deafening, Uzis and attack sirens pouring from speakers. The kids in his class bought bullhorns, very realistic hand grenades, and Righteous Red Wave iron-on emblems in the gift shop. He wanted a sticker that read THE RETURN OF CIVILITY—THE BEST KIND OF FREEDOM written over a rippling American flag, with the words REMAIN VIGILANT written beneath it. But his mother hadn't given him money for the gift shop, no wonder.

Of course, he knows now that the museum was propaganda. Still, he could pretend for a moment that this is what the Meltlands could be, a museum, researched for authenticity. "You remember what it was like before the Detonations?" he asks Bradwell.

"I lived out here for a little while with my aunt and uncle."

Partridge, whose mother had refused to leave the city, had only visited his friends' houses there. He remembers the sound of the gates—the low hum of electricity, grating gears, loud clunks of metal. Even though the houses in the gated communities were crammed next to one another, each with only a small swathe of grass, coated in a velvety, chemical sheen, they seemed desolate. "Do you still have pictures of it in your head?" he asks Bradwell.

"Not ones I want."

"Was this where you were at the end?"

Bradwell says, "I'd wandered away from the neighborhood. I was that kind of kid, always drifting away from where I was supposed to be."

"Most kids were kept indoors, out of the public eye," Partridge says. "I know I was." Children said things. They couldn't be trusted, and they repeated their parents like parrots. Partridge's mother told him, "If someone asks you for my opinion on something, tell them you don't know." She didn't leave him alone for long at a friend's house. There was always the fear of a virus, too, something contractible. The environment was compromised. The water systems were suspect, often tainted, the food stores contaminated. There were recalls. If not for the Detonations, Partridge had been taught in the academy, they still would have needed the Dome. It proved prescient. The Detonations— could his father really have been in on it from the beginning? He rarely spoke of the Detonations in the Dome, but when he did, he accepted it as a natural disaster almost. More than once he'd heard him say, "An act of God. And God was merciful on us," and "Thank you, Father, for we are blessed."

Partridge remembers one time when he and his mother arrived at a friend's house and the mother was gone. He wonders if the remains of that house exist somewhere nearby in this vast barren landscape. "Mrs. Fareling," he says, remembering her name.

"What?" Bradwell says.

"Mrs. Fareling was my friend's mother. We sometimes carpooled to things together. My mother liked her. She had a son my age, Tyndal. We showed up for a playdate at her house in a gated neighborhood, and she was gone. Another woman opened the door. 'State worker,' she said. She was there as interim care while Mr. Fareling looked for a replacement for his wife in the home."

"What did your mother do?" Bradwell asks.

"She asked what happened and the woman said that Mrs. Fareling stopped attending FF meetings, then church functions."

"Feminine Feminists," Bradwell says.

"Did your mother belong?"

"Of course not. She wasn't going to embrace conservative ideals. She thought it was bullshit, like saying, *Aren't we great the way we are! Pretty, feminine, nonthreatening.*"

"My mom despised the movement too. She fought with my dad about it." Partridge's friends' mothers were members of the FF. They always wore lipstick, which was pretty even though it sometimes gummed on their teeth.

"What happened to Mrs. Fareling?" Bradwell asks.

"I don't know." The woman said that rehab wasn't always permanent. She offered counseling: *Sometimes we can help when someone is affected by a sudden loss.* His mother refused. Partridge can almost remember the feel of her hand gripping his upper arm as she marched him to the car, as if he'd been the one to do something wrong. "On the way home, she told me that they built the prisons and rehabilitation centers and sanatoriums tall for a reason. So everyone knew that the only difference is that you live under their roof or in their shadow."

It's dusk and the shadows are growing darker. Beasts could be anywhere. They skirt a few melted jungle gyms and over a ribbon of flattened chain-link fence.

"Your parents," Partridge says to Bradwell, "how did they figure anything out if they said no to the Best and the Brightest in those Red Lobsters? They were on the outside."

"Luck," Bradwell says, "but I'm not sure if it's good luck or bad luck, now, looking back. My dad won a grant to study rituals in a remote Japanese fishing village and a family gave him a video recording of a woman who had survived Hiroshima, but had become deformed. Her arm was seared to a pocket watch. She was hidden because there had been others like her, people who'd fused in strange ways to animals, to land, to each other, and they were taken away by the government and never seen again."

"In the Dome, they like us to study ancient cultures. Cave wall drawings, shards of pottery, occasionally mummies. That kind of thing. Easier that way."

"I guess so." Bradwell looks at Partridge like he appreciates the admission. "Well, like a lot of historians, my father didn't believe that the atomic bomb was the sole reason for the Japanese surrender. Leading up to the surrender, the Japanese showed no fear of loss of life and sacrifice. My parents wondered if it wasn't the emperor's fear of these abominations created by the bomb. The Japanese were very homogeneous, an island culture. And this may have been too much for the emperor—not that they would be destroyed, but deformed, mutated. The generals were forced to surrender, and all of the people who were merged by the bomb were taken away to be studied. Because of MacArthur's censorship of the effects of the atomic bomb, the suppression of eye-witness accounts and oral histories, even scientific observations—what was basically a gag order on the Japanese—plus their own sense of shame... It all helped to hush up the true horrors, as well as the mutations."

They've come to a section of gate that's still standing. Bradwell climbs it first. Partridge follows. They both jump to the ground. Before them is just another stretch of charred remains and melted blobs of plastic.

"What about the United States?" Partridge asks.

"Do you really want to know? I've been told I'm too pedantic."

"I want to know."

"The US knew about the messy, unintended effects of the

bomb, and very quietly developed new sciences—what became your father's babies. Ones that would build up resistance to radioactivity in structures and allow them to control the effects of radiation. Instead of messy, unintended mergers, the US government wanted intentional mergers to create a superspecies."

"Coding. I've gone through some. I wasn't a ripe specimen for it, though." He's proud of this even though it's not as if he stood up to anyone. It's just a fact.

"Really?"

"Sedge was. I wasn't," Partridge says. "But how'd your parents get the info they needed?"

"One of the geneticists, Arthur Walrond, was a friend of my mother's, of Silva Bernt's. Walrond had a rowdy social life, drove a convertible, and had loose lips and a guilty conscience. One weekend he visited my parents, got drunk, and unburdened some secrets about the new sciences. It fit, of course, with my parents' theories. He started feeding them information." Bradwell stops and looks out across the charred remains of a gutted neighborhood. He rubs his head. He looks tired.

"What's wrong?" Partridge asks.

"Nothing. I just remember how he convinced my parents to get me a dog. 'He's an only child in a family of workaholics. Get the poor boy a mutt!' Walrond was doughy, short, duck-footed, but a fast talker with a sweet car, a lady's man, weirdly enough. He didn't have the necessary constitution for his life. He knew what they could do with the things he was working on. The government used the term *unlimited potential*, but he always added *for destruction*.

"He was sloppy. When the government found out he was leaking secrets, they gave him warning and enough time to kill himself before they showed up at his house to arrest him. And he obliged. An overdose." Bradwell sighs. "I named the dog Art, after Arthur Walrond. I had to give it up after my parents died. My aunt was allergic. I loved that stupid dog."

Bradwell stops and looks at Partridge. "Your father had my parents killed. He probably even gave the order. They were shot in their sleep before the Detonations, close range, silencers. I was sleeping in my bed. I woke up and found them."

"Bradwell," Partridge says. He reaches out, but Bradwell backs away.

"You know what I think sometimes, Partridge?" There are animal noises not far off, a yowl, a bird-like caw. "I think we were already dying of superdiseases. The sanatoriums were full. Prisons were being converted to house the infected. The water was already shot through with oil. And if not that, there was plenty of ammo, uprisings in the cities. There was the corn-fed grief, the unbearable weight of pie fillings. We were choking on pollutants, radiation. Dying one charred lung at a time. Left to our own devices, we were shooting ourselves with holes, burning alive. Without the Detonations, we'd have dwindled and finally clubbed each other to bright bloody death. So they speeded that up, right? That's all."

"You don't mean that."

"No," Bradwell says. "When I'm feeling a little optimistic, I think we could have turned it around. There were a lot of people like my parents, fighting the good fight. They ran out of time."

"I guess that passes for optimism."

"It wasn't bad to be raised by enemies of the state. I grew up jaded. After the Detonations, I knew not to go to the superstores like everyone else. I also knew that there wasn't relief coming. That's what everyone expected—army-issued water and blankets and urgent care. I had heard enough from my parents to know not to trust anyone. Better to go on the record as dead. And so I'm dead. Not a bad thing to be here."

"It's harder to die if you're dead."

"You know what's always stuck with me, though?"

"What?"

"I found a note from Walrond in my parents' things—a drunken scrawl. *The thing is—they could save them all, but they won't.* It's always bothered me. And then in this one article, someone's asked Willux about the radiation resistance of the Dome. He says, 'Radiation resistance has unlimited potential for us all.'"

"But it didn't. Not for everyone."

"Your father wanted near-total destruction so he could start new. Was he racing against those who were closer? Or those who were close to coming up with radiation resistance for all? Was he like the inventor of armor and then everyone got armor so he had to invent the crossbow—the escalation of *weapon, defense, better weapon, better defense*?"

"I don't know. He's a stranger to me now." For a brief second, Partridge wishes his father dead. Evil, he thinks to himself. His father isn't simply capable of evil. He has acted on it. Why? Partridge wonders. "I'm so sorry about your parents," Partridge says. He takes in the stretches of destruction in every direction. He staggers a little, trying to absorb the loss. And then his foot catches, and he trips on something.

When he regains his footing, he reaches down and picks up a metal object with three spokes fanning out around a sharp tip, caked in the dirt and ash. Bradwell walks back to him and stares at the thing in his hand.

"Is that a dart?" Partridge says. "I remember the kind thrown at a target, but never one that big."

"It's a lawn dart," Bradwell says.

Partridge hears the sound before he sees it—a whir that's nearly a buzz. He shoves Bradwell out of the way. They both land hard, the wind knocked out of them, as another dart thuds into the ground behind him. Bradwell staggers to his feet. "This way!" he says. They both start running toward a red-and-blue melt and squat down behind it.

The darts come quickly, whirring and thudding. Two darts

wedge into the plastic on the other side. And then everything's quiet.

Partridge looks around the melt and spots a dwelling propped up with bricks and walls supported by melts dragged from other yards. "A house," he says. "A short fence in front of it." Partridge remembers picket fences with little latches that swung open that penned trimmed dogs bouncing in the yards. But this fence is mostly sticks wedged into the ground, and on top of each stick something has been hung. He can't tell at first what the strange things are, but then he sees a blackened rounded cage—a set of wide ribs, some of the bones cracked, gone. Two sticks down, there's a broad skull. Human. Part of the skull is missing. Sitting in front of the house's remains are two skulls, lit from within by candles, like jack-o'-lanterns. Halloween. Partridge remembers wearing a box made to look like a robot. The Meltlands were famous for holidays, the trees strung with ghosts and Santas teetering on roofs. He sees what seems to be a garden, overturned dirt with stakes, but it's just more bones. These are splayed decoratively, hand bones spread to look like blooms. In another world, these things—picket fence, jack-o'-lanterns, gardens—meant home. Not anymore.

"What is it?" Bradwell asks.

"It's not good. They're proud of their kills." Another dart thunks into the plastic. "And they've got good aim. Are these the protectors?"

"Could be," Bradwell says. "If so, we surrender. We want to be captured and brought in. I won't know if it's them 'til I see 'em. And I need a better angle. I'm running to that melt there." Bradwell points up ahead.

"Try not to get hit."

"How many lawn darts can they have?"

"I don't want to know what they use once they're out of lawn darts, do you?" Partridge says, shaking his head.

Bradwell sprints. The darts come at him. He lets out a shout. He staggers, gripping his left elbow. He's been hit in the shoulder. He keeps running and throws himself behind the next melt.

Partridge takes off after him before Bradwell can tell him not to. He sprints and slides to a stop beside Bradwell, whose jacket sleeve is already bloody. Partridge reaches for the dart lodged in Bradwell's arm.

"Don't!" Bradwell says, rolling away.

"You've got to get it out," Partridge says. "What are you, afraid of a little pain?" He holds his arm down at the elbow. "I'll do it fast."

"Wait, wait," Bradwell says. "Do it on the count of three."

"Okay." Partridge leans on Bradwell's arm, pinning it to the ground, then wraps his hand around the dart. It's in deep. "One, two—" And he pulls it out, ripping some of the jacket too.

"Shit!" Bradwell cries. The wound gushes blood. "Why didn't you count to three?"

Paybacks, Partridge thinks, an impulse to get back at Bradwell for holding him in such contempt, for punching him when Pressia was first missing. He kind of hates Bradwell, but maybe only because Bradwell hated Partridge first. "We've got to wrap it up," Partridge says.

"Damn it!" Bradwell says, gripping his elbow to his ribs.

"Take off your jacket." Partridge helps Bradwell shrug it off. Partridge uses the small rip to tear the sleeve off and wraps the sleeve around the muscle of shoulder, tying it tight. "I wish I'd gotten a good look at them," Partridge says.

"Ah, you know what? I think you've got your chance." Bradwell points right in front of him.

And there is a set of eyes, low to the ground. A child is peeking out from behind the leg of a larger creature, wearing battle gear—metal chest plates made of mower blades, a helmet. A long braid curls over one shoulder. She's armed with weapons only recognizable in their parts—a bike chain, a drill, a chain saw.

"That's not bad," Partridge says. "Only one of her and a child. Two of us."

"Wait," Bradwell says.

Others drift in silently behind her. They're women too, and most of them also have children, either being held or standing next to them. More weapons—kitchen knives, two-pronged grill forks, skewers, weed whackers. Their faces are mottled with glass, chips of tile, bits of mirrors, metal, shards of flagstone, the sheen of plastic. Many of them have jewelry fused into their wrists and necks and earlobes. They must pick at the skin to keep it from growing over the jewelry, which is outlined in small dark red-crusted scabs.

"Have we been found? Was this the group you were hoping for?" Partridge asks.

"Yep," Bradwell says. "I think so."

"I think they're housewives," Partridge whispers.

"With their kids," Bradwell says.

"Why haven't the kids grown?"

"They can't. They're stunted by their mother's bodies."

Partridge has a hard time believing that the people who once lived in these homes were capable of survival. They were always followers who lacked the courage of their convictions. And those who were courageous, Mrs. Fareling, perhaps, disappeared. Are these the mothers and children of the gated communities, the ones who once delighted in plasticware? "Are we about to be beaten to death by a car pool?"

As the crowd moves closer, Partridge sees that the children are not just *with* their mothers. They're attached. The first woman they saw walks with an uneven gait. The child who'd seemed to be holding on to her leg is actually fused there. Legless, the boy has only one arm, and his torso and head protrude from her upper thigh. Another woman has eyes peering out from a bulbous baby head that sits like a goiter on her neck.

Their faces are angular and grim. Their bodies are slightly hunched as if ready to lunge.

Partridge pulls the scarf tight to make sure his unmarked face is hidden.

"Too late for that now," Bradwell says. "Just put your hands up and smile."

Still on their knees, they both hold their hands over their heads.

Bradwell says, "We surrender. We're here to see Your Good Mother. We need her help."

A woman with a hip-fused child steps up, pushing a knife-armored stroller up to Partridge's face. Another woman holding a long sharp pair of hedge clippers walks up to Bradwell and kicks him in the chest with incredible force. The hedge-clipper woman holds the blades in front of Bradwell's face, opening and closing the blades, glinting, sharp. The clipper has been fused to one of her hands, but the other hand pumps the blades. And then she puts her bare foot on Bradwell's sternum, opens the clippers wide, and holds them over his throat.

Partridge feels his arm jerk backward. He pulls out the meat hook and spins around, swinging over the head of a stunted child. The little girl's mother's hand is fused into the center of her daughter's back. He stumbles forward with the miss. The woman quickly puts a knee into his gut, uppercuts his chin, and holds a kitchen knife to his heart.

Her daughter laughs.

Partridge knows these women and their fused children are tactical and violent. They are soldiers. With his strength coding he could overtake half a dozen of them at once, but now he can see that there are more than a hundred. Their shadows shift. Other women move in quickly and strip them of their knives, the meat hook, their newly acquired lawn darts.

The woman with the kitchen knife grabs Partridge's arm with a grip that feels like it's embedded with rows of sharp teeth cutting into his skin. She pulls him to his feet with great strength. He looks at his pale arm, now smeared with blood, then glimpses her palm, which is shiny with shards of a mirror. She pulls an old dark pillowcase from her belt. Another woman, behind him, wrenches his arms and binds them so tightly that his elbows nearly touch behind his back. He glances at Bradwell, who's on his feet too now, also being bound.

The last thing Partridge sees before the pillowcase is thrown over his head is a gold cross and its thin chain embedded in a scalded chest.

And then there's darkness, his own moist breath muffled inside of the dark hood.

He thinks of the ocean. Did his mother wrap him in a blanket on the beach once? Did he hear the wind-rippled cloth batting his ears, tamping the constant roar of the ocean? What has happened to the ocean now? He's seen images of it, grayscale. It's turbulent and roiling. But grayscale will never capture the ocean. Neither will a static image. He closes his eyes and pretends that his head is in a blanket and the ocean isn't far off and his mother is near. He hopes he doesn't die.

A child cries out with the keening of a gull.

Pressia

ARABS

HALF OF INGERSHIP'S BONY FACE is fitted with a metal plate and a flexible hinge where a knot of jaw should be. It was fixed by someone who knew what they were doing, a pro. Not just a flesh-tailor like Pressia's grandfather. No. This was handled by some-one with real skills and instruments. The hinge allows Ingership to speak, chew, and swallow. Even so, his words come out stiff and labored. The metal tucks into the skin under his chin, and extends upward so far that it's impossible to see where the metal ends and the skin covering his skull begins because he's wearing a military cap. The other side of his head is clean-shaven, pink. The thought of his head scares Pressia because it brings to her mind the gun-shot, the jolt, the stutter of the boy's skull against the ground. She isn't a killer, but she let him get shot. He was going to die, yes. He asked El Capitan to do it. It was merciful. But this doesn't help. She's culpable.

Pressia is sitting across from Ingership in the backseat of a miraculously shiny black sedan. The sun is directly overhead. The orders indicated that El Capitan was to march Pressia Belze three miles to an old water tower, felled, its bulbous top cracked and blackened, where the car would be waiting. And when they arrived, the car was already there, looking so pristine it was otherworldly. The back window buzzed down, revealing Ingership's face. "Get in," he said.

Pressia followed El Capitan around to the other side. He opened the door. Pressia slid in first, then El Capitan got in and slammed the door. With his rifle slung over his shoulder and Helmud on his back, he had to hunch forward. Helmud was bulky and made the car feel crowded. Ingership glanced at him coldly, and it was almost as if he wanted to ask El Capitan to take Helmud off. Pressia imagined Ingership saying, *Can we put your luggage in the trunk?*

Instead Ingership said, "Get out."

"Who? Me?" El Capitan asked.

"Me?" Helmud said.

Ingership nodded. "You'll wait here. The driver will bring her back."

Pressia didn't want El Capitan to go. She didn't want to be alone with Ingership. Something about his mechanized speech and eerie calm unsettled her.

El Capitan opened the door, got out, slammed it, and then knocked on the window.

"Hit the button," Ingership said.

Pressia pressed a button on the interior handle and felt the electric vibration in her fingertip. The window disappeared down into the door.

"How long will you be gone?" El Capitan asked. Pressia could see his finger rubbing against the trigger.

"Wait for her," Ingership said, and told the driver to go.

The car jerked forward, spitting dust, and they were jettisoned forward. Aside from the ride in the OSR truck with her hands bound and mouth taped shut, Pressia hadn't been in a car for as long as she could remember. Did she even remember the sensation somewhere deep in her memory? She feared sliding out of the seat somehow. The wind was pouring in the window and with it the ash.

"Shut the window!" Ingership said, loudly.

Pressia pressed the button in the other direction, and up it went.

Now it's raining a little, and the sedan is so polished that the rain beads up and glides. Pressia wants to know where the car came from. It's sleek, untarnished. Did it survive in some kind of ultra-reinforced garage?

The driver keeps an eye on her through the rearview mirror. He's a meaty man, fat hands gripping the wheel. He has dark skin except where the burns are a deep, raw pink. They're drifting on the barren remains of a dilapidated highway. The road is mostly cleared of debris but still it's slow going. The landscape is desolate. They've long since passed the Meltlands, the burned-out prisons, rehabilitation centers, and sanatoriums. The road has given way to weeds and a set of ruts. Gauging the sun, Pressia knows they're heading northeast. Occasionally there are the decapitated posts of billboards, the melted shards of chain restaurants and gas stations and motels, the gutted bellies of eighteen-wheelers and oil-scorched trucks left on the roadside like the blackened ribs of dead whale carcasses. Every once in a while you see that someone has dragged the remains of things from the rubble and arranged a message, like: HELL IS WHERE THE HEART IS or, more pointedly, DAMNED.

And then the landscape grows bare. The Deadlands. They remind Pressia that she's lucky. Out here, all that's left is the scorched earth that might just stretch on forever in every direction. There is no road. Some small arid brush is the only vegetation.

But the Deadlands are ever so slightly alive. Occasionally, something will ripple under the surface, roaming Dusts, a creature that's become part of the earth itself.

The Deadlands set all of them on edge. The car is silently restless, as if the air is suddenly pressurized. A Dust rears up—large and bear-like but made of dirt and ash. The driver swerves, missing it.

Ingership sits up stiffly. He's made it clear that he has no intentions of talking about anything important, not yet at least. "You've never been out past the city, have you?" he asks, which strikes Pressia as nervous, idle conversation.

"No."

"It's best that El Capitan isn't with us. He really isn't ready. Don't tell him what you see out here. He'll only sulk," Ingership says. "You'll like it, Belze. I think you'll appreciate what we've done with the place. Do you eat oysters?"

"Oysters?" Pressia asks. "Like from the sea?"

"I hope you like them. They're on the menu."

"How did you get them?" Pressia asks.

"I've got connections," Ingership says. "Oysters on the half shell. They're an acquired taste."

Acquired taste? Pressia isn't sure what the term means, but she loves it. A taste is something that you can acquire? She'd love to simply be fed anything regularly enough to acquire a taste. She would love to acquire one taste and then another and another until she has a full collection of tastes. But no. She reminds herself that she can't trust these people at all. The outlands—is it where they'll beat information out of her?

They drive for more than an hour in silence. Dusts slip in front of the car, slithering like snakes. The driver runs them over, the creatures crunching under the tires. Pressia has no idea how long they'll continue on. All night? For days? How far do the Deadlands stretch? Do they have an end? If you head off in any direction, you will eventually come to them. No one has ever made it through them and back again. Not that Pressia knows, at least. She's heard that the Dusts there are worse than in the Rubble Fields. They're quicker, hungrier. They live on little and aren't weighted by stone.

If Ingership takes Pressia to the outlands to beat information out of her, will she be left in the Deadlands to die?

Finally, up ahead, there's a rise on the horizon—a hill? As they get closer, Pressia can tell that it has vegetation, some greenery, in fact. When the car makes it to the hill, it bears right, hugging a curve. The earth holds the hard memory of a road again. Once around the curve, Pressia looks down into a valley—farmlands surrounded by more Deadlands. There are lush fields, not exactly windswept wheat, but something darker, heavier, dotted with what seem to be small yellow flowers, rows of barren staked stalks, and other greenery heavy with unidentifiable purplish fruit. Among the rows, there are recruits in green uniforms. Some are rolling small plastic tank-holds and spraying down the vegetation. Others seem to be collecting samples. They limp and trudge, their marred skins exposed in the dim sun.

There are grazing fields of bulky animals that are shaggier than cows, with longer snouts, hornless. They teeter slowly on hooves out near a stand of greenhouses. The road twists along, leading to a yellow A-frame house and, a bit off the road, a red barn built up and painted brightly as if nothing had ever gone wrong. It's so astonishing that she can barely believe it.

Pressia remembers this kind of thing from Bradwell's clippings and, distantly, from her own memory.

Her grandfather knew farmers when he was a kid. "Agriculture is relatively new if you think of the entire *Homo sapiens* experience," he'd told her. "If we can reestablish that—creating more food than we need—we will reestablish our way of life." But the earth is scorched and hostile, the seeds mutated, the sunlight still blotted by dust and soot. People do better with small gardens tended in windows, from seeds of vegetation that didn't kill them. They can keep an eye on them, take them in at night so they don't get stolen. And they prefer the hybrid animals that they catch. The burden of feeding an animal, keeping it alive, is too much to ask of most people who are just trying to stay alive themselves. Each generation of animal has its own genetic distortions. One might make you sick, but his brother might not. Better to see a hybrid animal alive—see for yourself if it's really healthy—before eating it.

"This much food," Pressia says. "How is there enough sun?"

"There's been some tinkering in the coding. How much sun does a plant need? Can we alter that need? The greenhouses use mechanics, reflective surfaces to pinpoint light, conserve and shuttle it to the plants' leaves."

"Fresh water?"

"Same idea."

"What are these crops exactly?"

"Hybrids."

"Do you know how many people you could feed with all of this food?" Pressia means it as a statement of awe, but Ingership takes it as a valid question.

"If it were all edible, we could expand to serve one-eighth of the population."

"You can't eat it?"

"We have a few successes. Meager really. Mutations that pop up. Not usually our planned attempts."

"One-eighth of the population would eat it whether it was edible or not," Pressia says.

"Oh, no, not one-eighth of the *wretches*. This would be one-eighth of those in the Dome, to subsidize their dietary needs and eventually sustain them when they return to us," Ingership says.

The Dome? But Ingership is OSR. He's El Capitan's superior. OSR plans to overtake the Dome one day. They're building an army. "What about OSR?" Pressia manages.

Ingership looks at Pressia and smiles on one side of his face. "All will become clear."

"Does El Capitan know about this?"

"He knows without knowing he knows. How about you tell him that I live out here in a tent...like Arabs in the olden days in the deserts?" She can't tell if he's joking or not.

"Arabs," Pressia echoes, as if she's taken over the role of Helmud now. She thinks of her parents' wedding reception, her grandfather's description of the white tents and white tablecloths and white cake.

"Tent. Got it? That's an order." Ingership's voice is suddenly rigid, as if not only his face but his voice box too is partly metallic.

"Got it," Pressia says quickly.

It's quiet for a few minutes, and then Ingership says, "In my spare time, I tinker with antiquities. I'm trying to reclaim foods that have been lost. Still not quite perfected. So close." And then Ingership sighs deeply. "A little bit of old-fashioned civility here in the wilds."

Old-fashioned civility? Pressia couldn't even begin to understand what that might mean. "Where do you get the oysters?" she asks.

"Ah," Ingership says with a wink. "Little secret. Gotta keep something up my sleeve!" Pressia doesn't understand why he'd keep anything up his sleeves.

The driver parks in front of a set of wide porch steps, and Pressia remembers the lyrics to that recording her mother loved so much, her nightly lullaby—the girl dances across a porch, lonesomely.

And now a woman steps out of the house to greet them. She's wearing a bright yellow dress as if to match the house, and at first her skin looks so white it seems to glow. Is she a Pure? But then Pressia realizes that it is not her skin. It's a kind of stocking made of a thin, stretchy, almost shiny material. It covers every inch of her body and is fitted with gloves for her fingers and small neatly stitched holes for her eyes and mouth—and now that the woman is close enough, Pressia even sees holes at the nostrils. The woman is as rail-thin as Ingership. Her angular shoulders look like knobs of bone.

Ingership slides out of one side of the car, and Pressia follows.

As his wife calls out, "Delighted! Delighted you made it!" the stocking doesn't shift. It perfectly conforms to the muscles of her face beneath it—neither puckering around the lips nor pressing flat the nose. She wears a wig, a lightly fluffed blond wig that hides her ears and is held back by a wide clip at the back of her neck. She doesn't venture down the steps. Instead, she steadies herself by gripping the handrail.

Pressia follows Ingership up the steps and stands on the porch. Ingership kisses his wife on the cheek, but it isn't her cheek. It's the stocking-skin. "This is my fine wife!"

Ingership's wife is a little shaken by the sight of Pressia, as if she isn't used to seeing survivors. One of her ankles buckles in her pointy shoes.

Pressia hides her doll-head fist behind her back. "Nice to meet you," she says softly.

"Yes," Ingership's wife says.

"Oysters on the half shell?" Ingership asks his wife.

"Chilled and ready!" she says with a smile, the stocking of her face smooth and taut.

PRESSIA

OYSTERS

THE MOMENT THEY STEP INSIDE, Ingership's wife shuts the door and then presses a button on the wall that automatically extends rubber seals along the door's outline. To keep out the dust? Pressia wonders. If so, it works well. The walls are cream-colored and glossy. The wood floors shine. There's a painting of this exact farmhouse surrounded by hills of snow, all white and sparkling as if ash doesn't exist.

"Welcome to our humble abode," Ingership says, and then he runs a finger along a strip of white wood running, not quite waist-high, along the walls. He holds the finger up. It's lightly smudged with ash. He doesn't make the effort to unlock the metallic hinge of his jaw, and so he speaks through clenched teeth. "Icky?" he says to his wife.

She looks stricken. Her head bobbles slightly. "Icky!" she chirps.

Pressia has never seen so much elegance—a rug stitched with bright blue flowers, a banister carved to a curlicue at the foot of the stairs, and a golden ceiling. They turn into a dining room with a long table covered in a red cloth. The plates are set, the silver-ware shines, the walls are patterned with more flowers. A giant light is attached to the ceiling, made of glinting glass, not shards but finely cut shapes. Pressia can't remember the word for these lamps. She's heard her grandfather use it when she was playing with Freedle, and he decided to put a candle in Freedle's cage. It lit the room from above in a pretty way.

She thinks of Bradwell. She can't help it. What would he say about this display of wealth? He'd call it sick. *You know God loves you because you're rich!* She can hear him making fun of the place. She knows she should be disgusted too. Who, in good conscience, could live here knowing how everyone else lives? But it's a home—a beautiful home. She wants to live here. She loves the shiny rounded wood of the chair backs, the velvety curtains, the ornate handles of the silverware. Somewhere overhead there must be a bathtub and a tall fluffy bed. She could feel safe here, warm, peaceful. Is wanting that life so wrong? She can see Bradwell's expression in her head as he says, *Yes, actually, it is so wrong.* She reminds herself that it doesn't matter what Bradwell thinks of her anymore. She'll probably never see him again. The thought makes her chest ache again. She wishes it didn't. She wishes she didn't care.

There is a large manila envelope on the table with PRESSIA BELZE written on it in thick dark ink. It's ominous, but she's not sure why. Instead of worrying about it, she turns her attention to the food—a bowl of bright corn kernels shining with oil, what must be oysters on the half shell, tan globs set in glistening water atop rugged white shells, and eggs. Whole white eggs, shelled, and cut in half, their yellow yolks firm but still moist. Are these the antiquities that Ingership tinkers with—those *still not quite perfected*? *So close*? They look perfect to Pressia.

The table is set for six. Pressia wonders if anyone else is expected. Ingership takes a seat at the head of the table, and his wife—whose name Pressia was never given—pulls out the side chair to Ingership's left. "Here you are," she says. Pressia sits down and his wife helps by pushing the chair in, as if Pressia is incapable. She wedges the doll head under the table.

"Lemonade?" Ingership's wife asks.

Lemons—Pressia knows what they are, but she's never had lemonade. Where would she get lemons?

Ingership nods without looking at her.

Pressia says, "Yes, please. Thank you." It's been so long since she was mannered, she's not sure if she's said the right thing or not. Her grandfather tried to teach her manners when she was little, because he said it was how he was raised. His mother had told him, "In case you have to eat with the president one day." It was as if, without a president, the argument for manners fell apart.

Ingership's wife walks to the table with a shiny metal pitcher so chilled that its sides bead with moisture, and she pours each of them a glass. The lemonade is bright yellow. Pressia wants to drink it but waits. She decides it's best to do everything that Ingership does, in the exact same order. Maybe this will make him like her more, if he thinks she's like him in some way. In the brightly lit room, the metal of Ingership's face shines like chrome. She wonders if he polishes it every night.

Ingership picks up his white cloth napkin, snaps it open, and tucks it under his chin. Pressia does, too, one-handed. Ingership pulls down the brim of his military cap. Pressia doesn't have a cap and so she smoothes her hair.

When Ingership's wife lifts the plate of oysters, he raises two fingers, and she sets two shells on his plate. Pressia does the same. Ditto one scoop of oiled corn. Ditto three eggs. His wife then says, "I hope you enjoy the food!"

"Thank you, doll," Ingership says and then looks at his wife and smiles, proud of her. His wife smiles back. "Pressia, my wife was part of the Feminine Feminists back in our youth, you know, before..."

"Ah," Pressia says, although she doesn't recognize the term *Feminine Feminists* at all.

"She was on the board, in fact. Her mother was a founder."

"Very nice," Pressia says quietly.

"I'm sure Pressia understands the struggles," Ingership says. "She will have to balance her officer status with her femininity, of course."

"We believe in real education for women," Ingership's wife says. "We believe in achievement and empowerment, but why does that have to be at odds with simple feminine virtues—beauty and grace and a dedication to home and family? Why does that mean we have to swing a briefcase and be manly?"

Pressia looks at Ingership because she isn't really sure what to say. Is his wife reciting something that was once an advertisement? There is no real education for anyone anymore. Home life and family? What's a briefcase?

"Dear, dear," Ingership says. "Let's not get political."

His wife looks at the tight stocking on her fingertips, pinches at them, and says, "Yes, yes. I'm so sorry." She gives a smile, bobs her head, and starts to walk quickly to what must be the kitchen.

"Wait," Ingership says. "Pressia is a girl after all. She might like to see a real kitchen in all of its refurbished glory. Pressia?"

Pressia hesitates. Honestly, she doesn't want to leave Ingership. She's come to rely on him for cues to proper behavior, but she has to accept the invitation. It would be rude not to. Girls and kitchens. She's disgusted, but she says, "Yes! Of course! A kitchen!"

Ingership's wife looks intensely nervous. Her face, of course, is very hard to read, hidden as it is by the stocking, but she picks at the tips of the stocking on her fingers again nervously. "Yes, yes," she says. "This will be a real treat."

Pressia stands up, puts her napkin in her chair, and pushes the chair in. She follows Ingership's wife through the swinging door.

The kitchen is spacious. A large overhead light hangs above a long thin center table. Counters are spare, tidy, recently wiped down.

"The sink. The dishwasher," Ingership's wife says and points to a large black shiny box under the counter. "The refrigerator." She points to a large box with two compartments, one big on the bottom and one small on top.

Pressia walks to each thing and says, "Very nice."

Ingership's wife walks to the sink. When Pressia is at her side, she flips a metal handle with a ball on the end, and water gushes. She whispers, "I won't put you in harm's way. Don't worry. I have a plan. I'll do my best."

"Harm's way?"

"Did he not tell you why you're here?"

Pressia shakes her head.

"Here," Ingership's wife says, and she hands Pressia a small white card with a red line down its center—bright red, like fresh blood. "I can help, but you must help save me."

"I don't understand," Pressia whispers, looking at the card.

"Keep hold of it." Ingership's wife pushes Pressia's hand. "Keep it."

Pressia takes the card and puts it deep into her pant pocket.

And then Ingership's wife turns off the faucet. "And that's how it works! Pipes and all!"

Pressia looks at her, confused.

"You're welcome!" Ingership's wife says.

"Thank you," Pressia says, but it comes out more as a question.

She leads Pressia back out of the kitchen to the dining room. Pressia takes her seat.

"It's a beautiful kitchen," Pressia says, still confused.

"Isn't it?" Ingership says.

Ingership's wife gives a small bow and disappears back in the kitchen. Pressia hears pots banging.

"I apologize," Ingership says with a laugh. "She knows better than to talk politics like she did."

Pressia hears a noise in the entranceway and glances in that direction. There is a young woman wearing a stocking much like Ingership's wife's stocking, except not as pristine and clean. She wears a dark gray dress and boxy shoes. She has a bucket and sponge and is quietly wiping down the walls, especially the spot that Ingership deemed icky.

Ingership picks up an egg half and pops it into his mouth. Pressia does too, immediately. She lets it sit in her mouth for a moment, running her tongue along the slick surface of the egg, and then chewing. The soft yolk is salted. It tastes heavenly.

"You're wondering," Ingership says, "quite naturally—how? How is this possible? The house, the barn, the food." He whirls a hand in the air, indicating everything. His fingers look surprisingly dainty.

Pressia quickly eats the rest of her eggs. She smiles, tight-lipped, with her cheeks full.

"Well, I will let you in on a little secret, Pressia Belze. And it is this: My wife and I are liaisons between here and the Dome. Do you know what that means? Liaisons?" He doesn't wait for Pressia to answer. "We're go-betweens. Bridge builders. You know it was a lost cause here before the Detonations. The Righteous Red Wave was trying very hard and I am deeply thankful for the Return of Civility. But something had to give. The others struck first; even Judas was part of God's plan. You know what I'm saying here? There were those who embraced civility and those who never could. The Detonations, in some way, we must trust, were for the greater good. There were those who were prepared and those who didn't deserve entrance. The Dome is good. It watches over us like the benevolent eye of God, and now it asks something of me and you. And we serve." He glances sharply at Pressia. "I know what you're thinking. I must have been one who, in God's great plan, didn't deserve entrance into the Dome. I was a sinner. You were a sinner. But that doesn't mean we have to continue to sin."

Pressia isn't sure what to focus on first. Ingership is a liaison who believes that the Detonations were a punishment for sin. It's what the Dome would like the survivors to believe—that they deserved all of this. She hates Ingership, but mainly because he's got power. He's dealing in dangerous ideas, throwing around God and sin to benefit the powerful because he wants to be more powerful. Bradwell would probably cuff his throat and dent his metal face by pounding it into the wall, and then give him a lecture on history. But Pressia doesn't have that option. She sits at the table and glances at the manila envelope. Is this what Ingership is leading up to? Giving her the envelope? She wishes he would just get it over with. Does the Dome want something from her? And what happens to her when she refuses? She swallows the last of her eggs. She nods as if agreeing with Ingership, but really she's thinking about the eggs. She's tasted each one, *acquired* them into her stomach.

Ingership lifts an oyster, tips it up like a tiny cup of tea, and swallows it whole. He then looks at Pressia, as if goading her, or is it a test? "A true delicacy," he says.

Pressia picks up an oyster from her plate. She feels the rough edge of the shell on her fingers and then on her bottom lip. She tilts the shell up, and the oyster glides to the back of her throat and then down. It's gone so quickly, Pressia isn't even sure what it tasted like. Her tongue holds on to a bit of brine.

"Delicious, no?" Ingership asks.

Pressia smiles and nods.

Ingership slaps his hand on the table, triumphantly. "Yes, yes," he says. "The old world in your mouth for a moment, the most satisfying pleasure left to us." And then he slips one hand into his jacket and pulls a small photograph from an inner pocket. He puts it on the table and slides it to Pressia. "Do you know where we are?"

It's a picture of Ingership and his wife. They're standing in the corner of a white room. Beside them is a man about Ingership's age in a head-to-toe contamination suit. You can see that the man is smiling behind the small window covering his face. Ingership is shaking the man's thickly gloved hand. He's holding a plaque. His gaunt face with its shiny metal and his wife in her stocking are smiling grotesquely. They're both wearing all white. Have Ingership and his wife been into the Dome? Is that what life is like there? Contamination suits, faces behind small windows? Pressia feels her stomach lurch. Is it because of the picture? Has she eaten too quickly?

She pushes the photograph across the table to Ingership. A prickle of sweat breaks out across her back. She takes a sip of lemonade. It's the wildest thing she's ever tasted—sour and sweet at once. Her tongue arches up to the roof of her mouth. She loves it.

"It was a commendation ceremony in the Dome," Ingership says. He plucks the picture up and looks at it. "It's an anteroom really. We went back through a series of sealed chamber doors."

"Do they wear suits like that all the time?"

"Oh, no! They live in a world like the one we used to live in except safe and controlled and, and, and—pure." He returns the picture to the interior pocket of his jacket then pats it warmly. "The people in the Dome are, in a very measured way, having children. They will one day want to repopulate the earth. And they need people to test, prepare, secure, and—this is key, Pressia Belze—this is fundamental—*defend*."

"Defend?"

"Defend," Ingership says. "This is why you're here." He glances over his shoulder to see if the person is still there wiping the walls. She is. Ingership snaps his fingers, and she quickly picks up her bucket and disappears down the hall. "You see, a Pure has escaped the Dome. They actually expected the break and were preparing to let him go. The Dome doesn't want to hold anyone against their will. But if he was going out, they wanted to have him wholly supervised—outfitted with ear implants so they could hear him in case he needed help and with lens implants so that they could see what he sees and, if in danger, they could bring him home."

Pressia remembers her sighting of Partridge—his pale face, his tall and lanky body and shorn head, just as the whispers had reported. She knows Ingership's explanation is off, but she can't say how exactly. "Who is this Pure?" Pressia asks. She wants to find out how much Ingership knows, or at least what he's willing to tell her. "Why were they going to all this trouble?"

"That's officer thinking, right there, Pressia. It's what I like to see. He is actually the son of someone quite important. And he escaped a little earlier than the Dome expected, before he could be put under and outfitted for his own protection."

"But why?" Pressia asks. "Why would he want to leave the Dome?"

"No one has ever done so before. But this Pure, Ripkard Crick Willux—also known as Partridge—has good reason. He is looking for his mother."

"His mother is a survivor?"

"A wretch, yes, sadly. A sinner like the rest of us." Ingership sucks down an oyster. "This is the odd thing. The Dome has new information of her survival and now believes that she's in a burrow, a sophisticated but small burrow. The Dome believes she is there against her will, held prisoner. Dome forces are trying to locate this burrow with their advanced ground-level surveillance. The Dome wants to get her out safely before the burrow is destroyed. We also do not want the Pure to be hurt in the process. And because the Pure is not properly outfitted, we need someone to be with him, to guide and protect and defend him."

"Me?"

"Yes, you. The Dome wants you to find the Pure and stay with him at all times."

"Why me?"

"This I don't know. I have a very high level of clearance. But not all. Do you know something about this boy? Some connection?"

Pressia's stomach cramps again. She isn't sure whether she should try to lie or not. She realizes that her expression might have already given her away. She's a terrible liar. "I don't think so."

"Well, that's disappointing," Ingership says. Disappointing that she isn't connected or that she may be withholding information? She doesn't know which one he means.

"But you think his mother is really alive?" Pressia is flooded with hope. She could help save Partridge's mother. He was right after all.

"Very much alive, we think."

"Who is *we*?" Pressia says. "You keep saying *we*."

"I mean the Dome, of course. We. And that definition can include you too, Pressia." He taps his fingers on the table. "We'll have to get you prepared, of course. We have the materials here to do so. Of course, this will be civilized. My wife is preparing the ether." He leans into Pressia. "Can you smell it?"

Pressia sniffs the air and notices a sickening sweetness. She gives a shallow nod, suddenly too nauseous to offer much more. She feels hot in her stomach and chest. The heat flares to her arms and legs. Ether? "Something's not right," she says. She's dizzy now. She can't help but think of the boy in the woods. It isn't logical but she wonders if she deserves this as retribution for letting him die. Is this what happens to those who witness a murder and do nothing?

"Do you feel it?" Ingership asks. "Do you feel it throughout your body?"

Pressia looks at Ingership. His face is blurred.

"I wanted you to have this pleasure before your real mission begins. A small gift. An offering."

Is Ingership's wife preparing ether to put Pressia under? She has the strange card in her pocket—white with a stripe, of fresh blood? "The food?" Pressia says weakly, not sure what the gift has been.

"We don't have much time then. I feel it too." He rubs his arms, a quick rough motion. "One more picture." This time he reaches into the outer pocket of his jacket, just above his hip. He slides the picture to Pressia.

Pressia has to squint to focus. It's her grandfather. He's lying in a bed with a white blanket. He has some kind of breathing apparatus cupped to his nose, and she can see the fan in his throat, a smudged blur of motion in the shadow of his jaw. He's smiling at the camera. His face is peaceful and looks younger than she's seen it in as long as she can remember.

"They're taking good care of him."

"Where is he?"

"The Dome, of course!"

"The Dome?" Is it possible? She sees a bouquet of flowers in a vase on a bedside table. Real flowers? Scented? Her heart lifts. Her grandfather is breathing. The fan in his throat is pulling in clear air.

"But of course, he's an insurance policy to ensure you're motivated to do your job. Do you understand?"

"My grandfather," Pressia says. If she doesn't do as she's told, someone will kill him. She runs her hand over the doll-head fist hidden under the table. She feels another wave of dizziness. She thinks of her home. Freedle. If her grandfather is gone, where is Freedle?

"But you will be protected on your mission. Special Forces will always be on hand. Unseen, but not far off."

"Special Forces?"

"Yes, you saw them already. Did you not? They've already reported to the Dome that you and El Capitan have seen them. Incredible specimens. More animal than human but perfectly controlled."

"In the woods, those superhuman creatures...from the Dome? Special Forces..." The foods that she's eaten are the antiquities that he's been tinkering with, and now Pressia knows what he meant when he said they are *still not quite perfected. So close*, as Ingership put it. *So close*. They've poisoned her.

Pressia slips her hand under the lip of her plate, grabbing the handle of her dinner knife. She has to get out of here. She stands up, hiding the knife behind her thigh. Everything wheels around her for a moment and then sways. She tries to make out the letters of her own name on the manila envelope. It must contain her orders.

"Darling!" Ingership calls to his wife. "We're feeling the effects! Our guest..."

Pressia's stomach lurches. She looks around the room and then at Ingership's face. The real flesh of it is sunken. His wife appears, shimmering in her second skin except that her mouth is covered by a green mask. She's wearing pale green latex gloves over her gloved hands. And then the floor seems to shift under Pressia's feet.

Ingership reaches for her. She pulls out the knife, points it at his stomach. "Let me out of here," she says. Maybe she can wound him enough to make it to the door.

"This isn't polite behavior, Pressia!" Ingership says. "It's not one bit polite!"

She lunges at him but loses her balance, and as he reaches for her, she slices his arm. Blood rises quickly, a red mark on his shirt.

She runs for the door, drops the knife so she can grab the knob with her good hand, but it only clicks. It won't turn. She feels sick and dizzy. She falls to her knees and vomits. She rolls to her side, clutching the doll to her chest. Ingership appears above Pressia's head, and she stares up into his face, lit by the cut glass of the brilliant ceiling-bolted light fixture behind him. What was that kind of light called? What was it?

"I invited you to try all of the food," Ingership says. "But I didn't promise you could keep it. Tell me it wasn't worth it! Tell me!"

His military cap is gone, and now Pressia sees the strange puckering of skin where it meets the metal. He teeters, his arm bleeding, then staggers and for a moment Pressia fears that Ingership is going to come crashing down on her. But he reaches for his wife, clamps his hands on the stocking of skinny upper arms. "Get me to the bucket! I'm burning, darling. I can feel it in my limbs now. I'm burning bright! Burning!"

And then Pressia remembers the word. "Chandelier," she says. A beautiful word. How could she have forgotten it? When she sees her grandfather again, she'll whisper the word in his ear.

Chandelier, chandelier, chandelier.

EL CAPITAN

CAP

EL CAPITAN HAS BEEN LEANING AGAINST one of the heavy curved edges of the broken water tower, keeping an eye out for Dusts for so long it's now dark. Sometimes he hears ripples in the sand. He tries to shoot them but there isn't enough light and they're too fleeting to hit. The blasts seem to scare them off.

He's hungry and cold. His feet are swollen from pacing with his brother on his back. Helmud is asleep and deadweight. He kicks into a snore and El Capitan leans forward and then slams back, ramming Helmud into the hardened shell of the water tower. Helmud lets out a huff of air, a moan, and then whimpers until El Capitan tells him to shut up.

How long has Pressia been gone? He can't tell. He'd call in, but the walkie-talkie is dead.

When El Capitan finally sees the black car, the plume of dust trailing behind it, he's angry more than relieved. The car snakes across the Deadlands slowly. The motion must have a purpose. Is the driver moving erratically because he's afraid of some Dust rising up? Hard to say.

Finally the car comes to a stop. It's covered in dark sand. There's crusted mud on the tires. They've been somewhere fertile? El Capitan stands up and for some reason, Helmud starts whimpering again. "Knock it off, Helmud," El Capitan says, jerking Helmud around on his back. Helmud's neck makes a popping noise, but he's not dead. His neck does that sometimes.

The driver doesn't roll down the window. El Capitan walks up and simply opens the back door. No sign of Ingership, which isn't surprising. Ingership's visits are always quick. Pressia is leaning against the far window, legs crossed, a hand covering her eyes. Under the dim light in the car's ceiling, she looks shrunken and bruised. El Capitan climbs in, giving the door a hard slam. On the seat between them sits a manila envelope with Pressia's name on it, the seal torn open. It looks like it's been battered and wrung.

"We're going back to base, right?" El Capitan asks the driver.

"Depends," the driver says. "I follow the orders that Belze gives me now."

"What? Belze?"

"Ingership says so."

El Capitan has put in all these years, and Pressia Belze takes over? After one dinner? "Ingership told you to follow Pressia's commands over mine? Jesus!"

"Jesus," Helmud echoes.

"That's right, sir."

He scoots up to the front seat and lowers his voice. "She looks like hell," El Capitan says.

"Well, she's not dead," the driver says.

El Capitan sits back. "Pressia," he says softly.

Pressia turns and squints at him. Her eyes are red-rimmed and bleary.

"You okay?"

Pressia nods. "Ingership lives in a tent like olden-day Arabs."

"Is that right?" El Capitan says.

"Right?" Helmud says.

Pressia looks out the window, lifts her doll-head fist ever so slightly, and rocks it back and forth, like the shaking of a head. Is the doll speaking for her? She looks at El Capitan as if to ask him whether he understood the gesture. He guesses that she doesn't trust the driver, doesn't want him to overhear anything.

El Capitan nods then tests. "Did you have fun, live a little high on the hog?"

"It was lovely," Pressia says, and then again she wags her doll head. El Capitan gets it. Something's happened. Something bad.

"Are these your orders?" He touches the envelope.

"Yes."

"Do I have a role?"

"They want you to assist me."

The driver says, "I need your orders, Belze. Where to?"

"I don't like your tone," El Capitan says. He thinks of punching the driver in the head but decides not to. He doesn't want to upset Pressia.

"You don't have to like my tone," the driver says.

Pressia lifts the end of the envelope, dumping its contents: a single sheet with a list of orders, a photograph of an old man resting peacefully in a hospital bed, and there's a small handheld device. El Capitan hasn't seen a working computer in ages, only dead ones. Black screens, melted plastic, a few keyboards, and parts lodged in skin. "The blip," she says to El Capitan. "We have to find that blip. Male, eighteen years of age."

El Capitan picks up the handheld. He's so used to his walkie-talkie that it seems foreign. It's sleek with a shiny, almost oily screen. The screen displays terrain as if from an aerial view. And it does, in fact, include one small blue blip. The blip pulses, moving across the screen. El Capitan touches the blue dot, and the screen suddenly blooms before him into a close-up of the area around the blue flashing dot. There are words written on the screen— 24TH STREET, CHENEY AVE., BANK OF COMMERCE AND TRADE. Didn't his mother refer to the bank as the C&T? Was that his mother's bank? He remembers lollipops in a jar with a rubber-sealed cap and a maze-like line of people hemmed in by velvet ropes. But the streets are not what they once were. The screen shows the truth, a demolished city, overlaid with a map of the old city. "I know where this is," he says. "This blue blip here."

"Yes," Pressia says.

He scans the screen for a market that's started up recently nearby. It's not there. "This isn't up to date."

"Not completely."

"You know this blip?" El Capitan asks.

"It's a Pure. He broke out of the Dome through the air-filtration system."

El Capitan wants to kill a Pure. It's a simple desire as ordinary and forceful as hunger. "And what are we going to do with the Pure? Target practice?"

"We'll use him to lead us to his mother." Pressia squints at the horizon. "In the end, we will hand the Pure and his mother over to Ingership."

"And he's going to kill them publicly?"

"He's going to give them back."

"Give them back?"

"Yes."

To the Dome. El Capitan realizes that Ingership has been working with the Dome. It's as if he's known it without admitting it to himself. Of course, he thinks. This means that OSR doesn't even really exist. El Capitan remembers what it was like looking for the guns he'd buried, his brother dying on his back, how his blood pounded desperately through his body as he looked for landmarks. The world had been stripped, obliterated. His mother already dead, buried in the cemetery outside of an asylum. No bearings. He survived that, he quickly reminds himself. He says, "I'm glad to see that Ingership has earned your allegiance and trust."

"Absolutely," Pressia says, still looking out the window. El Capitan keeps his eyes on Pressia's doll head, which rises now, just an inch off the seat, and twists back and forth. She then turns and looks El Capitan in the eyes. "He has your allegiance and trust too, I hope?"

Is the driver listening and reporting? It doesn't matter. El Capitan can't respond. He can't even nod. This isn't the way he's going to go down. There's a fire in his chest. Helmud is restless, as if El Capitan's angry heat has spread to him through their shared blood. He's back there fiddling his fingers like an old lady nervously knitting baby booties.

"Where to?" the driver says.

Pressia shouts, "We'll tell you when we tell you!" El Capitan is proud of her, relieved to see some blood in her cheeks.

He looks at the handheld again. "You have a plan?"

She nods the doll head, and then says, for effect, "We'll follow the blip."

El Capitan puts his finger on the photograph and pulls it across the seat. "Someone you know?"

"My grandfather."

"Nice setup he's got there."

"Yes."

So, they have Pressia's grandfather, their hostage. This is the way they play it. El Capitan picks up the single sheet of orders. He skims it. They're to locate the Pure, gain trust, follow him to the target, his mother, hand the target over to Special Forces, which will arrive when called via walkie-talkie. "Special Forces?"

"The creatures who stole from your traps."

El Capitan tries to take this all in. He keeps reading. They are to protect the dwelling and all objects within it—at all costs—especially pills, capsules, vials. *Anything that appears to be medicinal.* Belze is in command. El Capitan is to aid and assist. He feels sick and trapped, like the recruits out in the pens. His fists are clenched. His chest feels clenched too.

"You know where we're going?"

She nods.

"I'm only going to follow orders if you really know what your mission is."

"As Ingership says, 'The Dome is good. It watches over us like the benevolent eye of God. It's asking something of me and you. And we will serve.'"

El Capitan can't help it. He laughs. "I've looked at it wrong all these years. Huh. That was stupid of me, right? The Dome isn't evil at all. We always thought they were the enemy and we'd have to fight them one day. Didn't we, Helmud?"

Helmud doesn't say a word. Pressia looks straight out the windshield. "No, we won't fight," she says. But El Capitan keeps an eye on Pressia's doll head. She lifts its knuckled head and lets it fall. Yes. They will fight. Pressia punches the leather seat.

"Okay," El Capitan says. One thing is clear, he's got to get rid of the driver. "Why don't you get the wind in your face a little?" He's never quite heard himself speak in a tone like this, gently, calmly. "You need to make sure you've got your legs under you. Take a little walk."

Pressia looks at him a minute then nods. She gets out of the car, leaning on the door for support, struggling a minute to stand upright. She holds her head with her good hand, as if she's dizzy. Then she shuts the door. El Capitan watches her turn the corner of the fallen water tower.

"What the hell?" the driver says, swiveling in his seat.

Helmud is agitated. He starts rocking on El Capitan's back. "Hell, hell, hell," he whispers. It's a warning. El Capitan knows it. Helmud is trying to tell the driver to ease up. But he doesn't. "Belze has a mission. You interfering with that mission? I should turn you in. Ingership will—"

El Capitan reaches around and punches the driver in the throat. The driver's head slams into his window. El Capitan gets out of the car, weighted by Helmud, and in a few quick strides, he opens the driver's door, pulls the driver out by the lapels of his suit. They stagger. El Capitan head-butts him, and throws him to the ground in the glow of the headlights. Helmud's forehead smacks the back of El Capitan's skull. El Capitan kicks the driver in the ribs, walks around the driver's curled body, and kicks him in the kidneys. He slips his hand around the gun in his belt, thinks of shooting him, but decides to let him fend for himself out here in the Deadlands.

The driver writhes on the ground and coughs a spray of blood, which flecks the sand. El Capitan pats the hood of the car. He remembers his motorbike, how it was almost like flying. He gets in the driver's seat, rubs the dash, grips the wheel with both hands. He used to know all there was to know about flying planes, and he knows he'll never get to. But maybe this will feel like it, just a little.

He buzzes the window down and whistles through his teeth. "Pressia?"

Pressia reappears, looking a little stronger.

"Get in the passenger seat. The driver's feeling a little incapacitated. I'm driving."

Pressia gets in the car and shuts the door. She doesn't ask any questions. The air inside the car's cavity seems electric. El Capitan hits the gas, puts it in reverse, drives backward, and then puts the car in drive. He pulls the wheel to avoid the driver. The tires spin and then catch, and the car jolts forward with a guttural rumble that he feels in his ribs, leaving a swirl of dust that twists in its wake where a Dust quickly forms. El Capitan sees it through the rearview mirror, lit by his taillights. And as if nearly animal and drawn by the driver's blood, the Dust lunges at the driver's body, which is lost in a frenzy of sand, kicking his cap across the Deadlands.

Partridge

MOTHERS

T<small>HERE'S A SMALL RIP IN THE SEAM</small> of the dark pillowcase over Partridge's head. He glimpses small bits of his surroundings, but not enough to know where he is. He's aware that he and Bradwell are being escorted by the heavily armed women and their children—sinew of muscle, larded haunches, strong arched backs—on all sides. One woman is leading. She has an old camping-style lantern, duct-taped to a stick and held high. It bobs, casting shadows on all of them. He can see how the women with children in their upper bodies stride. Those with children in their legs lurch and sway, gaits of exerted effort and drive. And some have no children, and, next to all of the others, they seem stripped, pared down, as if whittled to some smaller version of themselves.

The birds on Bradwell's back are still. They must be reacting to Bradwell's fear—or maybe he's not afraid in these situations anymore. Maybe that's one of the upsides of being dead. Maybe the birds just know when to keep quiet.

Every once in a while, Bradwell asks where they're going, and gets no answer.

The women are silent. When the children chatter or whine, they hush them or wrestle something from a pocket and pop it into the child's mouth. Through the rip, Partridge just sees flashes of the children, peering up from legs, clasped at a waist, draped with an arm. Their eyes are oddly bright, their smiles quick. They still cough, but unlike the children in the market, not with deep rattles.

Partridge can tell that the women are leading them out of a gated community away from the melts. The earth is more rubbled, once cement and tar, and so he assumes they're heading to what was once a strip mall. He twists his head so that the rip is in front of him. In addition to the lantern, another woman holds a flashlight that she uses to light the strip mall, moving quickly among the remains. There's part of a movie marquee; two E's and an L remain and Bradwell recalls eels—the electric kind. Were they fish or snakes? The other shops are unidentifiable—gutted of anything worth salvaging. Even glass and metal have been taken away. There are a few ceiling tiles and then, miraculously, the flashlight touches deep in the shadows, lighting one fluorescent tube that's still intact.

The echo of their steps is gone. They're heading toward something large and nearly solid. He can make out one of the monstrous fallen industrial buildings, one that once held prisoners or those like Mrs. Fareling who were hauled away or those dying of viruses. They move in a pack down the length of the wreckage.

One of the women says, "This was my home for three years. Women's wing. Chamber Twelve Eighty-four. Food under the door. Lights out after prayers."

Partridge shifts his head under the hood to see who is speaking. It's one of the childless women.

"I only had one prayer," another whispers. "Save us, save us, save us."

No one speaks for a long time. They keep marching until a

woman says, "Going down." And just then the ground disappears beneath Partridge's feet and he strikes a hard step, then walks down a set of stairs.

Partridge says, "Bradwell, you still here?"

"I'm here."

"Shut up!" It's one of the children's voices.

They file down into what must be a large basement, judging by the acoustics. The temperature cools quickly. The air is damp. The atmosphere is quiet and close. Partridge is shoved into a kneeling position, his hands still bound behind his back. The pillowcase is then ripped off, and it feels good to breathe in the open air, to have his full vision. A dozen or more women, still fully armed, some with children and some without, huddle around them.

Bradwell, now hoodless too, is kneeling beside him. He looks flushed and dazed.

Partridge tucks his chin to his chest, trying to hide his unmarked face. He whispers to Bradwell, "Was this the plan?"

"I think we're close," he says.

"Really?" Partridge says. "Close to what? Death?"

The center of the basement is bare and industrial-size, the kind of basement that would exist under a building, maybe a sanatorium. But the edges are packed with a collection of ordinary objects now warped, rusted, burned—big wheels, shovels, bowling balls, ball-peen hammers. There are also rows of folded metal cot frames, iron tubs, and metal mop buckets on rollers.

A woman stands in front of them. She's holding a blond child of maybe two or three, one arm fused to the child's head, protectively. Her other arm holds an ax head attached to a baseball bat. She says, "Deaths, what were you doing in Our Good Mother's land?"

Head still bowed, Partridge glances at Bradwell.

Bradwell says, "We're on a mission, and we've lost one. We need your Good Mother's help. It's a girl. Her name is Pressia. She's sixteen. We think OSR took her, but we're not sure."

"This is ordinary," the woman says. "OSR takes at sixteen, Death." She sighs wearily.

"Well, the circumstances aren't ordinary because he isn't ordinary." Bradwell looks at Partridge.

Partridge stares back.

"Show them your face," Bradwell says.

Partridge looks at Bradwell, wide-eyed. Is he a sacrifice here? A Pure. Was this Bradwell's plan all along? He shakes his head. "No," he says to Bradwell. "What are you doing?"

"Show them your face!" Bradwell says.

He has no choice. The women are waiting. He lifts his chin. The women and their children move in closer. They stare and gape.

"Take off your shirt," the woman says.

"It's just more of the same," Partridge says as one of the women unties his hands.

"Do it."

Partridge unbuttons a few top buttons and pulls the shirt off over his head.

"He's Pure," she says.

"Exactly."

The woman with the blond child says, "Our Good Mother will be pleased. She's heard the whispers of a Pure. She'll want to keep him. What do you want in return for him?"

"I can't really be completely traded," Partridge says.

"Is he yours to trade?" the woman says to Bradwell.

"Not exactly, but I'm sure we can figure something out."

"Maybe she will settle for a piece of him," the woman says to Bradwell.

"Which piece?" Partridge says. "Jesus."

"The Pure's mother is still alive, we think. He wants to find her."

"This may also be of interest to Our Good Mother."

"Meanwhile," Bradwell says, "could you put out word to all the mothers about Pressia? She has dark hair and dark almond-shaped eyes and a doll head instead of a hand. She's petite. She has a scar curved around her left eye—a crescent—and then burns on that side of her face." As Bradwell describes Pressia, Partridge wonders if he has feelings for her. Does he like her or does he simply feel responsible? It never dawned on him that Bradwell could fall for someone, but of course he can. He's only human. For a moment, he almost likes Bradwell, feels like they might have some common ground, but then, of course, he remembers that he's offering a piece of him to strangers.

She nods to Bradwell. "I'll put out word."

Pressia

spoke

Pressia isn't sure what happened to her in the farm-house. She passed out on the floor near the front door. She woke up in the backseat of the car, flying across the Deadlands. No more information. Was she given ether? Was she put under to have her stomach pumped because she'd been poisoned? Why would Inger-ship do that to her? Maybe because he's clearly insane, and his wife is too. How else to explain why she would tell Pressia that she won't put her in harm's way while she's poisoning her?

She has a bruised cut on the back of her head as if she hit it against the floor, maybe while struggling with Ingership? She fought. She knows that much. And now, every once in a while, she feels a sharp blow of pain in the top and back of her head, a brilliant shock. She doesn't feel right in any way. She's still nau-seous, her stomach airy and sour. Her vision clumps in dense pockets of fog. Clots of ghostly flowers that bloom and fade each time she blinks. Her hearing is muted as if she's listening to every-thing through a cup pressed to a wall. The wind hasn't helped. It whips up the dust to further blur her vision, and funnels through her ears.

And now the driver is gone. No looking back. El Capitan and Helmud are all she has. He's driving fast through the Deadlands closer to the city. Dusts occasionally appear in the headlights, and he plows through them. Their bodies spray into ash, dirt, and rocks.

She pulls the tracking device from her envelope. The blip is moving through part of the Rubble Fields in a perfectly straight line and with too much speed to be moving on the uneven terrain. She remembers Bradwell telling her that he catches the rat-like beasts by waiting at the ends of the small pipes that remain intact under the rubble, pipes only big enough for vermin. So Bradwell and Partridge must have found a chip, connected it to one of the rat-like creatures, and set it loose.

"We have to go to Bradwell's place, near the Rubble Fields," Pressia says. "That's the last place I saw the Pure."

"You know him?"

"Yeah, I do."

"Why didn't you tell me before?"

"Why would I?"

"Huh." He glances at Pressia as if he's now forced to rethink his assumptions.

"Huh," Helmud says, and he glances at her too. Now she can see Helmud twisting his fingers anxiously. El Capitan jerks his shoulders and mutters, "Knock it off."

"Knock it off," Helmud says back.

"You can't kill the Pure when we find him," Pressia says. "They aren't all bad. The Pure, this one we're looking for, he's good actually. He's got a heart. He's looking for his mother. I can relate to that."

"Me too," El Capitan says, and the gentleness of his voice—sad and lonesome—surprises her.

"Me too," Helmud says.

"We can't drive through town in this car," El Capitan says. "It'll draw too much attention."

"I know where Bradwell's place is," Pressia says. "I'll go."

"You're in no shape to make the trip on foot," El Capitan says. "Plus, one of us has to stay with the car. I don't want this beautiful piece of machinery destroyed by Dusts."

"Fine," Pressia says. "I'll draw you a map."

"I know a spot where we can keep the car out of sight," he says.

After a while, he pulls up to a billboard that's fallen but now stands propped on the stand that used to hold it upright. It serves as a lean-to garage. He parks the car.

Nearby, there's a collapsed roof that once stood over a row of gas pumps. They huddle beside it, hoping to find a break from the dusty wind. There's a fallen emblem of a *B* and a *P*, locked in a green circle. It once meant something. She's not sure what.

Pressia finds a metal spoke in the dirt that may have once belonged to a motorcycle. She was never good at drawing, but she could take apart her grandfather's watch and put it back together, fix Freedle's internal mechanisms, and make the small menagerie—the caterpillar, the turtle, the row of butterflies—because she was accurate and precise. She hopes that attention to detail pays off.

In ashen dirt lit by the headlights, she starts scratching a map, first an aerial view of the city. She points to the edge of the Rubble Fields, the location of Bradwell's butcher shop, marked with an X.

When El Capitan says he's got it, she starts on the second one—the butcher shop's interior, including the cooler where he's most likely to find things they've left behind and the extra weapons. She has to trust him, but she's not sure she does. He's hateful, really. But through all of his violence and cruelty, she sees someone who wants to be good. He didn't really want to play The Game, after all. In a different world, could he be a better person? Maybe they all could be. Maybe, in the end, that's the greatest gift the Dome can offer: When you live in a place with enough safety and comfort, you can pretend you'd always make the best decision, even in the face of desperation. The awful way he treats Helmud could be seen as hiding his love for his brother, something he can't show. Helmud is all El Capitan has and there's something deeply loyal about El Capitan—erratic and hot-tempered, but loyal. And that's worth something. She wonders how he lost his parents and if he thinks of them as much as Pressia thinks of her own parents and grandfather. But El Capitan is also vicious. And this is something that Pressia lacks. Did El Capitan know that by leaving the driver in the Deadlands he'd be eaten alive by the Dusts? Pressia isn't sure. She tells herself that there's a chance that the driver survived. But this is willful. She knows it's probably not true.

El Capitan stands up. "Let's go," he says. "I got it."

"Got it," Helmud says.

He pulls the rifle off his back and hands it to her. "Stay in the car, no matter what. Shoot anything that moves."

"Will do," she says, though she's not sure that she could. She gets into the driver's seat, shuts the door.

"If you need to take off, go ahead," he says. "The keys are right there in the ignition. I'll be fine."

"Fine," Helmud says.

"I can't drive."

"Better to have the keys than not to." He rests his hand on the hood. "Be careful." El Capitan has clearly fallen in love with the car.

"I'm not going anywhere," Pressia tells him. She feels she owes him. Who else would have helped her like this? She wouldn't have made it without him. "You got me this far."

He shakes his head. "Take care of yourself, okay?" He looks toward the grim skyline of the demolished city. "I'm following this buckle," he says. "I know this one. It'll take me close to the Rubble Fields. And I'll use it to find my way back."

Pressia watches him go, but her vision is shrouded. This stretch of Deadlands is made of ash. Dust ferrets and twists across the flat terrain. It's scarred with lots of asphalt clotting the earth, proof that a highway once ran through here. The last thing she sees is Helmud. He turns and waves his long thin arm. And then, within moments, El Capitan and Helmud fade into the murky vaporous distance. She has to cut the headlights. All goes dark.

EL CAPITAN

COOLER

EL CAPITAN SLIDES DOWN THE RAMP from the stunning pen, past the vats and shelves and railed ceiling. He reaches up and grabs a hook. "Jesus," he says to Helmud, "this place is perfect."

"Perfect," Helmud says.

"We could've survived on our own here, Helmud. Do you know that?"

"Know that?"

"This Bradwell is a lucky shit," El Capitan mutters.

"Lucky shit," Helmud says.

They'd gotten here quicker than El Capitan thought. The streets were quiet. The few people he came across quickly ran from him, dipping back into dim doorways or running down alleys. If they didn't recognize Helmud and him specifically, they saw the uniform, which is usually enough.

He is still moving as fast as he can. He admits that he loves that damn car. One of the reasons he beat up the driver was that he wanted to gun the engine through the Deadlands. So yes, he wants to get back to it, but also he wants it to keep Pressia safe. If he comes back and she's gone or only parts of her remain, he isn't sure he can take it. There's something about the girl. She's good-hearted. He hasn't met someone like that in a long time—or is it that he just stopped looking?

It's strange to have someone out there, waiting for him. There are stories, legendary ones, of lovers who died for each other during the Detonations. People who, like El Capitan, knew it might be coming. They'd made escape plans, had holdout supplies and meeting places. The meeting places, though, didn't work for these lovers. One would wait for the other. Maybe, according to the plans, you were only supposed to wait so long—half an hour, forty minutes—and then move on to safer ground. But these lovers always waited too long. They waited forever. They waited until the skies turned to red ash. He heard someone sing a song about lovers like this once and never forgot it. It was strange. The guy was just standing there on the street singing.

Standing on the station platform
nothing comes here anymore.
Watch the trails of vapor rise
and settle on the floor.
I see my ascending lover
glance at her watch and smile.
She knows that I've been waiting
for a lifetime and a while.
And then the wind it lifts her
and she breezes out of here.
I'm stuck with windblown ash
that fastens to my tears.
Ash and water, ash and water makes the perfect stone.
I'll stand right here and wait forever 'til I've turned to stone.

El Capitan had been younger, on patrol, when he heard the song. One of the other soldiers said, "Jesus, shoot him already." But El Capitan said, "No. Just let him sing." He never forgot the song.

He walks into the cooler and, sure enough, there's one of the rat-like animals in a cage, just as Pressia's map promised. He thinks of stealing it. It's plump. The smell of charred meat is strong. He hears Helmud start to make clicking noises as if he's calling to the animal. "Mmmm," Helmud moans.

"Yes, yes. Mmmm. But we can't get distracted."

The problem is that El Capitan doesn't know what he's looking for. Something out of place? Not easy to do when you've never been somewhere before. There are the two unstuffed armchairs, the footlocker, the metal walls, the railings, and hooks. There's a metal bucket of burned cloth, the charred remains of a backpack, and a small metal box. He picks up the box, opens it; it makes a strange plinking noise then goes dead. He shoves it in his pocket, just in case it's important.

He dips under a hook. There's the footlocker.

Helmud starts clicking again, calling to the small caged animal.

"Shut up, Helmud!" El Capitan says.

Helmud bucks, trying to get at the caged beast, which kicks El Capitan off balance. He falls to one knee. "Damn it, Helmud. What the hell?"

But then he feels a sharp stone in his knee. He stands.

And there on the ground is a piece of jewelry. It's a broken bird with a blue gem for an eye threaded on a gold chain. Will this mean anything to Pressia? He hopes so.

He picks up the necklace and puts it in his pocket. He then runs to the crawl space that Pressia had indicated on her map. There aren't as many weapons as she'd let on. Maybe that means Bradwell and the Pure are heavily armed. He reaches in and runs his fingers along the sharp blade of a knife. He grabs what must be a stun gun. He picks them up and puts them in his jacket. He takes one last deep breath—the cooked meat—and then goes.

Partridge

TWENTY

Y OU WERE GOING TO GIVE ME to them, like I'm your property,"
Partridge says. He and Bradwell are sitting on pallets side by side
on the floor of a small room, and, like the basement they were
in before, there's a strange collection of things lining the walls,
which makes the room feel even smaller than it is. It's as if the
mothers have stripped everything of any possible value from the
Meltlands and are hoarding it.

"I wasn't going to give you to them. I was going to trade you in.
It's completely different."

"In both scenarios, I'm theirs."

"But I backed them off that idea, didn't I?" Bradwell takes off
his jacket. The wound on the meat of his shoulder is swollen but
it's stopped bleeding. He balls up the jacket, making a pillow, and
lies down on his side.

"Yeah, they're going to settle for a piece of me. That's great. A
memento. What the hell?"

"You owe Pressia your life."

"I didn't know you'd take that so literally. It's an expression
where I come from."

"That's a luxury you can afford in the Dome. Not here. Things are life and death. Daily."

"I'm going to fight," Partridge says. "It's an instinct. I can't help it. No one's going to take a piece of me without a fight."

"I wouldn't suggest it with this crowd, but you do what you have to do." Bradwell punches his jacket as if plumping a pillow and closes his eyes; in a matter of minutes, he's breathing heavily, fast asleep.

Partridge tries to sleep too. He curls up on his pallet, closes his eyes, but can only seem to concentrate on Bradwell's erratic snoring. Partridge figures that Bradwell's learned how to sleep in the worst of circumstances. Partridge, on the other hand, has always woken at the slightest noise—one of the teachers on dorm patrol, someone out after hours on the lawns, the ticking of the air-filtration system.

He dips into sleep, lightly, then drifts to the surface of wakefulness again—Bradwell, Pressia, the meat locker, here and now, the dead old woman, the Death Spree, the mothers. He sees Lyda in his mind, her face in the near darkness of the Domesticity Display, her voice counting *one, two, three*. On the dance floor, she kisses him, soft on the mouth, and he kisses her back. She pulls away, but this time, she looks at him as if taking him in, as if she knows it will be the last she sees of him, then turns and runs off. He twists on the pallet. He's awake for a moment. Where is she now? And then his mind feels blanketed with sleep, and he dreams he's a baby. His mother holds him in her arms as her wings carry them through the cold, dark air. The feathers rustle, her wings buffeting—or are they Bradwell's birds? And is it dark because it's night or because the air is filled with smoke?

And there's the voice in the dark air, *sixteen, seventeen, eighteen* . . . Lyda counting in the darkened Domesticity Display, now full of smoke. But still he runs his finger down the blade. And Lyda says, "Twenty."

Pressia

EARTH

Pressia tries to keep watch for a shift of landscape, an arching rise of dark dusty sand, funnels, ripples. The car is half hidden by the felled billboard. The keys are in the ignition. She still feels the effects of the ether, which makes her feel heavy. She dozes, then wakes with a start.

She grips the gun tightly with her one good hand. She wonders if, because her sight and hearing are dimmer, her sense of smell is already keener. The scent of rot is part of the landscape. She thinks of the pale moist eggs from Ingership's dinner, the oysters. She feels sick again and quickly closes her eyes to regain some sense of balance in her head.

With her eyes shut, the image that appears in her head is of Bradwell and Partridge eating dinner at a large dining room table. Such things are possible now that she's seen Ingership's farmhouse, but not really, not ever, not for them. She imagines Bradwell's face, his eyes, his mouth. He looks at her. He's about to say something.

She opens her eyes. It's almost dawn. A hint of pale light is edging up in the east.

She hears something hiss—the movement of sand? If a Dust appears, she'll kill it. She has to. Is it wrong to kill something that wants to kill you?

In her cloudy vision, she sees a few bits of exploded tires, the skeleton of a delivery van rusting deep brown, and way off in the distance, when the wind dies for a moment and the ash settles, she sees the rumple where the horizon meets the gray skin of sky. Somewhere back there is the farmhouse, Ingership and his wife, her skin hidden in a stocking.

She looks for El Capitan's shape to emerge from the fallen cityscape behind her. Her doll-head fist, already blackened by ash, stares at her, expectantly, as if it needs something from her. She used to talk to it when she was little, and she was sure that the doll understood her. There's no one here to see the doll head. Not even the Dome, the benevolent eye of God. God is God. She tries to imagine the crypt again, the beautiful statue behind the cracked Plexiglas. "Saint Wi," she whispers, as if it's the beginning of a prayer. And what does she want to pray for? She wants to think of one of her grandfather's stories now—not the boy shot dead, not the driver eaten by Dusts, not the Dusts that may eat her.

And then there it is, a story. There was an Italian festival every summer, her grandfather told her. There were teacups so big you could sit in them and spin, and games you could play and possibly win a goldfish in a plastic bag filled with water. The fish looked magnified when they circled the bloated plastic bags, larger and then smaller and then larger again.

The ground swirls under the backhand of the wind, and Pressia doesn't like it. She blinks instinctively, trying to clear her vision, but this only makes it cloudier. The swirl and the wind seem to be at odds with each other. And then Pressia sees a pair of eyes. Her gasp is caught in her throat. She pushes the button on the door handle to make the window buzz down. Nothing happens. She has to turn on the car itself. She grabs hold of the keys. She twists the keys back and forth. There are only some hollow clicks. She pushes the key hard and the engine comes to life, everything shivering with energy. The Dust is still roiling and churning. She pushes the button. The window retracts. The ashen wind whips in. She lifts the gun and cocks it. Her hands are shaking. She hesitates, then tries to take aim.

The Dust drops to the earth. Gone again, but not far.

Pressia is frozen. The ash whirls in the car. She's poised to shoot, but she's never fired a gun before. She isn't an officer. She's just a sixteen-year-old girl. Even if she could give the Dome what they want, what would happen to Partridge? What would happen to El Capitan and Helmud? And her grandfather? She imagines him in the hospital bed, his smile, the blurred blades of the small fan lodged in his throat. Was there a stitch of worry in his eyes? Was he warning her?

What happens here when you're no longer of use? She knows the answer to this question.

She whispers, "Forgive me," because she feels sure that she's already failed her grandfather. She sees Saint Wi in her head, her delicate features. This is her prayer. "Forgive me."

And that's the moment when she feels the sharp tug on the gun. She pulls back, refusing to let go. The arms appear next. They're strong, earthen, not human, clawed. They grab her shoulders and start to pull her from the car. She tries to hold on to the gun, but she's no longer in position to shoot it. She uses the butt of the rifle to pound the Dust's chest.

She knows that the car is her best protection. She needs to stay inside of it. But the arms keep pulling her forward. She reaches back and jams the doll-head fist through the steering wheel, but in the process the gun is ripped loose.

The Dust's arms pull her close to its body. Here she smells the rot—it's sharp and mixed with the smell of rust. The Dust wrestles her loose from the steering wheel, pulling her upper body through the window. She braces her legs.

But then she looks up, over the Dust's shoulder. A ridge of sand behind this Dust defines itself into a spine with slats of ribs built into that spine.

The Dust is too strong. Her legs give. She and the Dust fly forward. It loses its grip. She lunges for the gun, picks it up from the ground, turns over on her stomach, and shoots. The Dust falls to the ground in small pieces.

The spiny ridge moves in then. She gets to her feet and takes aim but it slides underneath her, like a shark beneath a canoe. She turns and sees the ground heave like water churned by a storm. More Dusts are stirring, rising.

One Dust to her left is the size of a wolf. Another shoots up like a geyser, twenty feet high. She turns and fires, turns again and fires, not stopping to assess the damage. She's walking backward, trying to get to the car, seal herself inside it.

Where is El Capitan? Has he followed the wrong buckle in the ground?

Another wolf-size Dust lunges and then tackles her, crushing her body across the hard-packed earth. There is no muzzle and yet she feels its hot breath on her neck, her face. She punches it with the butt of the gun, in what she thinks may be ribs. The Dust lets out a grunt.

She scrambles away.

The spiny ridge swirls up Pressia's body, kicking the gun from her hand and pressing the air from her lungs. The gun skids to the feet of the wolven Dust.

Then she hears a shout. El Capitan?

The spiny ridge rears. A knife spins through the air and slices it. It goes slack and falls to the ground. The knife, a meat cleaver, thuds into the ground.

There is El Capitan. "I made a trip to the butcher's," he says.

There are Dusts everywhere now. Helmud jerking on his back, El Capitan slashes at three twisted pillars of sand with another knife and kills all three of them swiftly—slicing into their bodies. Whatever life was left in them hisses out, and the leftover ash and dirt rain across the Deadlands' floor.

Pressia shoots Dusts as quickly as she can. El Capitan is shouting to her, but with her muffled ears and the blasts, she can't make out his words.

Another Dust is on her quickly, pinning her down. It tightens its grip around her chest. She knees and punches its trunk, but it has her in a choke hold. Her neck muscles tensing against the hold, she drops the gun and tries to wrench herself loose. She can't breathe. El Capitan is there, suddenly. He grabs the Dust by the throat. He has a stun gun, presses it to what seems to be the head, pulls the trigger. The Dust falls.

Pressia gasps for air.

El Capitan grabs her hand and presses something small and hard into it. "Take it."

She can't speak.

"Maybe it's worth something."

Another Dust is upon them now. El Capitan grabs the rifle and fires. A nearby Dust hisses away.

She looks at the pendant necklace. She recognizes it immediately. It means Bradwell brought Partridge back to the butcher shop after she was lost. They may still be together.

But why is it broken? What happened to the other half?

She looks up. The Dusts are swarming. Pressia feels something grab her waist. She kicks as hard as she can. With each blow, there's a spray of dust and ash. She claws and jabs but still feels herself being slowly pulled down by the hungry earth itself. She tries to pull herself forward and sees an army of Dusts looming in the distance. Will this Dust pull her underground and feed on her? The dread of suffocation rises in her. She doesn't want to be buried alive.

The world around her stutters in her vision. It skips and jitters. She keeps fighting but she's been poisoned, put under, beaten. She's weak and hungry and thirsty. Her vision, already clouded, gathers darkly.

From her side, she shouts El Capitan's name. He calls back to her, and through the dirt kicked up by her struggle, she can see El Capitan, fighting Dusts, with Helmud on his back. He's still on his feet, but more Dusts are moving in. He's near the car. She can see the black shine. Dusts throw El Capitan into the side of the car. He falls to the ground. They will die out here.

She whirls her arms, pounds her boots into the Dust's body. She clenches her eyes shut and thinks of the swan's blue eye. A world gone blue, and now the throb in her ears and the pulse in her neck are blue and El Capitan is blue, the car, the Dusts. She turns toward the gray hills, blue now, and she looks for her mother's face, her father's face. She's aware that it's crazy. They're gone. But still her mind wants some comfort before she dies. Home. Where is home?

The earth is pulling her in. She feels the deep growl of Dusts rumbling through her body. She opens her eyes and the Deadlands are even more dead—ash, death, and dull sand.

She keeps fighting, her fist clenched on the pendant, punching, but it does no damage. She's exhausted. The envelope with her instructions and the tracking device are gone. The picture of her grandfather—she thinks of it now in her mind's eye. It's gone too, and it's as if it never existed. Where is he? What happened to Freedle? Will she ever see them again? Are El Capitan and Helmud dead now? Is it possible that they made it to the car?

She turns toward a drumming sound to see what she's sure will be her final sight. Pounding footsteps. A blur of ash, but then the shine of a child's face, a child being held by her mother. It's as if they are a lost vision of her very own mother and Pressia herself as a little girl, as if her mother has not been blown to bits through a plate-glass window.

"Pressia," her mother says. "Grab hold!"

There is a hand.

And then a pinhole is all that's left of her vision, and then that too is black.

Pressia

SACRIFICE

Pressia wakes up, her cheek set on something hard. Her head throbs. She sees a tire, its tread worn thin. But it isn't the tire of the long black car. She's in a room and the tire is miniature. It's connected to a motor with blades. A lawn mower? She wonders if she's dreaming, if this is some kind of afterlife. A basement devoted to lawn care? That's an afterlife?

She tries to sit up.

There are voices all around her, whispering. One speaks up nearby. "Wait." It's a woman's voice. "Take your time."

She rests again, lying on her side. She remembers the Dusts. El Capitan shooting his gun. The mother and child. She closes her eyes. "El Capitan and Helmud," she says.

"The two men in the car? Friends of yours?"

"Are they dead?"

"We were there for you, not them. Their life or death is of no consequence to us."

"Where am I?" She looks around and sees faces—women, children, a rotation as if she's in one of the teacup rides that her grandfather told her about. Their children are fused to their mothers' bodies. She stares at one and then the next.

"You're here. With Our Good Mother."

Mother? She doesn't have a mother. The room is cold and damp. She shivers. Bodies shift around her, and beyond the bodies, there are stacked boxes, melted toys, a row of distorted metal mailboxes, a half-melted tricycle.

Pressia pushes herself up. A woman takes Pressia's elbow and helps her sit upright on her knees. The woman holds a blond child of maybe two or three, one arm fused to the child's head, protectively. "This is Our Good Mother," the woman says, pointing straight ahead. "Bow to her."

Pressia looks up and sees a woman seated on a plain wooden chair, reinforced with plastic rope. She has a simple face, small and delicate, a mosaic of glass. There's only one light hitting her, and it makes the glass shimmer. Her pale skin has almost completely grown over the pearls around her neck. They look like a strand of perfectly shaped tumors. She's wearing a thin, almost gauzy shirt. Through it, Pressia sees the outline of a giant metal cross embedded in her stomach, chest, even up into the center of her throat, pushing back her shoulders. It forces her to sit erectly. She wears a long skirt and is armed with a simple cast-iron fire poker. It lies across her knees.

Pressia lowers her head, bowing, and stays that way, waiting for Our Good Mother to tell her when it's enough. At Our Good Mother's feet, there are Bradwell's weapons neatly arranged. This means he may be here. He's tied up in all of this somehow. Does this mean that after she disappeared, he tried to look for her? What about Partridge? Her heart starts beating hard in her chest. She's briefly flooded with hope until she realizes that this arrangement of weapons also means that Bradwell has been disarmed, maybe even shot and killed.

Did they leave the necklace for her to find? Are they gone?

The necklace. Where is it now?

The blood has rushed to Pressia's head, and she feels dizzy. Still, she doesn't move. She waits for the woman with the fire poker to say something, and finally she does. "Rise up." Pressia lifts her head. "You want to know," Our Good Mother continues, "as they all do, why a cross? Was I a nun? Devout? Fused in prayer? How?"

Pressia shakes her head. Her brain hasn't even gotten this far yet. The woman is talking about the cross in her chest? "It's none of my business," she says.

"Our stories are what we have," Our Good Mother says. "Our stories preserve us. We give them to one another. Our stories have value. Do you understand?"

This reminds Pressia of the first time she heard Bradwell speak in the basement, the idea of preserving the past. Bradwell—she can't imagine what it would feel like if she finds out he's dead. Our Good Mother is staring at her. She asked Pressia a question. Pressia can't remember what it was. She nods. Is this the right response?

"I will give you my story as a gift. I stood at a window, metal-framed," Our Good Mother says, running her finger over the fabric of her shirt along the metal cross lodged in her sternum. "With my face poised there, staring at the shuddering sky, one hand pressed to the glass." She holds out her hand, crusted with glass. "Can you see my near death in your head?"

Pressia nods. Her mother was killed in a rain of glass. "The weapons," Pressia says, pointing at them on the floor.

"Gifts," Mother says, "from the Death who brought us the Pure, who is also a Death. All men are Deaths to us. Surely, you know that."

Does this mean that they're alive or dead? Do these women kill all men they come across? Is that why they call them Deaths?

Then there's a commotion behind Pressia. She turns.

Partridge and Bradwell are being shoved into the room. They're here. They're still alive. Their hearts beating in their chests, their breath working their lungs. She's so relieved she feels like she might cry.

"Down, Deaths! Down before Our Good Mother!" the women shout.

Partridge and Bradwell kneel on either side of Pressia. They both look worse for wear. Their eyes wrung out, their clothes ratty and ashen. But still Bradwell smiles. His eyes shine. He's happy to see her and this warms Pressia's chest, her cheeks.

"Pressia," Partridge whispers. "They found you!"

So she hasn't been captured; she's been found? Have they been looking for her all this time? She was so sure that they would have parted ways. Partridge would have continued on his quest to find his mother, and Bradwell would have cut ties. He's survived because he hasn't let other people weigh him down. So what does it mean that he's come looking for her?

Our Good Mother claps her hands, and all the women and children bow and retreat out the door and up the stairs. Only one remains, the one with the spear-like broom. She stands at the door.

"We thought your two Deaths here were part of a Death Spree," Our Good Mother says to Pressia. "We don't take part in the sport, but when they occasionally intrude, we kill as many as we can before they disperse." She fits her small fingers into the handle of the poker.

"I'm glad you didn't kill them," Pressia says. This gives her hope that El Capitan and Helmud survived somehow. There's a chance.

"I am too. They're on a mission." Our Good Mother stands awkwardly; the rod of the windowpane fused to the center of her chest makes it necessary for her to pull herself up, using the arms of the chair. She walks stiffly. "We have helped them in that mission, in part because you are a female. We believe in saving our fellow sisters. But there's more. Something about finding the Pure's mother." She paces the room in a slow circle. "A Pure is of value to me," Our Good Mother says. "Sentimental value, if nothing else." She nods to the remaining woman, a guard really, who then walks to Partridge, points the tip of her broom-spear at his throat. "It seems to me that this isn't an ordinary quest, and that even this Pure is not an ordinary Pure. Who are you? Who are your people?"

Partridge looks at Bradwell, wide-eyed. Pressia knows what he's thinking—should he say his father's name? Will this spare his life? Or only make him more of a target?

Bradwell nods, but Partridge doesn't seem to trust the nod. Pressia wonders what's happened between them since she's been gone. Partridge doesn't move his head, but he looks over at Pressia. He swallows, the spear tip poised at his Adam's apple.

"Ripkard Willux. I go by Partridge."

Our Good Mother smiles and bobs her head. "Well, well, well." She turns to Pressia. "Do you see how he hasn't been forthright? He holds on to information, doesn't he? He has things to say that he isn't. Deaths do this. They can't be honest."

"I'm not withholding anything," Partridge says.

"Deaths do not speak to Our Good Mother unless addressed!" the woman with the broom-spear says and she thwacks him across the back.

Our Good Mother speaks only to Pressia now. "The Detonations hit and many of us were here, alone, in our houses or trapped in our cars. Some were drawn to the yards to see the sky or, like me, to windows. We grabbed our children to our chests. The children we could gather. And there were those of us who were imprisoned, dying. We were all left to die. We were the ones who tended the dying. We wrapped the dead. We buried our children and when there were too many to bury, we built pyres and burned the bodies of our own children. Deaths, they did this to all of us. We used to call them Father or Husband or Mister. We're the ones who saw their darkest sins. While we banged the shutters of our homes like trapped birds and beat our heads on prison walls, we watched them. We alone know how much they hated themselves, how shamed they were, their weakness, selfishness, their loathing, and how they turned that on us at first—and their own children—and then the world at once." She sits again in her chair. "They left us to die and we are forced to carry our children, our children who will never outgrow us, and we will do this forever. Our burden is our love."

The room is quiet. Pressia wonders for a moment what happened to Our Good Mother's child or perhaps children. She seems not to have one fused to her at all, only the metal cross, the glass of the panes. Were her children's bodies burned in pyres?

"Where did you go when you disappeared?" Our Good Mother asks.

"OSR captured me and put me in officer training. At first, I didn't know why. I went to an outpost, a farmhouse. An officer and his wife live out there and work for the Dome. They have crops of food."

"Inedible," Our Good Mother says. "We know of this. We've made it that far though not much farther. We watch."

"They have my grandfather. He's in the Dome. Hostage, I guess. I'm on a mission to get the Pure and his mother to Ingership. There are Special Forces out here, this wild superspecies. That's who we're supposed to hand Partridge and his mother over to."

"Special Forces? Outside the Dome?" Partridge says.

"The orders are to look for something medicinal when we find your mother," Pressia says. "They think she's in a bunker of some kind."

"If the Dome thinks she's here, that's a good sign, right?" Partridge says.

"It means we have to find her before they do," Bradwell says. "We've got competition."

"My mother and I can't go back. We can never go back."

"We can help," Our Good Mother says. "It's not my habit to talk to Deaths, but I must. There is a matter of payment. See, we found the girl, and if you want to make it out of the Meltlands alive to find your mother, you'll likely need our protection."

Pressia looks at Bradwell. Is it true that they need the mothers? He nods.

"I don't know if we have anything worthwhile to give," Pressia says.

Our Good Mother looks down at all the weapons. "Where did you get these?"

"A butcher shop," Bradwell says.

"Are you a butcher?"

"No. I found the shop when I was a kid, just after the Detonations."

"Do you want weapons as payment?" Pressia asks.

Our Good Mother looks at her and smiles. "I have all the weapons a girl could want." She holds out her hand. "Give me one to hold."

Pressia reaches down and lifts one of the knives, handle-first, and bows.

"Were you with your mother in the end?" she asks Pressia.

"Yes."

"Loss is loss is loss," she says, touching the blade. "You understand it or you don't."

"What kind of payment are you looking for exactly?" Pressia says.

Our Good Mother leans forward and speaks to Partridge directly. "We were watching you for some time before my women moved in. Do you know how many could have killed you by now and in how many different ways?"

He shakes his head.

"If you want to find your mother, you will need our help. The matter is whether or not you're willing to sacrifice for your goal."

Partridge looks at Bradwell and Pressia.

"It's your call," Bradwell says softly.

Our Good Mother points the knife at Partridge. "This is the way I see it. You have been here long enough, haven't you?"

"Long enough for what?" Partridge asks.

"To no longer be Pure."

"I don't know what you mean," he says. Pressia thinks of scars, burns, marks, fusing, and then, looking at the knife, amputations.

"Purity is a burden," Our Good Mother says. "That's what we've found. When you are no longer Pure, when you no longer have that to protect, you're free of it."

Partridge shakes his head violently back and forth. "I don't mind the burden."

"I would like my payment to also be a gift to you. I can end your Purity. You will never truly understand, but I can make you one of us, in some small measure." She smiles at him.

Partridge reaches for Pressia. "Tell her it's not necessary. We can think of some other kind of payment. I'm Willux's son. That could be useful, right? A direct line?"

"You're not in the Dome anymore," Our Good Mother says.

Pressia says, "No, we can think of something else."

Our Good Mother shakes her head.

Bradwell says, softly, calmly, "What are we talking about here?"

"Just a token," Our Good Mother says.

"What?" Bradwell says. "A finger?"

Pressia's stomach tightens to a knot. No more blood. No more loss, she says to herself. No.

"A pinky," Our Good Mother says, holding the handle of the knife with both hands. She looks at Partridge. "The women can hold you down."

Pressia feels wild, like there's an animal in her ribs clawing to get out. She can only imagine how Partridge feels. He looks at her desperately. Bradwell is the only one who seems to know that there's no way around this. He says, "It's a gift. You're getting off light. A pinky, that's all."

Partridge says, "I don't need a gift. I'm thankful for what I have. I'm glad that Pressia's back. That's enough of a gift right there."

Pressia wants to tell Our Good Mother to take something from her, but she knows that this would infuriate her. Our Good Mother hates Deaths. She would despise Pressia for any act of self-sacrifice. Then Pressia thinks: Shouldn't he pay? It's his mother after all. He came out here to find her, and what did he expect?

"They'll send us out with no protection," Bradwell says. "We'll never find your mother because we'll be dead."

Partridge is frozen, blanched. He's breathing hard.

Pressia looks at him. She states the plain truth. "We'll die."

Partridge stares at his hand. He looks at Bradwell. He's already put Bradwell's and Pressia's lives in danger. This is the least he can do, and he seems to know it. He walks to Our Good Mother and puts his hand on the table. "Hold it down," he says to Bradwell. "So I don't jerk away."

Bradwell holds Partridge's wrist so tightly that Pressia sees the whites of Bradwell's knuckles. Partridge presses his fingers together, exposing the pinky, alone.

Our Good Mother places the tip of the knife on one side of Partridge's pinky, raises the back of the knife, and in one swift motion lowers the back of the blade on Partridge's pinky, right at the middle knuckle. The sound—almost a pop—makes Pressia gasp.

Partridge doesn't scream. It happens too quickly. He stares at his hand, the fast-pooling blood, half of his pinky, disconnected. It must be oddly numb for a moment because his face is blank. But then his face contorts as the pain rushes in. He looks up at the ceiling.

Our Good Mother hands Bradwell a rag and a leather band. "Wrap it tight. Apply pressure. Keep it elevated."

Bradwell ratchets the leather band around Partridge's finger. He holds it in his fist, and then he presses the bright bloody rag to Partridge's heart. A bouquet. That's what Pressia thinks of—red roses, the kind of thing you'd see in one of Bradwell's old magazines.

Our Good Mother picks up the other half of his pinky, holds it in her cupped hand. "Take him back to your room. Women are waiting on the other side of the door to escort you."

"There's one more thing," Bradwell says.

"What is it?" Our Good Mother says.

"The chip in Pressia's neck," Bradwell says. "It's alive."

"No it isn't," Pressia says.

"Yes, it is," Bradwell says, emphatically.

"None of our chips are live. Who would ever care about us, stumbling around out here with nothing?"

"For whatever reason, they were herding you and Partridge together. It's obvious to me now," Bradwell says to Pressia. He turns to Our Good Mother. "Are there any doctors or nurses here? Someone skilled?"

Our Good Mother walks around Pressia and stops at her back. She takes a handful of Pressia's hair and lifts it, baring her neck. She touches a scar on the back of Pressia's neck, an old, dulled knot. Pressia feels a chill run down her spine. She doesn't want anyone cutting into her neck. Our Good Mother says, matter-of-factly, "You'll need a knife, alcohol, clean rags. I'll have it all delivered. You'll do it yourself, Death."

"No," Pressia says to Bradwell. "Tell her you won't do it."

Bradwell looks at his hands. He shakes his head. "The chip is in her neck. It's dangerous."

"You're a good butcher," Our Good Mother says.

"Actually, I'm not a butcher at all."

"You won't make a mistake."

"How can you be so sure?" Bradwell says.

"Because if you do, I'll kill you. It would be my pleasure."

This isn't comforting to Pressia. Bradwell looks even more nervous. He rubs the scars on his cheek.

"Go on," Our Good Mother says.

The woman with the broom-spear walks them to the door. Partridge looks a little loose in his knees, and Pressia isn't exactly steady herself. The woman opens the door, and before Pressia walks through it she looks back at Our Good Mother, who cradles one of her arms with the other arm, tilts her head, gazing at her left bicep. Pressia follows Our Good Mother's gaze, and there she sees the gauzy material of the shirt draw in and puff out—all that is left of her child, just an infant, the purpled lips, the dark mouth embedded in her upper arm, still alive, breathing.

PRESSIA

FAIRY TALE

THEY'RE ESCORTED TO A SMALL ROOM with two pallets on the floor. The woman locks the door behind them. Partridge slides down the wall to sit on his pallet. He holds the wounded hand to his chest.

Pressia can't sit down. Her head is ringing now. She has to have the chip removed by someone who isn't even a butcher? "I can't believe you think you're taking the chip out of my neck," she says to Bradwell. "You aren't. You know that, right? You're not even coming close."

"They know where you are at all times. Is that what you want? You love the Dome so much, I guess I shouldn't be surprised that you'd like to be their puppet."

"I'm not their puppet! You're paranoid. Crazy!"

"Crazy enough to come looking for you."

"I didn't ask you to do me any favors."

"Your grandfather did, though, and I've made good on that now."

Pressia feels like she's had the wind punched out of her. Is that why Bradwell came looking for her? Because he owed her grandfather a favor for stitching up his cheek? "Well, consider the debt paid off. I never asked to be anybody's burden."

"That's not what I meant," Bradwell says. "Let me start over."

"Quiet!" Partridge says. "Just shut up!" He's sitting there pale and shaken.

"I'm sorry about your finger," Pressia says.

"We've all made sacrifices," Bradwell says. "It was time he made one too."

"Nice," Pressia says. She hates Bradwell right now. He found her because he owed a favor. Nothing more. Why did he have to rub it in her face? "Really understanding."

"It's funny to see you in an OSR uniform," Bradwell says. "Look at those armbands. Are you an officer now? That's a really nice group of people. *They* are the ones who are really understanding!"

"I was abducted and they made me wear this uniform," Pressia says. "Do you think I like it?" Her voice is weak because she does like the uniform, and Bradwell probably knows it.

"Stop," Partridge says. "Bradwell's right, Pressia. They herded us to find each other. Who knows how long they've known where you are? The question is why you?"

Pressia sits down next to Partridge. "It makes no sense," she says. "I don't get it."

"One thing sticks with me from what Our Good Mother said." Bradwell crouches down and stares at Partridge. "You're holding something back. You're not being honest."

"What am I holding back?" Partridge says. "I've told you everything. I just had my finger cut off. Why don't you ease up?"

Pressia remembers the necklace. She checks her pockets and, in one of them, she feels the hard outline of the swan pendant, the edges of its wings. Did she have time to secure it before passing out? Did someone find it in her fist and put it in her pocket? She's relieved that she still has it. She fishes it out and holds it in her palm. "Did you two leave this for me? As a sign?"

Partridge nods. "You found it."

She recalls playing I Remember with Partridge, exchanging memories. She told him about the birthday pony, and he told her about a bedtime story, a bad king and a swan wife. A swan wife—like the swan pendant with its blue eye. Pressia looks at Bradwell. "Maybe it's not that he's holding back. It's just that he doesn't know what's important."

"And what is important?" Bradwell asks. "I'd love to know."

"What about the swan wife?" Pressia says to Partridge. "Tell me the story."

———

Partridge hasn't told the story of the swan wife aloud since that one time when he tried to tell it to his brother, Sedge, after the Detonations. Back then he could still remember his mother's laugh, but over time the air in the Dome was so empty, so vacant, that he felt like the smells and tastes and even memories were being eaten by a hollow pocket of air in his own head. Aribelle Cording Willux—all of the small traces of his mother were slowly disappearing. He knew it. Even only a week after the Detonations, he'd started to forget the sound of her voice. But now he's sure that if he could hear it, just one note of it, it would all come rushing back.

"The story goes like this." He starts to tell the story that he's been telling himself, alone, for years. "Before she was a swan wife, she was a swan maiden who saved a young man from drowning, and he stole her wings. He was a young prince. A bad prince. He forced her to marry him. He became a bad king.

"The king thought he was good, but he was wrong.

"There was a good king, too. He lived in another land. The swan wife doesn't yet know he exists.

"The bad king gave her two sons. One was like the father in that he was ambitious and strong. One was like her."

Partridge feels restless, and although he's weak, he has to get up and walk. He's barely aware of himself. He's touching things with his uninjured hand—the handle of a wheelbarrow, grooves and cracks in the cement-block walls. He stops and asks Pressia for the necklace. He holds it, just like his mother had told him to when she was telling him the story. He feels the sharp edges of the swan's wings. He goes on.

"The bad king put the swan wife's wings in a bucket down a dark old dry well, and the boy who was like the swan wife heard ruffling down that well. One night the boy climbed down the well and found the wings for his mother. She put them on, and she took the boy she could—the one like her who didn't resist her— and flew away."

But then he stops again. He feels light-headed.

"What is it?" Pressia asks.

"Keep going," Bradwell says. "Come on."

"He needs time," Pressia says, "to remember it."

But it's not that he's stuck. No. He remembers the story perfectly. The reason he stops is that he can almost feel his mother. The story released in the air also releases some part of her. He stops so that he can take it in and then it's gone. In these brief moments, he can remember what it was like to be a little boy. He remembers his boyish arms and his restless legs. He remembers the nubs of the blue blanket that they sat under at the beach house, the feeling of the swan pendant in his fist, like a big sharp tooth.

"The swan wife became a winged messenger. She took her one son with her to the land of a good king. She told him of the bad king's plan to take over the good king's land, that he would make fire roll down from the mountaintops to destroy everyone in its path. All of the good king's people would be destroyed in a ball of fire, and this new land—purified by fire—would belong to the bad king.

"The good king fell in love with the swan wife. He didn't force her to shed her wings. Here, she could be both maiden and swan. And because of this, she fell in love with him. He gave her a daughter—as beautiful as the swan wife, a gift.

"And he built a great lake to put out the fire as it rolls down the mountain. But because he was distracted by his love for her, the waters weren't ready when the fires came."

He starts to feel sick. His heart is kicking in his chest. He feels like he can't quite catch his breath, but he's trying to speak calmly. He knows that the story means something. Why hasn't he told them about the beach and the pills? He knows what it all means, doesn't he? His mother used to give them rhymed riddles so that they could have clues to where she'd hidden their birthday presents, hadn't she? His father had started the tradition while they were dating, while they were in love. The family liked riddles. What does this one mean?

"And so when the fire rolled down the mountain, the swan wife sought safety for her children. She carried her two children back to the bad king's land.

"She placed her daughter—whom no one knew—into the hands of a barren woman to raise.

"She returned her son to his crib—because he would always be treated like a prince.

"And then it was time for her to fly off to join the good king— because the bad king would kill her. But as she crawled away from her son, he reached for her and grabbed her feet with his hands, sooty from the fire. He would not let her go until she made a promise not to fly away. 'Burrow underground,' he begged her, 'so you can always be watching.'

"She agreed. She said, 'I'll make trails for you to find me. Many, many trails. All leading to me. You'll follow them when you're old enough.'

"She left her wings and crawled into the earth itself.

"And it was because of the boy's sooty hands that the swan has black feet."

His mother was a saint.

He likes this version of things.

His mother died a saint—except that now he knows she survived. He knew it by the way his father said, *Your mother has always been problematic*. He knew it by the way the old woman who was killed in the Death Spree said, *He broke her heart*. He knows it now.

The swan is not just a swan.

It's a sealed locket—*my phoenix*.

He says again, "She returns her son to his crib—because he will always be treated like a prince."

What were the little blue pills? Why did she force him to take them even when he was sure they only made him sicker? *No more pills*, he remembers crying. *No, please*. But she wouldn't stop. They had to take them every three hours. She would wake him up in the middle of the night. Why would she give him pills that would make him resistant? Did she want to save him? Did she know that, one day, he would have the chance to become a better version of himself—part of the superspecies—and did she want to render him useless? How did the pills make him resistant to changes in his behavioral coding? Why that and only that?

If she wasn't a saint, what was she?

A traitor?

He says again, "And that is why the swan wife has black feet," but this time it feels like a question.

———

Pressia isn't quite sure that she understands what she's heard. A fairy tale. That's all. Was she looking for more? No. It's meaningless.

Partridge looks at Bradwell. "You're thinking something about my mother."

"Aribelle Cording Willux," Bradwell says, as if he's a little amazed by the name itself.

"Just say it," Partridge shouts.

"Say what?" Bradwell says, and Pressia can tell that Partridge is right. Bradwell is the one holding back, as Our Good Mother would say. Not Partridge.

"You know something," Pressia says. "Are you going to lord it over us? Make us beg?"

Bradwell shakes his head. "The swan with black feet, it's a Japanese fairy tale. I was raised by a scholar of this kind of stuff. And that's not the way the old story goes. There is no second king. There is no third child—a beautiful daughter. There is no fire rolling down the mountain. And at the end, the swan is supposed to use her wings to fly away. Not underground."

"So?" Partridge says.

"So it's not just a little bedtime story. Your mother was giving you a coded message. You're supposed to figure it out."

Pressia feels tingling in the skin of the doll's head. She rubs it with her good hand to soothe the nerves. She wants to know what this story means, but she's afraid of it too. Why? She's not sure.

"I don't get it," Partridge says, but there's something about the story that Pressia feels deeply. The story is about separation and loss.

"But you *do* get it," Bradwell says flatly.

Pressia remembers what Partridge told her about the story. She says, "You thought your father was the bad king who stole her wings—you said so yourself." Her head feels heavy. Her heart is racing. That's not all of it. She can tell it's only the surface.

"I thought there was a reason she liked the story, on a personal level," Partridge says. "My parents didn't get along."

"And?" Bradwell says.

"You tell me," Partridge says. "You seem to have already figured it all out, as usual."

"She had two sons," Bradwell says quickly. "Then she took you to Japan as a baby, and she fell in love with the good king and had a baby. Who is the good king exactly? I don't know. But he was powerful. He had information."

Pressia glances at Partridge, whose body looks rigid—with fear or anger? Bradwell seems agitated, maybe even charged by all that he's heard. He looks at Pressia, then Partridge, and back again. She's supposed to know what's going through his mind. She doesn't. Why does he seem almost excited?

"Come on, Pressia," Bradwell says almost pleadingly. "You're not still just some little girl embarrassed by a doll. You already understand. You already know."

"A little girl? I thought I was a type or, better yet, just some debt you had to pay off." She touches the doll. "I don't need you to tell me who I am." But as she says it, she wonders if she still is a little girl in some ways. Just a few days ago, she was going to live her life in a cabinet in the back room of a barbershop. She was willing to retreat and live through clippings in magazines and dream of the Before and the Dome.

"You were never a type or a debt. Hear me out."

"Just stick to the story," Pressia says.

"Tell us what you really think," Partridge says.

"Okay," Bradwell says. "Here's my take. The man your mother had a child with, he was in on everything that the Japanese were doing—or trying to undo. Radiation resistance. Your mother fed him information. I agree with your mother's decision there. Some of the Japanese were really the good guys, if you ask me. My parents were on that side of things too." He pauses for a moment. "I barely remember my parents' faces." He looks at Partridge. "Why didn't you get more coding? Why weren't you a ripe specimen?"

"They tried to give me more coding. I was resistant. It didn't take," Partridge says flatly.

"How did your daddy react to that?"

"Don't call him that."

"I bet he went nuts," Bradwell says.

"Look, I hate my father more than anyone. I'm his son. I can hate him in a way that no one else can."

The room goes quiet.

Partridge says, "I hate my father's condescension, his reserve. I hate that I've never really seen him laugh loudly or cry. I hate his hypocrisy. I hate his head—the constant little shake of it, like he's always disapproving of me. I hate the way he looks at me like I'm worthless." Partridge glances around the room. "So was he happy that my body was rejecting coding? No. He wasn't."

"Because?" Bradwell says.

"Because he thinks my mother had something to do with it."

"He underestimated her," Bradwell says. "I think she knew all about Operation Phoenix and so did the person who gave her the pendant. That person had made Phoenix into a pet name, maybe reclaiming it somehow. She had to know what her husband and his people had in mind—mass destruction, Dome survival, and then eventually, after the earth regenerated enough, the emergence of his superspecies. And maybe she told the other side what he was up to. *The swan wife became a winged messenger*, right? They tried to put a stop to the plan, save some people. But at a certain point she knew they'd run out of time...I don't think Willux would care if she's alive or not—he left her for dead once already. Does he regret not killing her off? Is that all it is—revenge? Is he willing to use his only son just to make sure his wife is dead? Or does her survival mean that she knows something, a piece of information that he wants."

"You don't know him," Partridge says, but his voice is so soft that it has the tone of surrender.

Bradwell stares at the floor and shakes his head. "Look at what he's done to us, Partridge. We're the ones who can hate him in a way you can't."

Pressia looks at the doll-head fist, a reminder of a childhood she never really had. "What does this have to do with me?" She can't think clearly. Her head pounds. She knows that her life is about to shift, but she doesn't know how. She stares at the doll's fringe of plastic lashes, the small hole in its lips. Her cheeks burn. Everyone around her knows something. They don't want to say it. Doesn't she already know it herself? It's all there, in the bedtime story, but she can't see it. "Why did the OSR and the Dome want me to find Partridge? How did they even know I exist?"

Partridge sticks his hands in his pockets and looks at the floor. Has he already put something together, too? Maybe he's smarter than Bradwell's given him credit for.

"You're the little girl," Bradwell says. "In the fairy tale. You're the baby from the good king."

Pressia looks at Partridge sharply.

"You and Partridge," Bradwell whispers.

"You're my half brother?" Pressia says. "My mother and your mother..."

"Are the same person," Partridge says.

Pressia hears the sound of her own heart. That's all.

Pressia's mother is the swan wife. She may be alive.

PRESSIA

CHIP

PRESSIA CAN ONLY THINK OF ALL the things that may no longer be true—the entire childhood her grandfather invented. Is her grandfather even her grandfather? The giant mouse with white gloves at Disney World, the pony at her birthday party, ice cream cake, the teacup ride, the goldfish at the Italian festival, her parents' church wedding, the reception under a white tent. Was any of it true?

But she remembers a fish. It isn't the one from her grandfather's stories pressed into her memory. Not the fish in the plastic bag won at the Italian festival. No. There was a fish tank and a pocketbook tassel, and a heating duct under a table that seemed to purr. She was wrapped in her father's coat. She sat on his shoulders, dipping under flowering tree limbs. She knows it was her father. But the woman whose hair she brushed, who smelled sweet, was that her mother? Or was her mother the woman on the handheld recorder, the one singing about the girl on the porch and the boy who wants her to run off with him? Is that why it was a recording—because she couldn't be there? Because she had to return to her real family, her legitimate sons? Someone played that song for her dutifully, even when Pressia had grown tired of it. *A barren woman*, that's how Partridge put it in the story of the swan wife.

Those things were never a story. They're real. The song is in her head—into the Promised Land and the talking guitar and how he's going to spirit the girl away in his car.

The locks on the door unlatch from the outside, and the door swings open. It's the woman with the broom-spear. She has alcohol in a large bottle and a stack of neatly folded rags, gauze, another leather band like the one used to stop the bleeding of Partridge's amputated pinky, and something else—probably a knife—bundled in cloth. Bradwell takes them, and, without a word, the woman leaves, locking the door again with a series of clicks. Pressia closes her eyes for a moment, trying to steel herself.

"Are you going to be okay with this?" Bradwell asks Pressia.

"I wish someone else could do it. I don't want any more favors from you."

"Pressia," Bradwell says, "your grandfather isn't the reason I came looking for you. I just blurted that out. I don't know why. But it's not the whole story—"

She cuts him off. "Let's get it over with." She doesn't want to hear any more stories right now, especially not any in which Bradwell tries to redeem himself.

She lies on the floor, on her stomach, tucking her OSR jacket under her head. The bell she'd taken from the barbershop is still in the jacket pocket, forming a hollow pocket of air. She'd forgotten about it and now she's glad it's here—a reminder of how far she's come. She tucks the doll head under her chin. She closes her eyes, smells the floor—dirt, a smoky dust, faint traces of oil. Bradwell sweeps her hair to either side, exposing the back of her neck. His touch surprises her—it's so light, it's almost feathery.

Bradwell keeps saying, "It's okay. I'll be careful."

"Stop talking," she tells him. "Just do it."

"Is that what you're going to use? Jesus," Partridge says. She pictures all of Bradwell's butchery knives. "Did you put the alcohol on yet?" Partridge sighs. "You've got to keep it clean!" Is this what an older brother is like? Pressia wonders. Hovering around? Overprotective?

"Out of my light," Bradwell says.

"I don't want to watch," Partridge says. "Trust me."

She hears Partridge walk to the edge of the cramped room. He's shuffling nearby. He's processing all of this too, she figures. It changes who his mother is, doesn't it? Does a saint have an affair and a child by another man? She wonders how he's doing with this new version of his mother. It's easier to think of him than herself right now, but those thoughts barrel at her too. Why didn't her grandfather tell her the truth? Why did he lie to her all these years? But at the same time, she knows the answer. He probably found this little girl, and he took her in.

If she and Partridge have the same mother, and Partridge is white, then her mother has to be white—her mother, who went to Japan, who became a traitor, a spy? Her mother is the woman in the photograph on the beach and the same woman on the handheld computer screen, singing her a lullaby. Did she record it because she knew she was leaving her daughter? The photograph—her mother's hair kicked around by the wind, sunburned cheeks, a smile that seemed as happy as it did sad. Who then is the mother she's always imagined—the young and beautiful Japanese woman who died in the airport?

Her father has to be Japanese—the good king in the fairy tale—and so who is the young man that she's imagined as her father—the guy with the light hair whose feet pointed inward but played football on the lined fields in high school? Was it someone her grandfather loved? His own lost son?

All of this, she thinks to herself, is what she must tell her mother if she ever sees her, if she's truly alive—her life up to the moment she sees her again. That desire hasn't changed, only now she has hope—real hope—that she might actually meet her mother one day.

But can she really have faith that her mother might be alive? Her grandfather is the only one she's ever truly trusted in the world, and yet he's lied to her all these years. If she can't trust him, who can she trust?

Bradwell swabs her neck with alcohol. Rubbing alcohol or liquor? It's cold and gives her gooseflesh.

"The chips were a bad idea," Bradwell says. "My parents had enough conspiracy theories to know that they never wanted to have me chipped. They didn't want a megapower to know where everyone was at all times. Too much power. This chip makes you a target."

"Wait," she whispers. She's not ready yet.

Bradwell sits back.

She gets on her knees.

"What is it?" Bradwell says.

"Partridge," she says, quietly.

"Yes?"

She isn't sure what she wants to ask. Her mind is full of questions.

"What is it?" he says. "I'll answer any question you have. Anything."

His voice seems disembodied, as if he's only a dream, not real at all, as if he's a memory. Partridge has memories of his mother. Was she too young to hold the memories? *Memories are like water*, she remembers her grandfather saying. It's truer now than ever. Or does she not remember because her mother wasn't in her life very much? Was her mother the swan wife who gave her away to the woman who couldn't have children? "Do you remember me? As kids, did we ever meet?"

Partridge doesn't say anything at first. Maybe he's flooded with memories, too, or he's wondering if he should invent some story for her, the way her grandfather did. Doesn't he want to be able to fill in her lost childhood, like a real brother could? She would want to do this for him. Finally he says, "No. I don't remember you." But then he's quick to add, "That doesn't mean much, though. We were young."

"Do you remember your mother pregnant?"

He shakes his head and runs a hand over his hair. "I don't remember."

Her mind is flooded with questions. What did my mother smell like? What did her voice sound like? Am I like her? Am I different? Would she love me? Did she ever love me? Did she just let me go? "What's my name?" she whispers. "It's not Pressia. I was orphaned. My grandfather probably didn't even know me. His last name is Belze. It isn't mine. And it wouldn't be Willux."

"I don't know your name," Partridge confesses.

"I don't have a name."

Bradwell says, "You were given a name. Someone knows it. We'll find it."

"Sedge," Partridge says, and his eyes fill with tears. "I wish you could have met him. He'd have liked you."

Sedge is his dead brother. Her dead half brother. The world is frenzied—giving and taking. "I'm sorry."

"It's okay," Partridge says.

Pressia can't possibly miss Sedge, and yet she does. She had another brother. She had another connection in the world. And it's gone.

Pressia clears her throat. She doesn't want to start crying. She has to be tough now. "Why aren't you chipped, Partridge?" she asks. "Don't they have tabs on you?"

"Bradwell's right about the target. My father said that any son of his could become a target at any time."

"They put a simple tracking device in the birthday card; maybe there were others," Bradwell says. "We burned his things."

"But you put the tracking device on one of the rat beasts," Pressia says.

"How did you know that?"

"Figured it out." Pressia wants to get this over with now. No use putting it off. She lies down again on her stomach. "I'm ready."

Bradwell leans all the way to the floor—to whisper something to her? Pressia turns and rests her cheek on her hand. But he doesn't say a word. He simply tucks her hair behind her ear. It's a small gesture—so delicate, like the feathery touch she didn't think his large hands were capable of. He's just a kid. He's just a kid who's raised himself. He's tough and strong and angry—but tender, too. And nervous, she can tell by the rustling of wings on his back.

"I don't want to do this, Pressia. I wish I didn't have to."

"It's okay," she whispers. "Take it out." A tear slips over the bridge of her nose. "Take it."

Bradwell swabs her neck again, and then she feels his fingers on her skin. His hands are shaking. He must be bracing himself, because he takes hold of her neck and pauses. He says, "Partridge, I'm going to need you."

Partridge walks over.

"Hold on tight," Bradwell says. "Here."

There's a moment's hesitation. And then she feels Partridge's hand holding her head.

"Harder," Bradwell says. "Keep it steady."

Partridge's hands tighten like a vise.

Pressia feels Bradwell press his knee into her back. And then she feels Bradwell's hand again; he pushes his thumb and fingers into her neck, firmly this time, and then, in the space between, he digs in with a knife as sharp as a scalpel.

She lets out a shriek, a voice she didn't know she had. The pain feels like its own animal inside of her. The scalpel burrows deeper. She can't scream again, because her breath is gone. She tries to buck Bradwell from her back involuntarily. And even though she feels like the animal-of-pain has taken her over and she's become an animal, she knows not to move her head now.

"Stop," Partridge says.

But Pressia isn't sure if he's talking to her or to Bradwell. Has something gone wrong? He could paralyze her. They all know this. She feels the tickle of blood running down both sides of her neck. She's panting now. Her own blood is dotting the floor. She can see it start to pool, dark red. She is bracing herself for more pain. Her body takes on a deep core heat. She remembers the heat of the Detonations, waves of heat that kept coming. She remembers what it was like to be untethered for a moment, a child alone in the world. Does she really remember this? Or does she remember trying to remember? She can see the Japanese woman—young and beautiful—her mother who died, and she is now dying again because that woman isn't her mother. She's a stranger to her, a face singed to nothingness. Her skin melts away. She lies among bodies and luggage and overturned metal carts on wheels. The air is filled with dust, and the wave of heat comes again. And then there is a hand wrapped around her hand, her ears flooded with heartbeat. She closes her eyes and opens them and closes them. She once had a toy that was a set of binoculars with a button you could push that would make new scenes appear. She opens her eyes and closes them, then opens them, hoping for a new picture.

But it's still the dirty floor, the pain, the dirty floor.

She says, "Partridge, did our mother sing lullabies?"

"Yes," he says. "She did."

And that's something. It's a place to begin.

PRESSIA

EAST

THE BACK OF PRESSIA'S NECK IS padded with a gauzy cloth, moist with blood, and kept tight by a leather band tied around her neck like a choker to keep the padding in place. She applies extra pressure to the aching wound by sitting low on one of the mattresses on the floor and pressing her neck against one of the walls.

The chip, wiped clean of blood, is white. It sits on the floor like a lost tooth—something that was once deeply rooted inside of her now gone. And for some reason, it doesn't feel like she's free of it, but that she's lost another tether to someone in the world—someone who was watching over her—and this feels like something she should mourn even though she knows that the watching-over wasn't some kind of parental love at all.

Bradwell is all furious motion around her. The birds' wings on his back are pulsating. He pulls out a lawn mower then shoves it back into place. He picks up a hand trowel then stares at the ground.

Partridge sits next to Pressia on the mattress. "What's he doing?"

"He's in a frenzy," Pressia says. "I'd just let him go."

"Are you feeling okay?" Partridge asks Pressia.

The doll-head fist—she lifts it. The doll's eyes click open. Even the lids are covered in ash. Its lashes clumped. The small *o* of its mouth is clotted shut. She brushes over its plastic head with her good hand and feels her lost hand within it. This is how her mother seems to her now—a presence, numbed, riding under the surface of things. "As long as I don't move..." She doesn't even finish the sentence. She's angry at Partridge. Why? Is she jealous of him? He has memories of their mother and she doesn't. He got into the Dome. She didn't.

"So that's all it was," Partridge says, nodding at the chip on the floor. "A lot of trouble for something so small." He pauses and then says, "I didn't know," he whispers. "Not until you did. I'd never hold back something like that."

She can't even look at him.

"I just wanted you to know that."

She nods. It sends a sharp pain up her neck into the back of her head. "How do you feel about her now?" Pressia asks.

"I don't know."

"Is she still a saint? She cheated on your father," Pressia says. "She had a child out of wedlock, a bastard." She's never thought of herself as a bastard before. For some reason, she likes it. It has a certain toughness.

"I didn't come out here expecting simple answers," Partridge says. "I'm happy you exist."

"Thanks," she says, smiling.

"What's strange is that my father must have known. He's been watching you all these years so he had to have known. I wonder how he took the news?"

"Not very well, I bet."

Pressia folds the chip in her one good hand. Her eyes fill with tears. She thinks of the word *mother*—lullabies—and *father*—warm coat. Pressia has been a red dot on a screen, pulsing like a heartbeat.

Yes, the Dome has known she exists. They've kept tabs on her, perhaps all her life. But maybe her parents have kept tabs on her, too.

Bradwell asks Partridge abruptly, "Did your mother go to church?"

"We got swiped every Sunday like everyone else," Partridge says.

Pressia remembers the term *card-carrying*. It was something Bradwell had talked about during his mini lesson—the convolution of church and state. Churchgoers had cards. Their attendance was a matter of record.

"Not everyone," Bradwell says. "Not the ones who refused to go once it was turned over to the state and then were shot to death in their beds."

"Why did you ask the question?" Pressia asks Bradwell.

Bradwell sits down again. "Because the birthday card had religious wording. How did it go, Partridge?"

"Always walk in the light. Follow your soul. May it have wings. You are my guiding star, like the one that rose in the east and guided the Wise Men."

Pressia recognizes the star in the east and the Wise Men from the Bible. Her grandfather has whole sections of the Bible memorized; they were often recited at funerals.

Bradwell says, "But was this typical of your mom?"

"I don't know," Partridge says. "She believed in God, but she said that she rejected government-sanctioned Christianity *because* she was Christian. The government stole her country and God. Once she said to my father, 'And you. They stole you too.'" Partridge sits back as if he's just remembered this now. "Strange that was in my brain all along. I can almost hear her say it."

Pressia wishes that she had words from her mother that she could draw up from her memory, a voice. If her mother was the one singing her the lullaby, then she has something—lyrics, someone else's words.

Bradwell says to Partridge, "So maybe it's sincere."

"If it's sincere?" Partridge asks.

"It's useless," Bradwell says.

"If it's sincere, then it means what it means," Pressia says. "That's not useless."

"For us right now it is," Bradwell says. "Your mother wanted you to remember certain things. Signs. Coded messages, the necklace. So I was hoping this would lead us to her. But maybe it was her way of saying good-bye, of giving you advice to last a lifetime."

They're all quiet a moment. Pressia turns around and leans her back against the cool wall. If this was her mother's advice, what did it mean? *Follow your soul. May it have wings. Always walk in the light.* She imagines her soul having wings. She imagines following that soul. But where would it lead her here? There is nowhere to go. They're surrounded by Meltlands and Deadlands. And there is no untarnished light—everything exists beneath a gritty veil of ash. Pressia envisions the wind pushing the veil as if it rests over a woman's face and her breath billows the veil—her mother's face, hidden from view. What if her mother truly is alive, somewhere? How would you lead someone, knowing the world was about to be wiped clean of markers?

"You are my guiding star, like the one that rose in the east and guided the Wise Men," Partridge says. "Do you think she wants us to go due east?"

Bradwell pulls a map from the inside pocket of his jacket, the map they'd used to find Lombard. He spreads it out on the floor. The Dome, of course, is north, surrounded by barren terrain that gives way to some burgeoning woods before you hit the city. The Meltlands appear as gated communities in clumps surrounding the city to the east, south, and west. Then beyond that ring is a stretch of Deadlands.

Bradwell says, "Those hills in the east were a national reserve."

"And in the fairy tale, the swan wife burrows underground. Maybe she is in an underground bunker in those hills," Pressia says.

"So, tomorrow we head east," Partridge says.

"But that could be dead wrong," Pressia says.

"I don't like the expression *dead* wrong," Partridge says.

"East is all we've got," Bradwell says.

Pressia looks at Bradwell's face. She can see the light flecks of gold in his dark brown eyes. She's never noticed them before. They're beautiful—like honey. "It's all *we've* got?" Pressia says to Bradwell. "You've paid your debt, okay?"

"I'm still in this," Bradwell says.

"Only if you're in it for your own sake."

"Okay then, I'm in it for my own sake. I have selfish reasons. Does that work?"

Pressia shrugs.

Bradwell lifts her hand, opens her palm, his fingers on her fingers, and drops the necklace into her palm. "You should wear it," he says.

"No," she says. "It's not mine."

"But it is yours now, Pressia," Partridge says. "She would want you to have it. You're her daughter."

Daughter—the word sounds foreign.

"Do you want it?" Bradwell asks.

"Yes," she says.

Bradwell unlatches the dainty clasp. She swivels around, lifts her hair, careful of the bandage. He reaches over her head, holding the necklace with each hand. He locks the clasp. Once it catches, he lets go. "It looks nice," he says.

She reaches up and touches the pendant with one finger. "I've never worn a real necklace. Not that I can remember."

The pendant sits on Pressia's chest below the leather choker keeping the padding on the back of her neck in place, sitting in the dip between her collarbones. The gem gleams a brilliant blue. This necklace once belonged to her mother. It touched her mother's skin. What if it was a present from Pressia's father? Will she ever know anything about her father?

"I can see her in you now," Partridge says. "It's the way you tilt your head, the gestures."

"Really?" The possibility that she might look like her mother makes her happier than she'd have ever expected.

"That," he says, "right there, in your smile."

"I wish my grandfather could see it," she tells them. She remembers how, as he gave her the clogs, he said that he wished it were something more beautiful, that she deserved something beautiful.

Here it is, a small piece of beauty.

PRESSIA

PISTONS

Partridge is the first to fall asleep. He's lying down on his back, his injured hand over his heart. Pressia's on the other pallet, and Bradwell's on the floor; he insisted, but now Pressia hears him shifting around, trying to get comfortable.

"Enough. I can't sleep with your rolling around all night," she says. "I'll make room for you."

"No, thanks. I'm fine."

"Oh, so you get to do all the favors and get to be a martyr too? Is that how it works?"

"I didn't come after you just because I owed your grandfather a debt. I tried to tell you earlier, but you wouldn't listen."

"All I'm hearing now is that you're going to sleep on the floor, and I'm supposed to feel guilty about it."

"Fine," he says. He gets up off the floor and lies down next to her on the pallet.

She's lying on her back, but Bradwell can't—the birds are there, settling to sleep. He curls toward Pressia. For a moment, she can almost imagine that they're out in a field under stars, a clear night.

The room is quiet. She can't sleep. "Bradwell," she whispers. "Let's play I Remember."

"You know my story. I told it at the meeting."

"Think of something else. Anything. Talk. I want to hear someone's voice." She wants to hear *his* voice, really. As angry as he can make her, his voice now sounds deep and calming. She realizes that she wants him to talk because, whether she agrees or not, he's always honest and she can trust the things he tells her.

And so it surprises her that the next thing he says is, "Well, I lied to you once."

"You did?"

"The crypt," he says. "I found it when I was just a little kid before I came across the butcher shop. I slept there for days while people were dying everywhere. And I prayed to Saint Wi, and I survived. So I kept coming back."

"You're one of the people who prays for hope?" Pressia asks.

"I am," he says.

"That's not a terrible lie," she says.

"Nope. Not terrible."

"Did the prayers work? Do you have hope?"

He rubs his jaw roughly. "Ever since I met you, it seems like I've got more to hope for."

She feels heat rise in her cheeks, but she's not sure what he means. Is he saying that he hopes for something that has to do with her? Is he confessing he likes her, now that he's confessed his lie? Or does he mean something else? That she's made him see things differently?

"But that's not what you asked for," he says. "You wanted a memory."

"That's okay."

"Can you go to sleep now?"

"No."

"Okay, then. A memory. Does it have to be a happy one?"

"No," she says. "I prefer true over happy now."

"Okay then." He thinks for a moment. "When my aunt told me to get out of the garage, I did. I poked the dead cat in the box. And then I heard the motor turn over—and one shout. It was the noise my own father used to make when he'd skin a knuckle or wrench his back. I pretended it was his voice. I closed my eyes and imagined my father coming out from under the car with a heart-engine fused in his chest like a superhero. I imagined him coming back to life." Pressia can see Bradwell in her mind as a little boy with birds in his back, standing on a charred lawn, the dead cat in a box at his feet. He's quiet a moment. "I've never told anyone that before. It's stupid."

Pressia shakes her head. "It's beautiful. You were trying to imagine something great, something else, some other world. You were just a kid."

"I guess," he says. "You tell me something now."

"Obviously I don't really remember much from the Before."

"It doesn't have to be from the Before."

"Okay," she says. "Well, there's something I've never told anyone either. My grandfather knows, but he doesn't know, not really."

"What?"

"I tried to cut the doll head off when I was thirteen. Or that's what I told my grandfather. He stitched me up quickly. But he never asked me why I did it."

"Is there a scar?"

Pressia shows him the small mark on the inside of her wrist where the doll meets her arm. The skin on her wrist is etched with delicate pale blue veins and has a little rubbery give.

"Were you trying to take it off or..."

"Or," Pressia says. "Maybe I was tired. I wanted not to be lost. I missed my mother and father and the past, maybe because I didn't see enough of it in my head to keep me company. I felt alone."

"But you didn't do it."

"I wanted to be alive. That's what I learned as soon as I saw the blood."

Bradwell sits up and touches the scar with his fingertip. He looks at her as if his eyes are taking in her entire face, her eyes, her cheeks, her lips. Normally, she'd look away, but she can't. "The scar is beautiful," he says.

Her heart skitters. She pulls the doll head to her chest. "Beautiful? It's a scar."

"It's a sign of survival."

Bradwell's the only person she knows who would say something like that. She feels slightly breathless. She can only whisper. "Aren't you ever afraid?" She isn't talking about all the things she should be afraid of—heading back into the Deadlands tomorrow, the Dusts that rise up from that ground. She's talking about his fearlessness right now, calling the small scar beautiful. If she weren't afraid, she'd confess that she's happy to be alive because she has this moment with him.

"Me?" Bradwell says. "I get so scared that I feel like my uncle under the car, with pistons in my chest. I feel too much. It's like being drummed to death from within. You know?"

She nods. It's quiet a moment. They both hear Partridge mumble in his sleep.

"So . . . ," Pressia says.

"So?"

"Why did you come after me if it wasn't for my grandfather?"

"You know why."

"No, I don't. You tell me." They're so close that she feels the heat of his body.

He shakes his head and says, "I have something for you." He

reaches for his jacket. "We looked for you at your place. Your grandfather was gone."

"I know," Pressia says. "I know. He's in the Dome."

"They have him?"

"It's okay. He's in a hospital."

"Still," Bradwell says. "I'm not sure—"

She doesn't want to talk about her grandfather now. "What do you have for me?"

"I found this."

He pulls something from his jacket pocket and lays it on the spot where her ribs meet in an arch.

One of her butterflies.

"It made me think," Bradwell says. "How can something so small and beautiful like this still exist?"

Pressia's cheeks flush. She lifts the butterfly and holds it up so that she can see the pale light through its frail dusty wings.

"All the losses mount up," he says. "You can't feel one without feeling the others that came before. But this feels like an antidote. I can't explain it, like someone fighting back."

"They seem like a waste of time now. They don't even fly. You can wind them up and their wings flap but that's it."

"Maybe they just didn't have anywhere they needed to go."

LYDA

LITTLE BLUE BOX

To pass the time, Lyda reweaves her sitting mat over and over, but it never pleases her. She hums the tune of "Twinkle, Twinkle."

No one has come to visit, not her mother, not doctors. The guards arrive with food on trays, pills. That's all.

When Lyda woke up the morning after the redhead tapped out her message on the small rectangular window, the redhead was gone. Maybe she was crazy after all. Who would think that there were many people who thought they could overthrow the Dome? Tell him? Who, Partridge? Did the redhead think that Lyda could communicate with him? And why would Lyda tell him this if she could? The redhead must be crazy. Some people here are crazy. It's why these places exist in the first place. Lyda's an exception, not the rule.

There was another girl in the redhead's place that next morning. A new one, dazed with fear. And honestly, Lyda was relieved. What would she say to the redhead after her message? If she was ever going to get out of here, she couldn't be seen fraternizing with loonies, especially not revolutionary loonies. Revolutionaries didn't exist in the Dome. That was one of the nice things about it here. They didn't have to worry about those kinds of conflicts— like in the time before the Detonations—not anymore.

Lyda hasn't been taken back to occupational therapy either. As soon as the privilege was given, it was gone. She asked the guards when she'd be given permission again. But they didn't know. She could have asked them for more information, but that seemed dangerous. It was like admitting what she didn't know. She wants to seem like she knows something.

But then today, two guards show up before lunch and say they're taking her to the medical center.

"My relocation came through?" she asks.

"We're not sure," one guard says. It's a different guard. She has a partner waiting for her on the other side of the door. "Right now, no extra info. Just where to drop you."

Before she's escorted from her chamber, they cuff her, a plastic cinching device ratcheted so tight that she feels her pulse.

But then they pass two doctors in the hall. One whispers to the other, "Is that necessary? Think of Jillyce." Jillyce is her mother's first name. It seems so strange to hear them refer to her mother with such intimacy. They don't want her mother to see Lyda cuffed, the shame of it. Does this mean that she'll see her mother before she leaves?

As an act of mercy, they tell the guard to cut the cuffs. The guard is only a few years older than Lyda. She wonders for a moment if the guard once attended the academy, if they ever passed each other in the halls. The guard takes out a large, red-handled knife, fits it between the plastic cuffs and the inside of one of Lyda's wrists. Lyda imagines for a fleeting moment what it would feel like if the guard slit her wrist. She's still dressed in her white jumpsuit and head scarf. The blood would stain the white so brightly. They ask her to walk with her hands clasped in front of her and she does.

She looks for her mother as they leave the rehabilitation facility but doesn't see her.

The guards accompany her on a solitary train car, which stops in the medical center, and now they lead Lyda down another corridor. She hasn't ever been to the medical center, except to have her tonsils out and once for a little flu. Academy girls aren't coded. There's too much fear of damaging their reproductive organs, which is more important than enhancing their minds or bodies. Her chances of being approved for reproduction now are almost nothing. Those who are a bit older and don't reproduce can be taken in for enhanced brain coding. But she probably wouldn't be a good candidate for that either. Why enhance a brain that is psychologically compromised? She knows, too, that there's a chance of entering New Eden in her lifetime. At that point, won't everyone who can reproduce be needed for repopulation, maybe even those who've done time in a rehab center, like her? She still has hope.

The wallpaper is floral as if trying to pass for a hallway in someone's home during the Before. There's even a pair of rocking chairs, like it might be cordial to sit awhile and chat. This is supposed to set people at ease, Lyda supposes. Unlike the other girls who do so well in their lessons on small talk, Lyda has to memorize the list of appropriate questions just to keep up her end of the conversation. She always feels the panicked burden of conversation as if its end marked a greater ending. She thinks of what Partridge said to her when proposing that they dance. "Let's do what normal people do," he said, "so no one suspects." She's not normal. Neither is he.

But these little mock moments of domestic living wouldn't fool anyone, would they? Not with the fluorescent lights flickering and buzzing overhead. Not with the doors that sometimes yawn open, revealing a pallid room with a body cast set on a flat bed, bars on either side. Is there someone in the cast? She can never tell, not with the medical workers whizzing by in their masks and gowns and gloves.

Up ahead, there's a single-file line of academy boys. Her eyes flit quickly down their faces. Some recognize her; their eyes catch and go wide. One smirks. She refuses to look away. She's done nothing wrong. She lifts her head and steadies her eyes straight ahead, locking onto a call box mounted on the wall at the end of the corridor.

She hears her name, whispered. She hears Partridge's name, too. She wants to ask them what story they've been told— something, anything, even the lie that's being dispersed would be better than knowing nothing.

The guards turn at the end of the hall, and they finally arrive at a door. The nameplate next to the door reads: ELLERY WILLUX. Her breath catches in her throat. "Wait," she says. "I didn't know."

"If they didn't tell you, then it's supposed to be a surprise," says the guard who'd cut her cuffs loose.

"Give me a minute," Lyda says. Her palms have gone sweaty. She wipes them on the legs of the white jumpsuit.

The other guard knocks. "We're on time," she says.

A man's voice calls out, "Come in."

Willux is smaller than she expected. His shoulders are rounded, curled inward. She remembers him as robust. He used to be the one to give speeches behind microphones at commemorations and public meetings. But she realizes now that Foresteed took over all of that a few years ago without explanation. Maybe it's because Foresteed is younger and his teeth shine like he's swallowed the moon, as if he's lit from within. Willux has aged. So many of the most important men in the Dome seem toned, with a dense larded look to their guts, whereas Willux looks frail, his stomach a deflated paunch.

He swivels in his chair, situated in front of a bank of monitors and keyboards, and smiles softly. He removes a pair of glasses— are they for show? She can't remember when she last saw glasses. He folds them and holds them to his chest. "Lyda," he says.

"Hello," she says and she extends her hand.

He shakes his head. "No need for formality," he says, but she feels like she's been shunned. Or is it rebuked? Is she unclean now that she's been a patient in the rehab center? "Take a seat." He indicates a small black stool. She sits on the edge of it. He nods to the guards. "We'll talk in private," he says. "Thank you for delivering her here safe and sound!"

They bow lightly. The guard who cut her cuffs glances at her, as if trying to offer her some courage. And then they leave, shutting the door with a click.

Willux puts his glasses on the edge of his desk, next to a small pale blue box. It's just big enough to hold a cupcake. She remembers the cupcakes from the dance, the spongy texture, how each bite was almost too sweet, but how she marveled at the way Partridge ate such huge bites. He ate with abandon. She wonders if the box holds a gift of some kind.

Willux says, "I suppose you've heard that my son is missing."

Lyda nods.

"Perhaps you don't know that he's actually gone."

"Gone?" Lyda isn't sure what this means. Is he dead?

"He left the Dome," Willux says. "I would like to ensure his safe return, as you can imagine."

"Oh," Lyda says. Even the girls locked away in rehabilitation centers knew it. He's out there, somewhere. Should she act more surprised? "Of course you want him back. Of course."

"And there's a rumor that he was quite fond of you." He lifts his hand and smooths the thin hair on his head. His head, nearly bald, reminds her of a baby's head and the word *fontanel*, the soft spot on top of the infant's head where you can see the pulse and check for dehydration if the baby is sick. They've had many lessons on the proper care of infants. She always thought the word *fontanel* was more fitting for something exotic, like an Italian fountain. Willux's hand is trembling. Is he nervous? "Is this true? Did he have a thing for you?"

"I don't claim to know anyone's heart but my own," she says.

"Let me start more simply then," he says. "Did you know his plans?"

"No."

"Did you help him escape?"

"Not to my knowledge."

"Did he steal a knife from the display, and did you allow it?"

"He might have stolen something when I wasn't looking. I don't know. We were in the Domesticity Display together."

"Playing house?"

"No," Lyda says. "I don't know what you mean."

"I think you do." He taps the pale blue box with three fingers. She's afraid of the box now. "I don't."

He leans forward, lowers his voice. "Are you intact?"

She feels the heat rise in her cheeks. Her chest feels compressed. She refuses to answer.

"I can call and have one of the women check," he says. "Or you could just tell me the truth."

She stares at the tiled floor.

"Was it my boy?" he asks.

"I haven't answered your question," she says. "I'm not going to."

He leans forward then and pats her knee, then rests his hand there. "Don't worry," he says.

She feels sick. She wants to kick him. She closes her eyes; maybe she clenches them shut. His hand slides off her knee. She looks down at the tiled floor.

"If it was my son, we can still arrange for him to set this right— if, that is, we can find him and bring him home."

"I don't need to marry him," Lyda says, "if that's what you're asking."

"But maybe it would be nice? I mean, after all, with your recent history, you will be hard to place."

"I'll survive."

The room is quiet for a moment, and then Willux says, idly, "Will you survive?"

Her heart pounds in her ears. She realizes that her hands are clasped again, sitting on her lap, both gripping the other so tightly that her nails are digging into her skin.

"We have a plan and it requires your participation," Willux says. "You're going out."

"Where?"

"Out of the Dome to the other side."

"Out of the Dome?" It's a death sentence. She won't be able to breathe the air. She'll be attacked. The wretches will rise up, rape her, and kill her. Outside the Dome, the trees have eyes and teeth. The ground swallows girls who have any bit of their human shape left. They are burned alive at stakes and feasted on. This is where she's going. Out.

"Special Forces will bring you to a location on the outside, and you will lure my son back to us."

"You're sure he's alive?"

"Yes, at least as of the last few hours, and there's been nothing to indicate a change."

She feels some small measure of relief. Maybe she can lure him back. Maybe Willux would even let them get married. But of course, what will happen to her when they find out that he doesn't love her? That he was only being kind after she'd helped him steal the knife?

Willux claps his hands and calls out to some unseen assistant. "Roll section one twenty-seven—Partridge." Then he says to Lyda, "So you can see for yourself."

The computer screen stutters to life and Partridge appears. He's dirty, exhausted, bruised, but still Partridge. His light gray eyes, his strong white teeth—one slightly overlaps the other. He's being looked at through someone's eyes. A girl's eyes. Lyda can see the girl's body as she glances down and then back at Partridge.

Partridge whispers to her, "I didn't know. Not until you did. I'd never hold back something like that." Something like what? Lyda wonders. It's obvious that he knows this girl well. Lyda wishes that she could see the girl's face. The girl is no longer looking at Partridge. Her eyes scan the back wall cluttered with broken, gutted machinery. They're outside the Dome.

"I just wanted you to know that," Partridge says. And there's his face again, and his hand is wrapped in a bloody bandage and held up to his chest. He smiles at the girl.

The girl nods; evident from the bob of the camera angle.

"How do you feel about her now?" the girl asks. Are they talking about Lyda? She can't help but wonder. Why else show her this clip?

"I don't know," Partridge says.

The screen fades to black.

"He's hurt," Lyda says. "What happened to his hand?"

"A small injury. Nothing to worry about. We can correct almost anything here."

"Why did you show me that?"

"Just so that you can see he's alive and well!" Willux says.

She doesn't trust him. He showed it to her to make her jealous. The fact is that she's been lying to them and to herself. She kissed Partridge, not the other way around. He never told her that he loved her. It's all a lie. He can try to make her jealous if he wants to. She doesn't care. She never really had Partridge, so she can't really lose him.

But there's something else too. Partridge kissed her back, and when she pulled away, his face—it's inexplicable. He was astonished and happy. She thinks of his face now and smiles. Let Willux do whatever he wants to with all of his information. She remembers again Partridge whispering to her, "Let's do what normal people do so no one suspects." He was the one to say it. They were just pretending to be normal. They were set apart, different from the others. It was a kind of confession, a shared secret.

"Why are you smiling?" Willux asks.

"It's good news. Your son is alive."

Willux looks at her appraisingly, and then he lifts the pale blue box and hands it to her. "You will deliver this box to a soldier," he says. Again his hand shakes. "We hoped she would work with us, but she's already participated in the death and destruction of one of our own operatives." He takes a deep breath and sighs. "I've kept an eye on her for many years. A shiny lure for someone I hoped would retrieve her one day. She's proven pretty worthless."

A shiny lure so he could trap someone on the outside? Who? Lyda asks a simpler, more permissible question. "May I ask what's inside the box?"

"Of course," he says, and now she notes a tremor, ever so slight, a bobble of his head. "Take a look. I don't think it will mean much to you, but the soldier, Pressia Belze, will understand the message we're sending. It might help to convince her to refocus her loyalties. You can tell her that's all we have left."

Left of what? she wonders, but she doesn't ask. She doesn't want to open the box, but she has to know. She fits her hand over the lid and lifts it, rustling the pale blue tissue paper inside. She pulls it aside and, there, nestled in the tissue is a small fan with a dead motor, its plastic blades motionless.

PARTRIDGE

STRINGS

THEY HEADED OUT BEFORE DAWN. It's still early morning and they've come a long way. Six large women flank either side. A lot of the children are asleep, and heavier as a result, Partridge figures. One woman, whose fused child rides on her hip, supports the child's head by keeping it pressed to her chest with one hand, a butcher's knife in the other.

They walk in silence, passing blasted homes, rows of them completely gone, scorched foundations laid bare. Then they pass a few that are simply charred frames. Sometimes the bricks survived in part. Occasionally, the house is gone, but in its place, as if the setting of some disturbing play, there's a living room of brittle blackened foam, the spokes of a chair or the skull of a sink, too wrecked to be of value. Partridge can't concentrate. He's searching his memory for a fight between his parents, a moment of heated tempers, hostility, seething anger. His father knew his mother had another child, not his. He had to. He knew Pressia's location. He wanted her to find Partridge. Why? Does he have a flare for the ironic? Did he want to taunt his mother with both of her surviving children? Is it possible—even remotely—that his father wants to see his mother because he loves her, he wants her back, he needs to tell her that he forgives her? He knows it's a childish desire—two parents who are in love, a happy home. But he can't help it. His father did love her once, he had to. Her memory pains him. Partridge has seen it on his face.

They walk by more strip malls, ravaged, picked clean, and institutions—they're the worst. The stench lingers even though bodies have long since rotted away. The institutions offer no fairy tale. Partridge can't supply them with a swan wife or lost wings. They're proof of the oppression that preceded the end of it all, the Return of Civility.

It smells like death and rot. He remembers the strangely sweet, fecund smell of the dead body he found wrapped in reeds, the shepherd's wife, bound up. He tries to shake the image from his head.

There are other survivors out here. Partridge hears them—a hooting call, the sound of rummaging, an animal's low moan, and sometimes the women pause and listen, their heads all swiveling in the same direction. But no one attacks them.

The farther they travel, the less there is to see. The landscape is flat except for the distant hills in the east. The dirt has turned black. With nothing to bar it, the wind kicks up and rips along in dark sheets.

The women produce scarves from some unseen pockets and wrap their children's faces and their own. Partridge already wears a scarf. Bradwell covers his face with his arm. One of the women gives Pressia a scarf.

Partridge is keeping a close eye on Pressia. He's worried about her. She's been through so much, all at once. But Pressia is tough. Partridge knows it.

Eventually, the woman with the child's head pressed to her chest says, "This is as far as we go."

Partridge would tell her thank you, but he paid for this with his pinky. He can't muster the appreciation.

"Thank you," Pressia says.

Bradwell tells them to thank Mother for them. "We are indebted," he says and he looks at Partridge, who can only mutter, "Yeah."

The woman says, "Keep searching the ground. Look out for their eyes."

They begin to bow their good-byes, but then one of the women walks up to Partridge. She has long gray hair. She grips his arm and says, "If your mother is alive, tell her I said thank you."

"Did you know her?" Partridge says.

The woman nods. "You don't recognize him?" she asks. And there, hiding behind her, is a boy about eight years old. His hair is long and shaggy, his face shiny with burns. He looks at Partridge intently. "It's Tyndal," she says. "He doesn't speak."

Partridge stares at the boy and then back at the woman. "Mrs. Fareling?"

"I thought you'd recognize him because, well, he hasn't grown up."

Partridge feels unsteady. Tyndal is still a boy, a mute boy, fused forever to his mother. Partridge says, "I'm sorry."

"No," Mrs. Fareling says. "Your mother got me out of the rehab center. I don't know how. She pulled some strings, I guess. And I got a release. Something handed down. And by the time the Detonations hit, I was back at home with Tyndal."

"Tyndal," Partridge whispers, gazing into the boy's face as if still searching for him.

The boy gives a series of short and long nods, perhaps a kind of code.

"He wants to wish you good luck," Mrs. Fareling says, reading the nods.

"Thanks," Partridge says.

And then Mrs. Fareling reaches out and grabs Partridge and pulls him to her chest. She holds him, her fists gripping his jacket.

He hugs her. "She saved us," Mrs. Fareling says, crying now. "I hope she's alive."

"She is," Partridge whispers. "I'll tell her that you survived. I'll tell her that you're thankful."

Mrs. Fareling lets Partridge go. She gazes at him. "It's strange to hug you like that," she says. "I suppose, if things were different, Tyndal would be your size."

"I'm sorry," he says again, because there's nothing else to say. Nothing could make it right. He wishes his father could see Tyndal Fareling.

"It's time," she says. "Be well."

Partridge nods.

She pats his arm and so does Tyndal with his tiny hand.

"Thank you for everything," Partridge says. "Thank you."

Mrs. Fareling and Tyndal bow and walk on with the other mothers and children, back home again.

"Are you okay?" Bradwell asks.

"Fine," Partridge says. "I'm ready."

They each take out a knife and move on. But Partridge looks back. The women raise their hands to wave. He lifts his knife to wave back. And then a swift cloud of ash rises up, and he can no longer see the mothers. They are out here on their own now.

LYDA

OPEN

THE GUARDS FROM THE REHABILITATION CENTER are gone when Lyda emerges from Willux's office. Instead there are two male guards. They escort her to a solitary train car where she is passed off to a third male guard, heavily armed, bulky, with a small scar on his chin.

This guard travels with her through darkened tunnels. She sits in one of the seats, the pale blue box in her lap, watching the dark tunnel walls glide past the windows. The guard stands, his feet spread apart, firmly planted. He shifts his weight as the train switches tracks.

The guard must know she's going to be taken to the outside, but she isn't sure if he knows why.

"Will I be given a contamination suit?" she asks.

"No," he says.

"What about a mask?"

"And block that pretty face from view?"

"Have you ever escorted someone out of the Dome before?" she asks.

"A girl? First time."

He's escorted boys out? She's not sure she believes him. No one was ever said to have left the Dome before Partridge. Why would boys be sent out? She's never heard of such a thing. "Which boys?" she asks. "Who?"

"The ones you never hear from again," the guard says.

"What about Willux's son?" she asks.

"Which one?"

"Partridge, of course," she says a little impatiently. "He didn't get out this way. Did he?"

He laughs. "He wasn't ready for the outside. I doubt he's still alive." He says it as if he hopes he isn't alive, as if this would prove something.

The train slows to a stop. The doors open directly into a long white tiled hall. An intercom is attached to the wall of each chamber. He walks with her through the first three chambers. He says the word, "Open," and the door opens, they walk through, and the door closes behind them.

"There are three more chambers to go. You'll step through each door when it slides open. The final door will open to the outside. The loading dock is closed."

"The loading dock?"

"We're not as cut off as you'd think," he says.

"What do we load?"

"We unload," he says. "One day it'll be ours again." He means the earth itself, and she worries for a moment that he's going to launch into a speech about how they are the rightful heirs to paradise—temporarily displaced. He simply says, "We're blessed."

"Yes, blessed," she says, more out of habit than anything.

"Someone will be waiting for you," he says. "Special Forces."

"They send Special Forces out of the Dome?"

"They aren't human; they're creatures. Don't be surprised by their appearance." She's seen Special Forces before in stunning white uniforms, that small elite corps; they weren't creatures. They were half a dozen strong young men.

"What will this person look like?"

He doesn't answer. How can she prepare herself if he won't tell her what to expect? He glances at the intercom box and the eye fixed in the upper reaches of the ceiling. She takes this to mean he can't tell her, not allowed. He says, "I've got to pat you down. Standard procedure. Make sure you're only taking with you what's meant to go."

"Fine," she says though she hates it. "I'm supposed to bring the box with me and deliver it."

"I know." The guard pats down her legs, her hips, her lower ribs. "Arms up," he says. He's brusque, professional, and she's thankful for that. She's surprised when he holds her jaw steady with two hands and tells her to open her mouth. He peers inside, using a small handheld flashlight. He says, "Ears," and he turns her head. Again, the flashlight. He studies one ear and then, when he studies the other, he whispers, very softly, "Tell the swan we're waiting."

She isn't sure that she understands what he's just said. The swan?

"All done!" he says. "You're cleared."

She wants to say, *Waiting for what? And who is doing the waiting? Who is we?*

But she can tell by his abrupt tone that she can't ask questions.

He looks her in the eye and says, "Good luck."

"Thank you," she says.

He faces the door they've just come through. "Open," he says. The door glides open. He steps through it, leaving her. The door glides shut.

She's alone. She faces the door before her. "Open," she says. It does. She walks through it, and it closes quickly behind her. She does this once more and then she's standing before the final door. She's not sure what to expect. She sets the pale blue box down on the floor, pulls the white kerchief from her head, places it over her nose and mouth, and ties it at the back of her head.

She picks up the box, grips it in her hands. "Open," she says.

And there, before her, is a gust of wind, dirt, sky—and something cutting across that sky. A real bird.

PARTRIDGE

SMALL RIB CAGES

PARTRIDGE DOESN'T LIKE THAT IT'S QUIET. He doesn't like the way the wind has died or the way Pressia keeps saying, "Something's not right," and how this makes Bradwell nervous.

"Do you think we've timed this trip with some kind of feeding frenzy somewhere else?" Partridge says.

"Yeah, Partridge, maybe the Dusts are busy devouring a bus full of schoolchildren," Bradwell says. "Wouldn't that be lucky!"

"You know I didn't mean it like that," Partridge says.

The ground gets soft underfoot.

That's when Partridge sees a small creature, ash-colored, almost mouse-size, but not a mouse. It isn't furred. It's covered in sandy char, and its ribs look exposed, as if skinless. For a moment it darts across the ground then disappears into it, absorbed by earth. "What was that?"

"What?" Pressia says.

"It was something like a mouse or a mole." Partridge looks out to the blurred line where the dirt becomes underbrush that leads to the hills. He sees motion—not a mouse or a mole but instead a tumble of action, a roiling wave. "I think there's more than one."

And then, in an instant, there's a small rising cloud, just a foot high, rolling toward them.

"How many do you think there are?" Pressia asks.

"Too many to count," Bradwell says. The storm of small Dusts coming at them is accompanied by a high-pitched tone—not one squeal but many, all ringing out together.

The wind starts up again. Soon they're all leaning into the gusts. Pressia pulls two knives from her jacket. Partridge has a knife and a meat hook. His stumped finger throbs, but he's still got his grip. Bradwell has a stun gun and a small sharp knife. The ground is vibrating. The air smells thick and putrid.

"What are we going to do? Plan?" Partridge shouts.

"Stay here with Pressia!" Bradwell says, and with that he lifts his weapons and lets out a barbaric yawp. He charges the storm of small Dusts.

The Dusts, with their beady quick black eyes and partially exposed skeletons, move in a pack. Some are locked together, rib-cage-to-rib-cage, jawbone-to-jawbone. Some have fused skulls. Others are stacked on top of one another. And all of them are tied to the earth. It comes with them as they overtake Bradwell. They don't exist alone. They are Groupies that are also Dusts bound to the earth. With scrambling claws, they run up Bradwell's body, bringing with them what seems to be a hem of the earth, a dirt blanket that they could use to smother him.

It happens quickly. Bradwell is cutting the blanket of earth and small bodies with quick slices of his knife. The Dusts fall, but there are more, always more. He's covered in them, like he's trapped in a coat of small roving ashy beasts.

Pressia starts to run toward him, but Partridge shoves her so hard, she falls back. "I'll go."

Pressia shouts, "What the hell is wrong with you?" Her mouth covered with a scarf, her hair whipping around her head, she's holding her knife, and her doll-head fist is ready to throw a punch.

That's his little sister. It hits him with such force that he's momentarily stunned. His little sister. "Stay here!" he says.

"No!" she shouts. "I'm fighting."

There's no stopping her. As soon as Partridge starts running, she's after him. They charge to Bradwell and start whacking at the creatures with their knives and hooks. Partridge's body feels deeply strong and fast. The coding must be getting closer to full effect. But still there are too many of the small Dusts. He can't keep up. Bradwell staggers forward, then loses his footing. The blanket of earth covers his legs, immobilizing him. He twists his upper body, like a hooked fish, but it's no use.

The Dusts are on Partridge and Pressia now too. They have claws and sharp teeth. He can see the small dots of blood blooming on his shirt—Pressia's too—and the small Dusts have moved up Bradwell's back, attacking the birds beneath his shirt.

Bradwell cries out to Partridge and Pressia, "No, go back!"

But they keep fighting. They kick and flail, slicing the Dusts, shoving them off Bradwell.

But now the next wave of Dusts is rolling at them, chest-high. And behind the wave, there are pillars of Dusts rising. They seem to have heads, horns, spiked backs. Partridge is sure that this is the end. He'll never get any closer to his mother than this.

But then Pressia shouts above the high-pitched keening of the beasts. "He's coming! I hear him!"

"Who?" Bradwell says.

Partridge hears another strange sound too, a bass rumble running below the squealing—a growling motor and then a blasting horn.

A car, a miraculous black car, comes barreling through the waves of Dusts, plowing through them. There's a spray of ribs, teeth, shining eyes. The car skids to a sideways stop right in front of them. Partridge can barely see through the new gust of ash torn loose by the black car, but he hears a voice shouting at them from the car. "Get in, goddamn it! Get in!"

He isn't sure whether to trust the voice or not, but he's in no position to be choosy. He turns and sees Pressia help Bradwell to his feet. "Open the door!" Bradwell shouts at him.

Partridge runs for the door, opens it. Bradwell and Pressia jump in, then Partridge beside her. The car takes off before the door slams.

The driver sits close to the steering wheel because of something he's wearing on his back. He looks over his shoulder at Partridge, his face marred and burned. "That him, Pressia?" he shouts. "That the Pure?"

"Yes!" Pressia shouts. She knows the driver. "And this is Bradwell."

The driver yanks the wheel, hitting a Dust head-on, creating a cloud of ash that rains dirt and debris on the car. Wiry and lean, he moves like someone charged by a temper. Partridge grips the seat. In the Dome, they all rely on the rails. He barely remembers cars, and he's never been in a speeding car, driven by a maniac.

"I thought you two were dead," Pressia says.

"So did we!"

"This is El Capitan!" Pressia says.

Bradwell points to the windshield. "A herd of them! Jesus!" They hit a series of Dusts, each exploding against the car.

"Do we know where we're going to find the Pure's mother?" El Capitan says.

Partridge grabs the seat in front of him and pulls himself forward. "What do you know about my mother?"

And then as if from nowhere a head appears on the driver's back. A face—small, pale, and pruned with scars. He opens the small dark hole of his mouth and says, "Mother."

"Whoa!" Partridge says and rears back, slamming into the backseat.

The driver laughs, pulls the wheel so hard that Partridge bangs his head against the window.

"And that's Helmud," Pressia says. "His brother."

In addition to all the bites and scratches on Bradwell's body, one of the two seams running up the back of his shirt has split. Through the rip, Partridge sees one of the birds in Bradwell's back—gray shifting wings, some tinged with blood. There might be only three birds. Partridge had expected more what with all of their motion. Two shift restlessly. The calmest one, the one he sees clearly, has a beak drilled into Bradwell's muscle and skin, scarred with old burns. His skin puckers around its red beak. Its shiny dark eye is masked in black feathers. For a moment it seems as if the bird is looking at Partridge, startled—its eye beady and still—as if it wants to ask a question. It looks sickly and limp.

"One of the birds," Partridge says, his mouth pasty with ash. "It's injured."

"Your mother will have medicine," El Capitan says. "That's what the Dome wanted us to protect if we find her. I bet she'll have something that'll work on your injuries."

"Meds?" Bradwell says, looking at Pressia.

"If we ever do find her, they don't want anything in her possession damaged," she says.

It dawns on Partridge that he doesn't really know these people. He's stepped into the middle of their lives, and they're strangers to him. He doesn't understand them or this world they live in. Will his mother be a stranger to him too?

He looks out the window. They're moving fast. The flat blackened landscape is a blur. Is his mother alive in those hills? Did she tell him the story so that he would remember it all these years later? When was the last time he felt like he knew what he was doing? He stares at the cracked swan pendant hanging from the necklace around Pressia's neck. It sways with the rhythm of the jostling car, tapping Pressia's blood-flecked, soot-streaked collarbones. Its blue eye is small and fragile. What's it good for? What does it mean?

LYDA

IT

AFTER SHE STEPS OUT of the last compartment and the door slides shut behind her, there's the thunk of a heavy lock. But no one from Special Forces is there to meet her, as the guard told her there would be.

She looks out at the dark landscape, the swirls of ashy dust and, far off, twisted woodlands, and a city—toppled buildings, small but distinct smoke trails lifting into the sky. She's alone, holding the pale blue box in her hands.

She turns back to the Dome, gazes up at its massive sides. She knocks politely on the door, knowing that there isn't anyone on the other side. She hears a strange far-off howl from the woods. She doesn't turn around. She pounds with her fist. "No one's here!" she shouts. "No one's here to escort me!" She almost starts to cry and stops herself. She lets her fist slide down the door.

She turns then and notices the wheel ruts. They stop abruptly in front of the Dome, and she can make out the large rectangular seam of what might be the door to the loading dock, the one the guard had mentioned. Maybe he shouldn't have said something like that to her. Now she knows that the Dome isn't completely shut off. They're in communication with the outside. This goes against everything she's been taught. She shouldn't be allowed to know about the loading dock. But maybe the guard knew it didn't matter what she did and didn't know now—not if she was never coming back.

She takes a few steps forward. Her shoes slip in the grit. She's used to the tiled halls of the girls' academy, the stone paths through the turf, unmoving under her feet, and the rubbery grip of the rehab center's flooring. She's on a downward slope and so her pace naturally picks up, and she realizes that she is truly alone, under the eye of the real sun, under a bank of clouds that are limitlessly connected to the sky, the universe, and she starts to run. The girls' academy doesn't have any athletic teams although they do calisthenics every morning in the gymnasium for a full hour in matching one-piece jumpers—shorts and striped short-sleeved tops that zip up the front. She hates the jumpers and the calisthenics. When was the last time she sprinted like this? She's a fast runner. Her legs feel strong beneath her.

She runs for a while, closer and closer to the woodlands. And then she hears something buzzing, a low electric pulse. It comes from the stunted trees, but she can't tell which direction. She stops running but is surprised by how it feels like she's still in motion. The pounding of her feet on the earth is now the pounding in her chest. She scans the woods and then sees a large figure moving quickly, glinting. *Don't worry*, she remembers the guard saying. *They're creatures. They're not human.*

Was that supposed to be comforting?

"Who is it?" she shouts. "Who's there?"

The shape glints again, as if its skin reflects light.

And then it stands tall and walks out on long, muscular legs, almost spider-like in the delicacy of its movement. She decides that it's Special Forces because of its suit, which is formfitting and camouflaged with a dark mix of colors to blend with mud and ash.

Pale arms bulky with muscle are secured with weapons, shiny black guns that she has no name for. Its hands are too large for its body, but fitted perfectly into the guns' handles. She sees the glint of knife blades too, and they scare her more, as if it is also prepared for a more intimate killing.

Its face is thick-jawed, lean and masculine, although she can't quite think of it as male. Its eyes are narrow slits, hooded by a forehead that juts out. It stares at her then walks up close. She doesn't move.

"You're here to meet me?" she asks. "You're Special Forces?"

It sniffs the air around her and nods.

"Do you know who I am?"

It nods again. If it's not human, what is it? How did it come to work for the Dome? Is it a wretch that they've rebuilt for the Dome's protection?

"Do you know where you're supposed to take me?"

"Yes." The voice is human. In fact, it's shot through with melancholy and longing. He says, "I know you."

This is frightening. She can't say why. "I'm your charge," she says, hoping that this was what he meant. "Or maybe *hostage* is the better word?"

"Of course," he says, and then he turns and crouches. "I will carry you. It's fastest."

She hesitates. "A piggyback ride?" She's surprised she's used the term. It's been ages.

He doesn't respond, just stays still.

She looks around. She has no other options. "I have this box," she says. "I'm supposed to deliver it."

He reaches up and takes the box from her. "I'll keep it safe."

She pauses again but then climbs onto his back. She locks her wrists around his thick neck. "Okay," she says.

He sets off, hurtling through the woods, away from the city. His gait is fast and smooth and nearly silent. Even when he jumps large outcroppings of underbrush, he lands softly. Sometimes he stops abruptly, hides behind a stand of trees. Lyda hears the sharp yap of an errant dog, and someone singing. Singing! Here, outside the Dome, singing endures. The idea surprises her.

And now they're running again. The cold air fills her lungs. She's breathless. Her scarf covers her nose and mouth, but also her ears, creating loud tunnels of wind. Is this what it was like when people used to ride horses—all wind and trees and speed? She's on the soldier's back—her arms around his neck, her legs around his back, as if she were a child. But he's not a soldier. He's not wholly human. And she's not a child. She's an offering.

She hears the electrical buzzing sound. It's coming from all different directions. He stops, raises his hand to his mouth, and makes some kind of call that Lyda can't hear—maybe a sound out of her register. But she knows it's a call because she feels the vibration through his ribs locked in her knees. He stands stock-still.

"We'll wait," he says and bends to his knees, letting her get down.

She stands, feeling wobbly. "You know who we're looking for?" she says.

He looks at her sharply over his shoulder as if he's hurt by some kind of accusation. "Of course."

"I'm sorry," she says.

They wait awhile longer.

"How do you know me?" she says.

He looks at her through his narrow eyes. "I was," he says.

"You were what?" she asks.

"I was," he says again. "And now I'm not."

She sees clearly now that he's not old—just about half a dozen years older than she is, perhaps. His face doesn't resemble anything she's ever seen before—the thick brow, the heavy jaw—and yet could he have once been someone else? "Do I know you from the academy? Did you attend?"

He stares at her as if he's trying to remember something long lost.

"You were an academy boy. You became Special Forces. This is what they turned you into?" She thinks of the small, elite corps. This can't be what was done to them. It would be impossibly cruel. She lifts her hand. She touches one of the guns. She can see the place in his arm where the metal meets the folds of his skin.

He doesn't say a word, doesn't move. His eyes simply shift to her face.

"What about your family? Do they know you're here?"

"I was," he says again. "And now I'm not."

PRESSIA

LIGHT

PRESSIA FEELS LOST. The dust swirls around the car. The barren landscape stretches on before them. East. What was once a national preserve. That's all they have. And that might not even be a real clue. It might mean nothing. She says, "Smoke signals would help."

Bradwell looks at her sharply. "You're right," he says as if he's been thinking along the same lines. "The Dome would see smoke signals, though, but we need something like it."

"Recite it all again," Pressia says to Partridge. "The birthday card. Take it from the top. El Capitan hasn't heard it yet."

"It's useless," Partridge says. "There's nothing out here. There's nothing farther east but a hill and beyond that more dead barren nothingness. What are we doing out here, except risking our lives?"

"Recite it again," Bradwell says.

Partridge sighs. *"Always walk in the light. Follow your soul. May it have wings. You are my guiding star, like the one that rose in the east and guided the Wise Men. Happy 9th Birthday, Partridge! Love, Mom. Ta da!"*

"Always walk in the light," El Capitan says.

"The light," Helmud says.

"I've got nothing," El Capitan says.

"Nothing," Helmud says.

Pressia unclasps the necklace, pain slicing through the back of her neck. She stares at it in her palm, its blue jewel of an eye. She puts it up to one of her own eyes and squints through it, tinging the desolate land blue. She says, "How did 3-D glasses work? You know, the ones in the movie theaters that the people wore while eating from little paper buckets?"

"There were different kinds," Bradwell says. "Some used two different-colored lenses, one red and one blue, which made sense of a film that really had two images running at the same time. Other glasses were polarized, horizontal and vertical images being worked out by the lenses."

"Could someone send a light message that only people looking through a certain lens could see?" Pressia asks, musing aloud.

"In the Dome, there was this kid named Arvin Weed who sent messages to the girls' dorm shining a laser pen on the grass lawn of the commons," Partridge says, tapping the window with his knuckle, gazing off as if he's trying to picture the grass lawn now. "Some said he was trying to invent a type of laser that only his girlfriend could see."

"So if you want to be found and you can't use smoke signals," Pressia says, "you might use a kind of light that can only be seen through a certain lens."

Bradwell says, "What do you know about photons, Partridge? Infrared or UV? Do they teach a lot of science in the Dome?"

"I wasn't the best student," he says. "We have ways of detecting these kinds of light pretty simply. But Weed's right. There are other levels of light. He could send a beam right at his girlfriend— from his window to hers—and she could see it through a lens that only sees different frequencies of light out of our visual range. You know, two sixty-two, three forty-nine, three seventy-five." Pressia and Bradwell exchange a glance. No, neither of them knows this kind of thing. Pressia sees a twinge in Bradwell's face. She thinks of how much he loves to know things. They've both been robbed of an education that Partridge has taken for granted. Partridge doesn't notice. He goes on, "And they could need a lens to be detected. The beams would also have to be directed right at the person looking through that lens, right? Because lasers don't scatter light."

"It's like how dogs can hear whistles that are out of our hearing range," Bradwell says.

"I guess so," Partridge says. "I never had a dog."

"Light can exist on a spectrum that can be seen only through one kind of filter? Is that right?" Pressia says.

"Exactly," Partridge says.

Pressia feels a shiver run through her body. She holds the swan's blue eye to hers again. The landscape swims in front of her again, awash in blue light. "What if this isn't just the blue eye of a swan. What if it's our lens, our filter."

"*Always walk in the light,*" Bradwell says.

Pressia looks at the hills before them, and sweeps back and forth. She passes a small glinting white light, stops, and returns to it. The light sits like a beacon, like a star on top of a Christmas tree during the Before.

"What is it?" Bradwell asks.

"I don't know," she says. "A small white light." Pressia readjusts her view and sees another white light, flickering on top of another distant tree on the hillside. "Could it be her?" If this is the work of her mother, then it's the first real thing Pressia has ever known of her—on her own, without stories and photographs, and the murky past. Her mother is a flickering white light pulsing in trees.

"Aribelle Cording Willux," Bradwell says again, like the last time, a little awed and mystified.

"Can I look?" Partridge asks.

Pressia hands him the gem.

Partridge pulls himself to the middle of the backseat, up to the edge. He lowers his head and squints through the gem. "It's just a cloudy blue haze."

"Keep looking," she says. She isn't crazy. She saw the light. It was there, flashing.

And then he sees it too. Pressia knows he does. "Wait," he says. "It's straight ahead."

"If this is it, then once we're closer, we won't have the vantage point for it to lead us," Bradwell says. "We'll have to find some focus to keep us on the right trail."

"We've gotten this far," Partridge says.

"Maybe we'll get lucky," El Capitan says.

Helmud has a slack jaw but his hands still move nervously behind his brother's back. There's something in his eyes that makes Pressia wonder if he's smarter than he looks. "Lucky," Helmud says.

PRESSIA

SWARM

EL CAPITAN PARKS THE CAR in vines at the foot of the hills. He covers it as well as he can with clumps of plants he pulls from the earth, roots and all. He tells them which plants not to touch. "The one with the spikes on the tips of the three-pronged leaves, they're acidic. Coated in a thin film of it. They'll blister you." He points out a clutch of white flowering mushrooms. "Those are infectious. If you step on them and break them open, they'll send out spores." One group, he tells them, was part animal. "Vertebrate," he says. "They have berries that lure animals that they can choke and eat."

Pressia walks directly behind Partridge, who walks behind El Capitan, avoiding the most poisonous plants.

Bradwell insists on walking behind everyone, "to keep watch," but Pressia wonders if he's worried about her. She remembers the feel of his hand on her neck before he cut out the chip and the gentle touch of his finger on her wrist scar. And his eyes, the gold flecks. Where had they come from? It was as if they'd suddenly appeared. Beauty, you can find it here if you look hard enough. Every once in a while, in a quick shot, she'll remember how he looked at her, taking in her entire face. The thought of it makes her nervous, the same feeling as having a secret you hope no one ever finds out about.

They're in the brush, tromping uphill over thorny brambles and spiked vines, trying to stay true to the direction of the white light. Pressia feels unsteady, as if she has the legs of a newborn colt. The ground is unpredictably loose with gravel. She can hear the light noise of their blades tinking against one another as they walk. El Capitan huffs, and Helmud sometimes makes small noises on his back—little clicks and murmurs. Each of them loses their footing from time to time. The wind is stiff and cold. It helps to keep her alert. At their backs, the Deadlands writhe.

She's aware of her body more keenly now. Her vision is still a little milky, her hearing dimmed. Her head and neck wounds throb.

If she finds her mother, won't that mark her death? If they somehow get her mother to a safe place and don't hand her over to the Dome, they'll become targets, all of them. And if they fail and Special Forces gets hold of their mother first, Pressia will no longer be of use and she'll be killed.

She feels a well of dread in her stomach. She should be happy that there's a chance her mother is alive in a bunker in the hills. But if that's the case, why didn't she come for Pressia? The bunker isn't halfway around the world. It's right here. Why not leave the bunker and search for her daughter and bring her back? What if the answer is simple: *It was never worth the risk*? What if the answer is: *I didn't love you enough*?

Partridge stops so abruptly that she almost runs into his back. "Wait," he says.

They all stop and fall silent.

"I hear something."

It's a faint hum. The humming grows louder.

A hazy golden cloud descends upon them through the trees, and then suddenly there are wings beating around their heads. El Capitan bats the air. Pressia strikes what seems to be a swarm of large bees with heavily armored shells, like beetles. The hum fills her head, her chest. It vibrates through the surrounding trees. The insects are like a hive spinning around her head. Partridge smacks a few. They fall to the brambles.

But then she sees one of them—just one, stalled on the ground. It looks like Freedle, except not rusty and mottled. She picks it up in her hand, cupping it so it doesn't fly away. She knows this sensation immediately. A fat shiny insect crawling on her palm. Its wings fold in close to its body, like a cicada except that it's made of filigree metal, light and ornate. It has fine wire ribs and gears that churn slowly, a wasp's stinger—a golden needle like a tail—and small eyes on the sides of the head. "Wait. These are good," she says. The insect then lets out a familiar click and purr.

"How do you know?" Partridge asks.

"I've had one of these as a pet almost all my life."

"Where did yours come from?" Bradwell asks.

"I don't know. It was just always there."

"The birthday card," Partridge says. *"Follow your soul. May it have wings."*

"Do you think she sent them?" Pressia asks.

"If she did, then she knows we're coming," Bradwell says. "It's not possible."

"How else will we know exactly where to go from here on the ground in the hills? They're here to lead us the rest of the way," Partridge says. "It's part of the plan. It's just been a very long time coming."

"But anyone could have found that necklace and held it up," Bradwell says. "These insects could be leading the enemy to her."

The cicada twitches in Pressia's palm. She bends closer, opens her hand just enough so that she can see through the slits between her fingers.

Its gears speed up. It cocks its head. And one of its eyes flashes a beam of light into her left eye. She blinks. Her eyes tear. The locust tries again.

"A mechanical insect with a retinal scan," Partridge says.

"It's old world," Bradwell says. "But it doesn't seem to recognize Pressia's retinas."

Pressia hands it to Partridge. "You try it. If she sent it, it will recognize you."

A bead in the center of the insect's chest flickers. Its wings flutter.

"It knows who you are," Bradwell says.

The locust starts beating its wings.

Partridge flattens his palm and raises it up. "Let's see where it goes."

If these insects were sent by her mother, was Freedle a gift from her?

The insect, now aglow, flits into the air, dipping through limbs.

PARTRIDGE

PULSES

T HE LOCUSTS HAVE ALL SCATTERED EXCEPT for the one that did the retinal scans. It's a strange sensation, to be known for your retinas. Partridge assumes that his mother set this up before the Detonations, that she planned ahead and had his retinas recorded. How else? The specificity of her plan unnerves him. If she could do so much to prepare, why couldn't she have kept the family together? He wants to know what happened in the final days.

But her plan also feels scattered, buckshot. There were so many places they could have lost the trail that he wonders if his mother ever really believed that he would put all these riddles together. In his childhood, weren't there some presents he couldn't find without her help with the riddle she'd concocted for him? He supposes that the plan took shape out of desperation. She worked with what she had under constraints he couldn't imagine.

The insect is up ahead, flying quickly through the trees, much faster than they are. It's strange to see someone as gruff as El Capitan following a dainty winged bug, as if he's a butterfly collector.

Bradwell, Pressia, El Capitan and his brother—these are his friends now, his own herd. He thinks of the herd of academy boys as he last saw them, saying their good-byes in the coding center. Vic Wellingsly, Algrin Firth, the Elmsford twins—broad shouldered, low-voiced. They shoved each other around and went their separate ways. Partridge misses Hastings all of a sudden. Did he ever have lunch with Arvin Weed like Partridge told him to? Or did he try to join the herd? Have any of them thought much of Partridge since? He wonders what story they've been fed about his disappearance. Maybe they think he had a ticker put in and someone flipped the switch to put him out of his misery, just like they said.

El Capitan stops up ahead. He holds up one finger and points into the woods. Everyone freezes and looks. Partridge squints into the shadows. He sees a very quick shifting of light. A limb bobs. Leaves rustle. But no one is there.

"It's them," El Capitan says. "Special Forces. That's how they communicate with each other. Feel the electricity? It's like echolocation."

"Special Forces?" Partridge says.

"But how can they know we're here?" Bradwell asks.

"The chip is gone," Pressia says. "It doesn't make sense."

A pulse of electricity prickles his skin and crackles like static electricity. The buzz is in the air. Partridge tries to follow the pulse, which moves wave-like.

"They're part animal, part machine," El Capitan says. "They can sniff you out."

"But not miles away," Pressia says. "They were tipped off."

Partridge looks at Pressia. "Your eyes," he says. "The retinal scan should have picked up your eyes as well as mine. I mean, she probably got both of us scanned, right?"

"I don't know."

"Interference," Partridge says. "That's why."

There's a quick series of pulses now, crisscrossing the woods.

"What are you talking about?" Bradwell asks.

"Where have you been?" Partridge asks Pressia. "I mean, that car. That didn't survive the Detonations. It's from the Dome. So other stuff from the Dome is here, too. Right? What have they done to you?"

"At OSR headquarters, they dressed me, fed me, tried to make me shoot people, and eventually, when I was taken to the farmhouse, they poisoned me."

"Poisoned you?"

"I don't know what happened really. I passed out, they put me under with ether of some kind, and I woke up later in the car. I had a headache, and I felt out of it. Everything was blurry and my ears felt muffled."

"You're bugged," Partridge says.

"What do you mean?" Bradwell says.

"Her eyes, her ears. Jesus," he says. "They've seen everything she's seen, heard everything she's said." He looks at Pressia and wonders, for a moment, if his father is watching him now. He imagines that he's looking past her eyes and into the Dome.

Pressia whispers, "I got the chip taken out for nothing?"

"No," Bradwell says. "This is temporary, right? We can get her free of all this, can't we?"

"I don't know," Partridge says.

"The electrical pulses are getting stronger," El Capitan says, "which means they're closing in fast."

"Okay, let's stay calm," Bradwell says. "She's bugged. That's all."

"It's worse, actually," Partridge says. He doesn't want to say the next part, but he has to. "Your headache. Do you have a cut, a bruise?"

"I think I hit my head while I was fighting Ingership."

Partridge thinks of Hastings, how he was panicked about the ticker. Partridge told him it isn't real, that it is a myth. It's not.

"What is it?" Bradwell says. "What's wrong? Talk to us."

The pulses are coming even faster now. The crackling, buzzing electricity seems to be ricocheting around them through the trees.

"She's got a bomb in her head," Partridge says.

"What the hell are you saying?" Bradwell asks.

Pressia looks at the ground, as if she's remembering what happened at the farmhouse, putting pieces together.

Partridge says, "They've got a switch that they can flip, and if they do, her head will explode."

Everyone looks at Pressia. For a moment, Partridge wonders if she's going to start crying. He wouldn't blame her. Instead, she gazes solemnly back at them, her eyes steady, as if she accepts it. Partridge realizes that he still fights the idea that humans are capable of such evil.

Pressia looks away, uphill. Her vision catches on something. "It's stopped. It's hovering."

And there is the cicada, batting a small circle over one particular spot.

El Capitan runs to it and starts digging through the dirt with his bare hands. He wipes a crescent pane of thick glass. "It's here."

Partridge runs over and lies down on his stomach to look inside. It's dark, but there's a distant glow somewhere deep inside the earth. "This is it!" he says. "Get a rock. We can try to break in."

The pulses are almost constant. The electrical buzz whines, set at a higher pitch. There's no time to get a rock.

The bodies emerge, one by one, from the trees, until there are five of them. They're grotesque—monstrous thighs and swollen chests; their arms, thick with muscle, are fused with arsenals—and their faces are distorted, their craniums bulging distortions of elongated and protruding bones. Could these soldiers once have been academy boys, jostling across the turf greens, sitting through Welch's lectures in front of the art projector, listening to

Glassings make his dangerous asides? How many of them has the Dome done this to? Is this what they were going to do to Sedge? Was this future part of the reason he killed himself?

One of them knocks El Capitan to the ground with an elbow cross to his face. El Capitan falls hard. Helmud takes the brunt of the fall. The soldier rips El Capitan's rifle loose from his grip.

Another moves into view, partially hidden by billowing white cloth. But then Partridge sees that the white is clothing, a jumpsuit. A small figure, a shaved head, a face covered with a white scarf. A woman. The soldier—if that's what he can be called—is holding her around the waist. He pulls down the scarf.

Lyda—her delicate cheekbones now dusted with ash, her startlingly blue eyes, her lips, and dainty nose. "Why are you here?" Partridge asks, amazed, but he knows the answer, at least in part. She's a hostage. She's here to force him to make a decision. But what decision?

"Partridge," she whispers, and he sees that she's holding a blue box in her hands. He wonders for a moment if she's come all this way to give him something that she forgot earlier—a boutonniere for the dance? He knows that the thought is illogical, but he can't shake it.

She lifts the box. "It's for someone named Pressia Belze," she says, and she glances at everyone standing before her.

Pressia steps forward and walks to Lyda. Pressia clearly doesn't want to take the box.

Lyda is hesitant too. She says, "Are you the swan?"

"What did you say?" Partridge asks.

"Who here is the swan?" Lyda asks.

"Did someone tell you something about a swan?" Partridge says.

"They're waiting for the swan," Lyda says, and then she pushes the box into Pressia's hands. "That's all I know." She wants to get rid of the gift. She's scared of it.

Pressia looks at Lyda and then at the soldiers around her. The red target lights of their guns are trained on Pressia's chest. Her hands are shaking. She opens the box, fiddles with some tissue paper. She looks at what's inside, and Partridge can tell that, at first, it makes no sense to her. But then she looks up and lets the box fall to the ground. Her face has gone pale. She staggers backward and drops to her knees.

Lyda reaches for her or perhaps the box, but the soldier jerks her back.

"Get up!" the soldier shouts. Pressia looks up. The soldier has a red bead of light trained on her forehead. And then the soldier speaks more quietly. "Get up. Come on. It's time."

And it's in that softer voice—maybe the rhythm of the words—that Partridge hears his brother's voice, talking to him in the way he used to when Partridge was just a sleepy kid waking up, kicking sheets.

Get up. Come on. It's time.

Sedge.

PRESSIA

TUNNEL

AT FIRST PRESSIA TELLS HERSELF that her grandfather is not dead. They've taken out the fan, repaired his throat, and stitched him up. Pressia is still on her knees. She can't get up. She looks at the girl's face. A Pure. Someone Partridge knows. Someone he calls Lyda. "He's not dead," Pressia says.

"I'm supposed to tell you that it's all they have left," Lyda says gently.

The small set of fan blades looks polished, as if someone took their time. Pressia's grandfather is dead. That's what this means. And what does the light through the crescent window dug into the dirt mean—that her mother is alive? Is this the way the world works—endless taking and giving? It's cruel.

Still on her knees, Pressia grabs a fistful of dirt.

There's a bomb in her head. The Dome sees what she sees, hears what she hears. They've heard everything she and Bradwell said to each other last night—the confession of his lie, his desire to see his father with an engine in his chest, her scar. She feels stripped of all privacy. She looks at Bradwell; his beautiful face looks anguished. She closes her eyes. She refuses to let them see anything. She presses the doll head and her dirty hand to her ears. She'll starve them—the enemy, the people who killed her grandfather, who could kill her by exploding her head with a remote-control switch. But this makes it worse. She's punishing herself in order to punish someone else. *Kill me*, she wants to whisper. *Just do it*—as if she could call their bluff. The problem is that they aren't bluffing.

She looks at Bradwell again. He gazes at her as if he desperately wants to help her. He says her name, but she shakes her head. What can he do? They killed Odwald Belze, and then it was someone's job to polish the fan that had been in his throat and wrap it in pale blue tissue paper and find the perfect box. The people who did this are in her head. These are simple unalterable facts.

Pressia stands, her fist still clenching dirt. She's crying, silently. The tears work their way down her face.

Partridge looks dazed. His expression is a strange mix of fear and maybe anxious anticipation. He looks at the girl, Lyda, and the soldier beside her.

The beasts Pressia saw with El Capitan just days ago are soldiers. They were once human, once boys. She spots the cicada. It has perched on a furred leaf and tucked in its wings. Its light has faded.

The first soldier to arrive walks toward Partridge. Pressia is trying to listen, trying to pay attention. Her ears are ringing.

The soldier says, "Retrieve your mother. Do not disturb her quarters. Give her to us. We will give you this girl. If you do not, we kill the girl and take your mother."

"Fine," Partridge says quickly. "We'll do it."

"I can't fit through that window," Bradwell says.

"Neither can I," El Capitan says. "Not with this." He gestures to Helmud.

One of the soldiers walks to the window, which is slanted slightly upward to fit with the slope. He drops his knee into the glass, puncturing a hole. He punches the rest of it loose, barefisted, but he doesn't bleed.

The soldier says, "Only the Willux boy and Pressia."

"She might not be there," Pressia says. "She might be dead."

The soldier says nothing for a moment, as if he's awaiting confirmation of orders.

"Then bring the body," the soldier says.

The window is a dark crescent, dimly lit from within. Partridge goes in feetfirst. He has to tuck one arm down into the window and then drop. Pressia sits on the edge of the window, the ground littered with glass. She slips her legs in and, for a moment, lets them dangle. Then she feels Partridge's hands on her legs. She looks back one last time. There's El Capitan and Helmud, eyes darting wildly; the Pure girl with the shorn head, surrounded by the beastly soldiers who tower over her. And then there's Bradwell, dirt and blood on his face. He looks at her as if he's trying to memorize her face, as if he may never see it again.

She says, "I'll be back," but this isn't a promise that she knows she can keep. How can anyone promise that they'll return? She thinks of the smiley face she drew in the ash of the cabinet door. It's childish. Stupid. A lie.

She slides off the edge and falls through the window. Even with Partridge's help, she lands hard on the ground.

They're in a small room. The floor and walls are dirt. There's only one way to go—down a narrow hallway lined with moss. She looks up through the crescent window but only sees a bit of sky, coagulated by gray clouds and crosshatched by a few tree limbs.

A man's voice calls out down the hall, "This way!" A tall, narrow-shouldered figure appears at the end of the hallway. Backlit, his features are too dark to make out. She thinks for a moment of the word *father*. But it doesn't even register. She can't believe it. She can't believe anything.

She turns to Partridge and whispers urgently, "I need to know about the girl."

"Lyda."

"Are you going to hand over our mother to save her?"

"I was buying time. Lyda knows something. She knows the swan. Who's waiting for the swan? What does that mean?"

"Are you going to hand over our mother, if she's alive?" Pressia asks again.

"I don't think that will be my decision, in the end."

Pressia grabs his shirt. "Would you? Would you do it? To save Lyda? I did it. I sacrificed my grandfather. He's dead." Couldn't she have saved him? If she'd followed orders...

Partridge looks at Pressia intently. "What about Bradwell?"

The question catches her off guard. "Why would you even ask something like that?"

"What would you do to save him?"

"No one's asking me to hand over my mother to save him," Pressia says. Is he accusing her of having feelings for him? "So it doesn't matter."

"What if you were forced to choose?"

Pressia isn't sure what to say. "I'd rather hand over myself."

"But what if that wasn't an option?"

"Partridge," she whispers. "They can hear this, see it. All of it."

"I don't care anymore," he says. His eyes are teary, his voice shallow. "Sedge. My brother. He isn't dead. He's one of them."

"Who?" Pressia says.

"Special Forces," Partridge says. "He's one of the soldiers up there. They've turned him into—I don't know if he's really still in there. I don't know what they've done to his soul. We can't..."

Up ahead, there's the man's voice again. "This way." It's deep and unwavering. "We're here."

Partridge reaches out for her hand, but instead he grabs the doll-head fist. Pressia expects him to recoil, but he doesn't. He wraps his hand around the doll head, as he would her hand, and looks back at her. "Ready?"

PARTRIDGE

BELOW

THE DIRT FLOOR OF THE TUNNEL gives way to muddy tile, its grout black. The air is humid, smells mildewy. There are a few lights at the end of the hall. The cicadas flutter like moths, their metal wings clicking. Partridge holds his sister's doll-head fist in his hand. It is part of her. It isn't with her, but of her. He can feel the humanness of it—the warmth, the play beneath the skin of a real hand, alive. He feels a surge of protectiveness. Things could go badly from here on out. He knows he shouldn't feel so protective; Pressia's tougher than he is. She's been through so much more than he could ever imagine.

Their mother is here, somewhere. But will she be the mother he remembers? Practically everything he's known to be true—even her death—has been proven wrong. Still, she left all of these clues behind. She's led them here, which feels right, maternal.

The man at the end of the hall has stooped shoulders and a clean angular face. "You're a Pure?" Partridge asks, without thinking.

"I'm not a Pure. I'm not a wretch either," he says. "I survived in here. I would say I'm an American but that term no longer exists. I guess you can call me Caruso." He asks them if they'd like to see their mother.

"It's why I've come all this way," Partridge says.

"Right," Caruso says. "We wish you hadn't done that."

"Done what?" Partridge says.

"Left the Dome," Caruso tells him. "Your mother had a plan, either way."

"What were you planning if I stayed?"

"A takeover, from the inside out."

"I don't get it. A takeover from the inside out?" Partridge says. "It's not doable."

"Don't say too much," Pressia says. "I'm bugged."

"Bugged? Who's got her bugged?"

"The Dome," Pressia says.

Caruso stops and stares at Pressia. "Well, then, they can take a good, long look. Get an eyeful. What do I care? I didn't destroy the planet. I've got nothing to be ashamed of. We've lived here in defiance of them. We survived despite their best efforts." He turns to Partridge. "A takeover from the inside is doable if you have a leader in there."

"A leader on the inside? No one's capable of that. Who's this leader?" Partridge says.

"Well, you were supposed to be. Until you left."

Partridge feels a little unsteady. He runs his hand along the wall. "Me?" he says. "I was the leader on the inside? That doesn't make any sense."

"Come on," Caruso says. "Let your mother explain it to you."

They walk down the hall. The cicadas are now swirling around their heads.

The man stops at a metal door with a row of hinges running down its center. He looks down at the floor. "Be aware," he says. "Aribelle isn't the same. But she survived for you. Remember that."

Partridge isn't sure what this means. He looks at Pressia. "Are you okay?"

She nods. "Are you?"

He's terrified. He feels like he's standing on the edge of a ravine. It doesn't feel like he's going to become a son again or get some part of his old life back. No. It feels like the beginning of something unknowable. "Yeah," he says, "I'm okay," hoping he really is.

Caruso pushes a button, and the metal door folds to one side.

PRESSIA

CLOUDS

IN SOME WAYS, THE ROOM REMINDS Pressia of the little domestic scenes in Bradwell's magazines. There's an armchair with appliqué birds on it, a fuzzy wool rug, a small standing lamp, and drapes. But the drapes don't frame a window; they're underground. They hide more wall. It's the only possibility.

But it's not a little domestic scene at all because there's also a long metal table filled with communications devices—radios, computers, old servers, screens. None of them are on.

And running alongside the far wall, there is the most unusual thing of all, a long metal capsule with a glass cover. It's vaguely aquatic. She remembers her grandfather talking about glass-bottomed boats, *tourist traps*, he called them, that took you out through the swamps in Florida where you could count alligators lining the banks. It's strange to think of Florida now; that's where she was supposed to have been coming home from when her grandfather met her in the airport at the time of the Detonations. Disney, the mouse wearing white gloves. It never happened.

The metal capsule with the glass cover also reminds Pressia of Saint Wi, the statue of the girl in the crypt, the stone casket that was behind the Plexiglas.

And of course, it reminds her of her own cabinet, of home.

Is this where her mother lies?

A few cicadas followed and now circle the ceiling, and for a moment Pressia wonders if Caruso is insane. It wouldn't be that strange, having lived in confinement all these years. Is this a funeral? Is her mother really dead? Is this just a cruel joke?

Partridge must be thinking the same thing, because he turns and glares at Caruso who's lingering in the doorway. "What is this thing?"

"We have sixty-two of these," Caruso says. "We planned for air contamination and oxygen depletion. They're completely outfitted with oxygen. We didn't need them for that, but they've come in handy with viral contamination and general organ collapse."

"Sixty-two?"

"All we could get our hands on at the time. We had three hundred people here at one point. Scientists. Their families."

"Where are they now?"

"Your mother and I are the only ones left. Many died. Others branded themselves with scars to fit in with the other survivors and left. They still communicate with us. That's how we found out about your escape. Rumors. We weren't sure they were true until we picked up the light source on the gem."

"It sent light back?" Pressia asks.

"A refraction, yes."

Pressia isn't ready to look behind the glass. She stands slightly behind Partridge, letting him go first. He leans forward and draws in his breath. She can't see his face.

Pressia leans forward now. There is a woman's serene face behind the glass, her eyes closed. She is the woman from Partridge's photograph, their mother. Her hair is curly, dark but tinged gray, and it lies on the pillow in loose curls. She's still beautiful even though her skin is nearly papery and her eyes look bruised.

But then there is her ravaged body.

Her neck leads to collarbones, one of which is a steel rod that turns into a metal gear at the shoulder. Her arm is made of stainless steel. The metal is perforated as if from a colander, perhaps to keep it lighter in weight. In lieu of fingers, the arm narrows to a ball-bearing hinge where the wrist should be and ends in a pincer—two metal prongs. The other arm gives way to a prosthetic just above the elbow. It's wooden, thin, tan in color. It's been whittled to look like a real arm. Its dainty fingers are hinged. Leather straps keep it in place by attaching around the knotty bone of her shoulder.

Her legs are gone as well. She's wearing a skirt that ends mid-shin. Her prosthetic legs are skeletal—two bone-like spokes meeting at the ankles and then something closer to pedals for feet. Both are dented and nicked from use.

It's hard to explain but her limbs seem beautiful to Pressia. Maybe it's Bradwell's view that there's beauty in their scars and fusings because they are signs of their survival, which *is* a beautiful thing, if you think about it. In this case, someone built these arms and legs for her, the metal seams, the stitching in the leather straps, the covered bolts, the stippled design of the perforations. There's delicacy, care, love that's been poured into them.

Her mother is wearing a white shirt with a row of yellowed pearl buttons that matches the white skirt, and Pressia can't tell where the prosthetics end, but this is the way her own doll head works. It doesn't begin or end.

The buttons on her mother's cotton shirt rise and fall. Somewhere within her, there's a pair of lungs, a heart. The others who lived in the bunker were here during the Detonations, but her mother must not have been. For a moment, Pressia wonders if her mother was out trying to save wretches—a saint, just like Partridge thought all these years.

Caruso pushes a button on the edge of the capsule, and the top pops with some kind of pneumatic release.

Partridge grips the capsule's edge to hold himself steady.

Caruso steps back. "I'll leave you to talk."

Pressia thinks: Aribelle Cording, Mrs. Willux, Mother. What should she call her?

And then her mother's eyes open. They're gray, like Partridge's, like ashen clouds. Her mother sees Partridge's face, which is just above hers. She reaches up with her wooden hand and touches his cheek. "Partridge," she says and she starts to cry.

"Yes," he says. "I'm here."

"Here," she whispers. "Put your cheek on mine." And he does. Pressia realizes that her mother must want to feel his skin on hers.

They are both crying now, softly. And, for a moment, Pressia feels lost, as if she wasn't invited, as if she's intruding. Partridge pulls away from his mother. "And Sedge is here. He's overhead, aboveground."

"Sedge is here?" her mother says.

"And Pressia is here, too."

"Pressia?" her mother says, as if she's never heard the name before, and maybe she hasn't. It's not Pressia's real name anyway. It was made up. She doesn't know her real name.

"Your daughter," Partridge says. He reaches for Pressia, grabs her arm, and tugs her forward.

"How?" her mother says, and she hooks her pincer on a strap inside the capsule, pulls herself up to a seated position. She looks at Pressia, stares at her, confused. "It can't be," she says.

And Pressia lowers her head. She steps quickly backward, knocking into the table of electronics. One of the narrow radios topples, clattering loudly on the metal tabletop. "I'm sorry," Pressia says, and she reaches out with her hand and her doll-head fist to set the radio back into place. "I should be going," she says. "It was a mistake."

"No," her mother says, "wait." She points to the doll.

Pressia steps forward.

Her mother opens her hinged fingers.

Pressia lifts the doll's head and places it in her mother's wooden palm.

Her mother says, "Christmas." She touches the doll's nose, the lips. She looks at Pressia. "Your baby. I'd recognize her anywhere."

Pressia closes her eyes. She feels as if she's breaking open.

"You're mine," her mother says.

Pressia nods.

Her mother opens her arms wide.

Pressia leans over the capsule and lets her mother pull her to her chest. This is her mother—her *real* mother. She hears the beating of her mother's faint heart, the rise and fall of her fragile rib cage—alive. She wants to tell her everything that she's been holding on to—her memories like beads of a necklace. She wants to tell her about her grandfather and the back room of the barbershop. She remembers that she has the barbershop bell in her sweater pocket. She'll give it to her. It's not much of a gift. But it's something she can point to—*this was my life, but now my life has changed*. "What's my name?" Pressia asks.

"You don't know your name?"

"No."

"Emi," she says, "Emi Brigid Imanaka."

"Emi Brigid Imanaka," Pressia says. It's so foreign that it isn't a name really at all, but interlocking sounds that fit together perfectly.

Her mother's eyes lock onto the broken pendant. "So it was of use, after all this time," she says.

"You did plant it for us to find you?" Partridge says.

"I planted many things," she said. "I couldn't rely on any one trail of bread crumbs surviving the blasts, so I made as many as I could. And this one worked!"

"Do you remember the song?" Pressia asks.

"What song?"

"About the screen door slamming and the girl on the porch whose dress sways?"

"Of course." And then her mother whispers, "You're here. You found me. I've missed you. I've spent my life missing you."

PRESSIA

TATTOOS

AND THEN THINGS MOVE QUICKLY. "We don't have much time," Partridge says. "Not much time at all."

"Okay," Aribelle says to Pressia, "take the floral covering off that chair, and, Partridge, you pick me up and put me in it."

Pressia follows orders and pulls the floral print covering. Beneath it there's a cane chair fitted with wheels. The wheels are disks of pounded circular tin with rubber edging. The seat is padded with small canvas pillows. "I'm bugged," Pressia says. "Eyes and ears."

"The Dome?" Aribelle asks.

Pressia nods.

"What do they want?" Aribelle asks. Partridge lifts his mother's light frail body up from the capsule. He sets her in the chair. Her body clicks.

"They want what's here," Partridge says.

"In particular, medication. We think that's the main thing they're after," Pressia says.

Aribelle turns a crank on the side of the chair with her pincer, and a small engine attached to the back of the chair catches, then hums. The chair is motorized. Exposed pistons start pumping. "So they're breaking down," she says. "The classic signs are a slight tremor of the hands and head, a palsy. Eyesight and hearing weaken. The skin deteriorates next, becoming thin and dry. Eventually, bones and muscle erode, and organs fail. It's called Rapid Cell Degeneration and happens after too much coding. We knew it would."

"It's happening to my father," Partridge says, as if this is hitting him for the first time. "I thought he was just angry at me, shaking his head, almost unconsciously showing his disgust. But that's why he wants this medicine so badly."

Aribelle freezes for a moment; her entire body is rigid. "Despite all of the reports, part of me has always believed he was dead."

"Why?" Partridge says.

"I had my reasons."

"What reasons?"

She uses her pincer to fold down the collar of her shirt, revealing the skin just above her heart. There are six small squares, their outlines barely visible under her skin. Three of the squares pulse. Three don't. "We each embedded the others' heartbeats under our skin so we would know who was living and who was dead. A kind of pulsing tattoo." She points to the first two dead squares. "These two are dead. This one, here, Ivan, died very young, not long after we had the pulses embedded. This one not long before the Detonations, and your father's heartbeat," she says to Partridge. "It stopped pulsing shortly after the Detonations."

"He has scars on his chest," Partridge says. "I saw them once. A row of scars arranged just like that."

Aribelle takes a deep breath and lets it out. "He said that he was done with all of us. He was cutting us loose. And that's what he meant. He cut us out," she says, "with a knife. It makes sense. He wouldn't know if we were alive, but he was willing to sacrifice that knowledge to make us think that he'd died."

"And the survivors?" Pressia says.

She points to each of the pulsing squares one at a time. "Bertrand Kelly. Avna Ghosh. And Hideki Imanaka."

"My father?" Pressia asks.

She nods.

Pressia's eyes fill with tears. "You think he's alive."

"The fact that his heart is beating helps to keep me alive."

"Why the tattoos?" Partridge asks. "What linked all of you together?"

"Idealism." She moves to the table, turns on the computers. Screens light up. Radios crackle. "We were all recruited for the Best and the Brightest. Among that group there were twenty-two selected for an End-of-World scenario. This was in our late teens. We were kids still. From there, your father kind of chose an inner group. He was brilliant and lost. His mind, even before he took the enhancements, worked at a frenzied pace. I could only see in retrospect how mad he'd been from the beginning." She looks again at the swan pendant. "Your father, Pressia, he gave me that necklace. I knew the inscription inside it. The swan was important to us early on, the seven of us, a symbol. But then Operation Phoenix killed the swan and turned the symbol into a bird that could rise from the ashes. Ellery Willux's idea. Hideki, he wanted me to be the swan that became a phoenix and survived all of what we knew was to come. He called me his phoenix." She closes her eyes, spilling tears. "It started out so well meaning. We were going to save the world, not end it."

"But why did you even go to Japan to begin with?" Pressia asks.

"Imanaka, your father, was doing great work. The Japanese have a very intimate history with radiation, the bomb. They were ahead of everyone else in defense, resistance. His research dovetailed with my area, trauma repair through biomedical nanotechnology. And Ellery, Partridge's father, wanted me to go over to see if Imanaka was making any progress on reversal. He was afraid that he would degenerate one day. He wanted that information above everything else. My guess is that he still does. More urgently now than ever."

She glances at Pressia, very aware she's bugged. "There are other survivors out there. If Ghosh and Kelly and Imanaka are still alive, then there are more. Ellery wouldn't want news of this to circulate in the Dome. But I know it has to be true. I haven't been able to establish contact with anyone beyond a hundred-mile radius—radio wave, satellite . . . Nothing works. The Dome keeps all of those methods blocked. But I live on hope."

Pressia thinks of Saint Wi and Bradwell there in the crypt, kneeling before the small statue behind the cracked Plexiglas. Hope.

"You got resistance down, in some way, right? I mean, you did something to make me resistant to coding," Partridge says.

"Yes, but we didn't get it down fast enough. There was nothing we were going to be able to do to stop the Detonations—only defense and repair. We knew that it wouldn't really save many lives. People would still die in the destruction—a massive body count. But we could spare the survivors fusings and poisoning. We wanted to leach radiation-resistance materials into the public drinking water. But it was too risky. Doses that work on adults could kill a child. That's why I had to choose with you, Partridge. I couldn't make you completely resistant. You were only eight, and hardy enough for only one limited run of it."

"You chose my behavioral coding."

"I wanted that to be your own. The right to say no, to stand up for what's right. I wanted your character to be kept intact."

"And me?" Pressia asks.

She takes a long jagged breath. "You were a year and a half younger and small for your age. It was too risky to dose you. You were being kept in Japan, looked after by your father and his sister. I couldn't simply come home with a baby. I would have been sent to a rehabilitation center. That's where I would have died. I discovered what my husband was planning—full-scale destruction—and when I knew he was closing in on it, I sent for you. I had to tell my husband. I had no choice. He was furious. And there was more to it. I can't explain it all now—things about the past. Dark things that I knew to be true, things that he didn't want me to know. I couldn't live in the Dome. I had a plan for stealing the boys from him. I could tell that he was moving quickly—his brain so fevered—and I knew that he was making rash decisions and had massive amounts of power, no oversight. I needed to get Emi, I mean, Pressia here with me, safe in the bunker. There were delays, problems with passports. Your aunt was bringing you by plane. The Detonations were supposed to still be weeks away.

"But then, that day, your father called me, Partridge. He said that today was the day. It was going down earlier than planned. He wanted me to get into the Dome. He begged me.

"I knew he was telling the truth. There were already strange traffic patterns. People who'd been tipped off were getting in. Pressia's plane was finally coming in. I told him no. I told him to tell the boys that I loved them, every day. I said, 'Promise me.' He hung up the phone. And I drove to the airport as fast as I could, terrified. I got the call from your auntie that the plane had landed. I still thought we might be able to make it back to the bunker before the bombs. I parked the car and was running to Baggage Claim. I could see you through the plate-glass window, standing with your auntie—so small and perfect. My girl! I tripped on the pavement, got to my hands and knees, and I looked up. There was a flash of light. The glass shattered. And I was fused to the pavement—arms and legs. Some people had known where I was headed. They tracked me down. There were four tourniquets, a saw. I was saved. Beyond all expectations, I survived."

"Did you know I'd survived?" Pressia asks.

"You had a chip. Everyone who came into this country as a foreigner had to be chipped before entering.

"Our equipment after the bombings was sketchy. We could see chips moving on the screens, but not very well. When we located your chip, I used the information from your retinal scan, data your father had sent me from Japan. It was in one of the radiation-resistant computers and survived with minor problems. I had retinal scans for the boys too. I built small winged messengers. Our locusts. I sent them out, coded with your location, and they were chipped too. But they were destroyed before they reached the destination. Finally, though, one made it."

"I was chipped," Pressia says. "You knew where I was. You could have had someone come for me and bring me back here."

"Things were awful here. Confinement, disease, hostility. And how could I take care of you as I was? I couldn't even hold you." She lifts her prosthetic arms then points to a computer screen. It's a map that Pressia recognizes—the market, the Rubble Fields, Pressia's barbershop. "At the same time, the chip was a blip on the screen, and the locust was there too, always hovering nearby. Often the two blips were so close that there was no other explanation—you held it in your hand. And your blip began to tell a story. The blip was still at night, always in the same spot at the same time. It woke up and was active. It roamed some and returned to its spot, home. It was the story of a child who was cared for—a child with a routine. A healthy child. A child better off where she was. You were okay, weren't you? Someone took care of you, someone loved you?"

Pressia nods. "Yes," she says, tears streaming down her cheeks. "Someone took care of me and loved me."

"And then a few days ago, your blip wandered and didn't return. You're sixteen now and I worried about OSR. At the same time, we heard rumors of a Pure, and then that very old locust from the first flock returned. Your locust." She pulls open a drawer in a cabinet under the computer equipment. The drawer glows warm. It's an incubator, and lying on a small piece of cloth is Freedle. "It had no message. I thought it might just be some oddity, but with everything happening at the same time, I hoped it was a sign."

"Freedle," Pressia says. "Is he okay?"

"Tired from the journey, recovering. He's elderly. But someone's taken care of all of his delicate gears."

Freedle tilts his head and flutters a wing with a series of clicks. "I've tried to," Pressia says, touching his back with one finger. "I can't believe he made it here. My grandfather..." Her voice chokes on the word. "He's gone now. But he must have set him loose."

"You should leave Freedle here," Partridge says. "He'll be safer that way."

Pressia isn't sure why but this small fact—Freedle being alive—fills her with a strange sense of hope.

"Emi," Aribelle says, "I think I have to say things that the Dome can't hear."

"I'll go in the hall and wait." Pressia then turns to Partridge. She touches his sleeve. "Warn her," Pressia whispers. "Sedge. He's not the boy she remembers."

"I know."

Pressia walks to her mother and gives her a kiss on the cheek.

"We'll be quick," her mother says.

Partridge

CYGNUS

Y OU DON'T HAVE IT, DO YOU?" Partridge asks.

"Reversal for Rapid Cell Degeneration?" She shakes her head. "No. We were on to your father. We knew he'd broken from us, that he was dangerous."

"How did you know?"

"He betrayed me."

"Didn't you betray him too?" Partridge says it so quickly that it surprises him.

She glances at him. "Fair enough. But he wasn't the person he'd told me he was."

"We can't always be who we want to be." He thinks of Sedge. Can he ever be brought back? Can his mother save him?

"Look, there are things you should know. Your father took brain enhancements before they were fully tested, when we were all still young." She stares at the floor. "Leading up to the Detonations, his brain was fully coded. He said he had to enhance his brain so that he could make this new world happen. Humans worthy of paradise—a New Eden. I didn't see him much. He told me that he'd stopped sleeping. He only thought. His mind was on fire. The synapses were burning his brain, one minuscule firing at a time. But still he thought..."

"What?" Partridge asks.

"The Dome wasn't just a job. Domes were a lifelong obsession. You should have heard him lecture on ancient cultures when he was nineteen years old...He saw himself as sitting atop the pinnacle of human civilization. And he knew that the brain enhancements he'd taken would catch up with him. He thought he could find a way to fix it. Once he had that, he thought he could live on forever."

Partridge shakes his head. "You said you were originally in charge of biomedical nanotechnology for use in trauma. I know what that means." He thinks about Arvin Weed, rambling on about self-generating cells. "Why didn't you use those drugs on yourself? Didn't you have the ability to help bone cells create more bone? Muscle tissue? Skin? Don't you have those drugs here?"

"Of course I do. A variety. And there are some that you should know about. They're very powerful." She pulls open a drawer, and there, nestled into a row of grooves, are vials.

"Powerful in what way?"

"They're part of the answer to reversal. Your father needs what's in these vials, but he also needs another ingredient, which may or may not exist. One of the others in the group was working on it. And, most of all, he needs the formula on how to fit the two pieces together."

"Does the formula exist?"

"It did, a long time ago, but I don't know if it still does."

He thinks of the guns embedded in his brother's arms, Pressia's doll head, Bradwell's birds, El Capitan and his brother. "Can these vials undo fusings?"

She clenches her eyes shut, as if pained, then slowly flexes her pincer. She shakes her head. "No," she says, angrily. "They don't disengage tissue. They adhere and build it. Your father was going to release this biosynthesizing nanotechnology purposefully into the cocktail of bombs for the sole purpose of fusing survivors to the world around them, just to create a subhuman class, a new order of slaves, to serve them in New Eden once the earth was rejuvenated. I had to tell others. I had to leave him and try to find ways to save people. I failed.

"That's the real reason why I took you with me to Japan and where I met up again with Emi's—Pressia's father, one of the seven. I had to hand over as many of your father's secrets as I could."

"But why didn't you use any of those drugs on yourself?"

"For one thing, the drugs aren't perfected. They don't always know how to stop themselves. But also, Partridge, even if the drugs were perfect, you know why I wouldn't fix myself."

"No," Partridge says, exasperated. "I don't!"

"That would be like hiding the truth. My body is the truth. It's history."

"It doesn't have to be."

She looks at his hand. "What happened?"

"I made a small sacrifice," he said.

"Do you want to take it back?"

He stares at the bandage, the end darkened by dried blood. He shakes his head. "No."

"Then maybe you understand." She closes the drawer. "I've wasted so much of my life regretting things. So much of this is my fault, Partridge." She starts to cry.

"You can't blame yourself," Partridge says.

"I had to stop looking back. It was eating me alive. Seeing you and your sister, it helps me see the future."

"There's something else my father wants," Partridge says.

"What's that?" she asks, looking up at him. Her eyes are so much like his own, but different. He's missed her so much that, for a moment, he can barely breathe. He has to look at the floor to maintain his composure.

"He wants you."

"Me? Why? He doesn't have enough servants to wait on him?"

"Caruso out there said that I was going to be the leader from the inside. What did he mean?"

"Exactly that. You were going to be our leader, the one to take down your father and the Dome. We have sleeper cells inside. A vast network."

"Sleeper cells?" Partridge says.

"People inside the Dome who were with us," she says.

She drives the chair to the metal-topped desk. She opens a drawer with her pincer and pulls out a sheet of paper. It's a long list of names. "The Dome can't know this exists. It would jeopardize people's lives."

Partridge's eyes scan down the list. "The Weeds?" he says. "Arvin's parents? And Algrin Firth's father? But Algrin's supposed to go into Special Forces, elite training." He looks down the list farther. "Glassings," he says, and then he remembers the conversation he had with Glassings in his bow tie at the dance. "He called me on taking your things from the Personal Loss Archives," Partridge says. "He said that I could talk to him about anything I needed, that I wasn't alone."

"Durand Glassings," his mother says. "He's important. Our closest link to you."

"He's my World History teacher."

"He was the one who was going to lay it out," she says.

Partridge is astonished. "But I'm no leader," he says. "I couldn't command sleeper cells and take down the Dome."

"We were waiting to see a sign that you were ready. And we got one."

"What was that?"

"Ironically, it was your escape."

"What do we do now?" Partridge asks. "They want us to hand you over, along with everything here in your labs."

"And if we refuse?"

"There's a hostage," Partridge says. "A girl named Lyda." His voice is rough as he says her name.

"Lyda," his mother says. "She means a lot to you?"

He nods. "I wish she didn't mean so much."

"No you don't."

"She risked her life for me. I'm willing to risk mine for her. But I'm not willing to risk yours."

"Maybe we can give them what they think they want. I can take in some pills and by the time they find out they're worthless, maybe you all can get away, to safety," she says. "Buy some time. Eventually, though, you'll have to fight, Partridge."

"I can't. I'm not Sedge. He was the leader. Not me."

"*Was* the leader?" she says. "What's happened to him?"

"I was told he was dead. A suicide. He's alive, though. He's up there. He's on the other side—the soldier holding the hostage. The Dome has turned him into a machine, but also a kind of animal. I can't describe it. I can tell it's him, though, from his voice. I'd know it anywhere."

"I want to see him," she says.

"Does that mean you want to go up? Hand yourself over?"

"I'm not afraid of facing your father."

"But he could kill you."

"I'm mostly dead already."

"That's not true." There is something about his mother that is more alive than anyone he's ever met.

"You can do this, Partridge. You can take over and rebuild for everyone. A Pure, that's what they call you. But what does that really mean?"

He doesn't know how to answer. He wishes he did. He wishes the words sprang up from him. But there's nothing.

"Our communication with those in the Dome is very weak,

and since your escape it's stopped completely. If we knew that the people from within were still with us, that would help."

"They are," Partridge tells her. "They sent a message through Lyda. It was simple: *Tell the swan we're waiting.*"

"The Cygnus," she whispers.

And then, overhead, there's pounding. The cicadas stir and flit nervously around the room.

Machine-gun fire.

EL CAPITAN

ABOVE

EL CAPITAN HAS HIS HANDS ON HIS HEAD, and so does Bradwell, who is slightly downhill. They order Helmud to put his hands on his head too, but El Capitan tells them it's a waste, he's a moron. "Doesn't have a thought of his own in his demented head."

"Demented head," Helmud says.

The soldiers should know this. They've watched him and Helmud in the woods, where they seemed so elegant and strong and strangely peaceful. He spots the one who may have given him a plucked hen and eggs. He's sure it was the one who arrived holding the girl in white—so new to being outside the Dome that her clothes are whiter than any cloth he's seen since the Detonations. That soldier is the one who seemed to look at him sometimes in such a human way. Actually, he trusted all of them, but he was wrong to. They'll probably kill him and Helmud out here in the woods. All of them. And that will be the end of it.

They've been stripped of their weapons. They sit in a pile like kindling. The girl has gone placid. In fact, El Capitan wonders if she's in shock. She's pretty, dangerously so. Do Special Forces have sexual urges? Should the girl be worried? Or are they neutered like dogs?

The soldier who'd shown up holding the girl lets her go and walks up beside El Capitan. He finds the rungs of El Capitan's ribs above Helmud's thigh and digs in with the muzzle of the gun. The soldier says to the others, "I don't trust this one."

El Capitan wonders if this means he's going to shoot him. He braces, but instead the soldier just keeps the gun snug in his ribs.

"Noises on the perimeter," the soldier says. "Do a quick recon. I will maintain control." This one is the leader, clearly.

The other five soldiers do as they're told, immediately setting off, silently, through the woods, in different directions.

With his high-tech weaponry glinting up his arms, the soldier then whispers to El Capitan, "When they return, protect the girl. Take cover." The girl is meant to hear this too.

El Capitan wonders what this could mean. Is this soldier on his side?

"You'll do it?"

Is he going to turn on the other soldiers? Should El Capitan be prepared to reach for a gun? "Yes, sir," he says.

"Yes, sir," Helmud says. Sometimes when Helmud repeats, the echo feels like it comes from a twitch in El Capitan's own brain. Helmud isn't only his brother. They are one and the same. El Capitan looks at the girl again, this time seeing a ferocity in her eyes that wasn't there before. If this is their only chance, she looks willing to die for it.

And Bradwell, who stands with his fingers knit on top of his head, gives off a heated energy. He's restlessly fuming. He's ready for anything. El Capitan raises his eyebrows, trying to get his attention to let him in on the plan, but Bradwell just looks at him and mouths, *What?*

As silently as they left, the squad returns within a few moments of one another. They have nothing to report. No OSR. No wretches. No other beasts. All is quiet.

"Check your scanners," the leader says. "No mistakes. No errors."

And as they each look at their arm attachments, the leader shoves the girl into El Capitan's arms. El Capitan lifts her by the ribs, takes three or four running steps, and dives. Sedge opens fire on the other soldiers. Bradwell jumps to a crevice in the rock, taking cover. The closest soldier's chest erupts. He spins and sprays ammunition into the brush wildly.

The leader aims coolly with both guns on his forearms. He fires. And then sights unfold from his shoulders and gunshots blast, alternately from each weapon, kicking his shoulders back, one then the other, as if he's rocking.

Another soldier fires back in El Capitan's direction. The reports are almost simultaneous, and one soldier gets caught in the cross fire, shot in the skull.

Two down, El Capitan thinks. He starts to crawl to his rifle in the stack of weapons on the ground, but Lyda grabs him and pulls him down, forcefully.

"Wait," she says.

Bradwell has made it to the weapons first and picks up El Capitan's rifle with its clip of ammunition. He turns and starts blazing at the other three soldiers. One gets hit in the neck and lurches sideways, behind some rocks. The leader hits another one in the gut with two or three shots.

This soldier seems to understand as he drops down into the dust that he must fire on his leader, that there's something wrong. It's as if he realizes he has to override some programming. He loads his weapon and fires, hitting the leader in the thigh. The leader buckles, but does not fall. The soldier with the wounded gut retreats behind a tree.

El Capitan sees that the one Bradwell hit is reloading behind a huge, gnarled stump. He's overridden his programming, too, and he locks in on his leader. El Capitan can see from his protected position that the soldier is badly wounded, but will not lie down to die. The uninjured soldier has escaped, and El Capitan has a good idea that he's not a deserter. He'll be back.

Lyda says, "Get me a knife."

El Capitan crawls to the pile of weapons. He grabs a knife first and tosses it to Lyda, who catches it by the handle.

He sees Bradwell make a dash to finish off the man he wounded before the soldier can fire on the leader. Bradwell shoots him in the arm, striking the flesh of his bicep, blood glistening as it disappears into his uniform. Is he still fighting?

El Capitan reaches for another knife and a meat hook, but instead he's kicked in the stomach by the soldier bleeding from his belly. The blow is so hard that it lifts him from the ground. All the air has been knocked from Helmud's lungs; he gasps.

Bradwell charges the soldier who won't die. The soldier backhands him, knocking Bradwell to the ground. The soldier then grabs Bradwell by the shirt, but the shirt is so shredded that the soldier comes away with nothing but fabric. Bradwell, barechested, sprawled in the gravel and dust, kicks the soldier's knee, but the soldier barely flinches. Calmly, he levels the pistol lodged in his right arm, loads it, and aims at Bradwell, who curls to his side. The birds on his back go still.

El Capitan hears a report and thinks that Bradwell must be dead, but the soldier is the one who falls. El Capitan can see that the leader worked his way into a shooting angle as Bradwell's rush bought him some time to move on his injured leg. This leaves the soldier who grips his loosened abdomen. He looms over El Capitan, who scrambles backward, unarmed.

The leader shoots, blasting the soldier's hands and crippling his guns. The soldier howls. The guns in his shoulders take over as he turns to search for the leader. The bullets fly. One grazes Bradwell's shoulder—the one not already wounded—kicking his gun from his hands. Bradwell grabs his wound, seems dazed by the blood and noise. He staggers behind a rock, his eyes squeezed shut.

The leader shoots again, although he's lying on the ground, unable to get up, his blood pooling around him. His bullets perforate the soldier's chest and the guns on his shoulders. The soldier tries to shoot, but all his guns are jammed. He's weak, staggering in a circle. Crazed, his eyes lock on Lyda, and he lunges for her. El Capitan leaps onto the soldier's back, setting him off balance and taking him to his knees. It buys Lyda time to run, but otherwise it's useless. The soldier is so strong that he staggers to his feet. El Capitan holds on, choking him.

And then Helmud's skinny arms appear. He's holding a thin piece of wiry thread—something that seems to be made of wool and human hair. He casts it out and then pulls it around the soldier's throat. El Capitan grabs on to the wiry string too, and jerks with all of his weight and Helmud's. The wiry string gouges into the soldier's neck. Rearing back, he paws at it with his stubs.

And then Lyda appears. She stabs him in the lower stomach and then yanks the knife up as hard as she can.

The soldier staggers. She pulls the knife out, wipes it clean on her white jumpsuit, ready to stab again. But she doesn't have to. The soldier falls forward with El Capitan and Helmud on his back.

El Capitan pulls the string out with one hand and holds it—a bloody thing, now clotted with flesh. He remembers all the times he told Helmud to stop his nervous fiddling, that old agitated motion he made behind his neck. "Helmud," he says, "did you make this so you could kill me with it?"

And this time, Helmud doesn't repeat his brother's final words. His silence means yes.

For the first time in as long as he can remember, El Capitan is proud of his brother. "Damn it, Helmud! Shit! You've been planning to kill me!"

And then he hears noises. They all freeze and brace themselves. Maybe it's the soldier who got away doubling back.

But no, it's coming from the crescent window in the earth.

Two hands grip the sides of the window frame and then Partridge is pulling himself up, as if climbing from a grave.

PARTRIDGE

KISS

W HEN PARTRIDGE GETS TO HIS FEET, he takes in the carnage. El Capitan and Helmud are bloodied and bruised. Bradwell is bare-chested and bleeding again from the shoulder, but the other shoulder this time. He's on his knees, his head bowed, his chest heaving. Is he praying? His hands are clasped. Lyda's white jumpsuit is splattered and streaked with blood. She's breathless, stunned. She stares at Partridge with her bright blue eyes and then at all he sees.

And there are the bodies of soldiers. One's chest is exploded. Another, sliced up the middle, has bloody stumps instead of hands. One has been shot in the skull. There's a small hole in the back of his head, but as Partridge walks around him, he sees that his face is gone.

"What is this?" He feels sick, his knees weak. "What is this?"

And then he sees his brother, half hidden by underbrush. He runs to his side, falls to his knees. "Sedge," he says. The muscle of Sedge's right leg has been chewed through with bullets. There's blood under his ribs. It seeps into the knees of Partridge's pants.

"God," Partridge says. "No, no." His brother's chest rises and falls unevenly. He bends down to Sedge's head—his oversize skull and heavy jaw. "You're going to be okay," he whispers. "Mom is here. She's coming. You'll see her." Partridge yells to the others. "Get my mother! Help Pressia get my mother up here!"

Pressia is already aboveground. She looks at all the bodies. "My God," she says. "My God, no."

Bradwell staggers up and runs to her. "Pressia," he says, but she's obviously shaken, unable to respond to him.

El Capitan shouts to Bradwell, "Help me here!"

Together they lift Aribelle up from the window, her thin trunk and useless limbs. Caruso is pushing from below, but he doesn't follow her aboveground.

Partridge lays a hand on his brother's chest. The blood is wet and warm.

Sedge looks at Partridge and smiles. "Partridge," he says, "you're the one."

"No," he says, "it's you. It's always been you."

Partridge calls to Pressia again. "Is she here?" He turns and sees Bradwell cradling his mother. He carries her to Partridge, setting her down beside her two sons. Her eyes are wild.

"Baby, what happened to you?" Her voice is ragged and sharp. "Sedge. Look at me. Sedge."

"Look, Sedge," Partridge whispers. "It's her. She's here! She's really here!"

Sedge closes his eyes. "No," he whispers, "the story you told me. The swan."

"She's real," Partridge says. "She's here."

His mother takes a bottle of pills in her metal pincer and shoves them at Partridge. "Tell your father that he can have whatever he wants. He can have the pills. He can take me. Just not this. Not this." Her watery eyes skitter over Sedge's body.

Partridge takes the bottle and nearly falls backward. His brother is going to die. He's going to watch it happen. There's nothing he can do.

"Sedge!" his mother calls. Sedge's eyes catch hers and lock on. It's as if he truly sees her now, as if he recognizes her. His mother says, "Sedge, my baby!" And for a moment, Partridge thinks that maybe she can save him. There is hope in her voice.

Sedge smiles and then closes his eyes.

Partridge watches his mother as she bends over Sedge's body. She is giving him the kind of kiss on the forehead that she gave to both of them every night as children at bedtime.

And then, triggered by the flip of a distant switch, Sedge's head explodes, and, with it, Partridge watches his mother's face shatter.

The blood is a spray, a fine mist that fills the air.

Partridge hears nothing. He sees nothing but the bloody mist. He tries to reach for them, loses his footing, and then falls. He stands again. He turns a slow circle. His mother and his brother are dead.

Pressia is screaming. He can see her open mouth, her eyes wide with terror, the doll-head fist clasped to her chest. Bradwell is holding her up.

Partridge hears nothing.

Lyda is at his side. She has him by the arm. Her lips are moving.

El Capitan reaches for his shoulders. Partridge balls his fist and takes a swing. El Capitan dodges it, which sets Partridge off balance. He catches himself on a rock. Lyda is saying his name—he can read her lips. *Partridge, Partridge.* He stands. He yells her name, "Lyda!" But he can't hear his own voice.

El Capitan is speaking to him too. He's saying something loudly. Partridge sees the veins in his neck straining. Helmud closes his eyes, his lips muttering El Capitan's echo.

And then Partridge sees Pressia again. He locks onto Pressia's eyes. Pressia is bugged—eyes and ears. The Dome is watching;

his father is there. Partridge marches straight for Pressia, who is still screaming. He holds on to the flesh of her upper arms.

She closes her eyes.

"Open your eyes!" he shouts and the noise of his own voice floods his ears. "Open your goddamn eyes!"

Pressia looks at Partridge, and Partridge stares past his sister. He stares through the lenses of her eyes, into his father's eyes in the Dome. "I know you're there! I'm going to come for you, and I'll kill you for this! If I could, I'd rip out the part of you inside of me. I'd rip you clean out."

He stares up at the sky. His body starts to shake. He lets go of Pressia's arms. He looks again, and there is his sister's face. She stares at him, her face streaked with dirt and tears. It's his sister.

The bloody mist is gone.

PRESSIA

BLOOD

ONCE FREE OF PARTRIDGE, Pressia runs to her mother's body. Her jaw is gone. Her face is covered in blood, but one of her eyes is clear. The eye blinks. She's still alive. Pressia puts her hands on her mother's bloody chest; three of the six small squares are pulsing. Should she pump her heart? "She's alive!" she screams. "She's alive!"

Bradwell kneels beside her and says, "She's dying, Pressia. It's over. She won't survive."

Partridge is in the woods, deep in the woods. She can hear his choked sobs.

Her mother stares up at her.

El Capitan's voice says, "She's suffering. She could linger."

Her mother struggles to breathe. Her eye blinks furiously.

Pressia stands up. Bradwell does too. She turns to El Capitan.

He says, "Can you offer her mercy? Can you do it?"

Pressia looks at El Capitan and then at her mother, who starts to seize. Her bloody head is thudding against the dirt and rocks. "Give me a gun."

El Capitan hands it to her. She raises the gun, takes aim at her mother, draws in a breath, lets it halfway out, and then she closes her eyes. She pulls the trigger. She feels the blast run through her body.

Pressia is frozen. She stares. Her mother's face is gone. The three small, pulsing squares flicker and then stop.

"She's at peace," El Capitan says.

She gives the gun to El Capitan. She doesn't look back. She knows what she wants to remember. She starts to walk downhill.

"Let's move!" Bradwell shouts. "There's one more soldier out there somewhere!"

Leaves. Vines. The unfixed earth shifting underfoot.

I'm here, Pressia thinks. I'm in the next moment and the next. But who is she? Pressia Belze? Emi Imanaka? Is she someone's granddaughter or daughter? An orphan, a bastard child, a girl with a doll-head fist, a soldier?

She is rushing downhill, everyone jostling around her. In her mind's eye, her mother's face comes loose again, scatters, splintered bone, their heads—her mother's and Sedge's heads—so full of blood. Then it's everywhere—a film of blood on nettles, grass shoots, thorny weeds.

But they're all moving downhill now. Running wildly.

She wants to bury the bodies.

But, no.

There's one soldier still loose. He'll be coming after them.

Her grandfather was a mortician. He could have fixed them up nicely. He could turn a head to conceal a cracked skull. He could re-create a nose from a piece of bone. He could stretch the skin. He could make eyelids and stitch them closed. There used to be coffins with silk linings. Now he's dead and gone too.

Pressia is downhill. There will be no burial. They will be eaten by feral beasts. The burial is their own shroud of blood.

There's the car half covered in brush and vines, which El Capitan pulls off and throws to the ground. Partridge, Lyda, and

Bradwell stand by Pressia, breathless. Bradwell has made a bandage by ripping cloth from his pant leg. It's wrapped around his shoulder. The blood is dark. His shirt is gone. He's bare-chested. Partridge has offered his jacket, but Bradwell says he's burning up. The birds flutter, their bright beaks in deep, their masked eyes darting. She wanted to see them and now here they are—the gray fan of wings, the paler chests, their shining eyes, and their dainty claws, a bright red. She wishes she knew what kind of birds they are. She imagines him as a little boy, running through a flock. They lift and there's the blinding light. And the birds are with him forever. He offers her his hand.

"No," she says. She has to walk on her own.

She grips the barbershop bell hidden in her jacket pocket. She will never give the bell to her mother, proof of an old life. She won't tell her all of the stories she's saved. There wasn't time. She didn't even have the chance to tell her mother she loved her.

The girl in white is now streaked in red. Lyda. Partridge has her by his side. She holds him up more than he does her. He's saying, "But they wanted my mother alive. They wanted to interrogate her. It doesn't make sense." He's holding the bottle of pills tightly in his clenched fist.

Pressia is still the Dome's eyes and ears. They see everything she sees, hear everything she hears. But she doesn't understand what's happened. Do they? Is this what they'd wanted all along?

"Let's go," El Capitan says.

"Go," Helmud says.

Everyone climbs into the car. Partridge and Lyda are in the backseat. Pressia and Bradwell are in the front with El Capitan at the wheel. Helmud is gazing out at nothing. He's shaking.

El Capitan shoves the car in reverse. "Where to?"

"Pressia has to get free," Bradwell says. "Whoever did this to her has to undo it."

They back out into the Deadlands and now head south, around the hills.

"The farmhouse," Pressia says. "We need to be on the other side of this hill."

"How can a farmhouse exist out here?" Partridge asks. His voice is weary.

Pressia thinks of Ingership's wife, how she told her in the kitchen that she wouldn't put her in harm's way.

"They had oysters, eggs, and lemonade, these automatic rubberized seals to keep out dust, a beautiful chandelier in the dining room, and crops being sprayed down by field hands," she says, trying to explain, but as she does, she wonders if she's gone crazy. She sees her mother's face, the kiss she gives to her elder son. Pulling the trigger, her mother is dead. And it happens all over again, slowly, in Pressia's mind. Pressia curls forward, closes her eyes and opens them and closes them. Each time she opens them, there is the doll head staring at her. This was how her mother knew it was her. These clicking eyes and plastic lashes, the small nostrils and the hole in the center of the lips.

The Dusts rise up again, fewer here, as the land starts to give way to grass that roots it. Still the Dusts edge up and circle. El Capitan rams one and the others back away.

Bradwell shouts that he sees something. "Not a Dust. Special Forces."

They hug the side of the hill. And the soldier leaps from a jutting rock, landing with a thud on the roof of the car. Pressia looks up and sees the two dents made by his boots.

Bradwell grabs the rifle from the floorboards near El Capitan's feet, cocks it, points it straight up, and shoots, ripping a hole into the metal, shearing it wide open. The shot clips the soldier's leg. He thuds against the roof but holds on.

El Capitan tries to shake him loose, turning the wheel hard left, then hard right, but it doesn't work. The soldier appears at the passenger window, kicks it with his one good leg, splintering the glass. He reaches in and grabs Partridge by the throat, but Partridge has a meat hook and his own unusual speed. He reaches around the soldier's broad chest and hooks him between the shoulder blades.

The soldier lets out a guttural moan, loosens his grip, letting Partridge drop into his seat. The soldier still keeps his hold on the car. With his free hand he claws his back, trying to reach the hook. Bradwell rolls down the window, climbs halfway out of the car, cocks the gun again, but before he has time to fire, the soldier sees him, dives at him, pulling him from the car. They land with a thud on the ground and roll to a stop.

Pressia wants to scream—not Bradwell. She can't lose anyone else. She won't allow it. No more dying. She reaches for the handle. The door is locked. "Unlock it!" she screams.

"No!" El Capitan says. "You can't help him! It's too dangerous!"

She pounds the doll head on the door. "Let me out!"

Partridge reaches over the seat, grabs her arms, and pulls her back. "Pressia, don't!"

Lyda says, "Use the gun. Take aim."

Pressia grabs the gun and shoves her upper body out the window.

El Capitan turns the car around to give her a better line of fire. "Be ready when they separate. You might only get one chance."

The soldier is trying to stagger up, but his leg is stripped of muscle. He's also writhing against the pain from the hook still lodged in his back. He's got Bradwell by the throat, but Bradwell kicks the soldier's wound, elbows him in the gut, and scrambles to his feet.

Drawn to the soldier's blood, a Dust circles the ground around them like a vulture but from below. Plumes of ash rise, making it hard to see. Bradwell kicks the soldier's stomach. But the soldier grabs Bradwell and throws him. Bradwell lands hard, face-to-face with a Dust. He inches backward. The soldier pauses and seems to be assessing his leg wound.

Bradwell grabs the meat hook, wrestles it from the soldier's back. Once it's loose, Bradwell flies backward, landing hard.

Pressia takes her breath, lets it out halfway, and shoots.

The soldier spins and falls to the ground.

Bradwell gets to his feet, and, in one swift motion—the birds on his back a frantic blur of wings—he cuts the Dust clean through with the meat hook. He's beautiful, Pressia thinks—his wounded shoulders, as if he's been violently knighted, his tough jaw, his flashing eyes.

El Capitan pulls the car up to Bradwell, pops the lock, but Pressia's already pulled herself out of the window. She grabs Bradwell and helps him to the car. She opens the door. They both slide in. She slams it behind them then stares at Bradwell. She reaches up and touches a cut on his bottom lip. "Don't die," she says. "Promise me that."

"I promise that I'll try not to," he says.

El Capitan puts the car in gear and revs the engine.

She looks out the back window. A few more Dusts rush to circle the soldier. One rises and flares its back like a cobra. The soldier is quickly swallowed by the earth, gone.

Bradwell reaches up and lets his hand glide down her hair. She wraps her arms around him and listens to the pounding of his heart with her eyes shut tight. She imagines staying like this forever, letting everything else melt away.

Soon enough, Bradwell says, "We're here," and she lifts her head as they turn a corner and there are the rows of crops, then the long driveway that leads to the front porch steps of the yellow farmhouse. For a moment, she imagines they're on their way home.

But as they draw closer, she sees something small rippling from one of the windows—it almost looks like a small flag—a hand towel with a blood-red stripe down the middle. She reaches into her pocket and there's the card that Ingership's wife gave her in the kitchen, the sign. What does it mean? *You must help save me.* Isn't that what the woman said?

Partridge

PACT

His mother isn't dead. Sedge isn't dead. In Partridge's mind, they can't be. There's been a mistake, something he can sort out later. There were mistakes at the academy sometimes too, mostly errors in perception, human errors. His father is to blame. His father is human. This is a human error.

Or maybe it's a test. His father planted the blueprints, gave Partridge the photograph, hoping or maybe even knowing that Partridge would use the information. Maybe from that moment on, the bright flash of the picture being taken, all of this has been part of a plan to gauge Partridge's mental and physical strength; at the end everyone will emerge from their hidden spots, just out of his view, like an elaborate prank or surprise birthday party. It's an explanation that keeps his mother and Sedge alive. But even as he tries to hold on to this precarious feat of logic, he also knows that it isn't right. Another part of his brain keeps telling him that they're dead, gone.

The gauze wrapped around his left hand hides the tip of his missing pinky, but he starts to feel an ache as if it's there still, throbbing, when Pressia starts talking about the farmhouse. He doesn't believe her. How could he? A farmhouse out here? An automatic system to seal off the windows and doors to cut down on ash? A chandelier in the dining room? All of it surrounded by fields with workers spraying pesticides?

Any oyster at all—poisonous or not—would be a miracle of science. But there are labs in the Dome that are devoted to reinstating the natural production of food. The farmhouse has to be a product of the Dome. The two worlds are linked in ways he never could have imagined. The car that he's sitting in is proof. It had to come from the Dome. Where else?

When Pressia tries to describe it, Lyda says, "I saw the tire marks at the Dome. There's a loading dock. Trucks must move in and out."

Are they already testing the transition out of the Dome, back home to their rightful paradise, the New Eden? Partridge wonders. *Blessed.* In the Dome, they were *blessed.* Partridge remembers his mother's voice—*a new order of slaves.* His mother's voice is like a small slip of fabric that rustles lightly in his mind, and then he feels a swarm in his chest, sick with rage. She's injured, but Sedge is with her, and Caruso is tending to her, just like he did the last time she was almost left for dead. Human error. No, dead. Both of them, and Caruso will never come aboveground. He's the only one left. He'll die there one day—probably one day soon now that Partridge's father knows where the bunker is.

Mrs. Fareling—he thinks of her and Tyndal. He never got to tell his mother the message—that they survived. *Thank you.* There are so many things he didn't get to say, too many to count.

After Pressia says that they're getting close, Lyda turns to Partridge and whispers, "There's something someone wanted me to tell you."

"Who?"

"Just a girl I met while I was in the rehabilitation center," Lyda says, and she seems embarrassed to mention that she was there, but, of course, she was. That's where someone shaved her head. Partridge wants to ask her how much she's endured because of him. He wishes he could take it all back. But she doesn't want to talk about it now. He can tell. What she has to say is important. "She told me to tell you that there are many like her who want to overthrow the Dome. That's all she could say. Do you understand?"

"Sleeper cells," he mutters. Lyda is in deep. She's not just a hostage. She's a messenger. Does she know that she's working for his mother's side now? He wants to tell her everything his mother said about him being the leader, but he can't. His mind is too jumbled. "Yes," he manages to say. "I understand."

They now turn the final cutback. El Capitan pulls the car behind a stand of low bushy orchard trees, planted so close together their limbs are entwined. And there it is—a yellow farmhouse just as Pressia described it, and the dark lush rows of vegetation in a valley, an island farm, the Deadlands stretching in every direction around it like a sea of ash. There's a red barn with white trim and greenhouses. It disturbs him, the way it suddenly appears as if it's been ripped up from some other place and time, and screwed into the ground. There are no OSR soldiers working in the fields, but there are two ladders leaning against the face of the house, buckets poised on rungs, and two long poles on the ground. "Was someone scrubbing the house?" Partridge says.

Lyda says, "The thing that looks like a small flag in the window. It's a sign. I've seen it before."

"For the resistance," Bradwell says. "My parents had a real flag like that, folded in a drawer. It dates way back."

"Ingership's wife," Pressia says. "She's in trouble, I think."

"How did this house get here?" Partridge whispers.

"It's like a house in a magazine," Pressia says. "But sick, diseased on the inside."

"It's not like any old-fashioned Arabs in white tents," El Capitan says.

Pressia says to Partridge, "Bradwell needs your jacket." The heat of the battle has worn off, and Bradwell has started to shake. Partridge can see Bradwell's shoulders rattling. He takes off his jacket, which used to be Bradwell's anyway, and hands it to him over the seat. Bradwell puts it on. "Thanks," he says, but his voice sounds almost hollow—or is it that Partridge's hearing is off? He can't trust anything anymore—not what he sees or hears, not houses that appear out of nowhere, not misty blood or his sister's eyes.

"We can give Ingership the medications in exchange for getting all of this stuff out of your head," Partridge says. He's the only one who knows the truth—the medicine is a decoy, meant to buy time.

"What about Ingership's wife?" Pressia says. "Can we help her?"

"Isn't she the one who put you under?" Bradwell says.

"I don't know," Pressia says.

Fat birds, almost chicken-like, waddle across the road. They're grotesque, with two-clawed legs pitching them around awkwardly. They don't have feathers. Instead they seem to be covered in scales, as if the scaly skin that covers their legs has grown to cover their entire bodies. Their wings are bony things that edge up and down awkwardly at their sides.

"You didn't see those in the magazines," Bradwell says.

Partridge thinks of his father, diseased on the inside like this house. "When we walk up, hold the pills close to your head," he says to Pressia.

"No," Bradwell says, reaching over the seat and putting his hand on Partridge's chest. "That's too much."

"What?" Partridge says. "This is how he operates. He'd blow her up but not the pills." His father's a killer. He closes his eyes for a moment, as if trying to clear his vision. But he knows that his father didn't flip any switch until he saw that the pill bottle was in Partridge's fist, far enough away. "It's for her protection."

"He's right," Pressia says to Bradwell.

Partridge imagines his father watching on, knowing every word, every gesture. His father must be in communication with Ingership inside the house because, just now, two young soldiers in OSR uniforms walk out onto the porch. They're wretches, but well armed. They move to the edge of the porch and stand like sentries.

El Capitan squints through the windshield. "You know what pisses me off? These are my goddamn recruits. They can't even handle a weapon right. Works to our advantage, I guess."

"Pisses me off," Helmud whispers, his voice a rough whisper.

Bradwell says, "Okay, ready?"

Partridge wants to say more. He wants them to make a pact, here in the car, before they go in. But he's not sure what he'd have them swear to.

El Capitan says, "Hey, I forgot this." He tugs something from his jacket pocket and holds it up. "This belong to anyone?"

It's their mother's handmade music box, blackened from smoke.

"Take it," Pressia says.

"No," Partridge says. "You can have it."

"It plays a tune that only you two really know," Pressia says. "It's yours now."

Partridge takes it, rubs it with his thumb. The gritty soot smears. "Thanks." He feels like he's holding something essential, some part of his mother that he can keep forever.

"Are we ready?" Pressia says.

Everyone nods.

El Capitan puts the car in drive and guns it toward the house. The recruits don't shoot. Instead, they run and bang on the door. El Capitan slams on the brakes a little late, ramming the porch steps. Struck by the grille, they buckle and splinter.

They all get out of the car. El Capitan has his rifle. Partridge and Lyda have knives and meat hooks. Bradwell holds a knife.

Pressia holds the bottle of pills clenched in her hand, raised to her head, her knuckles pressed against her temple.

"Where's Ingership?" El Capitan shouts.

The recruits exchange a nervous glance but don't say anything. They're thin and, even with their seared skin, they look freshly beaten. Bruises and welts run across their exposed arms and face.

Just then an upper window slides open, one on the opposite side of the house from the red-stained hand towel. Ingership leans out, his arms stiff and chin high. The metallic plates on his face shine. He smiles. "You're here!" His voice is cheery, but he looks like he's been in a fight. On the exposed skin of his left cheek, there's a row of scratch marks. "Have any trouble finding the place?"

El Capitan cocks the rifle and fires. The shot sends a shock through Partridge's body. He sees the explosion again in his mind's eye—his brother, his mother, the air filled with a fine spray of their blood.

"Jesus!" Ingership shouts, ducking into the window. "That's not civilized!"

In a delayed reaction, one of the recruits shoots the side of their car.

El Capitan fires again, this time taking out a downstairs window.

"Stop!" Partridge says.

"I wasn't going to hit him," El Capitan says.

"Hit him," Helmud says.

"It's okay now," Partridge says. "We're not shooting."

"Your father could have this place surrounded," Ingership shouts at Partridge. "He could have already gunned you down. You know that, boy? He's playing nice with you!"

Partridge knows he's wrong. Special Forces is a very new elite corps. There were six, all dead now. He knows those who were next in line—the academy boys who were part of the herd. But they couldn't be ready for battle like Special Forces. There hasn't been enough time for that kind of transformation and training.

"He wants something and we have it," Partridge says. "It's that simple."

Ingership pauses. "You have the medication from the bunker?"

"Do you have the remote switch that explodes Pressia's head?" Bradwell counters.

"We'll make a deal," Partridge says.

Ingership disappears. There's some noise from the upstairs window. The two recruits on the porch keep their guns poised on them.

Then a deep buzz rises from the house, a release of the automatic rubber seals that keep out the ash.

The front door clicks and then swings wide.

In the upper window with the bloody hand towel, Partridge sees a white face—Ingership's wife?—then a pale hand pressed to the glass pane.

PRESSIA

BOATS

THEY STEP INTO THE FRONT HALL—the chair rails, white walls, the flowered runner, and wide stairs leading to the second floor. It floods Pressia with a sharp sense of being penned, trapped. She still holds the bottle to her head, her fingers stiff, her entire body aching. She looks into the dining room; again she's startled by the brilliance of the chandelier trembling over the long table. She hears footsteps overhead—Ingership's wife? The chandelier makes Pressia think of her grandfather, the picture of him in the hospital bed. She tries to remember that feeling of hopefulness, but then recalls the dinner knife in her hand, the latex gloves, the burning in her stomach, and how the doorknob wouldn't turn. It only clicked and then the click quickly becomes the trigger of the gun, the jolt of it in her arm, up into her shoulder. She squeezes her eyes shut for a second then opens them.

The two soldiers keep their guns trained on them. Ingership appears at the top of the stairs and walks down to greet them. A bit unsteady on his feet, he slides his hand along the mahogany railing. There are claw marks on one cheek. Pressia thinks of Ingership's wife. Is she locked in that bedroom? Was there a fight?

"Leave all your weapons here," Ingership says. "My men will too. We're not barbarians."

"Only if we can pat you down too," Bradwell says.

"Fine. But trust is an undervalued stock, if you ask me."

"Looks like you've been expecting us," Partridge says.

"There are things that the Dome chooses to tell me, and I'm one of your father's confidants."

"Really." Partridge sounds doubtful. And from what little Pressia knows about Ellery Willux, she doubts he has any confidants, much less Ingership as one. Willux doesn't seem like the confiding type.

"All weapons on the lowboy," Ingership says, pointing to the table along the wall.

They put down their guns and knives and hooks, as do the recruits, nervously. El Capitan pats down his own soldiers. He looks them in the eyes, but they look away. Pressia assumes he's trying to gauge their loyalty. They didn't shoot him when he opened fire in the yard. Only one of them shot the car. Does this mean that their loyalty is divided? If Pressia was one of them, she'd do what they're doing, which is playing both sides, trying to survive.

Bradwell pats down Ingership. Later, Pressia thinks she'll ask him what it was like. How much of him is real? Did the metal on half of his face exist all down one side of his body? It might, she thinks. Pressia wonders what Bradwell thinks of her now. Her cheek holds on to the memory of his warm skin, the pounding of his heart. Her finger remembers his cut lip. She told him not to die, and he promised he would try not to. Does he feel for her the way she feels for him—a headlong, heart-pounding rush? She's lost so much, and all she knows now is that she can't lose him. Not ever.

The soldiers pat them down, taking turns. Pressia stands next to Lyda. The soldiers run their hands over their bodies quickly.

"I don't like being shot at," Ingership says to El Capitan.

"Who does?" El Capitan says.

"Who does?" Helmud says.

"The soldiers will accompany me, just for good measure," Ingership says, "and the girls will wait in the parlor."

Pressia stiffens. She looks at Lyda, who shakes her head. The parlor stands to their left. It's filled with drapes and overstuffed furniture and throw pillows.

"No, thanks," Pressia says. She thinks of the back room of the barbershop, the cabinet that she once hid in. No more hiding. She thinks of the smiley face she drew in ash. Gone now, ash layered upon ash. She's not going back to hiding or being hidden.

"Wait in the parlor!" Ingership shouts so loudly that it startles Pressia.

Lyda glances at Pressia then says calmly, "We'll do what we want."

Ingership's skin burns brightly, the scratches flaring. He looks at El Capitan, Bradwell, Partridge. "Well?" He expects them to do something.

They look at one another.

Bradwell shrugs. "Well what? They gave you their answer."

Ingership says, "Well, I won't let their ugly stubbornness derail us." He turns on the stairs and begins to climb, taking each step one at a time. At the top of the stairs, he unlocks a door with a key on a chain in his pocket.

They step into what first seems to be a large, sterile operating room. Under the windows there's a counter of metal trays, small knives, swabs, gauze, and a tank of what must be anesthesia. They all pack in around an operating table. Pressia imagines that this is where they must have taken her to install the bugs and the ticker. She remembers none of it—except maybe the wallpaper. Pressia puts her doll-head fist up to it for a moment, keeping the pills close to her skull. The wallpaper is pale green with small boats. They look strangely familiar. Is this what she saw when she came to for a moment on the table, small boats with puffy sails?

"You perform a lot of surgeries in here?" Bradwell asks.

"Some," Ingership says.

The soldiers look anxious; they keep their eyes on Ingership and El Capitan, unsure who might bark an order at them next.

"Go collect my fine wife," Ingership says to one of them.

The soldier nods and disappears. There's a knock down the hall, voices, scuffling. A door being closed. He returns with Ingership's wife. Her hands and face are still covered with the full-body stocking, stitched to expose only her eyes and mouth and a full wig of honeyed hair. She's wearing a long skirt and white high-collared blouse stained with blood that's seeped up from her skin through the stocking and onto her clothes, like dark water-stains. Her body stocking is ripped on one hand so that her fingers are poking through. Some of the fingers are bruised bluish as if freshly twisted. This may be how Ingership got his scratches. The stocking is also torn on one side of her jaw, revealing pale skin, a dark bruise, and two welts that look almost like fresh burns. Pressia tries to remember exactly what Ingership's wife said to her in the kitchen. *I won't put you in harm's way.* Did Ingership's wife help Pressia? If so, how?

Ingership points to a small leather stool in a far corner. His wife scrambles quickly across the room and takes a seat. Once she sits, Pressia thinks she looks like a dummy wrapped in a stocking, the kind used for effigies of Pures. Kids like to do that sometimes, setting them on fire. But her eyes are very alive, flitting and blinking. She looks into all of their faces. Her eyes catch on Bradwell's face, as if she recognizes him and wants him to recognize her. But he doesn't seem to. She then looks at Pressia, fleetingly, and lowers her eyes again.

Pressia nods to her, unsure how to read her expressionless features.

She nods in return. And then she quickly lowers her gaze, keeping her eyes locked on her exposed fingers. Is Pressia supposed to save her?

"Was this once a baby's nursery?" Lyda asks quietly, perhaps to break the tension.

"We are not to reproduce," Ingership says. "Official orders. Right, dear?"

Pressia is confused. Official orders? Then Partridge and Lyda exchange a glance. They would know the rules well enough. Pressia figures some are allowed to reproduce, others are denied.

"The box?" Ingership says to his wife.

She stands and picks up something near the surgical instruments, a small circular metal container with a metal switch on hinges. It's connected to a long trail of wires fitted into an outlet in the wall. She sits on the leather stool again, holding it in her lap.

Bradwell lunges forward. "That's it, isn't it?"

The sudden movement frightens Ingership's wife. She clutches the switch to her chest.

"Steady now," Ingership says. "My sweet wife is skittish these days." He waves his hands near her and she flinches. "See?" She cowers like the dog that used to live near the lean-tos, the one Pressia used to feed sometimes, that was shot by OSR.

"We have what you want," Partridge says. "Let's just stay calm."

"Where do you think you're going to go from here?" Ingership asks Partridge. "This is what I don't understand. There is no future out here, but you could still go back, you know. You could do penance. Your father would return you to the fold. He'd have no use for these others." He waves at the rest of the group dismissively. "But you, you could have a life."

"I don't want to be brought into a fold. I'd rather die fighting."

Pressia believes him. She's underestimated him, maybe mistaking his lack of experience in this world for weakness.

"I bet you get your wish!" Ingership says lightly.

"Just disarm it, Ingership!" El Capitan shouts.

"And you," Ingership says. "You with the retard on your back. What will happen to you? You'll never win. Nothing you believe in actually exists. Your soldiers aren't even your own soldiers! It's the Dome's world still, wherever you look, as far as you can see."

El Capitan glances at the two soldiers. "Don't lose sleep over it, Ingership. You know I'll be fine."

"Fine," Helmud says.

"My wife has been acting up ever since your visit, Pressia. Very uppity. A cruel man would have sent her out to fend for herself in the wilds and die. But I was kind. I simply administered penance. And look at her now—so civil. If I told her at this moment to flip the switch, she would. Even though she's a very delicate creature by nature, she's obedient." He looks at his wife imperiously. This is all a show, but Pressia's not sure if it's for their benefit or the Dome's or if it's something more personal, playing out publicly with a captive audience.

Ingership steps toward Pressia, who tightens her grip on the pills held to her head. "What if I told you they're coming. They're on their way. Special Forces. Reinforcements. And not just half a dozen. No, a full platoon."

"You're lying," Lyda says. "If Willux wanted them here, he'd have brought them in already."

Pressia isn't sure if she's right or not, but she admires Lyda's conviction.

"Are you speaking to me?" Ingership says. He walks to Lyda and slaps her with the back of his hand. She spins and grabs the wall to steady herself. Pressia feels a wick of fury light within her stomach.

Partridge reaches out and grabs the lapels of Ingership's uniform. "Who do you think you are?" His grip is so tight that it's cutting off Ingership's oxygen.

Still, Ingership stares at Partridge coolly. "You're on the wrong side," he grunts. Without looking at his wife, he says, "Flip the switch."

"Don't!" Bradwell shouts.

Ingership's wife's fingers touch the switch lightly, nervously—the way a delicate creature would.

"She's still young," Bradwell says softly. "She's just lost her mother. Imagine. A child without a mother." Pressia understands what he's doing. Ingership's wife isn't allowed to have children. But once, they were expecting. Weren't they? Why else wallpaper a room the way one would a nursery? He's playing on this memory, this softness. "Have mercy on her. You can save her."

Ingership manages to shout one last time, "Flip the switch!"

She looks at her husband and then does as she's told. She flips the switch. Pressia draws in a deep breath, and Bradwell tackles Ingership's wife, knocking the box to the ground, where it shatters. Everyone in the room stiffens. There's no explosion.

Inside Pressia's ears, she hears a dull tick—just one in each ear—and then her ears are no longer so muffled. The lenses in her eyes go blank for a moment, and she sees nothing. But it doesn't last. Before she can even cry out, her vision is back and clear—no longer clouded.

Partridge releases Ingership, shoving him into the wall.

"What happened?" Partridge says.

"I'm alive. I can see and hear clearer. In fact, everything sounds loud—even my own voice." Pressia lets her hand with the pill bottle drop to her side.

Ingership's wife stands up. "I never activated the ticker. I switched the wiring. If anyone flipped the switch, it would only deactivate the bugs. I said I wouldn't put you in harm's way. I promised." She turns to Pressia. "You must take me."

"They'll kill us for this," Ingership shouts at his wife. He's breathless, slouching against one of the walls. "Do you know that? They'll kill us!"

"For now, they think she's dead," Ingership's wife says. "We have time to escape."

Ingership stares at his wife in total shock. "You had this planned?"

"Yes."

"You even dithered before flipping the switch while I was being choked so they would think you didn't want to kill her."

"I'm a delicate creature."

"You disobeyed me! You betrayed me!" Ingership shouts.

"No," she says, her voice sounding distant and airy. "I saved us so we could have time to escape."

"Escape into what world? To become wretches?"

Ingership's wife seems dizzy. She reaches for the drapes above the counter and hangs on to them for support. Her face contorts beneath the stocking. She lets out a cry.

Pressia looks at Lyda, a red mark and a cut on her cheekbone from Ingership's ring. "She saved me," Pressia says.

Ingership throws himself at the counter and pulls out a gun from the low cabinet. He stands, training it on Partridge. "I could kill you and now, without the eyes and ears, your daddy would never know." He shouts at his soldiers. "Grab them!"

But the soldiers don't move. They look at El Capitan, and then at Ingership.

El Capitan says, "They don't really respect you, Ingership, even with a gun. Do they?"

The soldiers are still frozen.

"I'll kill you myself, one at a time," Ingership says. He points the gun at Bradwell's face. "You think he doesn't know who you are?"

"What are you talking about?" Bradwell says.

"Willux knows everything about you and the people you come from."

Bradwell's eyes narrow. "My parents? What does he know about my parents?"

"Do you think he's going to let a son of theirs challenge him?"

"What does he know about them?" Bradwell takes a step

toward Ingership and the muzzle he's pointing at Bradwell's chest. "Tell me now."

"He wouldn't mind adding you to his collection. Little relics. I know that I, for one, would prefer you dead."

"His collection?" Partridge says.

Ingership's wife pulls too hard on the gauzy curtains. They pop loose from the hooks. She jerks back, nearly losing her balance. She turns behind her husband's back, seemingly trapped in the white gauze, cocooned, but there's something bright in her hand.

A scalpel.

She steps forward, the curtain dropping like a dress to the floor. She drives the scalpel into her husband's back.

He cries out, dropping the gun. It slides across the tile. Ingership arches and falls to the floor. Lyda picks up the gun and holds it steady, aimed at Ingership, who's writhing, the scalpel dug into his back. He smears his own blood.

Bradwell kneels next to him on the floor. "What about my parents? What has Willux told you about them?"

"Wife!" Ingership screams. But it's unclear whether he's calling desperately for help or out of anger.

"My parents," Bradwell shouts. "Tell me what Willux has said about them."

Ingership clenches his eyes shut. "Wife!" he calls again.

She reaches her fingernails into the rip in the stocking by her jaw and tears it from her face. A loud cry bursts from her chest. She pulls away the wig, showing her fine, matted, russet hair. Her face is covered in old scars, yes, but also fresh bruises, more welts and burns. Pressia can tell that she was once beautiful.

Ingership, on the bloody floor, shouts out, "Wife! Get the pills!"

"They're worthless," Partridge says.

Ingership rocks on one shoulder. "Wife, come here. I need you. I'm burning!"

Ingership's wife lurches to the wall. She rests her cheek against it and lightly touches the wallpaper, just one boat, just one.

For a moment, this seems like the dizzying end of everything. Bradwell stands up and looks down at Ingership. His eyes blink and stare off. He's dying. Bradwell won't get any information about his parents now. He walks over to Pressia and pulls her to him. She tucks her head under his chin. He holds her tightly. "I thought she'd killed you," he says. "I thought you were gone."

Pressia hears Bradwell's heartbeat again. It's like a soft drum. He's alive and Ingership is dead now; his eyes have gone blank. She thinks of her grandfather's work as a mortician, and she feels like she should say a prayer over the dead body, but she doesn't know any prayers. Her grandfather told her that they used to sing prayer-like songs at the funerals he oversaw. He said that the songs were for the mourners, to help heal them. She doesn't know any of those prayer-like songs, but she thinks of the song her mother used to sing to her—the lullaby. There's something about the nursery with no baby in it that makes her think of her mother, the image she saw on the screen, the recording of her voice. And Pressia opens her mouth and starts to sing softly.

Pressia's voice doesn't surprise Partridge. It's as if he's been waiting to hear it for many years. Her voice lilts with sadness, and it takes Partridge a moment to place the tune. But then he does. It is a song his mother sang to them at night. A lullaby that wasn't a lullaby at all. It was a love story. In Pressia's voice, he hears his mother's voice. She sings about a screen door that slams, a dress swaying. He remembers the night of the dance, the feel of Lyda's breath beneath the tight fit of her dress. She must be struck by the song too, because she fits her hand in his, the one wrapped in gauze, missing half a finger. He knows this isn't the end of the battle, but for a moment he can pretend it's over. He leans over to her and he says, "Your bird made of wire—did it ever go up in Founders Hall on display?"

Lyda is about to ask him what will happen to them now. Where will they go? What's the plan? But all her words are stuck. All that's in her mind now is the wire bird. It's a lonesome bird that swings beautifully in a wire cage. "I don't know," she says. "I'm here now." There is no returning.

Ingership's wife had been named Illia. She thinks of her name, of being Illia again. She isn't Ingership's wife because now he's dead. She thinks of Mary, the girl in the song, a girl on a porch. *Don't go*—that's what she wants to tell the girl. Her husband's blood is now on her shoes. She touches the boats on the nursery's wallpaper and remembers her father's boat, bailing it out with buckets as a little girl. She feels unsteady, as if standing in the rocking boat. She hears her father saying, "The sky is a bruise. Only a storm will heal it."

El Capitan looks at the soldiers. He imagines what they have to tell him. There are others living here, and their skins are probably as beaten as Ingership's wife's skin. They live somewhere on the land. They can't have much to eat that isn't poison. Some are surely dying. He puts his hands on the counter below the window to better shoulder his brother's weight. From here, he can see just a bit of the dim buckled remains of the old highway. The asylum graveyard was out here somewhere. He was there with his mother once in a thunderstorm. She was going to pick out her plot. He didn't go in. He stood behind the gate in the driving rain and waited for her, holding Helmud's hand because he was scared of the lightning. On the way home, she said, "I won't need a plot anytime soon. I'll die an old woman. Don't look so gloomy." But she would be going to the asylum for her lungs. The date was set, and they weren't sure when she'd return. "You're in charge 'til I come back, El Capitan." And he has been in charge of Helmud ever since. More than that, he is Helmud. When he hates Helmud, he hates himself. And when he loves his brother? Does it work that way, too? The truth is that Helmud's weight hasn't only made him stronger. It's kept him pinned to Earth, as if without Helmud, he'd have floated clean off the planet by now.

Helmud feels his brother's ribs between his knees, his brother's heart pounding in front of his heart. He says, "Down...roaring on. On the wind...climb in." His brother's heart will always reach every place he ever goes just before Helmud's heart. It's the way he will make it through the world—his brother's heart, a beat, then his. A heart on top of a heart. A heart leading. A heart following. Twin hearts, bound.

Bradwell remembers the song. Arthur Walrond, the drunk physicist, his parents' trusty leak, used to play it in his convertible. Bradwell remembers driving around with Walrond and the dog that Bradwell named Art after him, the wind whipping around their heads. Walrond is long gone, and so are Bradwell's parents. But Willux knew his parents. What would Ingership have said, if he were still alive? Bradwell wishes he knew. But he doesn't think about this for long because Pressia's voice slides him into this moment. Pressia's cheek is pressed to his chest, so he feels the song on his skin. The delicate vibration, the movement of her jaw, the thin cords of her neck, the voice box—that fragile instrument thrumming in her throat. A memory has formed and will stay on his skin like this: her soft quick draw of breath, each note held, the song lifting from Pressia's lips, her eyes closed to the future. It's an indulgence to think about the future, and he wouldn't if it weren't for Pressia. What if they can fight the Dome and win? Could he have a life with her? Not a convertible or a dog or a nursery with wallpaper boats. But something beyond this.

Partridge has to leave. It's too much to bear. His mother's dead. Her voice is a song in Pressia's throat.

Lyda's hand caresses his arm.

He shakes his head and pulls away. "No." He has to be alone.

He walks out of the room, across the hall. There's a door. He opens it and finds the communications room, all lit up, a huge blue-lit screen, a console of gauges, wires, keyboard, speakers.

He hears his father's voice, giving instructions. People respond to him, "Yes, sir. Yes." And then someone says, "Someone's there, sir."

His father says, "Ingership. Goddamn it! Finally."

Partridge says, "He's dead."

His father's face appears on the screen in front of the blue backdrop, his watery shifting eyes, the slight palsy of his head, his hands spread on the console before him. One of which is raw, a dark pink, scaly, as if recently scalded. He looks pale and breathless. His chest is slightly concave. Murderer.

"Partridge," his father says softly. "Partridge, it's over. You're one of us. Come home."

Partridge shakes his head.

"We have your good friend, Silas Hastings, and your buddy Arvin Weed has been extremely valuable. We'd have never known what he was at work on if we hadn't asked him a few questions about you. They'd both like to see you."

"No!" Partridge shouts.

His father whispers urgently, "That was a mistake in the woods with Sedge and your mother. An accident. It was reckless. But we're atoning for that now. All of that is ended." And now Partridge sees that the skin on his father's neck is also seared, as if it's only a thin pink membrane. Is his skin degenerating? Is this another one of the signs that his mother would have recognized?

Reckless? Partridge thinks to himself. Atoning? All of that is ended?

"And I brought you and your half sister together. Did you see that? A gift."

Partridge can barely breathe. His father *did* arrange it. He knew what Partridge would do. He treated him like a puppet.

"You've gotten what we need here. It will help so many. You've done well."

"Don't you know anything?"

"What?" his father asks. "What is it?"

"This is only the beginning."

"Partridge," his father says. "Listen to me."

But Partridge walks out of the room and starts running down the stairs. He opens the front door and, for no reason he can name, he runs down the porch steps and then up onto the roof of the black car. He stands there and looks out as far as he can see. It feels like a beginning.

He turns around and looks at the house, the large yellow bulk of it, the sky pressing in behind it all, and then the simple ripple of the blood-streaked hand towel. The wind, it still surprises him sometimes.

When the song is over, they're silent a moment. How long? Pressia can't tell. Time no longer has increments. It floods and fades. She walks to the window, and Bradwell stands behind her, wraps his arm around her waist, looks out over her shoulder. Neither of them can be far from the other now. Though neither of them has put words to this feeling between them, they're bound, more tightly because they've come so close to losing each other.

And life resumes because it has to. El Capitan and the soldiers lift Ingership by his arms and carry him from the room, his shoes dragging behind him, leaving streaks of blood.

Lyda has walked out of the room and now rushes back in. "Where's Partridge? Does anyone know where he went?"

No one does, and so she walks out again.

Ingership's wife picks up the curtain, folds it in her arms. She looks at Pressia and says, "You came for me."

Pressia says, "And you saved my life."

"I knew when I first saw you," Ingership's wife says. "Sometimes you meet someone and you know that your life will be different from then on."

"That's true," Pressia says—for her, it was true of Bradwell and Partridge. She'll never be the same.

Ingership's wife nods and then looks at Bradwell. "You remind me of a boy I knew once, but that was worlds ago." Her eyes look past him, unfocused and distant. She touches the soft cloth of the curtains, and walks out, down the hall.

This leaves Bradwell and Pressia alone in the operating room.

Pressia turns to face him. He kisses her on the lips, tenderly, and there's the heat of his skin, the pressure of his soft warm lips on hers.

He whispers, "It's your turn to promise not to die."

Pressia says, "I'll try not to." The kiss already seems like a dream. Did it happen? Was it real?

And then she remembers the silent bell. She reaches into her pocket and pulls it out. She cups it in her palm and hands it to him. "It's a gift," she says. "You think there's going to be time and then there isn't. It's not much, but I want to give it."

He lifts it, shakes it. It makes no sound. He holds it over one ear. "I hear the ocean," he says.

"I'd like to see the ocean one day," she says.

"Listen." He holds the bell to her ear. She closes her eyes. There's dim sunlight coming in through the windows; she can feel the press of it through her lids. She hears a muffled airy rushing sound—the ocean? "Is that what it sounds like?"

"No, not really," Bradwell says. "The real sound of the ocean can't be held in a bell."

Pressia opens her eyes and looks out at the gray sky through the windows. The wind shivers with soot, and then she hears Partridge's voice shouting their names.

There's the fresh scent of smoke. Something's caught fire.

Epilogue

*T*hey stand in a fallow field watching the farmhouse burn. Thin wires light up like cracks running across the façade of the house, brightly lit. Each wire sparks another. Pressia assumes that the house itself had a ticker, and somewhere in the Dome, its switch has been flipped.

The fire is efficient and quick. It goes up fast in great gusts of unfurling smoke and upward-spiraling cinders. The windows shatter. The curtains are lit up like flares; even the hand towel streaked with blood that was hanging outside the window is soon gone. The searing heat reminds Pressia of descriptions of the Detonations. Sun on sun on sun.

Lyda holds Partridge's hand tightly, like she's afraid he might run off again. Or is he the one holding on, hoping to stay where he is?

Bradwell and Pressia lean together, facing the fire, like a couple who've been dancing and the music has stopped, but they can't let go.

El Capitan has backed the car away from the porch. He and Helmud watch from behind the windshield. The soldiers stand on the far side of the car, letting it block them from the heat. Ingership's body is in the house. El Capitan shouted orders at the soldiers to leave it. "Easy funeral!" he said with a smile, though Ingership was never going to get a funeral.

The only one who looks away is Ingership's wife, Illia, who turns her back and keeps her eyes on the distant hill. Pressia looks at the side of her face, scarred and bruised. The stocking is a frayed collar around her neck.

They should go, but no one can move. The fire holds them there.

Pressia's memory of this day will blur. She can feel the details colliding in her mind already—a slow loss of facts, reality.

Finally, the house burns itself out. It's smoldering. The front half still stands. The door is wide open. Pressia takes a few steps toward the porch.

"Don't," Bradwell says.

But Pressia starts running. She's not sure why except she has an over-whelming fear of leaving something behind, of loss. Isn't there something that can be saved? She charges up the steps and into the charred foyer. She turns to the dining room. The chandelier has broken from the ceiling and through the table. A hole overhead gapes, and below it the chandelier sits like a fallen queen on a blackened throne.

Bradwell's voice comes from the door. "Pressia, we can't be in here."

Pressia reaches for the chandelier. She touches one of the ash-covered crystals. It's teardrop-shaped and still hot. She twists it from the chande-lier until it pops loose. It reminds her of pulling fruit from a tree. Did she ever do that as a child? She slips the crystal into her pocket.

"Pressia," Bradwell says gently. "Let's get out of here."

She walks to the kitchen, which has already collapsed. In the rubble, there are sparks. She turns and Bradwell is there. He grabs her by the shoulders. "We have to go."

That's when they hear the soft clicking, almost like the skitter of a rat's nails. They see a small light shining up through the wreckage. There is a buzz and a raspy whir. Pressia thinks of the noise of the fan that was lodged in her grandfather's throat. For a dizzy moment, she wants him to be alive and coming back to her.

Muscling up from the deepest part of the wreckage, where the floor has caved into the cellar below, is a small black metal box with robotic arms and multiple wheels. It burrows up, its gears hitching. The lights lining the top of the box flicker, then dim.

"What is it?" Pressia says.

"Maybe a Black Box," Bradwell says. "The kind of thing that's built to survive plane crashes, a recording of the flight and all the mistakes that were made so that those mistakes can't happen again." The beams overhead creak. Bradwell takes a step toward it.

The Black Box claws backward, away from him.

The wind is blowing now.

"Where is it trying to go?" Pressia asks.

"It's probably got a homing device."

A homing device. She knows that the Black Box is trying to get back to the Dome, but it reminds Pressia that she has no home, not anymore.

The beams pop and sigh. Pressia looks up at the ceiling. "It's going to give," she says.

Bradwell lunges for the Black Box, grabs it, and pulls it to his chest.

They run out of the back of the house, diving for cover in the tall grass, landing side by side. They're both breathless.

The house creaks; its boards whine and splinter. Then the beams buckle, and in a heavy exhale of dust the rest of the house, at last, caves in.

"Are you okay?" Bradwell asks.

Pressia wonders if he'll kiss her again. Is this the way she'll live from now on, wondering when he might lean toward her? "Are you?"

He nods. "We don't have a choice," he says. "We have to be okay, right?"

They're survivors. This is what they know. He stands up, reaches out his hand. She grabs it and he helps pull her to her feet.

They see the others in front of the house in the field. It's cold enough for their breaths to form ghosts in the air, barely visible through the rising smoke of the house.

Bradwell holds the Black Box against his ribs. He touches Pressia's face gently with the back of his rough knuckles then cups her face.

"You were only supposed to stick with us for your own sake, your own selfish reasons," Pressia says. "You said you had one."

"And I do."

"What's that?"

"You're my selfish reason," he says.

"Tell me we'll find something like home one day," she says.

"We will," he says. "I promise."

She realizes that she can love Bradwell in this moment so fully because she knows that this moment won't last. She allows herself to believe his promise and lets him hold her up. His hammering heart is as restless as the birds on his back, and she imagines how the soot will cover the earth again with a new dusting, black snow, a blessing of ash.

And then there's more shifting under the fallen house where it has collapsed into its own cellar hole. Another Black Box shoulders up, grinding its gears, and starts picking its way across the wreckage on spindly jointed arms. And then the cindered wood starts to shiver, and, one by one, Black Boxes pull themselves up from the char.

The End of Book One

ACKNOWLEDGMENTS

This novel drilled its way into my dreams. When I tried to look away, there were people who urged me not to, namely my daughter who kept telling me that I had to finish the book, that it was the best thing I'd ever written. When I confided in my friends Dan and Amy Hartman what I was at work on, they, too, kept pushing me back into this world. I'm thankful that they did.

I want to thank my father who tracked down tons of research for me—nanotechnology, history, medicine, slaughterhouses, light, communications, gems, geography, agriculture, Black Boxes...—who made architectural drawings of the Dome, drew up the top secret document *Operation Phoenix*, and sent me articles to read, things to consider, and I am forever indebted for the argumentative, thoughtful, and loving way he raised me.

Thank you to Dr. Scott Hannahs, PhD, director of DC Field Instrumentation and Operations at the National High Magnetic Field Laboratory at Florida State University, for briefly discussing with my father the feasibility of the construction of crystalline detectors. Thank you, Simon Lumsdon, for giving me a brilliant lecture on the basics of nanotechnology. I appreciate the information on burying guns posted by Charles Woods in *Backwoods*

Home Magazine, available at this link: http://www.backwoodshome.com/articles2/wood115.html.

I want to thank my husband, Dave Scott, who endures my fits of frustration and let me read these pages aloud to him, day after day, and who knows his way around a fight scene. I'm thankful for all of those who read early drafts—Alix Reid, Frank Giampietro, Kate Peterson, Kirsten Carleton, and Heather Whitaker, brilliant minds; and special thanks to my agents, Nat Sobel, Judith Weber, and Justin Manask, who believe in me, push me, and help me navigate the world. I'm thankful for Karen Rosenfelt and Emmy Castlen—I admire them so much and am honored that they responded to the novel as they did. I'm thankful for all of my overseas editors, and my editor here at home, Jaime Levine—thank you, thank you, thank you.

The research for this novel led me to accounts of the effects of the atomic bombs dropped on Hiroshima and Nagasaki. During the editing process, I found the nonfiction book *Last Train from Hiroshima* by Charles Pellegrino, which is not currently being sold by its publisher. It was a crucial read for me because of its depictions of those lost and those who survived. I hope a revised edition finds its way back onto shelves. And I hope, in general, that *Pure* directs people to nonfiction accounts of the atomic bomb—horrors we cannot afford to forget.

Julianna Baggott, critically acclaimed, bestselling author who also writes under the pen names Bridget Asher and N. E. Bode, has published seventeen books, including novels for adults, younger readers, and collections of poetry. Her work has appeared in the *New York Times*, *Washington Post*, *Boston Globe*, *Best American Poetry*, *Best Creative Nonfiction*, *Real Simple*, on NPR.org, as well as read on NPR's *Talk of the Nation* and *Here and Now*. Her novels have been book-pick selections by *People* magazine's summer reading, *Washington Post* book-of-the-week, a Booksense selection, a *Boston Herald* Book Club selection, and on the *Kirkus* Best Books of the Year list. Her novels have been published in over fifty overseas editions. She's a professor in the Creative Writing program at Florida State University and the founder of the nonprofit Kids in Need—Books in Deed.

Books by Julianna Baggott

Girl Talk

The Miss America Family

The Madam

Which Brings Me to You, co-written with Steve Almond

This Country of Mothers, poetry

Lizzie Borden in Love, poetry

Compulsions of Silkworms and Bees, poetry

The Prince of Fenway Park, for younger readers

The Ever Breath, for younger readers

Under the Pen Name Bridget Asher

My Husband's Sweethearts

The Pretend Wife

The Provence Cure for the Brokenhearted

Under the Pen Name N. E. Bode

The Anybodies Trilogy, for younger readers

The Slippery Map, for younger readers

The Amazing Compendium of Edward Magorium, for younger readers

READING GROUP GUIDE

JULIANNA BAGGOTT ON WRITING *PURE*

WHEN I STARTED WRITING *PURE*, I thought that it would be difficult to create an ash-choked, obliterated world of skeletal buildings, husks, detritus, rubble. But what turned out to be the more meaty challenge was trying to figure out what endures. I had to ask myself if love endures. What about hope and faith? What about beauty and art?

I started to see the world as Pressia does. Yes, the first image is of her hiding in a cabinet—a sixteen-year-old girl with a doll-head fist—but she's also a collector of odd things, a maker of mechanical toys, a barterer. She has a strong will to survive, an instinct to save people, and also, amid all of this loss, she still aches for something transcendent.

All of the wretches are burdened with loss, but they also have their own deep longing—for the past, the truth, home, and to know themselves.

These are things I long for still.

Pure is dedicated to my daughter. She's the age of the main character. I read her a very early snippet. She told me that it was the best thing I'd ever written and pushed me to write this novel. I don't know what struck her exactly. But it resonated. Maybe it's the idea that everyday life sometimes is polished up to look perfect—Dome-like—but, in truth, it can feel like an ashen waste-land. We all struggle at different times in our lives. Sometimes a post-apocalyptic novel simply feels like the honest emotional truth.

If someone, years ago, had told me that I would write *Pure* and, without getting a chance to read it, they simply described it to me, I would have thought it was a really dark book, beyond my imagi-nation. But novels in which people profoundly struggle are often the books that reach the most deeply for strength, rely on love, and inspire hope. That's the novel that I want to have written with *Pure*, the one I hope strikes you.

GROUP DISCUSSION QUESTIONS

1. What is the purpose of the Message that the Dome released after the Detonations? Why did they release it and what was its effect on the Wretches?

2. Would you rather be inside the Dome or outside?

3. If you could receive behavioral coding to make you smarter, faster, and stronger, would you want to? Partridge and the other boys in the Dome don't have a choice—they are forced to receive the coding whether they want to or not. Is this acceptable? Can you think of a situation where it would be appropriate to force behavioral coding on someone?

4. What do you think about Willux? Is he evil and power hungry, or is he genuinely trying to do what he thinks is best for society?

5. Discuss the relationship between Partridge and Bradwell. Why do they dislike each other?

6. Through various female characters, we get glimpses of the gender roles imposed by this society—the Mothers and their hatred of men, the Dome's refusal to let boys take art classes because they aren't "useful," and Ingership's wife's forced

participation in the *Feminine Feminists*. In describing an ideal woman, Ingership's wife explains: "We believe in achievement and empowerment, but why does that have to be at odds with simple feminine virtues—beauty and grace and a dedication to home and family? Why does that mean we have to swing a briefcase and be manly?" How does this fit with your conception of the ideal woman?

7. How would you feel if you suddenly met a long-lost sibling you didn't even know you had?

8. Bradwell tells Pressia that her scars are beautiful because they're a symbol of survival (page 319). Do you agree?

9. Discuss the relationship between El Capitan and Helmud. Why is El Capitan proud of Helmud when he realizes that Helmud was plotting to kill him?

10. Special Forces gives Partridge a choice: save his mother or save Lyda. In his place, who would you choose to save?

11. Discuss Aribelle. She was working against Willux, leading the resistance and studying biotechnology that could save lives—but in the process, she abandoned Pressia, Sedge, and Partridge. Do you think her actions were right, or wrong? Should she have gone into the Dome with Willux, Partridge, and Sedge? Once she located Pressia's chip after the Detonations, should she have taken Pressia into the bunker instead of leaving her with her adoptive family?

12. Do you think the swan story was an effective way for Aribelle to pass information on to Partridge? What else might she have done?

13. How does Pressia change throughout the book? Compare and contrast Pressia at the beginning vs. Pressia at the end.

14. Discuss the relationship between Pressia and Bradwell. How do you think their feelings for each other are impacted by the dangerous world in which they live? Would their relationship be different if they had lived before the Detonations?

We want our son returned...
If you ignore our plea, we will kill
our hostages one at a time.

Please turn this page

for a preview of

FUSE.

Wilda

Lying on a thin coat of snow, she sees gray earth meeting gray sky, and she knows she's back. The horizon looks clawed, but the claw marks are only three stunted trees. They stand in a row as if they're stapling the ground to the sky.

She gasps, suddenly, a delayed reaction, as if someone is trying to steal her breath and she's pulling it back into her throat.

She sits up. She's still small, still just a ten-year-old girl. She feels like she's lost a lot of time, but she hasn't. Not really. Not years. Maybe only days, weeks.

She tugs her thick coat in tight around her ribs. The coat is proof. She touches its silver buttons. There's a scarf tucked down into the coat, wound twice around her neck. Who dressed her? Who wound the scarf twice? She looks at her boots—dark blue with thick laces, new—and her hands fitted into gloves, each finger encased in a taut cocoon.

A curl of her dark-red hair sits on her jacket, her hair shining. The end of each strand is thick and perfect, as if newly cut.

She pulls up the sleeve of the coat, exposing her arm. Just as it was under the bright light, the bone is no longer warped. There are no thin plastic ridges bubbled along the skin. She isn't stippled with shards. Not even a mole or a freckle. Her skin is white—white, the way snow should be, maybe even whiter than that kind of snow. She's never seen really white snow with her own eyes. The light veins ride blue beneath the white. She touches the soft inner skin of one wrist to her cheek, then her lips. Smooth skin on smooth skin.

She looks around and knows they're close; she can feel the electricity of their bodies filling the air. She remembers what it was like when they first took her from the other strays; motherless, fatherless, they slept in a hand-made lean-to near the markets. She isn't sure why she was chosen, lifted into the air, clutched. One cradled her in its arms and hurdled across the rubble while the others bounded around them. Its breath chugged mechanically. Its legs pumped. Her eyes teared in the wind so that its angular face was blurry. She wasn't afraid, but now she is. They're here, their strong bodies buzzing like massive bees, but they're leaving her. She feels like a child in a fairy tale. In her mother's stories—she had a mother once—there was a woodsman who was supposed to take a girl's heart back to an evil queen, but he couldn't. Another sliced open a wolf to save the people eaten by a wolf. The woodsmen were strong and good. But they leave girls in woods sometimes, girls who then have to fend for themselves.

Light snow falls. She stands slowly. The world lurches as if it's suddenly grown heavy. She falls down to her knees and then hears voices in the trees, two people walking. Even from this distance, she can see the red scars on their faces. One wobbles from a limp. They're carrying sacks.

She tugs the scarf up over her nose and mouth. She's supposed to be found. She's a foundling; she remembers this word was used in the room with the bright light. "We want her to be a foundling." It was a man's voice, quavering over a speaker. He was in charge, though she never saw him. Willux, Willux, people whispered—people with smooth skin who weren't fused to anything. They moved easily around her bed, surrounded by metal posts where clear sacs of fluid were clamped and dripped into tubes, among little beeping machines, and wires. It was like having mothers and fathers, too many to keep track.

She remembers the wide light in the room, its brilliant bulb, so bright and close it kept her warm. She remembers how she first ran her hand over her skin and when she touched her stomach, it, too, was smooth. Her navel—the thing her mother always called the button of her belly, and what the voices in that room called her umbilicus—was gone.

She reaches up under her coat and shirt and runs her hand over her stomach. Like before, there's only a stretch of skin and more skin.

"Healed," the voices said behind white masks, but they were concerned. "Still, a success," they said. Some wanted to keep her for observation.

They will take more like her to be healed?

She starts to open her mouth to call to the distant figures carrying sacks, but her mouth doesn't open all the way. It's as if her lips are slightly stitched on either side—the edges sealed.

And what would she say? She can't think of any words. The words whirl in her mind. They're furred. She can't line them up or utter them. Finally she calls out, but the only words that form in her mouth are, "We want!" She doesn't know why. She tries again, to call for help, but again she shouts, "We want!"

They walk up, two young women. They're pickers; she can tell by the warts and scars on their fingers. They've touched a lot of poisonous bulbs, berries, morels. One of them has silver prongs, like those on an old fork, in place of two of her fingers. She's the one with the limp, and her face, though seared a deep red, is strangely pretty. Mostly because of her eyes, which glow a golden orange like liquid metal—stained by the brightness of the bombs themselves. She's blind. She clutches the other picker's arm and says, "Who's you?" It sounds like a birdcall. The girl heard birds in the bright room, recorded and piped in by the unseen speakers. Cooing, the girl thinks, and then she hears other birds in the woods. These birds have the kinds of calls she grew up with—not clear sweet notes as in the bright room, but scratches and rattles.

The two young women are scared of her. Can they already tell she's different?

She wants to tell them her name, but it's gone. The only words in her

mind are Fire Flower. That's what her mother used to call her sometimes; born from fire and destruction, she took root and grew. She's never
known her father, but she's pretty sure that he was lost in the fire and
destruction.

And then her name appears: Wilda. She is Wilda.

She puts her hand on the cold ground. She wants to tell them that she's
new. She wants to tell them that the world has changed forever. She says,
"We want our son." The words startle her. Why did she say this?

The young women look at each other. The blind one says, "What was
that? Who's son?"

The other, who has a ropey scar running down one cheek as if she'd
had a braid fused to her face now covered in a layer of skin, says, "She's
not right in the head."

"Who's you?" the blind one says again.

This time the girl says, "We want our son." These are the only words
that she can say.

The pickers look around suddenly, even the blind one. They hear the
electrical synapses now, firing through the air. The creatures who took
her are restless. "There's many," the one with the braided scar says,
wide-eyed. "They're protecting her. Can you feel 'em? They been sent by
our Watchers to look over her."

"Angels," the blind one says.

They start to back away.

But then Wilda pulls up her sleeve and exposing her arm—so white
it seems to glow. "We want," she says again, slowly, "our son returned."

PART I

Chapter Pressia

Moths

THE LOBBY AT OSR HEADQUARTERS is dotted with a few glowing lamps—handmade oil lamps strung from the exposed beams of the high ceiling. The survivors are bedding down on blankets and mats, curled together to keep warm. Their bodies hold a collective humid heat despite the fact that the tall windows haven't been boarded. Their bare casements are fringed with the gauzy remains of curtains. Snow starts to flutter and gust, flutter and gust, in through the windows as if hundreds of moths have been lured in by the promise of lit bulbs to bash themselves against.

It's dark outside, but almost morning, and some of the early risers are waking. Pressia's stayed up all night again. Sometimes she gets so lost in her work that she loses track of time. She's holding a mechanical arm she's just made from scraps that El Capitan brings her—silver pincers, a ball bearing elbow, old electrical cord to cinch it, and leather straps that have been measured to cuff the amputee's thin bicep. He's a nine-year-old with all five fingers fused together, almost webbed—useless. She whispers the boy's name hoarsely, "Perlo! Are you here?"

She makes her way through the survivors, who shift and

mutter. She hears a sharp, mewling hiss. "Hush it!" a woman says. Pressia sees something writhe beneath the woman's coat and then the silky black head of cat appears at the side of her neck. A baby cries out. Someone curses. A song rises up from a man's throat, a lullabye... *The ghostly-girls, the ghastly-girls, the ghostly-girls. Who can save them from this world? From this world? The river's wide, the current curls, the current calls, the current curls...* Pressia stops and listens. The baby goes quiet. Music still works, music calms people. *We're wretches but we're still capable of this—songs rising up inside of us.* She'd like the people of the Dome to know this. *We're vicious, yes, but also capable of shocking tenderness, kindness, beauty. We're human, flawed but still good, right?*

"Perlo?" she tries again, cradling the prosthetic arm to her chest. Sometimes in crowds like this she now looks for her father—even though she doesn't remember his face. Before Pressia's mother died, she showed Pressia the pulsing tattoos on her chest—one of which belonged to Pressia's father, proof that he's survived the Detonations. Of course, he isn't here. He probably isn't even on this continent—or what's left of it. But she can't help searching the faces of survivors looking for someone who looks a little like her—almond-shaped eyes, black, shiny hair. She can't stop her eyes from searching, no matter how irrational it is to believe she might one day find him.

She's made it all the way across the lobby and comes to a wall plastered with posters. Instead of the black claw, which once struck fear in survivors, this is a poster of El Capitan's own face— stern and tough-jawed. She looks down the row of posters, his eyes all lined up, his brother Helmud a small lump behind El Capitan's back. Above his head, it reads: *Able and strong? Join up. Solidarity will save us.* El Capitan made that up and he's proud of it. At the bottom, fine print promises an end to Death Sprees—the teams of OSR soldiers assigned to cull the weak, collect their dead in an enemy's field—and mandatory conscription at sixteen. For those who volunteer, El Capitan promises Food without Fear. Fear of what? OSR has a dark history. People were captured and hauled in, untaught how to read, used as live targets...

All of that is over. The posters have worked. There are more recruits now than ever. They show up throughout the day, wandering up from the city, ragged and hungry, burnt and fused. Sometimes, they come as families. He tells Pressia that he's got to start sending those back. "This isn't a welfare state. I'm trying to build an army here." But, so far, she's always talked him out of it.

"Perlo!" she whispers, walking along the wall, letting her hand slide over the rippled edges of the posters. Where is he? The curtains kick into the room. The snow is drawn in as if the large room is drawing in a deep breath.

One family has propped a blanket on a stick, creating a little tent to block the wind. She used to make little tents in the back of the burnt-out barbershop when she was little, with a chair and her grandfather's cane to prop a sheet, playing house with her best friend Fandra. Her grandfather called them *pup tents* and she and Fandra would bark like puppies. He'd laugh so hard the fan in his throat would spin wildly. She feels a pang of loss—for her grandfather and Fandra who are both dead, and her childhood which is dead too.

Outside the windows, guards keep watch at fifty foot intervals surrounding OSR's headquarters because Special Forces, released by the Dome, are multiplying. A few weeks ago, they were spotted bounding through the woods—their hulking figures bulked with animal muscle, their skin covered in something synthetic and camouflaged. They're agile, nearly silent, incredibly fast and strong, and well armed; their weapons are embedded into their bodies. They dart over the rubble fields, sprint among trees, light down alleys—quiet and stealthy, making routine sweeps of the city. They want Partridge—Pressia's half brother—most of all. Partridge is being protected by the Mothers, along with

Lyda—who is Pure, like Partridge, sent out of the Dome and used by the Dome as a pawn—and Illia, who was married to the top leader of the OSR, her twisted husband, whom she killed. They get bits of information from sketchy reports sent in from OSR soldiers who all deeply fear the Mothers. One report noted that the mothers are teaching Lyda to fight. She's just a girl from the Dome with no preparation for the ashen wilds, much less life with the Mothers, who can be loving and loyal but also barbaric. How is she holding up? Another report mentioned that Illia wasn't holding up. She'd been protected in the farmhouse all these years, and now her lungs are struggling with all of the ash.

Everyone who was there at the end of Pressia's mother's life has to be careful. They're the ones who know the truth about Willux and the Dome, and perhaps they have something that Willux is still after—the vials. Bradwell and El Capitan stripped as much as they could from her mother's bunker after she was gone. Partridge has the vials now and, hopefully, he's keeping them safe. They would mean a lot to Willux—with these vials and another ingredient and the formula of how to put them together, he could save his own life. Her mother's vials are potent yes, but, out here, they're too dangerous and unpredictable to be of use. They're beautiful and useless souvenirs.

How long can the Mothers keep Partridge hidden? Long enough for Partridge's father to die? This is the great hope—that Ellery Willux will die soon, and Partridge can take over from within the Dome itself. Sometimes Pressia feels like they're all held in a state of waiting, knowing that something is bound to give. She feels like she's waiting for the future to take shape.

Freedle flutters in the pocket of her sweater. She slips her hand inside and runs a finger down the robotic cicada's back. "Shhh," she whispers. "It's okay." She didn't want to leave him in her small bedroom, alone. Or was it that she didn't want to be alone?

"Perlo!" she calls. "Perlo!"

And, finally, she hears the boy. "Here! I'm here!" He scuttles over to her, weaving around survivors. "Did you finish it?"

Pressia kneels. "Let's see if it fits." She tucks the leather cuff around his upper arm, tightens it into place by the electrical cord laces. His fused hand can make a tapping motion. She tells him to apply pressure to a small lever.

Perlo gives it a try. The pincer opens and then closes. "It works." He opens and closes the pincer quickly again and again.

"It's not perfect," she says, "but it'll help, I think."

"Thank you!" he says so loudly he gets hushed by someone on the ground nearby. He whispers, "Maybe you can make something for yourself," he says, looking at the doll head. "I mean, maybe there's something…"

She tilts the doll so its eyes blink—one is slightly gummed with ash and so it clicks more slowly, out of sync with the other. "I don't think there's anything that can be done for me," she says. "But I get by."

The boy's mother whisper-calls for him. He whips around, raising the arm in the air triumphantly, and he darts off to show her.

And then there's a far-off gunshot, its rippling report. Pressia crouches instinctively and reaches into her pocket to protect Freedle. She lifts him and holds him to her chest. Perlo's mother pulls her son in close. Pressia knows it was probably an OSR soldier taking aim at shifting shadows. Errant gunshots aren't unusual. But that doesn't stop her chest from tightening around her heart. It's Perlo and his mother and a gunshot—the mix of it all and she remembers the weight of the gun in her arms, lifting the gun, taking aim. The gun went off in her arms. Even now her ears ring and she sees the bloody mist rising. It fills her vision. Red blooms before her eyes like the bursting flowers that shoot up in the rubble fields. She pulled the trigger, but now she can't remember if it was the right thing to do. She can't get it straight in her head. Her mother's dead. Dead. She pulled the trigger.

She walks quickly, sticking to the edges of the lobby, the posters stretching on and on. She cups Freedle gently. When she comes to a window, she looks out, carefully.

Wind. Snow. The clouds like clods of ash scuttling across the sky, she can see one bright star—a rarity—and below it, the edge of the woods, the brittle trees huddled and stooped. OSR soldiers are standing at fifty-foot intervals on the sloping hill. She can make out their uniforms, the occasional glint of a gun, the thin veils of their breath rising in the cold. And then she sees her mother's face lying on the forest floor and then it's obliterated. Gone.

Beyond the soldiers, her eyes stuttering through the trees. Is something out there—something that wants in? She imagines Special Forces hunkered down in the snow. Do they even need sleep? Are they, in part, cold-blooded, their skins covered in thin scrims of ice? It's quiet, eerily so, but still there's a certain coiled energy. It snowed three days ago—a fine dusting at first, it turned heavy—and now the lawn is iced, dark and glassy, in three inches or more and snow is flitting down.

She feels someone grab hold of her elbow. She turns. It's Bradwell, the double scars running up his cheek, his dark, dark lashes, his full lips chapped by the cold. She looks at his hand, all ruddy and rough. His broad knuckles are scarred and beautiful. How can knuckles be beautiful? Pressia wonders. It's as if Bradwell invented them.

But it's not like that between them anymore.

"Did you hear me calling you?" he says.

She feels like he's talking to her from underwater. Once, while the farmhouse burned, she had the courage to make him promise to find a home for them, but that was only because she didn't actually believe the moment would last. "What is it?"

"Are you okay? You look dazed."

"I just had to get an arm to a boy, and there was a gunshot. But it was nothing." She wouldn't admit to seeing bright red bursting before her eyes anymore than to her fear of falling in love with him. This is one thing Pressia knows is true: everyone she's ever loved has died. In light of that fact, how could she ever love Bradwell? She looks at him now and the words drum in her head: *Don't love him. Don't love him.*

"Have you been up all night?" he asks.

"Yes." She notices his hair standing up messy on his head. They both have the ability to disappear for days. Bradwell gets devoured by his obsession with the six black boxes that tunneled up from the char and rubble of the farmhouse and holes up for days on end in the old morgue where he now lives in the head-quarters' basement. Pressia gets wrapped up in making the prosthetics. Bradwell is still bent on understanding the past while she has devoted herself to helping people, here and now. "Have you been up all night too?"

"Um, yes. I guess so. It's morning?"

"Just about."

"Yeah, then I was. I had a breakthrough with one of the Black Boxes. One of them bit me."

"Bit you?" Freedle flits nervously in her hand.

He shows her a small puncture wound on his thumb. "Not hard. Maybe just a warning. It likes me now, I think. It started following me around the morgue like a pet dog." She starts walking down the hall and Bradwell follows. "I've taken them all apart, put 'em back together. And they contain information about the past—as far as I can tell—but they aren't wired to transmit. They aren't spies for the Dome or anything like that, which I had to rule out. If they ever had those abilities, they've been lost." Bradwell is on a tear, but Pressia isn't interested in the black boxes. She's tired of Bradwell's desire to prove his parents' Dome conspiracies right, his version of the truth, shadow history, all of that. "And this one, I can't explain it—this one is different. It's like it knows me."

"What did you do to make it bite you?"

"I was talking."

"About what?"

"I don't think you want to know."

She stops and looks at him. He shoves his hands in his pockets. The birds in his back flutter their wings, agitated. "Of course I want to know. It's how you unlocked the box, right? It's important."

He takes a deep breath and holds it for a moment. He looks at the floor and shrugs. "Okay then," he says, "I was rambling about you."

She and Bradwell have never talked about what happened at the farmhouse. She remembers the way he held her, the feel of his lips on hers. But can this kind of love survive in a world bent on survival? Love's a luxury. He looks at her now, his head bowed, his eyes locked on hers. She feels heat drill through her body. *Don't love him.* She can't even look at him. "Oh," she says. "I see."

"Nope, you don't see. Not yet. Come with me." He leads her down another hallway and then turns. And there, sitting by the door, waiting patiently, is a Black Box. It's about the size of a small dog, actually—the kind her grandfather used to call a terrier, the kind that likes to kill rats.

"I told him to stay and he stayed," Bradwell says. "This is Fignan."

Freedle noses up from her palm to see for himself. "Does he know how to sit and shake hands?" Pressia asks.

"I think he knows a hell of a lot more than that."

Chapter Partridge

Beetle

THE ROOT CELLAR SMELLS LIKE POOLED RAIN water and mildew. Bright red mold spores dot the walls and dirt floor. The walls are lined with the Mothers' jars of strange vegetables pickling in vinegar. Mother Hestra, heavily armed, paces overhead. Each of her footsteps reminds him he's locked underground. Sometimes, he feels like her footsteps are heartbeats and he's trapped in the ribs of some enormous beast. He wants out so badly sometimes he has to stifle a scream.

He hasn't seen Lyda in six days. Time is hard to measure while he's alone and bent over the maps of the Dome he's been making, with only a crack in a cellar door to measure the light of day occasionally interrupted by the skimpy meals the Mothers deliver— pale broths, clods of white roots, and occasionally a bite-sized cube of meat.

He tells himself that aboveground is no better—the wasted detritus of surburbia, a lot of what's gone. But, by God, he feels trapped and worse than the feeling of being trapped is the boredom. The Mothers gave him an old lamp so he has enough light to work by, and they've supplied large sheets of paper, pencils, and a sheet of plywood that he's set on the floor and uses as a hard-top desk. He's recreating the blueprints that he memorized to get out of the Dome, trying to get everything down as quickly as possible. But hour after hour, minute after minute, footstep overhead after footstep . . . the boredom becomes blinding.

The truth is he's forced to rely on the Mother's protection at least until he decides on a plan. Part of him wants to wait until his father dies. His father is weakening. Decades of brain enhancements have caused a palsy, and skin deterioration. Partridge's mother told him these were the signs of Rapid Cell Degeneration. Soon, his father's body will shut down. If that happens, it might be the perfect time to return. The Dome might respect Partridge as his father's legacy. His father has ruled like a monarch after all.

But the other part of him would like to take down his father while he's alive, defeat him for the right reasons. Don't the people of the Dome deserve to know the truth about what his father did? If he can get that truth to them and explain that there's another way to live—one in which they aren't just sheep following his father's orders, one in which they don't see the survivors as evil wretches who deserved their fate—they'd choose it over his father's reign. Partridge is sure of it.

He's got to find time with Lyda to make a plan. It feels inevitable that they'll go back, together.

Meanwhile, he wants to finish the maps, pushing through the solitary confinement, the blunt force of boredom, mold and spores, rationed food, and, stripped of all weapons, the awful feeling of needing the Mothers, who treat him like a child and, at the same time, a dangerous criminal. They still consider him the enemy, especially because he comes from the Dome; he's a Death—a man, worse a man from the Dome—and can't be trusted.

The Mothers are interested in the maps, which is why they've given him supplies, but Partridge wants to get them to El Capitan.

It's the one gift he has to give. They may never be of use; what are the chances El Capitan will ever form a viable army capable of taking down the Dome? Still, it's something he can contribute, a small gift. As he works on the maps, he lets his mind drum over all of the things his mother told him before she died. He's written down every word he could recall, all of it embedded with information, coded.

He puts his pencil down, opens and closes his fist. His hand's cramping, even his partially chopped-off pinky, which has healing to a shiny red nub. He rubs his fingers together, feeling the slickness of the waxy serum that the Mothers recently had him bathe in, as preparation for an upcoming journey. The waxy serum, extracted from a camphor tree and beeswax, is supposed to lock in his scent and mask it. His skin is stiff and shiny. There are reports that Special Forces have an excellent sense of smell, as do some of the other Beasts and Dusts. The Mothers never let Partridge and Lyda stay in one place too long. They're protective, yes, but also Mother Hestra told Partridge that they can't risk Special Forces closing in on Partridge, putting them all at risk. Nomadic living is best.

He wonders if Lyda has been bathed in the serum too. He's always afraid that, one day, she won't come on the journey to the next place. So far she always has, and maybe this is when they'll leave the Mothers and head back in, on their own. The Mothers won't want to let her go. They might have to escape. He tries to imagine the feel of her skin encased in this waxiness.

Sitting on the dirt floor beside him is his mother's metal music box, first found in her drawer in the Personal Loss Archives, Bradwell charred it in the butcher shop basement. But he made sure that Partridge got it back. A gift. Bradwell's more sentimental than Partridge thought, but when it comes to things your parents have left behind, he's got a soft spot. Partridge has rubbed the soot from the music box, but the gears are still blackened.

Because all of its parts are metal, it still works though it's off-key and a little more muted now. It's the only thing the Mothers let him keep—maybe because they're mothers themselves. He lifts the box, winds it, lets it play—the notes tinking in the close damp air. He misses his mother. He missed her for so long before he saw her again—for such a short time—he's gotten good at missing her. Maybe it's why he's so good at missing Lyda. Years of practice.

When the notes die out, he looks at this most recent map, a cross-section of the Dome's three upper tiers—Upper One, Upper Two, and Upper Three and three subfloors called Sub One, Sub Two, and Sub Three, which include a section for the massive power generators. The ground floor is called Zero—home to the Academy where he spent most of his time.

He misses the Academy with relentless longing, even though he knows he shouldn't. He shouldn't want to be back in his dorm room, hanging out with Hastings, begging Arvin Weed for his notes, hoping to avoid the herd—a group of boys who pretty much hate him. He even misses his classes. He thinks of Glassings, his history teacher, in that moment he pulled him aside in the hallway outside of the dance. Partridge was just about to steal the knife so, in retrospect, it was the moment when he could have turned back, continued on with his familiar life.

That's not how it went. Somehow he ended up here, powerless.

The irony is he has the vials, his mother's life's work—the vials are powerful. His father murdered for them—Pressia's adoptive grandfather, as well as his father's own oldest son and the woman his father supposedly loved, Partridge's mother.

The vials remind him of what his mother wanted him to become—a revolutionary, a leader.

Partridge walks to the jars and picks one up, third from the corner jar. Under it there's a narrow, deep hole, and a few beetles skitter away. He fits his hands down in and lifts a tightly wrapped bundle, lightly caked in moist dirt. He carries the bundle to his cot and unwraps his mother's vials, four of them attached to syringes with hard plastic covers over the needles. Bradwell and El Capitan took them from his mother's bunker after the farmhouse burned, along with anything else that might be of use—computers, radios, medicine, supplies, guns, ammunition. Afterward, it seemed smart to split the group in two—El Capitan, Helmud, Bradwell, and Pressia went to headquarters; and Lyda, Partridge, and Illia with the Mothers because they have the greatest ability to keep Partridge hidden and heavily guarded. If one group was found by Special Forces, at least the others could carry on. The Mothers didn't allow Partridge to keep any of his mother's things. Bradwell and El Capitan took the bulk of his mother's stuff, but Partridge hid the vials under his jacket.

He checks each vial. They're cool to the touch. Partridge's mother took Partridge to Japan as a baby at Partridge's father's urging, because the Japanese were ahead of everyone else on creating biomedical nanotechnology to repair trauma from detonations, in particular self-generating cells that would move into the body to repair it.

From a very young age, Partridge's father used brain enhancements—so much so that he lit up his brain with firing synapses—and now he has the telltale signs of Rapid Cell Degeneration—a palsy and skin deterioration, which will lead to organ failure and death. It's not just him. Partridge remembers how, in the Dome, anyone who is sick, old, or weary is quickly whisked away to a cordoned-off wing of the Medical Center. In the last few weeks, he's realized one very dark truth: Rapid Cell Degeneration will also eventually affect Special Forces and all of the Academy boys who've been enhanced, including, eventually, Partridge himself, one day.

Before his mother died, she told him that if what's in these vials is paired with another substance as dictated by a formula—a formula that's gone missing—then this concoction could reverse

Rapid Cell Degeneration. At the time, he'd been so overwhelmed with emotions—he hadn't seen his mother since he was a little boy. He'd thought she was dead, and here she was, after all these years. But now, when he recalls it, he tries to concentrate on what she actually said, in particular the three things needed to reverse RCD—the contents of these vials, another ingredient that she said *someone* had been working on, and the formula to put it all together.

His mother showed him a list of people within the Dome who were on her side. Arvin Weed's parents, Algrin Firth's father, even Durand Glassings. They're part of a network within the Dome. When Lyda was sent out of the Dome as bait to lure Partridge, one of the people in the network whispered a message to her, *Tell the Swan we're waiting.* When Partridge told his mother this, she whispered, "The Cygnus," which he still doesn't understand.

She told him that the liquid in these vials contains powerful cell-generating material. But, too, that the serum is unwieldy, imperfect, dangerous.

Holding one of the vials up to the dim light, he wants to know how, exactly, this liquid is unwieldy, imperfect, and dangerous. What would happen, for example, if it touched a living creature's skin? He wants to test it. Why? Doing something would feel better than doing nothing. And now that the idea is there in his head, there's no talking himself out of it.

First, he'll needs something living to test the serum on.

A beetle.

He walks to the jars again and pulls one out quickly. Again, a few beetles dash off, but he cups his hand over one of them. It has a glossy, green back and a bright-red head spiked with thornlike horns. Its legs fan out, knotted, bristled with spikes. He holds it in place until he feels the beetle tickling up his fingers.

"Sorry," he whispers to the beetle. "I really am."

He carries it to the plywood, opens his mother's music box,

gently nudges it into the box, and closes the lid. The beetle's legs scratch the box. He wishes Arvin Weed, the boy-genius of the Academy, were here. God, Partridge regrets not paying attention in labs.

He picks up one of the syringes, uncaps it. The needle shines. He knows that this means he'll waste a drop—just one though.

He upends the music box. The beetle starts skittering across the plywood, but he pinches it, and holds it delicately in place.

While its legs scurry, getting nowhere, a sharp tail curls up from under its wings, revealing a swaying stinger. Its small rounded black eyes seem wet. Partridge looks at the needle, starts to depress the stopper when his finger and thumb poised on either side of the beetle's shelled back are covered with tiny prickles of searing heat. The burning moves up his fingers into his hand, and the shock of it causes him to shout.

Quickly, he moves the needle toward the beetle, but his hand feels rigid with pain. He releases his hold on the beetle. It clicks across the plywood, but not before a drop of liquid from the needle falls, landing—thick and wet—on one of the beetle's hind legs. The leg goes limp from the thick wet trap of the liquid, but the beetle drags itself forward.

The shout has alerted Mother Hestra. Her knuckles rap the cellar door. "What was that noise?"

Partridge wraps the syringes, his burning hand blotched now, and he crawls to the jar, lifts it, and slides the bundled syringes in the hole. The beetle pulls itself under the plywood to darkness.

The cellar door opens wide with a clang. Mother Hestra is backlit, dimly.

"What's the noise down here?" she asks.

"It's a chant from the Academy. It can get too quiet down here." He rubs his burning hand but then stops. He doesn't want any more questions.

Mother Hestra has thick body. Her son, Syden, a five-year-old, is permanantly fused to her leg. She's wearing furs stitched together and fitted to the shape of her body with a hole for the boy's blotched head, just above her hip. Most of the Mothers are double-beings, fused to children, and Partridge has never gotten used to it. During the Detonations, the Mothers were holding their children or protecting them from the bright flashes, bent to them, tending to them. Partridge can't quite imagine being stunted in that form, never growing up, always locked into place within the confines of your mother's body. Syden's face has begun to age. Will he grow old like this?

Mother Hestra glares at Partridge. One of her cheeks is seared with words—a backward script burned into her skin during the Detonations—the impression of a blackened tattoo. Partridge doesn't let himself stare at it long enough to try to read it. It'd be rude. "Well, stop with all that," she says.

"I was just going to sleep anyway."

"Good. We leave in the morning. I'll call on you early."

"Lyda and Illia are coming to?" He'd rather not have Illia coming along. She's crazy. He can't fault her. She was locked away in the farmhouse, abused by her husband, forced to hide her scars beneath a stocking made to look like a second skin. Recently, she's reverted to wrapping herself in swathes of cloth—because she's ashamed of her skin? Or is it simply a habit? She murdered her husband—a scalpel to the back, and it messed her up good. Lyda is the only one he wants to see. Lyda.

"Lyda, yes. Illia? I don't know," Mother Hestra says.

"Where are we going?" Partridge asks.

"Can't say." And with that, she heaves herself out of view. The cellar door slams shut. For a second, Partridge is blinded by the news. No more confinement. He'll see Lyda tomorrow. They'll be together. He can talk to her about going back. Everything will be different, but it's coming. He can feel it. God, he misses her.

That's when he hears the rasp, low and heavy. And then there's a noise like a shovel in dirt. But that's not it either—a thick scraping noise.

He's feels like he's not alone.

His mother's music box lies in the dirt. He reaches for it, and sees the long black talon, on a thin spoke—the leg of an insect— a massive insect—sticking out from under the plywood. *Not the beetle*, he says to himself. *Not the beetle*. Because it's too big to be the beetle's leg. Still, there's rasping.

He puts his hand on the plywood and begins to lift it. The leg crimps, disappears from view.

He takes a breath and yanks the plywood so hard it flips over; he forgets he's been coded with extra strength sometimes.

There's the beetle. Its tail clicking against its own shell, its wings convulsing wildly and uselessly, the rasping, as it struggles for breath.

And its one spiny, thick, massive leg.

The liquid in the vial worked. The cells of its leg weren't injured and so, with incredible speed, the cells didn't repair trauma, they built on healthy tissue and bone, even the ornate spikes on this one hind leg have ordered themselves perfectly. And, for some reason, this seems familiar to him—the delicacy of rebuilding a small limb?

Partridge doesn't want to touch it. His hand still tingles with heat. *Unwieldy, imperfect, dangerous.* That's what his mother called the serum. The beetle's leg jerks uncontrollably, gouging a claw-mark in the dirt.

And Partridge feels a strange rush of power. He made this happen with one tiny drop of liquid. His head pounds and his ears ring, and he thinks of his father's power. What did the old man feel when the Detonations hit—blast after blast of bright blinding light pulsing around the Earth?

My God, Partridge thinks. What if Partridge's father loved the power of it all? What if it made him feel like he was lit up? What if it felt like this small infinitesimal moment expanded exponentially, infinitely, inside of him?

The beetle's wings fold in tightly to its body. The leg spasms a few more times, and then the beetle digs its powerful leg into the dirt like a knife and pushes itself up. Its small legs dart beneath it, and then the massive leg contracts, then extends. The beetle springs into the air and flaps its wings. The leg is too heavy for the wings to support. It falls to the ground, but the massive leg is there to soften the landing. It contracts again, springs forward, flaps, lands, contracts, springs forward…

The beetle is no longer what it was moments ago.

It's a new species.

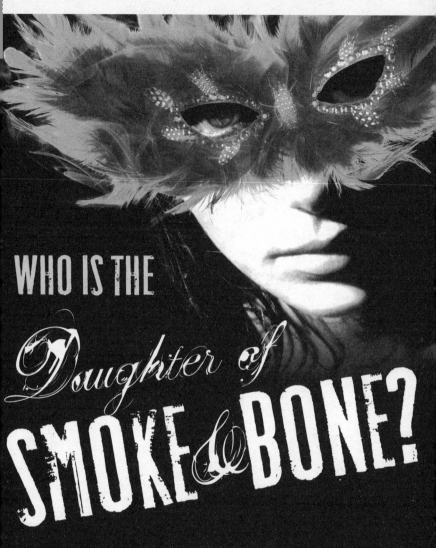

WHO IS THE

Daughter of

SMOKE & BONE?

From National Book Award finalist **LAINI TAYLOR**—now in paperback!

"Thrillingly fresh and new…you won't want to put it down."
—*Entertainment Weekly*

LITTLE, BROWN AND COMPANY

DAUGHTEROFSMOKEANDBONE.COM

BOB514